Extraordinary Praise for

DALE BROWN

and The Patrick McLanahan Series

"**D**ale Brown is a superb storyteller."
—W.E.B. Griffin

"**E**xciting and intelligent entertainment."
—Mark Greaney

"**T**he best military adventure writer
in the country today."
—Clive Cussler

"**B**rown puts readers into the cockpit. . . .
Authentic and gripping."
—*New York Times*

"**F**illed with detailed descriptions of weapons
and aircraft, as well as Brown's trademark action and suspense."
—*Library Journal* on *Arctic Storm Rising*

"**T**he brisk plot showcases the latest military
technology and warfare techniques. . . . Brown
consistently entertains."
—*Publishers Weekly* on *Arctic Storm Rising*

"**S**pectacular. . . . The action builds to an exciting climactic battle. . . . Brown shows once again why he stands out in the crowded military thriller genre."

—*Publishers Weekly* on *The Moscow Offensive*

"**A**n off-the-books mercenary unit is the world's best bet against unchecked Russian aggression. . . . A fun read that really shines with the author's convincing knowledge of military aircraft."

—*Kirkus Reviews* on *The Moscow Offensive*

"**A** very smart, timely, and terrifying political thriller. . . . Current, spot-on, and full of bone-crushing action, Dale Brown's *The Moscow Offensive* is one of his best novels to date, and a sure bet to please action junkies who also like heaping sides of politics and next-gen tech."

—The Real Book Spy

"**A** tense, atmospheric thriller with a ripped-from-the-headlines plot, *Price of Duty* moves at a breakneck pace. Highly readable, enormously entertaining, its twists and turns will keep you glued to the pages."

—Karen Robards

"**B**rimming with action and political intrigue. . . . First-rate."

—*San Francisco Chronicle* on *Rogue Forces*

Also by Dale Brown

ARCTIC
STORM
A NOVEL # RISING

DALE
BROWN

wm

WILLIAM MORROW

An Imprint of HarperCollinsPublishers

Excerpt from *Countdown to Midnight* copyright © 2022 by Creative Arts and Sciences LLC.

ARCTIC STORM RISING. Copyright © 2021 by Creative Arts and Sciences LLC. All rights reserved. Printed in the United States of America. No part of this book may be used or reproduced in any manner whatsoever without written permission except in the case of brief quotations embodied in critical articles and reviews. For information, address HarperCollins Publishers, 195 Broadway, New York, NY 10007.

First William Morrow premium printing: January 2022
First William Morrow hardcover printing: May 2021

Cover design by Richard L. Aquan
Cover photographs © Peter Lane/Alamy Stock Photo (F-22);
© Shutterstock

Print Edition ISBN: 978-0-06-302323-9
Digital Edition ISBN: 978-0-06-301505-0

William Morrow and HarperCollins are registered trademarks of HarperCollins Publishers in the United States of America and other countries.

22 23 24 25 26 BVGM 10 9 8 7 6 5 4 3 2 1

IN MEMORIAM

Once again, this novel is dedicated to my son, Hunter Dale Brown. My fondest memories of him are when I gave him his first bath in my kitchen sink when he was about a week old, with his mom looking on in terror; his high school graduation party on the shores of Lake Tahoe; his Eagle Scout court of honor; and collaborating on my novel *Strike Force* when he was just nine years old, tossing ideas back and forth as I drove him home from school.

Like his old man, Hunter was quiet, a little shy, and fiercely loyal to those who got to know him. He was a hard worker, the go-to IT guy, a great teacher, and the best son Diane and I could have ever wished for.

Life is nothing but the soul's never-ending journey through time and space, and I'm happy that Hunter's came into our lives. We love and miss you, big guy. Enjoy the rest of your journey.

We had discovered an accursed country. We had found the Home of the Blizzard.

—Sir Douglas Mawson, polar explorer

I will find a way out or make one.

—Attributed to Robert Peary, Arctic explorer

ACKNOWLEDGMENTS

Again, a big Thank-You to Patrick Larkin for his expertise, talent, and support.

CAST OF CHARACTERS

AMERICANS

CAPTAIN NICHOLAS "NICK" FLYNN, U.S. Air Force
intelligence officer, assigned undercover to
Wizard One-One, an HH-60W "Jolly Green II"
combat search-and-rescue helicopter

CAPTAIN SCOTT "FX" DYKSTRA, U.S. Air Force,
command pilot, Wizard One-One

TECHNICAL SERGEANT CARL "ZEE" ZALEWSKI, U.S.
Air Force, pararescue jumper assigned to Wizard
One-One

CAPTAIN KATE "GHOST" KASPER, U.S. Air Force,
copilot, Wizard One-One

STAFF SERGEANT BILL WADE, U.S. Air Force, flight
engineer and gunner, Wizard One-One

TECHNICAL SERGEANT MIKE CAMARILLO, U.S. Air
Force, pararescue jumper assigned to Wizard
One-One

"ANDERSON WHITE," head of an OGA "Other
Government Agency" (CIA) black ops team

SERGEANT FIRST CLASS ANDY TAKIRAK, Alaska Army
National Guard, senior noncommissioned officer
assigned to Captain Nick Flynn's Joint Force
security team

PETE JOHANSSON, civilian maintenance supervisor, Barter Island Long Range Radar Site, Kaktovik, Alaska

SMITTY WALZ, civilian electronics technician, Barter Island Long Range Radar Site

MARTA MCINTYRE, civilian cook and "gofer," Barter Island Long Range Radar Site

SENIOR AIRMAN MARK "M-SQUARED" MITCHELL, U.S. Air Force, communications specialist assigned to Flynn's Joint Force security team

PRIVATE FIRST CLASS COLE HYNES, U.S. Army, assigned to Joint Force security team

TRIG JENSEN, hermit trapper working the Arctic National Wildlife Refuge in Alaska

MIRANDA REYNOLDS, head of the CIA's Directorate of Operations

JONAS MURPHY, U.S. Director of National Intelligence

BILL TAYLOR, U.S. Secretary of Defense

REAR ADMIRAL KRISTIN CHAO, U.S. Navy, head of the Pentagon's operations directorate

GENERAL FRANK NEARY, U.S. Air Force, Chief of Staff

STAFF SERGEANT PEGGY BAKER, 176th Air Defense Squadron, Alaska Air National Guard, radar specialist, Joint Base Elmendorf-Richardson, Alaska

LIEUTENANT COLONEL CARMEN REYES, 176th Air Defense Squadron, Alaska Air National Guard, operations center supervisor, Joint Base Elmendorf-Richardson

SPECIALIST RAFAEL SANCHEZ, U.S. Army, Carl Gustaf 84mm recoilless rifle gunner attached to Flynn's Joint Force security team

PRIVATE WADE VUCOVICH, U.S. Army, assigned to
   Joint Force security team

MAJOR JACK "RIPPER" INGALLS, 211th Rescue
   Squadron, Alaska Air National Guard, HC-130J
   Super Hercules pilot

CAPTAIN LAURA "SKATER" VAN HORN, 211th Rescue
   Squadron, Alaska Air National Guard, HC-130J
   copilot

GENERAL KEITH MAKOWSKI, U.S. Air Force,
   commander, North American Aerospace Defense
   Command (NORAD)

CAPTAIN AMANDA JAFFE, U.S. Air Force,
   Information Integration Officer, RC-135V
   Rivet Joint ELINT (Electronic Intelligence)
   aircraft

TECHNICAL SERGEANT PHILIP KIJAC, cryptologic
   language analyst, RC-135V Rivet Joint aircraft

COLONEL LEONARD HUBER, U.S. Air Force,
   commander, Third Wing, Joint Base Elmendorf-
   Richardson

CAPTAIN CONNOR "DOC" MCFADDEN, U.S. Air Force,
   F-22 Raptor fighter pilot

LIEUTENANT ALLISON "CAT" PARILLA, U.S. Air Force,
   F-22 Raptor fighter pilot

MAJOR KING, 176th Wing, Alaska Air National
   Guard, liaison officer to Third Wing

LIEUTENANT GENERAL DAVID ROSENTHAL, U.S.
   Air Force, commander, Alaskan Command
   (ALCOM), Joint Base Elmendorf-Richardson

PRIVATE FIRST CLASS TORVALD PEDERSEN, U.S. Army,
   designated rifle marksman for Flynn's Joint Force
   security team

AIRMAN PETER KIM, U.S. Air Force, assigned to Joint Force security team

STAFF SERGEANT TIM WAHL, Alaska Air National Guard, HC-130J Super Hercules loadmaster

PRIVATE NOAH BOYD, U.S. Army, assigned to Joint Force security team

PRIVATE MIKE SIMS, U.S. Army, assigned to Joint Force security team

PRIVATE FLOYD LEFFERT, U.S. Army, assigned to Joint Force security team

PRIVATE GENE SANTARELLI, U.S. Army, assigned to Joint Force security team

RUSSIANS

COLONEL ALEXEI PETROV, Russian Air Force test pilot in charge of the PAK-DA prototype stealth bomber flight test program

MIKHAIL IVANIN, CEO of the Tupolev aerospace and defense company

GEORGY REMIZOV, Tupolev corporate test pilot

DMITRI GRISHIN, oligarch and CEO of *Severnaya Zvezda Stolitsa* (North Star Capital), one of Russia's largest industrial and financial conglomerates

DR. VIKTOR OBOLENSKY, neurologist employed at the Bekhterev Private Clinic in Moscow

MAJOR OLEG BUNIN, Russian Air Force test copilot for the PAK-DA stealth bomber flight test program

PAVEL VORONIN, confidential assistant and troubleshooter for Grishin

SERGEI BONDAROVICH, ex-Spetsnaz major now
  working for Voronin

PIOTR ZHDANOV, president of the Russian Federation

MAJOR GENERAL VASILY MAVRICHEV, Russian Air
  Force, commander of the Long-Range Aviation
  Force

LIEUTENANT GENERAL YVGENY ROGOZIN, commander,
  Russian Air Force

MAJOR VALENTIN YAKUNIN, Su-30 fighter pilot

CAPTAIN IVAN SALTIKOV, Su-30 fighter weapons officer

KONSTANTIN YUMASHEV, head of the Federal
  Security Service, the FSB

GENNADIY KOKORIN, Minister of Defense

ADMIRAL NIKOLAI GOLITSYN, commander, Russian
  Navy

SERGEI VESELOVSKY, head of the Foreign Intelligence
  Service, the SVR

ALEKSANDR IVASHIN, head of the General Staff's
  military intelligence agency, the GRU

MAJOR VADIM KURYOKHIN, Russian Air Force, Su-35S
  fighter pilot

CAPTAIN ILYA TROITSKY, Russian Air Force, Su-35S
  fighter pilot

COLONEL IOSIF ZINCHUK, Russian Air Force,
  commander, Tu-142 maritime reconnaissance
  aircraft

CAPTAIN SUKACHOV, Russian Air Force, Tu-142
  defense systems operator

LIEUTENANT GORSHENIOV, Russian Air Force, Tu-142
  second navigator

CAPTAIN YURI BASHALACHEV, Russian Air Force,
  Tu-142 bombardier-navigator

CAPTAIN ARKADY TIMONOV, Russian Spetsnaz special forces, commander, reconnaissance-attack team outside Joint Base Elmendorf-Richardson

LIEUTENANT LEONID BRYKIN, Russian Spetsnaz special forces team outside Joint Base Elmendorf-Richardson

CAPTAIN FIRST RANK MIKHAIL NAKHIMOV, Russian Navy, commander, SSBN BS-64 *Podmoskovye*

SENIOR LIEUTENANT ANATOLY YALINSKY, Russian Navy, diving officer, SSBN BS-64 *Podmoskovye*

MAJOR GENNADY KORENEV, Russian Spetsnaz special forces, commander, Raven assault force

CAPTAIN PRIMAKOV, Russian Spetsnaz special forces, second-in-command, Raven assault force

COLONEL GENERAL ANATOLY GRUZDEV, commander, Russian Strategic Rocket Forces

CANADIAN

PETER GOWAN, Royal Canadian Air Force, deputy commander, North American Aerospace Defense Command (NORAD)

ARCTIC
STORM
RISING

PROLOGUE

LATE JULY

Rays of summer sunlight streamed through rows of windows set high up along one drab concrete wall of the huge assembly hall. They lit sections of a large, futuristic-looking blended-wing aircraft: the first flyable prototype of Tupolev's top secret PAK-DA stealth bomber. A protruding nose and the large, rounded cockpit canopy surrounded by narrow engine intakes along the wing's leading edge explained the nickname it had acquired in construction, *Skat*, or Devilfish. So did the multiple elevons and other control surfaces lining the wing's trailing edge. Seen from above, the aircraft's unusual configuration gave it the look of a manta ray gliding silently across the ocean floor.

Intended to match and even surpass America's operational B-2 Spirit and next-generation B-21 Raider stealth bombers, the PAK-DA was a subsonic aircraft with a planned range of more than twelve thousand kilometers. Two powerful NK-65 turbofan engines, each producing more than sixty thousand pounds of thrust, would enable it to carry thirty metric tons of payload—both long-range stealth cruise missiles and shorter-ranged air-to-air missiles for self-defense—in internal weapons bays. The bomber's own stealth characteristics, new sensor systems, electronics, and flight controls were designed to allow its wartime crew of four to penetrate advanced enemy air defenses without being detected. All told, this prototype was the culmination of a top secret research-and-development program that had already consumed many years and hundreds of billions of rubles.

Russian Air Force Colonel Alexei Petrov slid out through an opening on the aircraft's belly and dropped nimbly onto the assembly hall floor, ignoring the ladder fitted to the hatch. In his midforties, the veteran test pilot was still trim and fit, though flecks of gray dusted his dark brown hair. Smiling broadly, he nodded to the knot of Tupolev design engineers, senior executives, and company test pilots waiting for him. "My congratulations, gentlemen. You've built a beautiful machine. I'm looking forward to putting it through its paces in the weeks and months ahead."

His praise for their work drew answering smiles from the engineers and executives. In contrast, the rugged faces of Tupolev's own experienced civilian pilots stiffened slightly at the unwelcome reminder that they were being bypassed. Desperate to show the world that Russia could still compete militarily with the United States and China, the Kremlin had ordered this new strategic bomber program accelerated by every means necessary. Delivering the PAK-DA prototype directly to Petrov and his team without the usual sequence of carefully monitored corporate test flights would shave months off the process of certifying the design for full-scale production and deployment to operational regiments.

"When would you like us to arrange the formal handover?" Mikhail Ivanin, Tupolev's burly CEO, asked carefully.

"As soon as possible," Petrov replied. "But not here in Kazan. Let's take care of that business down at Chkalov instead."

The other man pursed his lips. The Air Force's Valery Chkalov flight test center was nearly nine hundred kilometers south of Kazan. Named after one of the old Soviet Union's most famous and daring test pilots, the range was now specially equipped to handle experimental advanced stealth aircraft. Transferring the bomber prototype there right away would definitely speed up the process of validating its flight characteristics and systems. Unfortunately, it also meant assigning Tupolev's own specialist mechanics to the distant base for a prolonged period. They would be needed to train Air Force ground crews to maintain the PAK-DA's complex avionics and advanced radar-absorbent coatings. The hassle factor for the company and its employees would be high. So would the added expense. Then again, Moscow's orders were clear: whatever Petrov and his team wanted, they would get.

Glancing at the unhappy faces of Tupolev's own pilots, Petrov threw them a bone. "Your guys can bring the bomber down. After all, it's only fair that they have the honor of taking the Devilfish up for its first flight."

With a curt nod, Ivanin crooked a finger, signaling the senior company flier over to join them. Georgy Remizov was a short, stocky, round-faced man a few years older than Petrov himself. He'd flown high-performance combat aircraft for the Air Force before resigning to join Tupolev when Russia's post-Soviet military went through one of its periodic belt-tightenings. Perfunctory introductions completed, the CEO excused himself. "For now, I'll leave you to work out the details with Georgy, Colonel. But feel free to contact me if you need anything else."

Then he hurried away, almost as though he feared Petrov would make some new outrageously expensive demand if he lingered any longer. The two pilots watched him go with some amusement. "Chief Executive Ivanin has a superb head for numbers and budgets," Remizov murmured.

"But he's no aviator?"

"I think he sometimes wishes we built locomotives or automobiles instead of aircraft," Remizov confided. "I hear he gets airsick above the fourth floor of any building."

With the Tupolev test pilot pacing him, Petrov strolled toward the nearest exit from the huge aircraft assembly hall. The armed guards posted there stiffened to attention. He threw them a casual salute and then glanced down at the shorter man. "Well? Any questions?"

Remizov shook his head. "None." A lopsided smile flashed across his face and then vanished. "I anticipated your . . . request. I've already worked out a flight plan with contingencies for any possible teething troubles. We'll never be more than a few minutes' flying time from potential abort fields during the whole trip south to Chkalov."

"Very good," Petrov said in approval, and he meant it. The first few flight hours were always the most dangerous in any new aircraft. No matter how thoroughly you scrubbed a revolutionary design in wind tunnels and computer simulations, things could still go badly wrong under real-world conditions. "I appreciate your attention to detail."

Remizov shrugged. "I had a good teacher." This time his smile was more genuine. "I served under your father as a junior pilot, Colonel." He shook his head admiringly. "The general was one tough son of a bitch, that's for sure. Without mercy for fuckups. But we were sharp as razors by the time he finished with us." His eyes narrowed as he quoted from memory, " '*Train hard. Plan thoroughly. Act fast. Those are the keys to victory.*'"

Petrov hid a grimace. Would he never escape his father's shadow? Even now, years after the old man's final heart attack finished him, devoted acolytes of Hero of the Soviet Union, Major General Vladimir Petrov, seemed to turn up wherever he went. It was maddening, even if understandable. As a young lieutenant, the older Petrov had won his spurs and his medals as a "volunteer" flying secret combat missions against the Americans over North Vietnam and then again against the Israelis during the October War in 1973. Credited with several kills, he was renowned as the top-scoring Russian fighter pilot since the Korean War. In later years, he'd risen rapidly in rank, leading ever-larger frontline Air Force units equipped with the best aircraft. If his heart hadn't given out, the famous Major General Petrov could easily have someday commanded all of Russia's aerospace forces.

In sharp contrast, Alexei Petrov knew with some bitterness that his own career, though marked by praise, promotion, and medals for peacetime flying exploits, would never match that of his father. At his age, this assignment to lead the PAK-DA stealth bomber flight test program represented his last real chance to shine. But once he finished vetting the new aircraft and its systems, he would undoubtedly be shunted off to a desk and relative obscurity somewhere inside the Ministry of Defense bureaucracy. After that, he could look forward to wasting years dealing with dull reports before finally being put out to pasture on a wholly inadequate state pension.

Oblivion and poverty—not exactly attractive prospects, he thought coldly as he made his farewell to Remizov and left the vast Tupolev factory. Which made it much easier to contemplate taking a very different path in life. And imagining how the course of action he was now considering would have horrified his father—always so rigidly attentive to his duty—made it even more appealing.

A couple of hours outside Kazan, Petrov swung his IRBIS touring motorbike off the crowded highway and onto a narrow, tree-lined road. He opened the throttle, smoothly accelerating as the track curved back to the west. The sensation of speed as trees flashed past, more blurs than distinct shapes, was exhilarating. Through openings in the woods on his right, he caught glimpses of an enormous stretch of dark blue water, the vast Cheboksary Reservoir created by damming the Volga River. Off on the left, wheat and barley fields surrounded small farming villages. Apart from a couple of old tractors trundling across the fields and faded clothes drying outside run-down cottages, there were few signs of people.

A few kilometers farther on, he slowed and pulled in behind a silver-gray late model Mercedes sedan parked just off the road. Dismounting, he stripped off his helmet and unzipped his jacket. Even in the shade provided by the trees, the summer heat was oppressive.

At his approach, the driver of the Mercedes slid out from behind the wheel. With a silent nod, he opened the sedan's rear door. A slight bulge in the man's dark business jacket revealed the presence of a shoulder holster.

Petrov raised an eyebrow. So even here in this

rural backwater, his host felt the need for a body-guard. Perhaps such vigilance was an inevitable by-product of the acquisition of great wealth. If so, he thought with satisfaction, he might someday soon learn the value of caution himself.

He slid into the back of the air-conditioned Mercedes and nodded politely to the older, heavier-set man waiting there. "Everything is on track," he said confidently.

"There were no problems at the factory?"

Petrov shrugged. "The Tupolev guys are pissed, but no one's willing to stick his neck out to protest openly."

"They are wise," the older man said, with the hint of an icy smile of his own. Dmitri Grishin was one of Russia's most powerful oligarchs, a man who had made his fortune through close ties to Moscow's political, industrial, and defense elites. Either on his own or through intermediaries, he owned significant stakes in many of the nation's most successful and profitable enterprises. "Our president does not appreciate having his decisions questioned."

"Fortunately for us," Petrov agreed, matching the oligarch's wry expression. His eyes narrowed. "What about the other elements of our special project? Are they moving ahead?"

Grishin nodded smoothly. "My people have everything well in hand. They've found a valley deep in the wilderness in Alaska that's perfect for our purposes. All will be ready when you are."

"What about the Americans?" Petrov asked. "Is

there a chance they could stumble across your team at work?"

The oligarch shook his head. "Relax, Colonel. The Alaskan wilderness is enormous and almost entirely uninhabited. I doubt anyone's even visited the site we've found since the end of the last Ice Age, more than twelve thousand years ago. The Americans won't see a thing."

Reassured, Petrov slid back out of the Mercedes and then leaned back in. "Until the snows fall, then."

"And the icy winds blow," Grishin agreed. He glanced up at the younger man. "Fly safe, Colonel. We both have a lot at stake here."

Petrov shot him a grin. "Don't worry. I'll take care of the PAK-DA prototype like it was my very own."

Moments later, as he stood watching the limousine pull away, Petrov felt a sudden stab of pain lance through his left temple. "Fuck," he muttered. He'd been resolutely ignoring a mild headache since leaving the Tupolev plant. But now it was getting worse. Frowning, he fumbled out a couple of aspirin tablets from a packet in one of his pockets and then pulled out a stainless steel hip flask. Embossed with the badge of the Soviet Union's Red Air Force, it was the one item he'd inherited from his father that he genuinely valued.

Impatiently, he downed the aspirin with a swig of vodka and then recapped the flask. This was no time for illness. Not when he was so close to making sure that *he* would be the one everyone remembered in the future.

ONE

AUGUST

Its shadow lost among jagged black peaks and spires of hardened lava, the dark gray U.S. Air Force HH-60W Jolly Green II helicopter flew low across the desolate wastes of southern Libya. Specially designed for service with CSAR (combat search and rescue) squadrons and named in honor of the HH-3E Jolly Green Giant made famous during Vietnam War rescue missions, this was the newest variation of Sikorsky's versatile UH-60 Black Hawk series. Like its predecessor aircraft, the HH-60G Pave Hawk, the Jolly Green II was equipped with a hoist and retractable midair refueling probe. But upgraded avionics, engines, weapons, armor, and larger fuel tanks dramatically increased its capabilities, including extending its unrefueled range to more than seven hundred miles.

The helicopter's nose dropped sharply, descending fast as it sped down a bleak slope of black volcanic rock and sand. Along the horizon to the southwest, the terrain shifted dramatically—morphing into a seemingly endless, golden-orange sea of Saharan sand dunes. Heat waves rippled across a landscape baked by the harsh rays of the desert sun high overhead.

Seated behind the HH-60's cockpit and facing outward, Captain Nicholas Flynn felt his stomach floating as the helicopter raced downslope at more than 160 knots. Through the cabin window in front of him, he caught blurred glimpses of massive boulders zipping past not more than a few feet below. That only increased the sensation of uncontrolled speed. He swallowed hard and crossed his arms over the straps holding him in his seat. "Oh, what fun," he muttered, realizing too late he was on the intercom.

"What's the matter, Nick?" the cheerful voice of the pilot, Captain Scott "FX" Dykstra, asked through his headset. "Don't like flying?"

Through gritted teeth, Flynn shot back, "Flying, I don't mind. I just prefer my sky with a little less ground in it."

Dykstra chuckled. "See, there's where I gotta disagree with you." The helicopter banked hard left and then right again, as he steered around a massive ledge of basalt jutting out at an angle from the softer soils around it. "Clouds are pretty and all, but high altitude's a happy hunting ground for hostile interceptors and missiles. Down here just above the dirt is the sweet spot, where any bad guys only get a couple of seconds to react before we scoot on past and out of sight."

"Oh, I understand the theory," Flynn said, bracing himself as the HH-60 slewed sharply upward again and then leveled out a hundred feet off the desert floor. "It's the practice that scares the shit out of me."

A new voice came on the intercom circuit. This one belonged to Technical Sergeant Carl Zalewski, one of the two PJs, or pararescue jumpers, riding with him in the Jolly Green II cabin. "Please tell me you're not being literal, sir. Our guys just washed this bird before we took off from El Minya. If we bring it back all dirty, they're gonna be seriously upset."

Flynn found himself grinning. "Just talking figuratively, Zee. Fear not, my camos retain their pristine nature, without any unsightly new brown blotches."

That drew a quick laugh from the rest of Wizard One-One's crew. There were five of them all told: Dykstra; his copilot, Captain Kate "Ghost" Kasper; their flight engineer, Staff Sergeant Bill Wade; Zalewski; and the other PJ, Technical Sergeant Mike Camarillo.

"Geez, Nick, if you're gonna freak out, I might have to assign Wade to monitor you in between engine checks," Dykstra joked. "It'll give him something to do besides wail and gnash his teeth about his missing guns."

"I am not wailing, sir," the powerfully built flight engineer said in mock protest. "Just sitting here sobbing quietly."

Before they'd lifted off from El Minya, an Egyptian Air Force training base in the Nile Valley, ground personnel had hurriedly removed the helicopter's two door-mounted .50-caliber machine guns. Stripping the weapons and their mounts shaved off close to a thousand pounds of weight. Even with the HH-60W's larger fuel tanks, every option to lighten its load and extend its range counted. This emergency search-and-rescue mission to a crash site in southern Libya was at the very outer edge of the helicopter's capabilities—already requiring one midair refueling just to get them this far.

Up to five hours ago, the crew's primary focus as part of the Sixty-Fourth Expeditionary Rescue Squadron had been on weeks-long joint training exercises with their Egyptian and other allied counterparts. That had changed the moment they received a flash transmission reporting the crash of a U.S. Air Force C-130J Super Hercules deep in the Sahara Desert, some miles from the nearest inhabited place, the Wath Oasis. Despite being nearly nine hundred miles away, they were the closest trained CSAR group. Parachuting in a team might have been faster, except that no one in their right mind wanted to drop a handful of rescuers into the unknown without a way to pull them out in a hurry if trouble erupted. So now the Jolly Green II and its specialist crew was en route to do what they could for any survivors from the aircraft that had gone down. Of course, as hours went by without radio contact from the crash site, it was looking less and less likely that anyone had made it out alive. But someone still had to go check.

Wizard One-One's pilots, Dykstra and Kasper, were combat-tested veterans of several daring mis-

sions to extract wounded U.S. and allied personnel under fire and deep in hostile territory. Bill
Wade was along to keep the helicopter's engines,
hydraulic systems, and other equipment operating
smoothly during an extraordinarily long and gru-
eling flight. And as pararescuemen, Zalewski and
Camarillo were graduates of one of the toughest
training programs in the entire U.S. military—
nearly two years' worth of rigorous courses covering
emergency medicine, parachuting, mountaineer-
ing, combat diving, wilderness survival, tactics, helicopter operations, and half a dozen other valuable
specializations. If there were injured survivors still
trapped in the wreckage of the C-130J turboprop,
their expertise would be crucial to extracting the
wounded and getting them back to base alive.

Nick Flynn's own role in the mission was less
clearly defined. After graduating from college with
an ROTC scholarship, he'd undergone intensive
training to qualify as a Special Tactics Officer in the
Air Force Special Operations Command—earning
the right to a scarlet beret, similar to the maroon
beret worn by the rest of Wizard One-One's crew.
But there the similarities ended. Thanks to an ear
for languages and a gift for quick study, he'd been
quietly recruited into Air Force intelligence operations shortly after completing the STO course.
He'd come to Egypt with the squadron as one of
its combat rescue officers. But that was just a cover
story. His real mission was to gather HUMINT,
human intelligence, on the Egyptian and other foreign nationals involved in the exercises—focusing

on those who might someday be recruited as potential intelligence sources. Or, conversely, on those
who might be open to working with terrorists or
other groups hostile to U.S. interests.

Ostensibly, his language skills were the reason
he'd been assigned to this flight. None of the others
in the helicopter crew knew enough Arabic to liaise
with locals if that proved necessary. But the lieutenant colonel in charge of the Sixty-Fourth had
his own motives in putting Flynn aboard. "You're
a spook, Nick," he'd said quietly. "And whatever's
actually going on out there is really fucking spooky.
Right now, no one higher up the chain of command
will tell me what the hell one of our C-130s was
doing off on its own so deep in Libya. All I'm getting is static about how I don't 'need to know.' Well,
that's bullshit. So there's no damn way I'm sending
my folks out on a limb without a specially trained
pair of eyes and ears along to ride herd on this situation. Which is where you come in."

Flynn couldn't disagree with that line of reasoning. More than a decade after the brutal civil war
that ended Colonel Muammar Gaddafi's authoritarian rule, Libya was still a cauldron of rival armed
factions. There was no real central government,
only fluctuating coalitions of regional groups, tribal
militias, and die-hard Islamists. Chaos and conflict
were the stuff of everyday life throughout most of
the fractured country. That was especially true in
the sparsely populated far south, hundreds of miles
from Libya's more densely inhabited coastal strip
along the Mediterranean. All of which made the

region the very last place you'd expect an unarmed U.S. Air Force cargo plane to be operating.

Reflexively, he patted the M4A1 carbine slung from his tactical body armor. Whatever they found at the crash site, this sure wasn't going to be another boring day spent schmoozing Egyptian, Saudi, Iraqi, and other foreign officers over endless cups of tea.

A soft ping through his headset signaled an update from the helicopter's navigation computer. From her position in the cockpit's left-hand seat, Kate Kasper relayed the new data as it appeared on one of her big multifunction display panels. "Heads up, whiz kids. We're about eight minutes out from the estimated crash site. Check your gear and stand by."

Flynn took a quick pass through the accessory pouches attached to his body armor. Extra magazines for his carbine and Glock 19 sidearm. Check. His Panasonic Toughbook tablet field computer was ready to go with a full battery. So were his pocket laser range finder and multiband tactical radio. He was set.

In the pair of seats behind him, Zalewski and Camarillo were doing the same thing with their personal weapons and trauma kits. Satisfied with those, the PJs went rapidly through the array of compact cutting and lifting tools packed in their individual rucksacks.

"Two minutes," Kasper called. "Radar's picking up objects on the ground about six miles out, at our twelve o'clock."

"I don't see any smoke," Dykstra commented

matter-of-factly. "Any fires must have burned out by now."

Flynn leaned back in his seat, craning his head sharply to look through the helicopter's forward cockpit canopy. With all the heat haze, it was difficult to make out many details. But there was definitely a blackened scar stretching across the orangish desert sand. At one end of the scar, he could see a big, crumpled gray cylinder partially buried nose-first in a large dune. A debris field of torn and bent pieces of blackened metal—scorched wing panels, twisted propellers, and shattered engine mounts—stretched away for hundreds of feet on both sides of the wreck.

Dykstra whistled softly. "Looks like that Herky Bird slammed in almost horizontally. The wings ripped off, but the fuselage seems mostly intact." He tweaked the cyclic, pedals, and collective to reduce their airspeed as the Jolly Green II swung through a gentle, level turn to come in behind the downed C-130.

Abruptly, as they came out of the turn, Flynn spotted a twin-turbine helicopter, a Russian-manufactured Mi-17 medium transport, sitting parked on the sand not more than a hundred yards from the Super Hercules's torn fuselage. Oddly, its desert camouflage paint scheme showed no obvious national markings or other identifiers. Several Western-looking men in civilian clothing were visible around the helicopter and the C-130 wreckage. Some carried a mix of small arms and wore military-grade body armor.

"Son of a bitch," Kasper muttered. "We've got company."

A new voice crackled over the helicopter's ARC-210 communications system. *"Wizard One-One, this is Rocking Horse Six. Suggest you land on the other side of the wreck. We'll confer further once you're down."*

"Copy that, Rocking Horse," Kasper acknowledged tightly. Her fingers danced across her multifunction display, inputting the call sign they'd been given. She switched back to the intercom. "The computer confirms that 'Rocking Horse' is legit. But that call sign belongs to an OGA."

Flynn snorted. OGA was military jargon for "Other Government Agency." In practice, that usually meant the CIA's clandestine service and its paramilitary contractors.

"You know anything about these guys or what they're up to out here, Nick?" Dykstra asked, making small adjustments to the helicopter controls to veer off and circle back around toward the suggested landing site. "Wearing your other hat, I mean?" That was a not-so-subtle reference to Flynn's covert status as an Air Force intelligence officer.

"Not a doggone thing, FX," Flynn said truthfully. His hands moved to the quick-release buckle on his seat straps. A rotor-whipped cloud of swirling sand and dust billowed up as the HH-60 flared in and then settled lightly on its main landing gear. His eyes narrowed in concentration. "But I can promise you that's about to change."

TWO

AN HOUR LATER

All three U.S. Air Force crewmen aboard the downed aircraft were dead. Confirming that had required Zalewski and Camarillo to painstakingly work their way into the half-buried nose of the big cargo turboprop, first digging through compacted sand and then carefully cutting through jagged layers of impact-crushed metal. Once they'd gotten close to what was left of the C-130's cockpit, they'd spotted the broken remains of its two pilots and loadmaster wedged in amid the twisted wreckage of instrument panels, wiring, consoles, and seats.

"How's it look, Zee?" Flynn asked when Zalewski wriggled back outside to report.

Stretching cramped shoulders, the big pararescueman shook his head gravely. "Bad, sir. A real mess. It's gonna take a hell of an effort to get the bodies out." He stripped off his helmet and gloves, then rubbed a weary hand through his short-cropped, sweat-drenched hair before taking a long swallow through the tube of his hydration pack.

Under the late afternoon sun, it was well over one hundred degrees Fahrenheit, and it was even hotter inside the C-130 wreck's tight, confined spaces.

Flynn nodded. He lowered his voice. "So what do you think? Was this crash an accident? Or enemy action?"

Zalewski's forehead wrinkled in thought. "If I was a betting man, sir, I'd put my money on bad guys," he said at length. "The Herc's forward section is all torn up. Even more than I'd expect from the impact when it smacked into this sand dune."

Flynn frowned. "Like maybe the plane was hit by a missile?"

"Either that, or else somebody set off a bomb right behind the cockpit," Zalewski suggested. He jerked a thumb over his shoulder toward the C-130's tail section. "Once we get 'em back to the tech experts, info from the flight data and cockpit voice recorders should pin down exactly what happened."

"Yeah." Flynn glanced away along the top of the massive, miles-long dune, which rose a couple of hundred feet above the crash site. His jaw tightened. About a hundred yards away, a handful of figures in white robes and head coverings crouched on the crest, watching all the activity around the wrecked airplane with undisguised curiosity. The first locals from the nearby oasis had appeared while Camarillo and Zalewski were cutting their way into the cockpit. More seemed to be arriving with every passing minute. He turned back to the big PJ. "You know, I think it'd be a good idea if you and Camarillo got those black boxes out soonest.

Before this place turns into Grand Central Station at rush hour."

"That will not be necessary, Captain," someone said from close behind him.

Flynn turned around to find one of the civilians who'd flown in ahead of them aboard the unmarked Mi-17 helicopter. The other man was almost skeletally thin. He'd introduced himself earlier as Anderson White—a name that was almost certainly fake, but which certainly matched his pale, washed-out eyes, gray crew cut, and thin, almost colorless lips. Whoever he really was, he was definitely the one calling the shots for the black ops team.

"And why is that, Mr. . . . White?" Flynn asked, adding a deliberate pause to show that he wasn't buying the other man's obvious alias.

"My team will retrieve those data recorders and make sure they get to the right people," White said flatly, ignoring the dig. "I suggest your people focus on recovering those remains. It would be best if you leave everything else to us. This is not your show."

Flynn didn't like the sound of that at all. He deliberately allowed a little more of his native Texas drawl to slide into his voice. "Maybe *y'all* are forgetting this was a U.S. Air Force C-130."

"Flying under my agency's orders," White countered smoothly. "And carrying a cargo we provided. Which makes everything on that aircraft aft of the cockpit solely our jurisdiction."

Flynn fought down a scowl. Virtually the only piece of information the OGA black ops team had provided was that the Super Hercules had been coming in so low over this part of the desert because it was on approach to an old Libyan Air Force runway south of the Wath Oasis. A quick check of the map and data files loaded into his field tablet showed that was part of a base Gaddafi had built inside the Aouzou Strip—a sixty-mile-wide swath of territory along Chad's border with Libya. Rumored to be rich in uranium deposits, the Strip had been the spark for nine years of military clashes between the two countries back in the late 1970s. It was just the kind of disputed turf that seemed likely to draw in some of the world's bad actors, especially those interested in acquiring potentially fissionable ores for full-fledged nuclear weapons or improvised dirty bombs.

Right after they'd landed, he'd grabbed a quick look inside the C-130's largely intact cargo compartment. Within a couple of minutes, one of White's tough-looking paramilitary security personnel—whose tats and beard marked him as ex–Special Forces—had not so gently backed him out again. But not before Flynn got the chance to check out a few of the crates the big turboprop had been carrying, discovering what looked like a shitload of Russian-made small arms, ammunition, RPGs, and land mines.

He raised an eyebrow at White. "Your jurisdiction? Meaning what, exactly?"

"Meaning that you're going to stand back and let my team complete its work without further interference," the other man replied. He checked his watch. "From what I've been told, they should be done rigging the cargo and the aircraft with explosives in approximately one hour." His lips thinned even further. "Which is why I suggest you rev your own unit into higher gear and get those bodies out, ASAP. Once our charges are set, we're not going to sit around waiting on you and your people."

Flynn stared at him. "You're going to blow the wreck up?"

White nodded. "We're going to sanitize this site, Captain. And thoroughly. This mess needs to be cleared up before any more unwelcome visitors arrive—say the international press, or members of several of the factions who claim they're in charge of this godforsaken region."

"Because otherwise they'd find evidence that you've been running guns to a different splinter group? Here in Libya? Or south in Chad?" Flynn said pointedly.

"A provocative assertion," the other man acknowledged. His voice took on an edge of its own. "But since the matter is highly classified, I strongly suggest you let it drop. Here and now."

"Or what? You'll have to kill me?"

White smiled narrowly. "You've been watching far too many bad movies, Captain Flynn. We don't kill people to protect our secrets these days. Well, not often, anyway." He shrugged. "We prefer nonlethal measures."

"Like what?" Flynn pushed with a wry smile of his own. "Amnesia drugs? MiB-style memory zappers?"

"Nothing so technical," the other man said

coldly, dropping any pretense at affability. "Now we rely on leaks to our allies in the media. We can count on them to shit all over people's careers and reputations until everyone who matters is convinced our targets are either crazy or dirty." His pale eyes glittered. "Trust me on this—you really do *not* want to find out what it's like being on the receiving end of one of our smear operations. So just back the fuck off."

Flynn stiffened and then felt Zalewski's big hand land on his shoulder.

"The guy's not worth the trouble, sir," the PJ murmured. "Let it go. For now."

Reluctantly, Flynn let himself be guided away. He glanced up at the technical sergeant. "You're not going to give me some heartfelt lecture on the perils of wrestling with a pig, are you?"

"Hell no," Zalewski said. He grinned. "I'm a suburban kid. Bacon and pork chops are as close as I ever get to pigs." Then he nodded back over his shoulder toward where White stood watching them walk away. "But I've got a pretty good built-in detector for creepy sacks of shit. And that guy's pegging the top of the meter."

"What's your read on his security detail?"

The PJ shrugged. "Mostly solid. Definitely ex–meat eaters." He used the slang for Special Forces troops who took part in dangerous combat missions instead of training allied soldiers and local militias. "I figure their new Secret Squirrel bosses pay a lot more than ours do, though."

Flynn thought about his monthly check with all

its assorted deductions and nodded. "Safe bet, Zee."
He checked the crest of the dune again. Another
couple of robed men had appeared and joined the
others observing them. His eyes narrowed. "Can
you make that hour deadline to get the bodies out?"

"It'll be tough," Zalewski admitted.

"What if I give you a hand? I'm checked out on
some of your extraction gear."

The PJ shook his head. "Appreciate the offer, sir.
But it's real tight inside that part of the wreck. As it
is, me and Mike are having to take turns clearing a
good-sized opening into the cockpit." He followed
Flynn's gaze and nodded. "Anyway, I kinda figure
we could use a good pair of eyes out here. Watching
the watchers, if you get my drift."

"Yeah, I'm not real happy about having an audience, either." Flynn was uncomfortably aware that
they didn't have enough spare personnel to maintain
a secure perimeter around the crash site. Most of the
OGA black ops team was busy around the C-130's
cargo compartment. And Wizard One-One's flight
crew—Dykstra, Kasper, and Wade—were fully occupied watching over their own helicopter. The
same went for the Mi-17's two pilots. White had
posted one of his ex–Special Forces contractors on
guard near the tail section of the downed plane, but
otherwise there was just him.

Flynn's subconscious had started sending up
flares the moment Zalewski confided his suspicions
that this crash wasn't an accident. Well, he decided,
it was high time he started paying attention to those
danger signals from his lizard brain. Whoever had

brought the cargo plane down might have bigger plans—plans that could prove dangerous to the health of Mama Flynn's dark-haired boy . . . and every other American in the vicinity. Which made it imperative that he take a long, hard look at their surroundings and tactical situation.

So, as soon as the PJ squeezed back inside the C-130's damaged forward fuselage, Flynn made the long trudge upslope to the top of the dune. Loose sand slid out from under his combat boots with every step. By the time he made it, he was drenched in sweat. Little swirls of sand danced along the knife-edge-like crest, kicked up by occasional gusts of wind that were as hot and dry as if they had come straight out of a bake oven. His shadow stretched away to the left, lengthened by the sun slanting lower in the west.

Squinting against the glare, he raised his binoculars and scanned across the sea of dunes toward the Wath Oasis. Its tiny cluster of buildings marked the only source of water for more than sixty miles in any direction. Any trouble was likely to come from that direction.

There were tracks down the nearest slope off to the south, heading this way. They continued across the desert floor, coming to an end among a small herd of camels tethered down at the base of this sand dune. They were about a couple of hundred yards from his position on the crest. Two more of the white-robed locals squatted close to the camels, evidently guarding them.

Flynn focused in on them. Under those head

wrappings, it was hard to get a good look at their faces, but they appeared to be young and fit, certainly not more than thirty years old. The hard work needed to survive in this waterless, harsh climate aged people fast.

Slowly, he lowered the binoculars. Come to think of it, he hadn't seen any women or children among those who'd arrived to gawk at the wrecked Super Hercules and the Americans working the crash site. Nor had he noticed any of the elders who ordinarily controlled the daily life of this region's semi-nomadic clans.

A flash of movement off to the south caught his eye and Flynn got his binoculars back up just in time to catch sight of another white-robed man stationed high up on the next dune over. He was vigorously waving at a rider mounted on a camel that had just lumbered over the crest. Unlike the others, this rider was dressed in the bright-colored clothes favored by local women. Obediently, she turned the head of her beast around and disappeared down the other side again. Apparently satisfied, the watcher sank back on his haunches.

"Crap," Flynn muttered. Somebody out there was definitely controlling access to this area—making it off-limits to any but able-bodied young men. That almost certainly spelled trouble. Turning quickly, he half trotted, half slid back down the dune's loose slope.

He found White supervising his team's activity near the tail of the wrecked C-130.

"What is it this time, Captain?" the gray-haired

intelligence officer snapped in exasperation. "I thought I made it clear that this is my bailiwick, not yours."

With an effort, Flynn controlled his temper. "We may have bigger problems than jurisdictional squabbles, Mr. White," he said evenly.

"Such as?" the other man asked skeptically.

Rapidly, Flynn ran through his observations and his reasoning. "It's likely this aircraft was deliberately brought down here, either by a missile or a bomb. And my bet is that whoever's responsible is gathering a force to finish the job," he concluded. "Which means we're all in the crosshairs."

"And you're basing this remarkable theory solely on the absence of women and children watching us work?" White said in disbelief. "For God's sake, man, get a grip. The nearby clans are primitive herdsmen. They're also devout Muslims. So it's hardly surprising that they're discouraging their wives and young children from mingling with armed infidels like us—especially since as far as they know we're recovering the mangled victims of an air crash." His lip curled slightly. "I suggest you calm down. The last thing any of us need is for you to go off half-cocked and provoke some unfortunate incident."

With that parting shot, he waved a hand in dismissal. "Consider your concerns noted, Captain. Now, if you don't mind, I have serious work to do." Then he turned away to confer with one of his paramilitary contractors who'd been planting demolition charges.

It took almost every ounce of self-control Flynn possessed to stop himself from just hauling off and decking the black ops team leader. Instead, he took a deep breath, spun on his heel, and headed toward the landed HH-60W at a rapid clip. If, as he suspected, shit was about to get real here, he needed to make sure Dykstra, Kasper, and the others were clued in and alert.

He came around the tail section of the C-130 and saw the gray-painted helicopter sitting peacefully on its landing gear. The soles of Bill Wade's boots were visible through the open side doors. While they were grounded, the flight engineer had some equipment panel popped up to run a routine maintenance check. But Dykstra and Kasper weren't hanging out near the cockpit, where he'd expected to see them.

Instead, the two pilots had moved off a few yards nearer to the edge of the massive sand dune—ostentatiously positioning themselves between the bird and some of the white-robed tribesmen who were now drifting closer down the slope while talking loudly and exchanging broad, cheerful gestures. Both Dykstra and Kasper had their hands on the M4A1 carbines slung from their battle gear. They were very carefully *not* pointing them at the locals. Yet. But they were clearly focused on any possible threat from the men approaching the helicopter.

Which was why neither of them had noticed the tribesman in bulky robes coming around the other side of the Jolly Green II's fuselage. Unlike the others, this man was anything but casual in his movements. He was walking slowly, but very deliberately, toward the helicopter's open cabin.

That is so not good, Flynn thought, feeling abruptly cold despite the bone-dry heat. He increased his pace to intercept the tribesman. "*Alsalam ealaykum ya sidiqi. Hal yumkinuni musaeidatuk bashi'an?*" he called out politely in Arabic. "Peace be upon you, my friend. Can I help you with something?" The local Teda clans had their own Nilo-Saharan language, Tedaga, but he didn't speak it. And Arabic was the de facto lingua franca throughout North Africa.

Surprised, the robed man swung toward him and stopped. "Ah, *la*. Ah, no," he said hesitantly. "*Shukrana jazila. Ana jidi.* Thank you. I'm fine."

Fine, my ass. Flynn could hear that the tribesman's voice was slurred. He'd also gotten close enough to see that the other man's pupils were dilated. The son of a bitch was drugged, he realized. Bad. Bad. Very bad. His right hand dropped to the Glock 19 pistol he carried in a chest rig on top of his armor. "*'Akhraj min hna! Alan!*" he snapped. "Get out of here! Now!"

The tribesman's eyes widened in sudden panic. He fumbled at the opening to his robe, pawing for something inside.

Flynn caught a split-second glimpse of wires and a bulky vest. He reacted instantly. With his left forearm, he slammed the other man's hands aside. And in that same action, he drew his pistol, slid his finger inside the trigger guard as he swung it on target, and fired twice. Both 9mm rounds hit the tribesman squarely in the face, tore through, and exploded out the back of his skull. Already dead, the would-be suicide bomber dropped to his knees and then slumped to the ground.

With the ear-splitting crack of the two shots he'd fired still ringing in his ears, the world around Flynn seemed to blur into slow motion as adrenaline flooded his system. He slid the Glock back into his chest holster and grabbed his M4A1 carbine instead.

Through the HH-60W's open door, he could see Bill Wade looking back over his shoulder at him in stunned surprise. On the other side of the helicopter, Dykstra and Kasper were doing the same thing, caught completely off guard by the sudden eruption of violence.

Beyond them, the group of white-robed men who'd been ambling down the sandy slope had also frozen in their tracks. But they were no longer smiling. Instead, their expressions were taut, with their eyes narrowed and intent—the look of men determined to kill.

"Hostiles! On the dune!" Flynn yelled as he sprinted forward at an angle to get a clear shot. "Take cover and engage, for Christ's sake! This is an ambush!"

Now the remaining tribesmen were grabbing the weapons they'd hidden under their robes, awkwardly dragging out a mix of Soviet-era AK-47s and AKMs. One of them yelled an order, waving his arm wildly toward the grounded American helicopter.

Oh my God, Flynn realized. That smart bastard

wanted to just overrun them. It was a good plan. If the attackers got in close enough to overwhelm them with superior numbers, it was all over. So he needed to stop their assault before it started. He dropped to one knee, brought his sights onto the shouting tribesman, and squeezed off three quick shots. Bright red splotches blossomed across the man's white robes, and he went down hard.

The enemy doesn't have body armor, Flynn thought, fighting to stay in control. Score one for the good guys.

For a second or so, the white-robed men stared down at the body of their leader in shocked surprise, but then they threw themselves prone and started firing downhill. Most of their 7.62mm rounds went high and smacked into the helicopter's bullet-resistant armor panels, ricocheting off in all directions. One hit Bill Wade in the stomach as he scrambled out through the door. The combination of Kevlar and ceramic plates stopped the bullet from penetrating, but the impact knocked the flight engineer down. Another round ripped through his leg as he fell. More AK rounds tore up sand around where Dykstra and Kasper had already gone prone.

The two pilots shot back. Neither was an expert marksman, but they both had enough training to avoid the rookie mistake of aiming too high when firing up a slope. One more tribesman slumped over, drilled through the head. His assault rifle fell from his lifeless hands.

Suddenly, a blinding flash—brighter than the red-tinged afternoon sun—lit up the crash site.

WHAMMM.

And a huge shock wave slammed Flynn face-first into the ground with enormous force.

Blearily, he spat out blood and grit and raised his head just high enough to see a fire-laced cloud of oily black smoke rising beyond the wrecked C-130. Someone, probably another suicide bomber, had just blown the hell out of the black ops Mi-17.

Trailing smoke, a rocket-propelled grenade skimmed just over the downed Super Hercules and arrowed on to impact a couple of hundred yards beyond the HH-60W. It went off in an orange flash and a fountain of sand. The sight dragged Flynn out of his daze. Somebody out there on the other flank had an RPG launcher. And if they scored a hit on this last intact helicopter, he and the other Americans still alive at the crash site were royally screwed. Their enemies weren't going to sit on their asses and wait while the Air Force flew another search-and-rescue helicopter all the way from Egypt.

His hearing was coming back a bit, just enough to let him pick up the harsh, staccato rattle of automatic-weapons fire coming from the other side of the downed cargo aircraft. Some friendlies over there must have survived the suicide bomber's detonation.

On this side, the surviving white-robed attackers were also starting to stir, recovering from their own daze. Another few seconds and they'd be back in action.

Flynn scowled. The longer this fight went on, the worse it was going to get. It was time to end this—at least here. Rolling over, he tugged a ball-shaped M67 fragmentation grenade from one of his equipment pouches. Quickly, he flicked its safety clip away with his left thumb, twisted the pull ring, and yanked it out to release the pin. One swift glance over his shoulder showed him his target. Without hesitating, he reared back and lobbed the grenade high into the air, rolling back onto his stomach with the same fluid motion.

"Frag out!" he screamed, hoping like hell that Dykstra and Kasper could hear him through their own blast-deafened eardrums.

As soon as the grenade left his hand, its safety lever flipped open and fell away. The grenade itself soared on through a smooth arc until it thudded down high up on the dune, several yards above and beyond the little knot of prone tribesmen. Then gravity took over and it rolled downhill, right into their midst.

Flynn buried his face in the sand again.

Craaack! The grenade exploded, sending lethal, razor-edged fragments sleeting through a fifty-foot radius.

Flynn looked up. Through a small puff of dirty gray smoke drifting downwind, he saw the results. Three of the five remaining attackers were motionless—ripped into blood-soaked corpses by dozens of pieces of steel. Two staggered upright. Scarlet streaks down their faces and shredded robes showed that they hadn't escaped the blast unscathed, but they still clutched AK-47s in their hands.

He grabbed his M4 again. "*'Iisqat al'aslihat alkhasat bik!* Drop your weapons!" he shouted.

Instead, they whirled toward him, apparently still determined to carry on this fight.

"Assholes," Flynn muttered. Gritting his teeth, he squeezed off six more rounds. Hit multiple times, the two white-robed men crumpled to the sand and lay still. They were either dead or dying, he decided. Painfully, he scrambled back to his feet.

The sound of gunfire from the other side of the C-130 seemed to be trailing away—fading from a near-continuous crackle of shots to isolated *pop-pop-pop*s. With his carbine up and ready to fire, he moved warily off in that direction.

Greasy black smoke from the burning Mi-17 made it difficult to see much. Bodies, some in white robes, others in camouflage uniforms, were scattered in all directions. He spotted White's gray-haired, skeletal form lying huddled near the shrapnel-torn tail section of the wrecked Super Hercules. Whether the man was dead or simply unconscious wasn't clear, and Flynn wasn't inclined to go check . . . not just yet.

At least one of the former Special Forces contractors was still alive, though seriously wounded and pretty clearly in shock. He was trying to apply a combat tourniquet to his own mangled right thigh . . . but his blood-soaked hands were shaking too badly.

"Hang on, trooper," Flynn murmured, kneeling beside him. He set his M4A1 down. "I've got this."

Quickly, he slipped the tourniquet band through the buckle, pulled it tight, and wrapped it around the man's leg. Then he carefully twisted the tourniquet rod, further tightening everything down until the blood pulsing out through gashed flesh slowed and then stopped.

"Thanks, man," the wounded man said weakly. "Thought I was fucked." But then his eyes widened as he saw something looming over Flynn's shoulder.

Crap. He desperately grabbed for his weapon and whirled around, already knowing it was probably too late. One of the tribesmen had emerged from the thick black curtain of smoke, with a rictus grin like the Angel of Death plastered across his face, and an AKM pointed straight at Flynn's head. The Libyan's finger was already tightening on the trigger.

Crack.

The tribeman's chest exploded, torn apart by a 5.56mm round fired at close range. He fell in a boneless heap and bled out across the sand.

Zalewski appeared out of the smoke, still holding the short-barreled carbine he'd fired one-handed. The big PJ's left arm, apparently broken, hung limp at his side. Flecks of dried blood were spattered across his camouflage and body armor. Grimly, he prodded the Libyan he'd shot with the toe of his boot. "Pretty sure that was the last of 'em," he said softly.

Flynn breathed out. "Sure hope so, Zee." Slowly, he got back up. "And . . . thanks."

Zalewski looked away from the dead tribesman and toward him. Lines of pain and exhaustion were drawn across his broad face. "What are your orders, sir?" he asked. "That we're bugging out, I hope." He nodded at the burning helicopter. "Because if there are more of these bastards out there, that smoke's going to draw 'em like flies to rotting meat."

The big man's warning agreed with Flynn's own somber assessment. They might have destroyed this first band of attackers, but there was no telling how many more enemy fighters were lurking at the nearby oasis—waiting to see the results of their carefully planned ambush. And with so many dead and wounded of their own, the smart move for Wizard One-One's survivors and what little was left of the black ops team was to abandon this crash site . . . and fast.

Thirty minutes later, Nick Flynn sat with his legs dangling outside the open door of the heavily loaded HH-60W helicopter. Rotors beating hard, the CSAR bird lifted slowly off the ground, fighting for altitude as it flew east into the darkening sky. Bone-tired, he held on tight to the doorframe, craning his head to scan the desert rippling past below them—watching closely for any sign of another enemy ambush. Behind him, injured men were crammed into every available space inside the Jolly Green II's cabin. There hadn't been room or payload capacity to bring away any of their dead.

Between them, the black ops team and Wizard One-One's crew had lost more than half their

strength. Bill Wade would probably lose his leg.
Mike Camarillo was dead, gunned down by the terrorists just outside the wrecked C-130. Zalewski's
arm was fractured, snapped when he'd been tossed
around inside the downed turboprop's crumpled
fuselage by the suicide bomb blast. Most of the
ex–Special Forces veterans working for White had
been killed, some by the bomb, the rest during the
ensuing close-quarters gun battle—but they'd gone
down hard, taking most of the attacking tribesmen
on that flank with them.

White himself was still alive, though he'd been
shot in the chest. Apparently, the AK round had
missed his heart, assuming he actually had one.
Right now, the intelligence officer was propped up
against the rear bulkhead, swathed in bandages, but
conscious and glaring at Flynn.

"Fast movers at ten o'clock high," Dykstra reported over the intercom.

Flynn looked up and spotted twin contrails ar-
rowing westward across the sky, coming their way.

"*Wizard One-One, this is Hammer Three-Five,*" a
crisp voice called over the radio from one of the two
U.S. Air Force F-15E Strike Eagles vectored to this
location. "*Can you confirm the target is clear?*"

"Wizard One-One confirms the target is clear,
Hammer Three-Five," Kate Kasper replied. "Anyone still breathing down there is a bad guy."

"*Copy that,*" the Strike Eagle pilot acknowledged.
"*Target locked.*" And then, "*GBU Thirty-eights away.*"

Flynn blinked, not sure if he'd actually seen
several small specks falling off the distant F-15s or

not. GBU-38s were five-hundred-pound gravity bombs converted to precision-guided munitions by bolting on control surfaces and combined inertial guidance–GPS systems. Once released at high altitude, they were capable of steering themselves to targets up to fifteen nautical miles away.

He leaned farther out the door, staring to the west and silently counting seconds. It should be any moment now—

"*Impact*," the Strike Eagle pilot reported.

Orange flashes rippled across the desert in rapid succession as bomb after bomb plummeted down out of the sky and detonated. Huge clouds of smoke, sand, and debris billowed high into the air. When they drifted away, there were only overlapping craters where the wrecked C-130, its cargo of illicit weapons, and the burned-out black ops helicopter had once been.

Flynn sat back with a sigh.

"Don't get too comfortable, Captain," White said bitterly. "Your recklessness triggered this disaster. And I'm going to make sure you don't just walk away from the mess you've created."

For a moment, Flynn stared back at the pale-eyed intelligence officer. Was the other man really serious? Or just desperately hunting around for someone else, anyone else, to take the fall for his own obvious failure? Then he shrugged and looked away. Let White stew in his own rage and pain. There wasn't any point in arguing with the man right now. There'd be time enough to make sure the facts were straight when they were all debriefed.

Instead, he closed his eyes and leaned back against the door, steeling himself for the long flight to an emergency extraction point deeper in the Sahara.

But deep inside, Nick Flynn couldn't quite shake a growing sense of unease . . . and the uncomfortable awareness that not all enemies necessarily wear different uniforms or speak different languages.

THREE

SOME WEEKS LATER

Doing his best to control his nerves, Captain Nick Flynn followed the uniformed Pentagon police officer escorting him down a long basement corridor. Overhead LED lights glowed brightly, illuminating a bare concrete floor and walls painted a faded institutional green. Other than a firm, but polite "Follow me, sir" uttered right after they met at the entrance, the sergeant hadn't said a single word to him. Nor had any of the multitudes of people hurrying onward in all directions paid him the slightest attention. More than twenty-five thousand military personnel and civilians were employed inside the enormous building. And in a place where Army, Air Force, and Marine generals and Navy admirals were a dime a dozen, a junior officer, even one with a police escort, apparently didn't rate so much as the flicker of an eye.

Maybe it was a trick of the poetic imagination he'd inherited from his Irish immigrant grandfather, a teller of many tales, but something about this silent procession through the bowels of the

Pentagon struck him as eerie—as though he were nothing but a ghost drifting through this massive military bureaucratic machine. Jet lag brought on by an overnight flight from the Middle East only intensified this weird sense of disembodiment, as did the preemptory orders he'd received to report here today for "further debriefing on the Wath Incident."

Flynn honestly wasn't sure what more there was to analyze about the tribal ambush and its aftermath. He and the other survivors had spent days with Air Force and DoD investigators. Every observation, word, and action they could recall had been relentlessly probed, questioned, and challenged in an effort to develop a clearer and more detailed picture of how the attack unfolded and how it was repelled. The precision-guided munitions used to destroy the downed C-130 and its cargo had also obliterated every scrap of physical evidence, so all that was left were differing and imperfect human memories.

With Flynn in tow, the gray-shirted police officer turned right into a narrower hallway, one of the five concentric rings that ran around each floor of the huge building. Two Marine sergeants in camouflage battle dress uniforms stood on guard outside a door a few yards farther on.

"This is Captain Nicholas Flynn, USAF, reporting here as ordered," the police officer announced. "You have him?"

The older of the two Marine noncoms nodded. "I relieve you of the responsibility, Sergeant," he said formally. Without any further word, the policeman turned around and walked away.

Curiouser and curiouser, Flynn thought, raising an eyebrow in surprise. He offered the two sentries a dry smile. "So I'm your 'responsibility' now? Is that some kind of new DoD code word for 'prisoner'?"

"Couldn't say, sir," the younger Marine sergeant replied woodenly. He held out a hand. "May I have your cell phone, please?" He nodded toward the door and its adjoining electronic card reader and ten-key pad. "That's a secure room. Per SOP, no personal electronic devices are allowed inside."

Wordlessly, Flynn handed over his phone and watched the guard stash it in a lockbox. Then he stood still while the noncom patted him down, making a final check for any additional prohibited devices. He glanced at the door. The usual alphanumeric code used to identify rooms inside the Pentagon had been covered over by another sign: I-CON (T).

"Icon?" he asked.

"Intelligence Conference," the older sergeant explained.

With the (T) signaling that it was only a temporary use of this particular facility, Flynn realized. Maybe even just for today's scheduled exercise in once again plowing the same stony ground of trying to figure out exactly what had gone wrong in the Libyan desert.

The Marine swiped his ID card through the reader and rapidly punched in a code on the pad. With an audible click, the door unlocked. "Go right on inside, sir," he said. "They're waiting for you."

Which was probably pretty much what the Babylonian guards had said to Daniel right before they shoved him into the lion's den, Flynn decided warily. He took a quick look around the room as he entered. Five men were seated behind a long table. Four of them were military. The fifth was a beefy, overweight civilian in a dark suit, a collared white shirt, and a red silk tie.

A couple of the Pentagon brass, a colonel and a major general, were from the Air Force. The other pair were Army, both of them brigadier generals. Oddly, and in Flynn's view, ominously, no one else in the room had a name tag or an ID badge on his uniform or coat. That was totally against all regulations. What the hell was going on here? He took a closer look at the civilian at the far end of the table. Everything about the guy shouted high-ranking CIA executive. You could take the man out of Langley, but you couldn't take the shadowy aura of Langley out of the man.

Definitely worried now, he came to attention. "Captain Nicholas Fl—"

"Take a seat, Captain Flynn," the Air Force two-star said quietly, interrupting. He indicated the lone chair set in front of the table.

Working hard to keep any expression off his face, Flynn did as he was told. His mouth felt as dry as dust. Suddenly, this setup seemed a hell of a lot more like a trial than it did a routine intelligence debrief. More than ever, he thought, this was a time to be cautious.

As though he'd read his mind, the major general

shook his head. "Relax, son. This is not an official UCMJ proceeding."

Which was very cold comfort, Flynn concluded. Proceedings conducted under the Uniform Code of Military Justice at least had protections for those involved, including the right to legal counsel if necessary. He leaned forward slightly in his chair. "May I ask exactly what the purpose of this meeting is then, sir?"

The general glanced briefly at the men seated next to him before turning his attention back to Flynn. "Consider this more of an informal, inter-agency discussion, Captain," he said. "Together with our colleague from the CIA here, we're simply trying to find a mutually agreeable way to handle this unfortunate situation before it spins further out of control. And we'd appreciate your coopera-tion in that effort."

Spinning out of control? How so? Flynn won-dered. From the moment they'd landed back at El Minya, everything that had happened in Libya had been classified top secret. Under direct orders from higher up, he and all the other survivors had already signed mounds of official paperwork swear-ing to keep everything hush-hush.

"Maybe you missed the news out there in the back of Bumfuckistan, Flynn, but our bid to keep this quiet has failed. Some son of a bitch somewhere leaked," the civilian behind the table growled. "So now we've got members of Congress and the me-dia screaming their heads off—demanding to know why a U.S. aircraft crashed in Libya and exactly how so many Air Force personnel and other Americans ended up dead or badly injured in a firefight with the locals."

"So what are you going to tell them?" Flynn asked bluntly, realizing as soon as the words were out of his mouth that he should have kept his mouth shut. His earlier resolution to be cautious had been the smart play. This was like walking blindfolded through a minefield.

"As little as possible," the CIA executive snapped back. His jowly face had reddened. "This was a highly sensitive, need-to-know operation, and those clowns on Capitol Hill, except for the people we can trust on the intelligence committees, do *not* need to know one goddamned thing. That goes double for the press." He glowered at Flynn. "Which brings us right back to you. Because from our perspective, *you're* the one who landed us all neck-deep in the shit."

Flynn gritted his teeth. *Keep your temper in check,* he warned himself. *Don't rise to the bait.* "Whoever told you that got it wrong," he said, far more calmly than he felt.

"Your own testimony is that you fired the first shot," the CIA officer reminded him. "Killing that first tribesman is what triggered everything else. The ensuing battle. The horrendous casualties our team and yours took. And all of the political and national security fallout we're facing now."

"I *killed* that Teda clansman because the bastard was about to detonate a suicide bomb," Flynn snapped.

The other man shrugged. "So you claim. But there's no real evidence to prove that any bomb ever existed."

"Except that second suicide bomber who did succeed in detonating his vest," Flynn said tightly. "The one who blew your Mi-17 helicopter to hell and gone. Remember him?"

"Again, there's no hard evidence for your assertion." The CIA officer's expression was contemptuous. "For all we know, once the shit hit the fan and our security contractors started exchanging fire with the locals, stray rounds might have set off the helicopter's fuel tank. Or maybe they detonated some of the explosives our team brought with them to sanitize the site."

"You see our problem, Captain Flynn," the Air Force general said. "Without forensic evidence from the battlefield, assessing what really happened boils down to deciding which of the two conflicting narratives we accept—yours or that of the Agency case officer who was also present."

"Mr. *White*," Flynn bit out.

"Correct," the CIA executive agreed. "And our Mr. White is an extremely experienced operative, with years of field experience." He steepled his hands and looked over them at Flynn. "Tell me, Captain, before this unfortunate incident, how many times have you been in combat?"

"None," Flynn admitted, struggling to keep his voice even. He saw now where this was going. He'd walked into a Red Queen's court right out of *Alice in Wonderland*, where the order of the day was "sen-

tence first, verdict afterward." With the press and
Congress on the warpath, the Pentagon brass and
the CIA were both looking for a scapegoat, someone they could blame if their continuing efforts to
cover up the full extent of the disaster failed. And
given the choice between a junior Air Force captain
without any political influence and a ranking intelligence officer who could probably blow the whistle
on a lot of questionable covert operations if he felt
threatened, there wasn't much doubt about whose
head would roll.

Confirming his suspicions, the CIA representative turned his head toward the Air Force two-star
presiding over this irregular kangaroo court. "Ideally, we'd prefer that Flynn here be held incommu-
nicado in some stockade. The last thing any of us
want is him being available to testify in front of any
congressional hearings . . . or blabbing to journalists."

Jesus Christ, Flynn thought, scarcely able to believe his ears. Just how far did these guys think they
could go? Did they seriously imagine they could
imprison any U.S. citizen, let alone a serving officer
in the U.S. military, without trial or review? Forget
Alice in Wonderland, this was starting to sound a lot
more like the opening of *The Man in the Iron Mask*.

The Air Force general glanced at his Pentagon
colleagues and then cleared his throat. "In our
judgment, that would be . . . inadvisable. We don't
think it's necessary in this case to go so far outside
the regulations." He looked briefly at Flynn and
then turned back to the CIA's representative. "Nev-

ertheless, we agree it would be in the best interests of the Department of Defense and our national
security to make sure what happened at the Wath
Oasis fades quickly from the public consciousness."

"What are you offering?"

"This episode is already highly classified. Which
means that any unauthorized disclosure to the media or Congress is a serious felony, punishable by
years in federal prison. Should Captain Flynn decide to do so anyway, in some fit of whistleblower
zeal, we are also prepared to convene an immediate
court-martial to try him for various crimes, including the unprovoked use of deadly force resulting in
the killing of numerous civilians, fellow U.S. Air
Force personnel, and other American citizens."
Here at least, the general had the grace to offer
Flynn an apologetic look.

After a moment, the CIA man shook his head.
"My agency needs something more concrete."

"Which is why we're also going to transfer the
captain to a new duty post," the general continued.
"One that's about as far from the District of Co-
lumbia as it's possible to get. He won't be talking
out of school to anyone from there, at least not
easily . . . or undetectably."

"Flynn could resign his commission," the CIA
executive pointed out. "I've seen his records. He's
completed his active-duty service obligation. And
once he's out of the Air Force, all you've got as a
hold on him is that top secret classification rating."

Flynn sat rigid, half in shock and half in fury at
the way these . . . pompous *assholes* . . . were so cava-

lierly debating the best way to wreck his life and his military career.

The Air Force general shrugged. "Any request Captain Flynn makes to resign can be denied on the grounds that the needs of the service come first. A year or year and a half should be long enough for this mess to die down and be forgotten."

The CIA man thought about that for a moment and then nodded sharply. "Fair enough. That meets our needs." With a cursory nod to the assembled Pentagon brass, he climbed heavily to his feet and left. He didn't spare a glance for the young officer whose career he'd just helped destroy.

One by one, the somber-faced Army brigadiers and Air Force colonel took their own leave and walked out of the room, leaving Flynn and the Air Force major general behind. From start to finish, not one of them had said a word.

Of course not, Flynn thought bitterly. *They'd all made up their minds on how this was going to end before I even got here. Why waste time and breath pretending this whole proceeding was anything but window dressing for a predetermined outcome? And pretty shoddy window dressing, at that?*

"I'm sorry about this, son," the general said at last, breaking an awkward silence. He stood up. "Really, I am." He shook his head. "Look, I know this isn't much consolation, but incoming rounds don't care whose side you're on, or whether your intentions were smart or stupid. Think of this as some random bullet that just happened to have your name on it. That may not be fair, but it's reality.

So take your medicine. Do the job we're assigning you. And for God's sake, don't rock the boat or shoot your mouth off again. Then, in a year or two, when this has all blown over, we'll let you resign your commission and start over again in the civilian world. And I can guarantee that a lot of corporate doors will be open to a young man like you with an honorable discharge."

Flynn ignored that unsubtly dangled carrot. Instead, carefully controlling his voice to hide his anger, he simply asked, "So where am I being exiled to . . . sir?"

The general didn't hesitate. "One of the North Warning System's long-range radar sites. At Kaktovik, Alaska."

"I'm not exactly qualified to manage radar systems," Flynn pointed out bluntly.

"We know that, Captain," the general agreed. He shrugged. "The North Warning System is largely automated anyway, with any necessary maintenance or upkeep handled by civilian contractors."

Flynn frowned. Then what the hell was he being sent to do? Play poker with bored civilian radar technicians?

"Congress has been bitching about potential security threats to our early-warning air defense radars," the general explained. "They're worried about possible Russian commando raids or sabotage. So we've agreed to explore the formation of small Joint Force security teams for these sites."

"And that's where I come in," Flynn guessed flatly.

The general nodded. "That's where you come in. We're putting you in command of the first experimental Joint Force security detail."

Christ, Flynn thought bleakly, they were assigning him to glorified sentry duty at a post well above the Arctic Circle. He shivered inside. If they'd tried for a thousand years, these bastards couldn't have picked a better place to punish him for the crime of making the CIA's covert ops gurus look like fools. For a Texas boy who'd grown up seeing snow only on occasional ski trips, the thought of Alaska's sub-zero winter temperatures and endless dark nights was downright hellish.

FOUR

EARLY OCTOBER

Set in a quiet side street in the heart of Moscow's Meshchansky District, the Bekhterev Private Clinic occupied a five-story glass-and-concrete office building. Its namesake, Vladimir Bekhterev, born in 1857, was known chiefly as one of Russia's most famous neurologists, a rival of Ivan Pavlov, and also for his probable murder on the orders of Josef Stalin. Asked to examine the dictator in 1927, Bekhterev had privately warned colleagues that Stalin was a paranoiac. He died suddenly and mysteriously the following day. After the fall of the Soviet Union, Russia's new rulers reinstated him in the pantheon of national medical heroes. The Bekhterev Clinic had been sponsored by profit-seeking investors as part of that rehabilitation process. And now its cadre of highly trained doctors and neurosurgeons provided discreet and expensive medical services to Russia's government and business elites.

One of those specialists, Dr. Viktor Obolensky, had his office on the clinic's fourth floor. Delicate watercolors on its dark-paneled walls, the doctor's elegant oak desk, comfortable leather chairs, and richly colored Oriental rugs created an aura of luxury that was a far cry from the dingy, run-down atmosphere of state-run medical offices and hospitals. His usual patients, men and women of influence and wealth, valued the difference.

Right now, Colonel Alexei Petrov didn't give a damn about his surroundings. His whole attention was focused on the MRI images Obolensky had just shown to him to explain his diagnosis. Slowly, he looked up from the blue-tinted pictures to focus on the neurologist. "There is no possibility of a mistake?"

Apologetically, Obolensky shrugged his shoulders. He wore an expensive, immaculately tailored Italian suit under his regulation white coat. "I'm afraid not, Mr. Kuznetsov. The indications are unmistakable."

Petrov took the blow in silence. The name Kuznetsov, the Russian equivalent of Smith, was the pseudonym he used for his visits to the clinic. He was also paying cash for these tests and consultations, since the last thing he wanted was a paper trail his Air Force superiors might be able to follow. Now, more than ever, he was glad that he'd taken precautions. "And the prognosis?" he asked at last, not sure if he really wanted an answer.

"Not good," the doctor admitted bluntly. "A combination of radiation treatment and chemotherapy might slow the progression. At least to a degree. But the location and size of this malignancy make surgery . . . inadvisable." The corners of his mouth turned down. "I wish I could give you better news. Unfortunately, this is not a case where there is even the slightest margin of doubt."

Petrov took a short, sharp breath. "I see." For a brief moment, darkness seemed to veil his vision. He cleared his throat uncomfortably. "And the likely time frame?" he asked, noticing with a trace of cynicism that he'd chosen a deliberately distanced, almost clinically sterile way to phrase his question. No doubt that was common for people in his position.

Again, Obolensky shrugged. "My best estimate would be anywhere from six months to a year. Perhaps eighteen months at the outside." He nodded at the sheaf of MRI images still clutched in his patient's hands. "The precise progression of tumors of this kind varies widely from individual to individual. Regular scans would let us track its growth more closely, of course."

And fatten your pocketbook, too, Petrov thought bitterly.

The neurologist looked somber. "If you have any serious responsibilities in your work, it would probably be best to let your associates and your employer know the situation as soon as possible."

"In case I drop dead suddenly?" Petrov felt his mouth twist into a thin, wry smile.

Obolensky shook his head. "That is unlikely. But the frequency and severity of your headaches is likely to increase over the coming months. I can prescribe medication to alleviate some of the pain, but these medicines naturally have significant side effects. As time goes on, it may become more and more difficult for you to concentrate. Or to handle complex, difficult problems."

"I see."

"If you prefer, I can brief the necessary people for you," the neurologist said hesitantly. "These kinds of conversations are often painful. Sometimes a relatively disinterested, scientific approach is best."

Petrov smiled thinly again. "That would require me to waive my right to doctor-patient confidentiality, would it not?"

"Yes, it would," Obolensky admitted. He steepled his hands. "I fully understood your desire for privacy early on, Mr. *Kuznetsov*." His tone left little doubt that he knew the name was phony. "But you can see that the situation has changed. Sooner or later, those for whom you work will realize you aren't well."

And the doctor was concerned that they would blame him for helping hide the bad news, Petrov realized. For all Obolensky knew right now, his patient was a high-level financial director or senior government executive—someone whose illness-induced mistakes could cost billions of rubles or cause a terrible political scandal. None of the promises of patient confidentiality made by the Bekhterev Private Clinic would protect it in such a case. All of which gave Obolensky every reason to start digging to find out Petrov's real identity if he refused to cooperate.

Understandable or not, Petrov thought coldly, that was something he simply could *not* risk. "I take your point," he said at last. "Look, it's already Friday. What if I put together a list of names and numbers over this weekend? I should be able to get it to you by Monday morning."

Relieved, Obolensky sat back. "Thank you. I appreciate your confidence. And you can rely on my discretion."

Petrov smiled more genuinely this time. "Oh, of that, I have absolutely no doubt, Doctor."

LATER THAT EVENING

Humming softly along with the Korean pop music wafting from his Lexus luxury sedan's premium sound system, Dr. Viktor Obolensky turned off the main thoroughfare and onto a narrow private road that led to his country dacha. He was looking forward to a couple of days away from his office and importunate patients. As a medical specialty, neurology paid exceedingly well, but all too often it meant dealing with desperate people who wanted to see him as a miracle worker—as someone who could save them from a tragic fate otherwise decreed by genetics or by some random cosmic ray that had sleeted through their brains and condemned them to death.

This far outside the city, he had no close neighbors, and the woods lining both sides of the road were already pitch-dark. Glowing a spectral white in his high beams, row after row of slender birch trees appeared briefly and then vanished in the blackness.

Abruptly, there was a muffled *bang* from his right front tire. The steering wheel jolted under his hands and then tugged hard to the right.

"*Sukin syn!*" Obolensky muttered, wrestling the car back straight and braking to a stop. "Son of a bitch!" One of his tires had just blown out.

Still grumbling under his breath, he switched off the ignition—leaving the headlights on—and climbed out onto the graveled road. It was too dark to make out anything outside the arc of the sedan's beams. With a sigh, he pulled out his cell phone and activated the flashlight. Using it to light his way, he moved around the front of the Lexus and leaned over to inspect the damaged tire.

And then the world flashed bright red as a terrible blow smashed into the back of Obolensky's head. Blood spattered across the sedan's shiny, polished side panels.

Dazed, he dropped to his knees. His right hand fluttered upward, weakly feeling for the site of the injury.

His attacker brutally slapped that away and caught him in a tight hold, dragging his head hard back into an armpit. Suddenly terrified, Obolensky fumbled at the arms that gripped him. It was too late. A single quick, powerful twist snapped his neck—killing him instantly.

The attacker, dressed in dark clothing and gloves, a face mask, and a hood, knelt briefly beside the corpse. He scooped up the dead man's cell phone from where it had fallen. Then, quickly and efficiently, he went through the doctor's pockets, retrieving his keys and wallet. Satisfied, he got back to his feet, opened the car door, switched off the headlights, and tapped a control to pop the Lexus's trunk.

It required only a couple of minutes' more work for him to manhandle the body over to the trunk and stuff it inside. With a little luck, he thought, it would be at least a couple of days before anyone investigated the abandoned car and found Obolensky's corpse. And with a bit more luck, it would look enough like a robbery gone wrong to satisfy the local police.

Sweating slightly despite the cool night air, Colonel Alexei Petrov used the dead man's cell phone flashlight to survey the scene one more time. It was vital to make sure that he hadn't forgotten anything that would raise unnecessary questions or lead back to him. Beneath his mask, a slight, confident smile crossed his face. There was nothing. Just a few scuffed footprints around the front of the sedan and faint smears of dried blood that would match that of the victim, not him.

Finished, Petrov turned away and headed back through the darkened forest to where he'd parked his nondescript rental car. Part of him regretted killing Obolensky. But he knew the act had been necessary. Nothing could be allowed to interfere with the project he had undertaken. That was true now more than ever. Dmitri Grishin, the oligarch who was backing his plan, believed he was primarily motivated by money. This was not the time to disabuse him of that notion.

FIVE

THE NEXT DAY

Barter Island sat just off Alaska's desolate Arctic coast. Roughly four miles long and two miles wide, it was a snow-covered, treeless plain. On a narrow spit just off its northern shore, there was a large mound of heaped-up whale bones. Not far from the mound, the tiny village of Kaktovik occupied the island's northeastern quarter. Around two hundred people lived in its assortment of cabins and prefab houses, most of them Iñupiat Alaska natives.

A thousand-foot-wide saltwater channel separated the island from the mainland, and there were no roads connecting the island to the nearest inhabited place, Prudhoe Bay. Close by Alaskan standards at least, since Prudhoe Bay was more than 110 miles to the west. The only real way in or out for people and freight was by air. An old military runway, perched right on the edge of the Beaufort Sea and subject to periodic flooding during storms, had been abandoned in favor of a relatively new 4,500-foot-long gravel strip built on slightly higher ground in the center of the island. A converted school bus provided routine transportation into town for arriving passengers.

This afternoon, the bright yellow airport bus had been rented by the U.S. military's Alaskan Command to bring Captain Nick Flynn and his newly formed security team to the Barter Island Long Range Radar Site, about a third of a mile outside Kaktovik. The twelve men, a mix of Alaska National Guardsmen on active duty and regular U.S. Air Force and Army personnel, had flown in earlier aboard a C-130J transport plane dispatched from Anchorage's Joint Base Elmendorf-Richardson— now 640 miles away to the south.

Alaska was astoundingly big and empty even by Texas standards, Flynn thought moodily, staring out the windows of the bus as it bumped along a rutted gravel track. Their two-hour flight here had carried them across a vast landscape of dense forests, sheer snow-capped mountains, and wide-open tundra flatlands. All told, there were fewer than seven hundred and fifty thousand people scattered across an enormous expanse more than twice the size of Texas. He frowned, remembering one of his college history classes. Back in the 1700s, Voltaire had famously dismissed Canada as just "a few acres of snow." Nick wondered what the French philosopher would have thought of Alaska—judging by what he'd seen during the flight up here, it was basically a few hundred *million* acres of snow.

His breath fogged the bus window. This was only the beginning of October, but winter had already arrived on Barter Island. The highs were in the low twenties, with temperatures plunging below zero after dark. This far north, the sun was currently visible for only about ten hours a day. Toward Halloween, it would be above the horizon for just six and a half hours. And then, by late November, the island would find itself wrapped in the perpetual Arctic night—from which it would not emerge for more than six long weeks.

Just imagining that unending spell of frozen darkness was bad enough. But Flynn had a sinking feeling that reality would be even worse. He looked over his shoulder at the soldiers and airmen he would be commanding under those grim conditions. Bulky in military-issue cold weather parkas, trousers, and boots, they were scattered down the length of the bus. They occupied separate bench seats, as though determined to keep their new comrades at arm's length for the time being. Most of them looked about as gloomy on the outside as he felt inside.

His frown deepened. These men weren't a cohesive team yet, just a collection of individuals hurriedly thrown together from a grab bag of other units across Alaska. Boarding the C-130 for the flight here was the first time any of them had ever really met. He shook his head. Everything about this assignment was half-assed. Apart from their names, his only source of information about the soldiers and airmen now under his command were the personnel files he'd downloaded onto his tablet shortly before takeoff. And he hadn't had any real time to dig into those records yet.

Flynn had a depressing hunch, though, that he wasn't going to find a lot of glowing adjectives in their personnel evaluations. Most commanding officers, ordered to "volunteer" men for this kind of long-term detached duty, would be very careful to select those who wouldn't be particularly missed— the oddballs, misfits, and even disciplinary hard cases. One corner of his mouth quirked upward. He might not be looking at his very own Dirty Dozen, but the odds were good that he'd just been saddled with the Dingy Eleven.

Or maybe that should be the Grimy Ten, he thought, after a quick glance at the grizzled noncom seated right across the aisle from him. From the top of his broad, weathered face to the tips of his rugged combat boots, Sergeant First Class Andy Takirak, Alaska Army National Guard, had the look of a tough, thoroughly squared away military professional. Nor would the prospect of spending a winter in the middle of the Alaskan wilderness hold any terrors for the older man, Flynn decided. After all, this was his own native country.

According to his file, Takirak was a member of the Bering Straits Iñupiat tribe, distantly related to the indigenous peoples of the North Slope like those who lived in Kaktovik. In civilian life, he worked as a wildlife guide and hunter around the Prudhoe Bay oil fields. He'd been assigned to the Joint Force security team as its scout and senior NCO. And unlike the rest of them, the sergeant was a genuine volunteer. He'd offered to go back on active service the moment he'd heard the scuttlebutt about an experimental unit forming for duty along the barren Arctic coast.

Flynn wasn't quite sure if that made Takirak crazy, or incredibly dedicated . . . or a bit of both. But he *was* sure that he was going to have to rely heavily on the National Guard sergeant's expertise and survival skills to help whip the rest of this raw collection of individuals into a cohesive and efficient unit. He strongly suspected the Pentagon higher-ups who'd exiled him to Alaska expected him to fail in that task. He planned to prove them wrong—even if he privately thought the whole concept of creating special security units like this was a waste of manpower and resources. Any serious Russian attack on the North Warning System's radars would probably be carried out by bombers and long-range cruise missiles—not up close and personal by Spetsnaz commandos or saboteurs.

"There's the station, sir," Takirak said quietly, pointing ahead through the bus's salt-streaked windshield. Flynn leaned forward, studying the complex of buildings that was slated to be their duty post for at least the next six months.

The Barter Island Long Range Radar Site sat on a low coastal bluff, overlooking the cold, gray Beaufort Sea. A faint glimmer of dazzling white along the distant northern horizon hinted at the pack ice beginning to creep down from the Arctic Ocean. At the west end of the station, a raised platform held a white protective dome for the AN/FPS-117 active electronically scanned array air search radar. From a distance, it looked oddly like two-thirds of a golf ball resting on a flat-topped tee. As they got closer, its true size became more apparent. The top of that large dome rose nearly fifty feet above the flat, snow-covered tundra. And from the briefing he'd been given, Flynn knew that powerful motors inside the dome could rotate the entire fifteen-ton radar array through a complete circle in as little as ten seconds.

A string of connected, prefabricated buildings ran east from the radar platform. Rust streaked their metal roofs and siding. When the station was first built in 1953 as part of the old Distant Early Warning Line, it had been much larger, with barracks housing more than 150 U.S. Air Force officers and enlisted men. Now, those barracks and other outbuildings were gone, torn down when the Barter Island site had been modernized to become part of the U.S. and Canada's new, largely automated North Warning System. The structures that were left contained generators, equipment and vehicle storage, and working quarters that were still far too big for a handful of resident civilian contractors.

With a high-pitched squeal of brakes, the bus pulled up in front of the ramshackle building closest to the elevated radar platform and stopped. A rusty white sign over a door identified it as the GRAND FIVE-STAR BEAUFORT SEA VISTA INN.

"*Jeezus*," one of the soldiers sitting behind him muttered. "Welcome to Barter Island LRR, boys. You will never find a more wretched hive of scum and villainy."

Flynn tamped down on a grin, recognizing the classic *Star Wars* quote.

"I prefer the outtakes version, myself," another said with a sardonic edge to his voice. "The one where Alec Guinness just says, 'It's a fucking shithole. A fucking shithole.'"

"Yeah, well, he must have been thinking about this goddamned place, all right," a third soldier growled. "Christ, I need a drink."

"Then you're out of luck, pal," the first man told him. "'Cause Kaktovik is a dry town. No alcohol allowed. Not even beer."

That triggered a chorus of subdued groans, which ended abruptly when Sergeant Takirak casually turned around in his seat and gave them the "look" so beloved of veteran noncoms. When delivered by a skilled professional, the "look" was said to be capable of putting the fear of God, eternal damnation, and thirty days in the stockade into the heart of even the most hardened reprobate. From the sudden, absolute silence that descended across the bus, Flynn judged that Andy Takirak was just such a professional.

He studiously ignored the byplay. His ROTC instructors had spent a lot of time and energy drumming into their students' heads the proposition that half the job of figuring out how to be an effective officer was in learning what *not* to hear and what *not* to see. Besides, griping about their quarters, meals, and pay was a time-honored privilege of enlisted personnel. He didn't mind bitching, so long as it didn't exceed the traditional bounds.

As soon as the driver opened the bus door, Flynn was the first one outside. His breath steamed in the ice-cold air and his boots crunched across a layer of snow mixed with gravel. A light, freezing wind tugged at his scarlet beret. It carried the mingled smells of salt, fuel oil, and rusting metal.

Three civilians in winter coats and boots emerged from the building and strolled over to join him. Two were men, one of them tall and heavyset, the other short and wiry. The last was an older woman with short-cropped gray hair and a round, friendly face.

"Captain Flynn?" the tallest man said. "My name's Johansson, Pete Johansson. I'm the maintenance supervisor here." He nodded to the shorter man. "And this here is Smitty Walz. He's my electronics whiz. But he doesn't say much, do you, Smitty?"

"Nope," the short man agreed.

"And I'm Marta McIntyre," the gray-haired woman told him with a pleasant smile. "Mrs. Marta McIntyre. I'm the general gofer around the station—the cook, supply officer, and housekeeper all in one." Her smile widened. "Plus, I keep Smitty and Pete from killing each other on the rare occasions our satellite TV dish goes on the blink."

Flynn grinned appreciatively at her. "How do you do that, Mrs. McIntyre? Tranquilizer gun? Martial arts expertise?"

She sniffed. "Not me. I just climb up on the roof and fix the darned thing."

"Marta's a piddler," Johansson said. Then, seeing Flynn's look of incomprehension, he explained. "That's station lingo, Captain. A piddler is someone who sees stuff that needs doing and just goes right ahead and does it." He shrugged. "This is a big place and with just the three of us to keep it running, we're all pretty much self-motivated."

Mrs. McIntyre nodded. "And now that you and your troops are here, I guess I'll be cooking for you, too. At least, that's what those high muckety-mucks down at Elmendorf are hoping." She turned to watch Sergeant Takirak and the others filing out of the bus. Under the noncom's soft-spoken orders, they immediately began unloading their personal gear, equipment, and weapons from the vehicle's luggage compartment. "Unless, you'd prefer living on those MREs I hear so much about."

Flynn shook his head quickly. "No, ma'am. We'd be thrilled to eat whatever you put in front of us." The armed forces' Meals Ready to Eat were fine. In the field. If you didn't have anything else. And if you were seriously hungry. But in his opinion, anyone who'd choose MREs over home-cooked food had either lost all sense of taste or had some other serious psychological problems. Besides, from the look of Johansson's waistline the odds were good that Marta McIntyre was a decent cook.

"I'll have Smitty show your guys where to stow their personal gear," the station superintendent told him. "The rest of your equipment arrived a couple of days ago. We've stashed it in the vehicle maintenance bay for now."

Flynn nodded. The orders creating his Joint Force security team specified that it was expected to actively patrol the area around the radar site. That included the mainland as soon as the surrounding lagoons iced over. To make that possible, the supply sections at Joint Base Elmendorf-Richardson, or JBER, had provided a mix of snowmobiles, cross-country skis, and snowshoes. Teaching his men and himself how to use them was going to be one of his top priorities.

"And while they're doing that, I'll give you a tour of your quarters," Mrs. McIntyre said. She jerked a thumb at the rusty sign over the station door. "That bit about it being five-star accommodations may be baloney, but really this place isn't so bad." She swept her gaze across the barren, snow-covered landscape around them and then shrugged. "Well, on the inside, anyhow."

A couple of hours later, Flynn stepped outside. The sun was a distant bright dot on the western horizon. The wind had picked up, and high gray clouds were moving in from the north. It already felt much colder among the lengthening shadows. Shivering, he pulled the hood of his cold weather parka over his scarlet beret and tightened the coat's Velcro wrist straps down around his gloves.

Then he crunched across the frozen tundra to the edge of the bluff where Andy Takirak stood alone, looking out to sea. The National Guard noncom had a pair of binoculars around his neck.

"See anything, Sergeant?" Flynn asked as he drew up beside the other man.

Takirak grinned. "Miles and miles of nothing,

sir." He took a deep breath and let it out in a cloud of steam. He waved a hand at the low gray-green waves rolling toward a gravel beach only a few feet below them. Chunks of drift ice floated in among the waves. "All the way from here to the North Pole and beyond. No people. No roads. No cars. No houses. Just the seals and the polar bears hunting them out there on the ice cap, living and dying the same way they have for hundreds of thousands of years."

"Which you don't mind?" Flynn wondered, hearing the unmistakable happiness in the other man's voice.

"No, sir," Takirak admitted. "Up here above the Arctic Circle is where I feel the most alive." His grin turned sheepish. "I read in a magazine somewhere about some famous writer who said hell was other people. May not be that way for most folks. But it kind of is for me. Which makes being out in the wilderness like this a little bit of heaven."

Flynn couldn't think of much to say to that. He shrugged his shoulders. "I guess that's a natural attitude for anyone raised up here."

"Maybe so. But I wasn't brought up in Alaska, Captain," Takirak told him. He looked out to the sea again. "My parents died when I was real little. Some kind of accident, I guess. All I got from them was my native name, *Amaruq* . . . Gray Wolf." He pointed at his short, gray-flecked hair. "Suits me better now."

Flynn laughed.

"Anyway, my other relatives must have been too

poor to keep me, because I got shipped off to a foster home down in the Lower Forty-Eight." Takirak turned his head toward Flynn. "I didn't make it back to Alaska until I turned eighteen and hitchhiked in across Canada." His smile returned. "Then I joined the Guard the next year and haven't looked back since. I figured getting Uncle Sam to pay me to tote a rifle and spend a lot of time outdoors was a sweet deal."

Flynn nodded with a grin of his own. "Guess so, Sergeant." He burrowed deeper into his jacket. "Speaking of spending time outdoors, I think the sooner we start getting the men used to operating in this climate, the better."

"Yes, sir. You've got that right." Takirak looked over his shoulder at the radar station behind them. "It's real easy for guys to huddle up inside once there's snow on the ground. Gets even easier as the dark comes on and everything ices up," he warned.

Flynn grimaced just thinking about it. He wasn't immune from that same natural urge to hibernate. Their quarters inside the station were surprisingly comfortable. Besides an industrial-sized kitchen and dining area, there was even a rec room with a TV, a pool table, and a popcorn machine. And he'd already overheard some of the enlisted men hoping their new CO wasn't really a gung-ho type, despite his Special Operations Command beret. "Suggestions?" he asked.

"That we start off with an hour of PT at zero-seven-hundred hours, tomorrow morning," Takirak said.

"Which is more than an hour before the sun even comes up," Flynn pointed out.

"Yes, sir, but we can't let the position of the sun dictate anything from here on out. Working days have to start and end when we say they do, not when there's sunlight outside," the other man said patiently. "Anyway, we can use the vehicle maintenance bay. It's got decent overhead light."

"But no heat."

Takirak's eyes crinkled with laughter. "Trust me, sir. We'll all be sweating plenty by the time PT's done."

Flynn thought about that and matched the older man's smile. "I take your point. And after PT?"

"Breakfast to replace the calories we just burned off," the sergeant said. "And after that some kind of working detail or maybe a route march across the tundra to acclimate."

"We need a firing range," Flynn said slowly, thinking it through. The team was equipped with a variety of small arms and heavier weapons, including one of the new, very lightweight M3E1 Carl Gustaf 84mm recoilless rifles and an M249 light machine gun. Issued fresh from stores, all of their weapons would need to be zeroed in to be effective in combat conditions. "Somewhere out on the western end of the island, where there's no chance of any stray rounds hitting anything or anyone by accident."

Considering that there was nothing between here and Prudhoe Bay except the occasional rock, that wouldn't be much of a challenge.

Takirak nodded. "Yes, sir. We can put a range together out that way without much trouble." He cocked an eyebrow. "If I may ask, exactly how much time are you planning to spend on weapons training?"

"As much time as it takes to qualify every man in this unit as a marksman or above," Flynn said simply. "We both know the odds are probably about a million to one that we're ever going to come face-to-face with any Russian Spetsnaz commandos up here. But if we do draw that short straw, I want to make damned sure our guys come out the other end alive. And that our enemies end up dead." Aware that he sounded a little overzealous, he shrugged. "Plus, shooting live ammo is a hell of a lot of fun. And a really good way to break up the monotony."

"Amen to that," Takirak agreed appreciatively.

SIX

A FEW DAYS LATER

Several thousand meters above the winding trace of
the Volga River, three Russian aircraft slid southeast
through a moonless night sky. Two were twin-tailed
Su-34 fighter-bombers assigned as chase planes
to the third, much-larger plane—the manta ray–
shaped PAK-DA stealth bomber prototype. Weeks
of rigorous tests had validated the experimental
aircraft's flight characteristics and confirmed that
its stealth features made detection and tracking
by radar and infrared sensors extremely difficult.
Now the program had moved on to check out the
bomber's advanced navigation, attack, and defense
systems.

Inside the PAK-DA's relatively spacious cockpit,
Colonel Alexei Petrov tweaked his stick slightly to
the left. Responding immediately to his control
inputs, the bomber rolled into a gentle turn. The
Su-34s flying a thousand meters off each wingtip
matched his maneuver perfectly. Infrared sensors
fed their images directly to the face shield of his

flight helmet—turning the inky darkness into a green-tinted version of full daylight.

He smiled under his oxygen mask. Flying at night like this made it more difficult for any foreign intelligence agents stationed near the Chkalov Test Center to track this new aircraft. It also offered an excellent opportunity to evaluate the sensors and software that Tupolev's engineers touted as providing unparalleled situational awareness to the bomber's crew. So far, he had to agree. A quick press of a switch on his stick allowed him to toggle rapidly between any of the cameras mounted around the PAK-DA's nose and wing—giving him the equivalent of a full, 360-degree view. And all without the need to actually turn his head or lose sight of any of the vital flight information provided by his HUD, his heads-up display.

Seated next to him in the right-hand seat, Petrov's copilot, Major Oleg Bunin, checked one of his large multifunction displays. It showed a detailed, digitized map of the terrain ahead of them. Variously shaped icons glowed across the map. One blinked green. "Coming up on the target evaluation range in two minutes." Bunin, stockier and slightly taller than his commander, tapped the screen with a gloved finger. "The range is locked in to our navigation system."

A new steering cue appeared on Petrov's HUD. It slid right and then centered as he rolled out of the turn to the east and leveled off. His left hand slid the throttles forward. "Going to full military power."

The roar from the bomber's two massive NK-65 turbofans deepened as it accelerated, racing ahead now at more than a thousand kilometers per hour. Both Su-34 chase planes easily kept pace. The fighter-bombers were capable of attaining supersonic speeds well above those possible for the larger, longer-ranged aircraft.

"Sixty seconds out," Bunin reported. "Activating targeting radar and other sensors." His fingers tapped at another of his displays. Instantly, the PAK-DA's active electronically scanned array Ku-band radar powered up. Like the AESA radars carried by America's B-2 stealth bombers, its signals were designed to be difficult for any enemy to intercept.

Almost immediately, new icons blinked onto Petrov's HUD. They showed the positions of possible targets—camouflaged tanks, armored personnel carriers, artillery pieces, surface-to-air missile launchers, and bunkers—scattered across the test range. Some of them were real. Others were decoys that had been carefully constructed to produce apparently genuine radar and thermal signatures. "Engage our target discrimination program," he ordered.

Obeying, Bunin set a piece of sophisticated computer software running. It rapidly analyzed data collected by the bomber's radar and other sensors, ferreting out the slightest inconsistencies. "The TDP program is running."

One after another, target icons vanished as the software weighed them in the balance, judged them

to be fake, and locked them out of the system—
ensuring that no missiles or bombs would be wasted
on mere decoys. As they disappeared, Bunin highlighted several of the remaining high-priority
targets for the bomber's advanced attack software.
Acting autonomously, the computer selected the
weapons most likely to kill each target and assigned
them on its own, without human intervention.

A countdown timer flashed into existence on
Petrov's HUD. "Attacking in ten seconds," he said
calmly. His thumb settled over the weapons release button on his stick. The timer clicked to zero.
Petrov pressed the switch. "Weapons away!"

A high-pitched whine permeated the cockpit
as the bomber's internal bay doors cycled open.
Graphics showed simulated missiles and guided
bombs leaving the bays and plunging toward their
designated targets. When they were gone, the bay
doors whined shut again.

Satisfied, Petrov throttled back to reduce speed
and keyed his mike. "Chkalov Test Center, this is
Ten' Odin, Shadow One," he radioed. "Attack complete. Repeat, attack complete."

"*Copy that, Shadow One*," the mission controller monitoring this series of tests acknowledged.
"*Stand by for our evaluation.*"

Data links between the bomber prototype and
the test center allowed the technicians there to follow every action taken by the PAK-DA's flight crew
and its computers in real time. Right now, they were
checking the evaluations made by the bomber's target discrimination program. Had it successfully

identified which targets were real and which were cleverly crafted fakes?

"*Shadow One, this is Chkalov,*" the controller said, sounding pleased. "*We score that as a complete success. Every target selected was legitimate. And every target discarded by your computer was a decoy. There were no observed errors.*"

Petrov and Bunin exchanged triumphant glances. While Russia's stealth bomber was primarily intended as a strategic strike platform to hit high-value fixed sites—enemy command centers and air bases, for example—they'd just demonstrated an additional capability to conduct attacks on well-camouflaged tactical targets. That made the PAK-DA a match for America's B-2s, which had been used for years against terrorists in Afghanistan, Libya, and Syria.

"Understood, Chkalov," Petrov said. He glanced across the cockpit at his copilot. "What's left on our checklist, Oleg?"

"Just one more computer test," Bunin told him, reading a menu of action items from one of his displays. "We need to verify the handoff between our primary and secondary computers in case of trouble."

Petrov considered that. Because the bomber prototype relied so heavily on computers to manage its advanced fly-by-wire flight controls, weapons, defenses, and sensors, it was equipped with redundant backup computer systems. If its crew lost their main computer, either because of battle damage or some other malfunction, secondary systems were supposed to take over automatically. They'd successfully demonstrated this switching capability several times on the ground. Now it was time to make sure it worked when it counted, in the air.

"We'll head back to the barn," he decided. "And conduct that last test on our way."

He rolled the PAK-DA into another turn, this time back around to the northwest. A new steering cue appeared. They were roughly one hundred kilometers from the test center's Akhtubinsk military airfield, approximately eleven minutes' flying time at their present speed.

"Standing by to shut down the primary computer," Bunin said. His fingers were poised over a menu on his largest MFD.

"Permission granted," Petrov replied.

Bunin tapped one of the icons on his screen and then used the virtual keyboard that appeared in response to enter a code confirming his instruction. Tupolev's software engineers wanted to make sure no one could shut down the aircraft's computer systems with a simple accidental finger swipe.

Immediately, every multifunction display in the cockpit went dark.

And stayed dark. So did Petrov's HUD.

"*Der'mo,*" he snarled. "Shit." When they'd tried this out on the ground, the secondary computer had taken over so fast that all they'd noticed was a slight flicker on the screens. "Bring the secondary computer up manually."

"Yes, Colonel," Bunin said. He flipped open a

panel on the console set between them and pushed a system reset button. Nothing happened. He tried again, but all the screens stayed blank.

"Go back to the primary computer," Petrov ordered.

Bunin nodded and punched the main computer's manual reset button. Again, there was no response.

Turbulence buffeted the bomber. Caught by a sudden gust, it banked slightly to the right. Instinctively, Petrov tried to level out again. The stick felt dull and mushy in his hand. Like all flying wings and many other advanced military aircraft, the PAK-DA prototype was inherently unstable. It relied heavily on computerized fly-by-wire systems to make the adjustments to its elevons and rudders that were necessary to maintain controlled flight.

Well, this was bad, Petrov thought. But not necessarily lethal. After all, he'd practiced for just such an event in simulators many times. Coolly, he instructed Bunin, "Switch to the backup manual flight controls."

His copilot opened another panel on the central console and flipped a new series of switches. His eyes darted toward Petrov. "Our manual flight controls are active."

Gingerly, and then with more force, Petrov tugged his stick to the left and pushed down hard on the rudder pedals. The aircraft responded sluggishly, but finally it came back level. "Christ," he muttered. "This thing handles like a drunken pig without the computers." He keyed his radio mike again. "Akhtubinsk Tower, this is Shadow One. We've lost both flight control computers. I am declaring a mission abort."

"*Understood, Shadow One,*" the control tower replied right away. "*We lost your data link at the same time. We're clearing the field now. Emergency vehicles are on standby.*"

Quickly, Petrov shifted his attention to the two Su-34 chase planes. "*Opekun Odin i Dva eto Ten' Odin.* Guardian One and Two, this is Shadow One. Close on me. I've lost all instrumentation and I'm returning to Akhtubinsk immediately. But I'm going to need your eyes."

Unable to hide their concern, both chase plane pilots acknowledged. The twin-tailed aircraft rolled in to within fifty meters, one on the bomber's left side and one on its right. Their red, green, and white position lights glowed brightly in the darkness.

"Give me a reading on my airspeed, altitude, and heading," Petrov said calmly.

"Shadow One, your airspeed is five hundred kph. Altitude thirty-eight hundred meters. Your heading is now three-two-one degrees," one of the Su-34 pilots reported.

"Understood," Petrov replied. "What's my most direct heading back to the airfield?" That earlier, inadvertent roll to the right had thrown them a little off course. And with the computers down, so was their digitized navigation system.

"Come left to three-one-four degrees."

Sweating under his helmet, Petrov muscled the stick and rudder pedals to raise control surfaces on the trailing edge of the bomber's right wing, while simultaneously lowering rudders and elevons along its left wing. Slowly, the big plane banked left a few degrees. Straining, he reversed the process to level off again on the correct heading.

Carefully, the Su-34 pilots and weapons officers coaxed the stricken PAK-DA prototype back toward the test center's Akhtubinsk field. Their constant commentary on altitude, attitude, airspeed, and the observed positions of the bomber's wing rudders and elevons blurred through Petrov's mind as he fought to keep the inherently unstable aircraft in control. Without the fly-by-wire system, even small adjustments required enormous effort.

Under the strain, time seemed to stretch out almost unbearably for most of the return flight. Seconds felt like minutes. Minutes dragged like hours. But then, as they came in on final approach, with the airfield's bright lights blazing ahead of them through the cockpit canopy, everything sped up. And Petrov's whole world narrowed down to a tight cone directly ahead of the aircraft.

"*I confirm that your landing gear is down, Shadow One,*" one of the Su-34 pilots radioed.

"Copy that," Petrov replied tightly.

"*Two hundred meters, descending at ten meters per second. You're coming in a little hot. Airspeed is three hundred ten kph.*" The Su-34s were sticking to the bomber's flanks as if they were glued there, gliding down out of the sky beside it as though they planned to land, too.

Petrov blinked away a droplet of sweat. The double strand of runway lights seemed to be rushing at him like a runaway freight train. Reacting instantly, he reduced his throttles and heaved back on the stick to raise the bomber's nose a degree or two. His rigid neck and shoulder muscles felt as though they were on fire.

"One hundred meters, down at eight meters per second. Angle of attack looks good, Shadow One. Split drag rudders full open. Airspeed two-ninety kph," he heard a chase plane report through his headset.

And then they were over the runway itself. Parallel white bars painted along the concrete strip loomed up and then vanished beneath the cockpit, growing ever bigger as the PAK-DA lost altitude. Abruptly, the heavy bomber dropped the last couple of meters and touched down with a sharp jolt. Instantly, the Su-34 chase planes on either side hit their afterburners and climbed away at high speed.

Petrov chopped back on his throttles to reverse thrust and then braked hard to shed their remaining speed. With its turbofan engines howling, the big aircraft rolled down the runway. Slowing fast, the PAK-DA prototype came to a complete stop about fifteen hundred meters from its touchdown point. Through the cockpit canopy, he could see flashing red and white lights as several emergency vehicles converged on their stationary bomber.

With a sigh, he shut down their engines and sat back.

Beside him, Bunin stripped off his flight helmet. The younger man's thick mop of hair was soaked with sweat. His teeth gleamed briefly in the darkness. "That was some seriously shit-hot flying, Colonel," he said in unfeigned admiration. "I think you just saved the whole stealth bomber program—not to mention a twenty-billion-ruble experimental aircraft. Oh, and our lives, too, for whatever they're worth. I suspect our masters in Moscow are going to be very, very happy with you."

Wordlessly, Petrov nodded. Inside, he smiled. Without realizing it, his copilot had just managed to put his finger on the whole point of tonight's little exercise.

SEVEN

THE NEXT DAY

Mercury City Tower's glowing, bronze-tinted reflective glass made it stand out among the five other ultramodern skyscrapers that formed Moscow's International Business Center. Slanting, steplike recesses along one side of the building gave the nearly 340-meter-high tower a unique, tapered look that only added to its apparent height. And inside its reinforced concrete-and-steel exterior, high-end restaurants, stores selling luxury goods, business offices, and opulent apartments filled the seventy-five floors soaring above the ground.

Two hundred meters and forty-four stories above street level, the corporate headquarters for one of Russia's largest and most successful industrial and financial conglomerates, *Severnaya Zvezda Stolitsa*, or North Star Capital, occupied three full floors. In theory, North Star was a shareholder-owned corporation. In practice, it was completely controlled by its chairman and CEO, Dmitri Grishin.

Grishin maintained a palatial private office on the topmost of those three floors. Floor-to-ceiling, east-facing windows offered him an unobstructed view of a loop of the Moskva River, the centuries-old Arbat District, the Kremlin's redbrick walls, and much of the sprawling metropolis beyond. On good days, he savored the view.

Today was not such a day.

Grishin glowered down at the report he'd just finished reading. Irritably, he scrawled his signature across the last page, closed the folder, and tossed it onto a growing stack of similar documents. Early on in his quest to amass wealth and power, he'd learned the importance of closely monitoring the decisions made by his subordinates. Staying near the top of the heap in Russia's chaotic, ever-churning business and political climate required an almost infinite capacity for hard work and careful attention to even the smallest details. As a result, senior managers across his far-flung corporate empire were expected to provide weekly summaries of their operations—production costs and profit figures, personnel moves, interactions with federal, local, and foreign officials, consumer feedback, and a host of other useful data.

Unfortunately, none of the reports he was studying now made pleasant reading. For months now, persistently low world oil and natural gas prices had been wreaking havoc with Russia's economy, which depended heavily on the energy sector. More than a sixth of the nation's GDP came from oil and gas, along with half its government revenues, and more than two-thirds of its export income. Because of depressed prices affecting those industries, incomes were down, unemployment was sharply up, and the broader economy was sliding fast toward a severe recession. And aware of the growing strains on government finances, foreign creditors were increasingly reluctant to lend money to Moscow except at exorbitant interest rates.

Grishin's frown deepened. The worsening slump threatened both his own personal wealth and Russia's political stability. In the past, his fellow countrymen had proved willing to surrender their freedoms in return for a measure of prosperity and security. The current government's increasingly obvious failure to live up to its end of that bargain was dangerous. Already, there were protests and demonstrations in the streets of Moscow, St. Petersburg, and other large cities. They were peaceful so far, but the slightest spark could turn them violent. Worse still, there were unpleasant rumors that the Kremlin might soon be forced by its fiscal woes to cut pay and pensions for the armed forces and the police. And if unrest spread through the two strongest pillars of the state—the military and law enforcement—Russia's ruling elites could lose their grip on power in the blink of an eye.

The oligarch had no illusions. Although he had been one of the earliest and strongest supporters of his nation's authoritarian president, Piotr Zhdanov, he knew the Kremlin leader would not hesitate to sacrifice even his closest allies to save his own skin and position. "Lightening the sleigh"—throwing the weak overboard for the wolves to devour first—was an old and cruel Russian tradition. Under serious threat, Zhdanov would eagerly seize the opportunity to toss the mob a scapegoat or two. And during an economic crisis, blaming the nation's troubles on "criminal capitalist billionaires" was an obvious play.

Finished with his depressing reading, he signed the last report and sat back with a heavy sigh. The omens all pointed in the same dark direction. His status, his fortune, and even his personal safety and that of his immediate family were all increasingly at risk. He looked up from his desk, noticing that outside his office windows, the morning's weak sunshine and pale blue skies had yielded to looming gray clouds. Wonderful, he thought dourly. Even the weather matched his mood. From the look of those clouds, Moscow's first real snowfall of the season was on the way.

Then Grishin laughed harshly. *Enough moaning and pissing, Dmitri*, he told himself. He had no intention of sitting frozen in fear, like a mouse transfixed by the hungry, burning gleam of a cat's eyes. His determination to act first against the threats he saw emerging had been the genesis for the audacious, highly risky scheme he had privately code-named *Akt Ischeznoveniya*, Vanishing Act.

Leaning forward again, he picked up a secure internal phone. Teams of professionals checked and rechecked North Star's communications and computer networks every day to make sure they were safe from unauthorized access by corporate rivals and snooping government agencies. Like all rich and powerful men in Russia, Grishin had many secrets that were too dangerous to share. "Send in my visitor," he ordered tersely.

Moments later, his office door buzzed and then swung open to admit a tall, fit man in his early thirties. From the stylishly tailored shoulders of his Savile Row bespoke suit to the narrow tips of his expensive, Italian leather dress shoes, Pavel Voronin appeared to be the consummate, high-level corporate courtier. He had been educated overseas at the best schools in the United Kingdom and the United States, and it showed. Anyone meeting him for the first time would have pegged him as a polished yes-man—more used to crafting bland, inoffensive memos and massaging delicate executive egos than engaging in the rough-and-tumble, red in tooth and claw, real world of Russian business infighting.

The facade the younger man presented to others amused Grishin.

In reality, Voronin was his top troubleshooter— in all senses of the word. Outwardly genial and cultured, he was actually ruthless, driven, and completely amoral, willing to go to any lengths needed to accomplish whatever task he'd been assigned. In the bad old days of the Soviet Union, he would have been snapped up by the KGB or the GRU at a relatively early age and trained in the dark arts of "wet work," murder and assassination. Fortunately, Grishin's talent scouts had spotted him before Russia's revamped intelligence bureaucracies realized the depths of his ambition and skills. And there was no doubt that the younger man found working for his current patron far more interesting and lucrative than government service. To enhance his effectiveness, only a handful of the oligarch's closest aides knew that Voronin worked for North Star Capital. On his rare visits to the Mercury City Tower, he used Grishin's own private executive elevator.

Currently, Voronin was responsible for handling the operational details involved in Vanishing Act. That included acting as Grishin's discreet liaison with Colonel Alexei Petrov. As their plan drew ever nearer to activation, it was no longer safe or sensible for the two of them to meet in person, or even by phone or email.

Grishin nodded brusquely at the single chair in front of his desk. He waited while the younger man sat down and crossed his perfectly creased trouser legs. "I hear there was an unfortunate incident during the most recent PAK-DA prototype flight?"

With a hint of a smile, Voronin nodded. "So there was." He shrugged nonchalantly. "Apparently, a simple, easily fixed programming error created a very dangerous situation—one that could easily have led to the loss of the aircraft and its crew." His smile widened. "Fortunately, Colonel Petrov's flying skill, courage, and dedication to duty saved the entire stealth bomber program from catastrophe."

Grishin nodded. "That is excellent news." He raised an eyebrow. "I hope the colonel's merits are appreciated by his superiors?"

Voronin nodded. "My sources inside the Kremlin assure me that the powers-that-be fully understand the bullet they just dodged. Losing the PAK-DA prototype would have been an utter political and strategic disaster. In fact, I hear that President Zhdanov himself phoned Petrov to offer his thanks and congratulations." His pale gray eyes gleamed with amusement. "As of this moment, our illustrious national leader is convinced that the colonel is someone who can do no wrong."

"And this computer glitch?" Grishin pressed. "The one that caused all this trouble?"

"Investigators are already digging into its origin," Voronin said calmly.

"Will that be a problem?"

"No," Voronin said simply.

Grishin eyed him. "You seem very confident of that, Pavel."

"Tragically, the Tupolev software engineer responsible for that piece of flawed code is no longer available for interrogation," Voronin explained. "Apparently, he accidentally fell out of a window last month. According to the police report, he was heavily intoxicated."

"How . . . unfortunate," Grishin commented dryly.

Voronin shrugged again. "Alcoholism is the sad national curse of our beloved Motherland, is it not? Certainly, it serves as a useful explanation for a multitude of sins."

Slowly, Grishin nodded. Inwardly, he felt a momentary chill. There were times when the younger man's casual willingness to kill unnerved even him. Then again, he reminded himself, Voronin's cold-blooded efficiency was a survival trait—and one that profited his employer as well. After all, there were no prizes for second place in the high-stakes game they were currently playing, only disgrace, humiliation, and, in all probability, execution for treason.

EIGHT

With his face and eyes protected from subzero temperatures by a thermal mask and ski goggles, Captain Nick Flynn looked down and saw an expanse of tundra rushing up at him. Although the gray light filtering through a layer of thick clouds made it difficult to judge distances with any precision, that ground sure looked like it was getting closer fast. Really fast. He released his attached weapons case and rucksack so that they fell away into the freezing air and swung loose below his feet, still connected to him by a long strap. Then he forced himself to relax, bent his knees slightly, tucked his chin in, and gripped the risers.

A small puff of white billowed up when his equipment packs hit the ground. *Thousand-one, thousand-two,* he counted silently.

Thump.

His boots thudded into the snow. Instantly he let himself buckle and rolled sideways to absorb the landing shock. At that same moment, a gust of wind caught his collapsing parachute canopy and snapped it back open wide. Dragged behind the chute, he slid across the tundra in a glittering spray of fine ice crystals and powder snow.

Great, Flynn thought with a mental grin. Now he got an impromptu sleigh ride across the frozen ground. Unbidden, that old song "Over the river and through the woods to Grandmother's house we go" began playing in his head. But his grandmother's house was about three thousand miles south of here, and there wasn't any snow in Central Texas, especially not in October. Hurriedly, he hit one of the two release assemblies on his harness to spill air out of the parachute. That brought his wind-driven skid to a halt.

Overhead, the C-130 turboprop he'd just jumped from was already a diminishing dot in the distance, with the roar of its four engines fading fast. And across the wide-open, white landscape, eleven more men came drifting down out of the cloud-covered sky. One by one, they thumped to the ground, raising little spurts of snow of their own. Counting them off, he breathed out in relief. Although he'd been the first one out of the plane, everyone else in his small unit had followed him off the aircraft's rear ramp.

Having someone refuse a jump wasn't usual, but it could happen, and Flynn knew he hadn't yet gotten to know these men well enough to judge the odds of anyone pulling that kind of boneheaded stunt at the last second. As it was, he'd had to practically beg to get permission for his unit to participate in

this practice airborne drop and field exercise. Only
the fact that all of them, whether Army, National
Guard, or Air Force, had already earned their jump
wings earlier in their military service made it even
thinkable. But having an aircraft head back to Joint
Base Elmendorf-Richardson with one of his stray
sheep still aboard would have given the Pentagon
and CIA assholes still gunning for him even more
ammunition.

Getting back to his knees, Flynn reeled in his
fluttering canopy arm over arm. Quickly, he bundled up the material before stuffing it into a bag
clipped to his parachute harness. It took seconds
more to struggle out of the harness itself and retrieve his weapons case and rucksack. Pulling out
a pair of snowshoes and strapping them on took
even more time. Finished at last, he stood up with a
grunt and heaved the heavy rucksack onto his back.
As a final measure, he slung his M4 carbine over
the white camouflage smock he wore on top of his
parka.

He brushed snow off his goggles and mask and
scanned his wider surroundings. Right before they
jumped, the C-130's crewmen had rolled a pair of
large cargo pallets out the open rear ramp. The
pallets were loaded with a couple of snowmobiles
and towable sleds, plus additional supplies of food,
fuel, and ammunition. They'd come down under
multiple parachutes, and it looked as though they'd
landed intact about three hundred yards from his
position.

By now, several members of Flynn's team already had their own gear on. In ones and twos, they headed toward the equipment pallets—crunching awkwardly through ankle-deep snow. Others were still wrestling with balky parachutes or fitting themselves out with cross-country skis or snow-shoes.

It didn't surprise Flynn to see that Sergeant Andy Takirak was the first man to reach their heavier gear. Despite being older than anyone else in the unit by at least fifteen years, the veteran National Guardsman was one of the most physically fit. And his decades of experience in this kind of terrain and harsh climate showed. Compared to everyone else, he moved over the frozen tundra with surprising speed and grace.

By the time Flynn reached the first pallet himself, Takirak had already stripped off its protective tarpaulin. "How's everything look?" he asked.

The noncom gave him a thumbs-up. "Good, sir," he confirmed. "There's no damage to this snow machine or sled that I can see."

Flynn nodded. Alaskans always referred to snowmobiles as "snow machines," since they used them more for work than recreation. He reminded himself to start doing the same. Like Texans, longtime Alaska residents had their own lingo. And if he didn't want to stand out all the time as what they called a cheechako, a clueless tourist, he needed to remember to use local words and phrases when possible. "After all, when in Nome—" he murmured, privately enjoying the horrible pun.

"Sir?" Takirak asked, sounding puzzled.

"Never mind me, Andy," Flynn said, glad that his mask hid his reddening face. "Just talking to myself."

"Might want to go easy on that right now," the older man said with a faint suggestion of amusement of his own. "Yakking to the walls will come natural enough to all of us by the time the serious winter sets in."

As more soldiers and airmen arrived, Takirak put them to work offloading the small two-man vehicles, sleds, fuel cans, ammunition boxes, and other supplies and prepping them for use. There was less grousing than usual. Some of that was probably due to the usual adrenaline rush conferred by surviving a jump out of a perfectly good airplane. A bit more might be owed to the vast stretch of empty country in which they now found themselves. As far as the eye could see in all directions, they were the only living human beings. There were no trees or signs of other vegetation. Effectively, their little band was all on its own in a flat, almost featureless plain of snow and ice, broken only by a range of low, rocky hills halfway to the northern horizon. Their voices were instinctively hushed, as though they were awed visitors wandering around inside the echoing interior of a huge cathedral.

In fact, it wasn't until they were almost finished emptying the two pallets that Senior Airman Mark Mitchell—M-Squared to his friends—finally got up enough nerve to ask the question that had to be on everyone else's mind. "Say, sir? Uh, where's everybody else? Did those Herky Bird pilots screw up their navigation and drop us in the wrong place?"

Flynn put down the boxes of MREs he'd carried over to one of the sleds and turned his head to meet the red-haired airman's mildly worried gaze. Mitchell had earned his jump wings during a stab at the Air Force's pararescue course. He'd been bounced for what his personnel file dryly called "attitude adjustment issues." Based on Flynn's personal observation over the past several days, that probably meant the airman had pulled one prank too many on his instructors. After a succession of other scrapes in various units, he'd been "volunteered" to serve as the new Joint Force team's communications specialist. In the field, that meant carting around the team's AN/PRC-162 manpack radio and sticking close to his new commander's side at all times.

Mitchell's curiosity and concern were natural. The training and readiness exercise they'd piggybacked onto involved four other C-130s carrying more than three hundred paratroopers belonging to the Army's Fourth Brigade Combat Team (Airborne). By rights, this snow-covered plain should be filled with other soldiers assembling into platoons and sorting out their own gear.

"We're on the right drop zone," Flynn assured the airman, raising his voice slightly so that everyone could hear him. "The rest of the troops are jumping onto a DZ closer to Deadhorse. Their COs have their own training exercise plans for their units. But I've got something different in mind for us."

Another soldier, Private First Class Cole Hynes, pushed forward. Short and square shouldered, Hynes had a temper that had cost him his sergeant's stripes a few months back. Apart from his pugnacity, his soldier skills were first-rate. On the team's improvised firing range at Kaktovik, he'd proved able to rapidly put rounds on target at six hundred yards with their M249 Para light machine gun. "Just how far from Deadhorse are we, sir?" he asked with a frown, eyeing the miles and miles of untouched snow in all directions.

It was time to pull the pin on his unwelcome surprise, Flynn realized. Except for Takirak, he'd kept the details of this planned field exercise close to his chest. He'd done so precisely because he didn't want any of his troops to duck out before climbing aboard the C-130 by "accidentally on purpose" twisting an ankle or coming down with some mystery illness. The Spanish conquistador Hernán Cortés had motivated his men to conquer or die by burning the ships that had carried them to Mexico. His task today was considerably simpler, which was probably just as well because it would be damned hard to set anything ablaze on this frozen, treeless plain. Instead of defeating a hostile empire whose fighting forces outnumbered his by a hundred to one, all he wanted to accomplish was toughen up his men physically and teach them to make the best use of their winter gear, snowshoes, and skis before the harsh Arctic winter fully set in and made this type of training too hazardous.

"We're roughly fifty-nine miles from the airport

at Deadhorse," he announced calmly. "That's as the crow flies." He paused to make sure they were all focused on him. "Or, in our case, as the man marches." He checked his watch. "In approximately seventy-two hours, a plane will land there to ferry us back to Kaktovik. It will take off again sixty minutes later, whether we're on board or not. So that's how long we've got to finish this little jaunt."

Hynes, Mitchell, and the others stared at him in consternation. "You're shitting me," someone muttered from the back of the little knot of soldiers.

"Nope," Flynn assured him. He glanced at Takirak. "I'm dead serious, aren't I, Sergeant?"

The noncom nodded stoically. "Yes, sir." A dry smile darted across his weathered face and then disappeared. "Only fifty-nine miles in three days? With clear weather in the forecast?" He shook his head. "Heck, that's practically a stroll in the park."

"Yeah, but it's a pretty fricking cold park, Sarge," Mitchell pointed out.

"Which is why you're wearing all of that fancy winter gear provided by Uncle Sam, courtesy of the generous taxpayers of these United States," Takirak reminded him. He looked around the circle of dubious faces. "So quit your bitching and get organized, ladies. I want both pallets unloaded and all of this extra gear stowed on the sleds in ten minutes. Because whether you're happy about it or not, we're hiking north to Deadhorse. So there's no sense in wasting more daylight." He glanced at Flynn. "With your permission, sir?"

"Carry on, Sergeant," Flynn agreed. He stepped

back out of the way as the knot of soldiers and airmen broke up and went to work again. Thank God for an experienced NCO, he thought for what had to be the hundredth time over just the past week. Loner himself or not, the National Guard sergeant had the right touch when it came to handling what was still more a prickly bunch of individuals than a solid military unit.

In the end, it took closer to fifteen minutes to organize the march column to Takirak's satisfaction, but at last they moved out north across the tundra—tromping steadily toward the low hills along the northern horizon. The noncom and another man were a few hundred yards out in front as scouts. Bringing up the rear, two more men drove the snow machines and towed sleds piled high with their extra supplies, puttering along at very low throttle to keep pace with the soldiers on foot ahead of them.

At the head of the central column, Flynn settled his rucksack across his back and started off. Mitchell came next, bowed slightly under the weight of his own gear and their radio. "Man, I thought I was joining the Air Force, not the fucking Foreign Legion," he heard the communications specialist grumble under his breath. "All this 'march or die' shit is gonna get old real fast."

Flynn looked back over his shoulder with a grin. "It's not actually 'march or die,' Airman Mitchell."

"No, sir?" the radioman asked.

"Nope," Flynn continued. "Not enough sand, for a start."

"Hell of a lot of snow, though, sir," Mitchell pointed out.

Flynn nodded. His grin widened. "That's why it's more like 'march or freeze your ass off.'"

Mitchell snorted. "Anyone ever tell you that you're kinda mean, sir?"

"All the time, ever since I was a kid," Flynn said, still smiling. "And that was just my mother."

THREE DAYS LATER

Flynn concentrated on putting one snowshoed foot in front of the other. After three days and nearly sixty miles of marching north across this frozen landscape, the rhythm had become second nature to him. His breath puffed out in a little cloud of steam that drifted away on the icy breeze. He looked back at his men. Though their shoulders were bowed down under the weight of their rucksacks, they were all in position in the column and moving easily, almost gracefully, through the snow.

The first day's march had been the roughest on all of them, except for Andy Takirak. Within the first few miles, every step had been painful and every breath an agony as they sucked in bone-dry air chilled to just above zero. By the time they made camp, his little band of soldiers and airmen were too tired even to bitch about the situation he'd dropped them in. Only the National Guard sergeant had seemed disgustingly cheerful when he prodded them awake the following morning, hours before sunrise. Everyone else had been wrapped in misery, all too aware of aching feet, calves, and shoulders.

That had changed sometime during the second day's even longer hike. One moment, Flynn felt like all he could do was focus on taking the next painful step—slogging along in an endless procession of discomfort where sheer willpower was the only thing keeping him moving. Then, suddenly, he'd felt his head come up and his shoulders go back. His breathing had eased, too. Oh, his feet and back still hurt . . . but it no longer mattered. Or at least not as much. A quick check of the march column had showed that the rest of his team was experiencing something similar. Even their usual crappy jokes and banter had started to bounce back and forth again.

"They're over the hump," Takirak had said matter-of-factly during their next rest break.

Flynn had nodded, understanding what the older man meant. The "hump" was that almost indefinable psychological moment when you realized that what had seemed impossibly difficult was doable after all. There was a hump somewhere in every challenging situation, and if you managed to get past it you learned a lot about yourself . . . and the others who'd been there with you.

Like all good things, that brief moment of elation had faded again under the strain of marching so far and so fast. But it lingered inside every man as a source of confidence and renewed strength. They knew now that they were going to make it—that they'd reach Deadhorse on time if they just refused to give up.

A droning roar off to the east brought Flynn's head up again. There, coming in low, on its final approach to the airport, was an Alaska Air National Guard C-130J turboprop. He glanced at his watch.

From behind him, Mitchell asked, "Is that our ride, sir?"

Flynn nodded, feeling a grin starting to spread on his face. "That it is, Airman. And right on time." He moved off to the side of the column of marching men and raised his voice. "Well done, guys! You did it."

Answering smiles spread along the line of weary, unshaven faces. Bringing up the rear, with his light machine gun draped over his shoulder, Hynes pulled down his thermal mask. "Hey, Captain," he asked. "Is that it? Aren't you going to make some long, inspiring speech?"

Flynn shook his head. "Hell no, PFC." He nodded toward the runway, now visible just a few hundred yards ahead of them. The Super Hercules had landed and was taxiing down the strip. "Hear those propellers?"

"Yeah?" Hynes said curiously.

"Well, that's my speech," Flynn told him with a laugh. "Know what they sound like to me?"

"Victory?"

"Yep," Flynn agreed. "Victory . . . and hot food, showers, and clean sheets."

That drew whoops and cheers. Hynes and the others grinned even wider. "Roger that, sir!"

NINE

SOME DAYS LATER

In a whirling flurry of rotor-blown snow, a large twin-engine helicopter settled heavily onto the tundra. Painted white with red stripes, it was a Boeing Vertol 234 heavy-lift helicopter—the civilian version of a military CH-47 Chinook. As its turboshaft engines spooled down, both rotors gradually slowed and then stopped moving. The rear ramp whined down and thudded into the snow, revealing a compartment crammed full with nearly eleven metric tons of cargo. A couple pieces of small construction equipment—walk-behind, smooth-drum, compaction rollers—were strapped down closest to the opening. Large sections of folded white fabric and long aluminum stringers filled the rest of the fuselage from floor to ceiling.

Kept comfortable despite the cold by his fashionable gray-and-blue Rossignol ski jacket, Gore-Tex pants, and waterproof boots, Pavel Voronin strode down the ramp and around to one side of the big helicopter. As it climbed above one of the neighboring peaks, the morning sun threw his shadow far across a dazzling white field.

Several men were already headed his way from out of a clump of dwarf black spruce and willow trees. Behind them, a handful of carefully camouflaged tents nestled among the trees.

Voronin nodded a greeting to their leader, a lean, wiry man carrying a scoped rifle, who trudged up to join him while the rest moved on to start unloading cargo from the helicopter. "*Zdravstvuyte*, Sergei Bondarovich."

"Welcome to *Voron'ye Pole*, Crow Field," Bondarovich replied. Like the others on this small, covert operations team, he had served in Russia's elite Spetsnaz special operations forces. Before he left the military to work for Dmitri Grishin and North Star Capital, he had attained the rank of major.

"Crow Field?"

Bondarovich shrugged. "We had to call this place something."

"True," Voronin agreed. Almost none of the hundreds of mountains, ridges, valleys, rivers, and streams inside the enormous Arctic National Wildlife Refuge bore official names. The absence of identified places on maps made the wilderness seem even more alien and inaccessible—a trackless region the size of Scotland that was virtually untouched by humans or any of their works and words. But Bondarovich's choice made sense since the little icebound stream bordering this concealed camp eventually joined one of the rare exceptions to that rule, the Old Crow River. And, he thought, when one considered how North Star planned to use this remote valley, calling it Crow Field was even more apt.

He moved off to the side, making way for the first drum roller as it trundled down the helicopter ramp and turned toward the camp. A shallow trail of densely compacted snow and ice marked its passage across the tundra. Pleased by this first evidence of the construction equipment's effectiveness, he knelt and pushed at the trail with his gloves. It felt solid, unyielding to the touch.

Voronin got back to his feet. "That should do the trick," he commented.

"No doubt," Bondarovich said. "Once you give us the go-ahead to start full-scale operations, we'll start clearing the valley floor of any obstructions and compacting the snow layer to the required depth."

"How long will you need?"

Bondarovich pulled at his chin. "Three days at a minimum," he said. "But more likely four. Or even possibly five. We're down to only about seven and a half hours of sunlight already, and we lose more than nine minutes every day. If we rig lights to keep working after it gets dark, we could easily blow our cover here."

Voronin nodded his understanding. There were no other settled places anywhere near this valley. Lights glowing here at night, in what should otherwise be unbroken darkness, would stand out like a sore thumb to any passing aircraft, triggering any number of inconvenient questions. Currently, the local Canadian authorities in the little town of Fort

McPherson believed the heavy-lift Vertol 234 helicopter's job was ferrying supplies north to an environmental group that was supposed to be studying the effects of climate change on the Beaufort Sea coast. Nothing could be allowed to shake that conviction, especially with Grishin and Petrov's high-risk, high-reward plan moving rapidly to fruition.

A low warning whistle from the edge of the camouflaged encampment interrupted his thoughts. He looked up in surprise and saw a lone figure with what looked like a hunting rifle slung over one shoulder slowly hiking down a snow-covered slope at the western edge of the valley.

"Ah," Bondarovich said with a wry grin. "It seems our unwanted guest has decided to show himself at last."

"What unwanted guest?" Voronin demanded.

"An American. A hermit fur trapper working this part of the refuge," the ex-Spetsnaz major said calmly. "We've been aware that he's had us under observation for the past couple of days."

Voronin's mouth tightened in exasperation. "And you let him do this? Knowing the stakes involved?"

Bondarovich shrugged. "The American knows this territory like the back of his own hand, and he's wary of strangers. I saw no point in spooking him unnecessarily."

"Do you have any more information about him?" Voronin snapped.

The other man nodded. "I had Makevič check him out," he confirmed. Besides being an experienced bush pilot, Felix Makevič had worked as a deep-cover GRU agent in Canada for years before switching his employment and loyalty to Grishin and North Star Capital. "His name is Jensen. Trig Jensen. And his only contact with the outside world is through bush pilots who fly into his isolated camp from time to time. Not more often than every three or four months, if that."

"Does he have a radio or a satellite phone?" Voronin pressed.

"Only a one-way radio that he uses to listen to gospel music from a religious station outside Fairbanks," Bondarovich answered. "This fellow Jensen is a throwback, a man trying to live almost entirely on his own, outside the modern world."

"For that I give thanks," Voronin answered sardonically. With the ex-Spetsnaz major at his side, he moved out to meet the trapper at the edge of the camp.

Up close, Jensen was a short, broad-shouldered man. His full brown beard was streaked with gray. Hard blue eyes peered out at them from under a fur-lined hood. He certainly didn't waste any time with meaningless courtesies. "What the hell are you folks doing up here?" he demanded. "With your goddamned, noisy helicopter and all? You're going to scare away the game for twenty miles or more. Damn it, this is a wildlife refuge. It's totally off-limits to all of this techno bullshit."

"I do apologize, Mr.—?" Voronin said smoothly, in utterly unaccented American English, pretending that he didn't know the other man's name.

"Jensen."

Voronin nodded gratefully. "Mr. Jensen." He spread his hand. "I sincerely regret any inconvenience or disruption of your work, but I assure you that our efforts here have official status."

"Exactly what kind of *official* status?" the trapper growled, somehow managing to make the word "official" sound like profanity.

"We're here as part of a federal climate change research project," Voronin answered patiently. "And I can assure you that any unintended degradation of this pristine landscape will be completely repaired once we're finished here."

Jensen snorted. "Easy to promise. Tough to do." He glared at them. "You got any proof of this story of yours?"

"Certainly," Voronin replied. He unzipped his ski jacket slightly and dug out an ID card from one of its inside pockets. Forged by highly paid experts in Moscow, it identified him as James Henderson, an official with the federal Environmental Protection Agency. While the trapper examined it through skeptical eyes, he went on. "In a way, I'm very glad that we've met. My research team here could use your obvious familiarity with the ground and the local wildlife." He smiled. "And naturally, you would be generously compensated for your time."

"Uh-huh," Jensen said cynically. He hawked and then spat off to the side, before tossing Voronin's forged ID back to him. "Look, Mister Whoever You Really Are, I didn't come all the way out here on my lonesome to grub for pay. And certainly not from the goddamned government." His eyes narrowed to slits. "Or from anybody else, for that matter. So, if it's all the same to you, I'll just be on my way and leave you fellas in peace." Without waiting for an answer, he turned and stalked off—plodding determinedly back up the nearby slope through snow that was more than a foot deep.

Voronin stood watching the American go. When he was out of earshot, he glanced at Bondarovich. "Do you think he believed me?"

The other man shook his head. "*Net shansov v adu.* Not a chance in hell."

"A pity," Voronin commented dryly. Without taking his eyes off the fur trapper, now more than a hundred meters away, he reached out. Understanding his intent, Bondarovich handed him his scoped rifle. Briefly, Voronin inspected the weapon. It was a C14 Timberwolf, the civilian bolt-action rifle the Canadian military had selected to convert for use by its snipers. He nodded in appreciation.

Then he chambered a round, raised the rifle to his shoulder, and smoothly sighted through the scope. Gently, he squeezed the trigger.

Craack.

Struck squarely between the shoulder blades by a .338 Lapua Magnum round moving at nearly nine hundred meters per second, Jensen went down in a spray of red blood against the snow-white landscape. The American writhed once and lay still, sprawled like a rag doll on the hillside.

Voronin studied the dead man for a moment longer. Slowly, he lowered the rifle. "Make sure the body isn't found."

"That won't be a problem," Bondarovich assured him. "By the time anyone notices this American is missing, he'll have vanished forever."

"You seem very confident of that," Voronin said.

Bondarovich nodded. "This Arctic wildlife refuge contains nearly eighty thousand square kilometers of wasteland. No search party can cover that kind of ground. For all that anyone will ever know, Jensen might as well have been snatched by the *Na'in*."

"The *Na'in*?" Voronin asked.

"A mythical monster of the local native tribe, the Gwich'in," the ex-Spetsnaz major explained. "Translated, it means 'the Brush Man,' a creature that wanders the woods alone in search of human prey."

THAT SAME TIME

Tupolev's manta ray–shaped PAK-DA stealth bomber prototype streaked low across a darkened landscape west of the Don River. Occasional pockets of light marked small farming villages, and a string of glowing beads stretching from east to west outlined the path of the A-260 highway between Volgograd and the Ukrainian border near Donetsk. An advanced digital terrain-following system allowed the aircraft to stay as low as one hundred meters off the deck—climbing and diving in tiny increments of a few meters at a time as it raced across the steppe's low, rolling hills and shallow ravines. Abruptly, it banked sharply to the right and soared higher, gaining altitude fast.

Inside the cockpit, Major Oleg Bunin kept his eyes on his displays. "We are executing an attack program," he reported. His hands were in his lap, away from any controls.

From the left-hand pilot's seat, Colonel Alexei Petrov nodded. "Copy that." The altitude bar on his HUD stabilized at five thousand meters as their aircraft rolled back out of its turn and leveled off. Fighting the instinct to regain active control over the bomber, he locked the fingers of his own hands across his stomach. "Our engines are throttling back," he announced, seeing the settings change without any input from him.

"Target selection," Bunin said quietly, watching his own screens shift yet again. "Range one thousand kilometers." He glanced across the cockpit. "That's the dummy missile complex south of Ryazan."

A blinking green icon flashed into existence in Petrov's vision. It turned solid a second later. "The target's coordinates are downloaded to our practice missile."

With a high-pitched whine, the doors of a weapons bay in the fuselage behind them slid open. And then the stealth bomber shuddered slightly as a single Kh-102 cruise missile weighing 2,400 kilograms released and fell away into the air. Seconds later, a seven-and-a-half-meter-long finned shape zoomed away to the north-northwest.

"Good engine start on the missile," Petrov confirmed. Right on schedule, the Kh-102's turbofan engine had ignited as it dropped toward the ground. He breathed out in relief, as did Bunin. A failure would have created an embarrassing impact crater somewhere on the grassy steppe below them, but nothing worse, since the practice cruise missile was armed only with a mock payload. In wartime, that Kh-102 would have been armed with a 250-kiloton thermonuclear warhead—twelve and a half times more powerful than the Fat Man atomic bomb dropped on Nagasaki.

New menus flickered onto Bunin's multifunction displays. "Attack judged complete," he murmured. "We are returning to base."

In confirmation, the PAK-DA banked hard again, turning back toward the airfield at Akhtubinsk. From the start of this mission, the aircraft had been operating entirely under computer control, relying on its autonomous systems to handle every detail from takeoff to its precise flight path to target designation and weapons launch. Essentially, its human pilot and copilot were along on this particular test flight only in case something went wrong with the computers or their operating systems.

Throughout the flight home, Petrov kept his attention resolutely focused on his HUD indicators, ready to take back over at the slightest sign of trouble. In one sense, he welcomed the success of this first real test of the prototype's autonomous systems. It would allow him to push his proposal for a full-scale combat exercise. But he still found the experience of being reduced to a mere spectator aboard the bomber unpleasant, even a bit unnerving. After all, by training and inclination, he was first and foremost a pilot, not a nursemaid for some incomprehensible blur of digital ones and zeroes inside the circuits of a highly advanced thinking machine.

Suddenly, a sharp pain stabbed through his left temple. It felt as though someone had punctured his skull with an ice pick. The glowing numbers and icons on his HUD blurred in his vision, becoming unreadable. *Damn it*, he thought desperately. Not now. His teeth ground together as a second wave of agony flared through his head. Trying hard not to groan out loud, he unzipped a pocket on his flight suit and grabbed a couple of the powerful pain pills he'd stashed there before takeoff. Aware that he was sweating, he popped them into his mouth and swallowed them whole. He coughed dryly as they scraped down his throat.

"Are you all right, Colonel?" Bunin asked. The bomber copilot looked concerned.

Petrov forced himself to grin. "No problem, Oleg," he lied. "Just a slight headache." He shrugged. "I had a little trouble sleeping last night, that's all."

"So what was her name?" Bunin asked, grinning back. The worry faded from his friendly, open face.

"A gentleman never tells," Petrov retorted. His headache dialed back a bit as the fast-acting drugs took effect. Now it was more a sensation of steady, unrelenting pressure than of pulsing, stabbing torture. The indicators on his HUD swam back into focus.

"Just so long as it wasn't that hot blonde," Bunin laughed. "You know, the curvy captain in Operations?" His hands sketched out what he considered the officer in question's most obvious assets. "Because I've already got my eyes on her."

Half closing his eyes against the dull pain still squeezing his head in a vise grip, Petrov settled back against his seat. Beside him, his copilot droned on and on, outlining an elaborate scheme to woo and seduce the young woman. Although he nodded encouragement from time to time, inside he was far, far removed from any real interest in Bunin's sex life. Unfortunately, he thought coldly, the late and unlamented Dr. Viktor Obolensky had been right. His headaches were definitely increasing in both their frequency and severity. With that in mind, perhaps he should be more grateful that the PAK-DA bomber's autonomous systems had just demonstrated their operational readiness. The time could be coming, and much sooner than he hoped, when he might be forced to rely very heavily on the prototype's soulless computer programs to carry out his secret plans.

TEN

A FEW DAYS LATER

Set high on a hilltop just west of the Vltava River, Prague Castle was a sizable complex of several Renaissance and Baroque-era palaces and towers, a Gothic cathedral, and other churches and convents that could be seen looming on the horizon from almost everywhere in the Czech capital. Long a seat of government, culture, and religion, tourists thronged to its picturesque grounds and world-famous museums throughout the year.

One of those art museums, the Riding School, stood not far outside the north gate, bounded by scenic gardens on either side. Centuries before, the large, red-roofed Baroque hall had been built so that the Holy Roman Emperor Leopold I and his courtiers could exercise their horses indoors in bad weather. Stucco reliefs of leaping steeds, lances, and other weapons still decorated the front above its main doors. Inside, under high ceilings and wooden rafters, the works of various modern painters and sculptors were periodically exhibited.

Miranda Reynolds paused just inside the entry to assess her surroundings. Dozens of life-sized, though oddly distorted, human sculptures filled the gallery. Some were painted entirely red or green or blue. Others were a pallid white or gray. Still others wore long strands of fake hair that morphed strangely into clothing. A handful of visitors drifted through the large space, admiring the bizarre atmosphere created by the ultramodern art installation.

To anyone who didn't know her well, Reynolds appeared to be a successful, middle-aged Western corporate executive on a business trip to Prague. Her perfectly coifed dark hair matched her understated, but obviously expensive, blazer, slacks, and shoes. A simple gold necklace and the barest hint of lipstick completed her carefully curated look. Certainly no one outside the arcane confines of the world's intelligence agencies would have guessed that she was the current head of the CIA's highly secret Directorate of Operations.

A bearded man in jeans and a windbreaker brushed past her on his way out of the museum. "You're clear," he muttered softly, carefully not looking in her direction.

Without acknowledging the report, Reynolds strolled nonchalantly toward one of the sculptures near the far end of the hall. It portrayed an elderly woman with upraised hands and an eerie, expressionless gaze. A tall, well-dressed younger man was there ahead of her. He had been moving slowly around the carved figure, apparently intent on examining it from every angle.

Politely, he stepped back to make room. They stood together in silence for several moments, each looking at the sculpture. Then he shot a sidelong glance in her direction. "I understand the experts claim this is one of Zoubek's finest works," he said with a slight smile. "Having seen it now up close, I think I agree."

Reynolds shrugged. "Personally, my tastes run more to Calder."

His smile widened a little at the agreed-upon recognition phrase. He lowered his voice. "I assume your coming here means that my patron's proposal intrigues your agency, Ms. Reynolds."

"Perhaps," she said with a terse nod. In ordinary circumstances, no high-ranking CIA official would ever agree to a clandestine rendezvous like this on foreign soil. The risks were simply far too high. Intelligence agency executives at her exalted level were accustomed to dispatching worker bees—case officers and their agents—to do the hard and dangerous work, while they stayed safely sheltered at headquarters. But the tidbits of secrets about Russian stealth aircraft and weapons passed along to her through a chain of cutouts were so tantalizing that she had decided this meeting was worth the gamble.

That was especially true now, when the CIA was viewed so unfavorably by the president and his closest advisers. The huge media and congressional black eye Langley had sustained over that mess in the Libyan desert a couple of months ago hadn't helped matters any, Reynolds thought gloomily.

Boiled down to its essentials, the agency needed to score a massive success if it were to regain its influence over national intelligence policy anytime soon. That went double for Miranda Reynolds. Like sharks, the rivals who coveted her position in charge of the CIA's covert operations unit scented blood in the water. They were already circling, waiting for the right moment to strike.

She was no stranger to the ritual. Years before, she'd maneuvered her own predecessor out of office and into retirement in the wake of a blown operation in Afghanistan. With that in mind, however, she had no plans to yield so tamely to the same kind of internecine Agency coup. If anybody wanted her chair, they'd better be ready for a fight—and if arming herself for that inevitable confrontation required coming all the way to Prague for this mysterious rendezvous, so be it.

"Well, I think you'll find what I can offer you reasonably interesting," the elegantly dressed young man said. "Perhaps even worth your long trip from Washington." Graciously, he offered her a folded art brochure.

Reynolds glanced inside the brochure and saw a photograph of a large blended-wing aircraft with obvious stealth features. It bore clear similarities to speculative media and Pentagon illustrations of Russia's rumored PAK-DA strategic bomber. But there were also significant differences. For one thing, the images she had seen all showed an aircraft with raised winglets at the outer edge of each wing. According to analysts, these winglets would reduce turbulence, but they would also increase the hypothetical stealth bomber's radar cross-section. Their presence had seemed to suggest Russia's aeronautical engineers hadn't yet fully solved the stability problems inherent to any tailless flying wing design.

If so, it was clear that this was no longer the case. This photo showed a plane without winglets, one very similar to America's B-2 Spirit and B-21 Raider stealth aircraft. More important, it showed the bomber prototype in flight, with a twin-tailed fighter close by to provide a sense of scale. The image was clear enough to provide U.S. intelligence analysts with a wealth of new data. Carefully, she refolded the brochure and slipped it into her purse. "Reasonably interesting, indeed." She turned her apparent attention back to the sculpture of the old woman. "And your price for more?"

He smiled gently. "Not so much, compared to its value. Shall we say, something on the order of what your government routinely spends in just four or five hours in a single day?"

Reynolds arched one of her finely sculpted eyebrows in sheer incredulity. That would put the price tag at well over two billion dollars—20 percent of the CIA's current operating budget and close to 3 percent of what the U.S. government spent annually on its entire alphabet soup tangle of civilian and military intelligence organizations. She sniffed in disgust. "For images, specifications, and data we might be able to obtain ourselves through other means? Or that could easily be faked? You must be joking."

Without waiting to hear more, she started to turn away. Whether she'd been lured to Prague by a con artist or a lunatic was relatively unimportant. Her first priority was to cover her tracks fast and get out on the earliest possible flight to the States. If her rivals inside the agency found out she'd been wasting her time playing Jane Bond, amateur field agent, they'd have all the ammunition they needed to pull her down.

"You misunderstand me, Ms. Reynolds," the young man said soothingly, holding up a hand. "My patron proposes providing you with something far more tangible for your scientists and aviation engineers to examine—perhaps even something on the order of the Hakodate Incident of 1976."

Hakodate Incident? What the hell was he talking about? Hurriedly, Reynolds ransacked her knowledge of intelligence history. She knew there was something, some sort of massive intelligence coup linked to that phrase, which sounded vaguely Japanese. Something about a plane, she thought. A Russian plane. And then, when she made the connection, her eyes widened involuntarily.

In September 1976, a Soviet pilot, Lieutenant Viktor Belenko, had flown his MiG-25P Foxbat fighter to Hokkaido's Hakodate Airport and announced his intention to defect. The U.S. and its Japanese allies had eventually returned the MiG-25 to the USSR, but not before they'd stripped the Soviet jet down to its constituent parts—gathering incredibly valuable data about Soviet aircraft design, electronics, and manufacturing techniques in the process.

For a long, uncomfortable moment, she stared back at the tall young man, completely unsure how she should react to this veiled proposition. Was he seriously signaling the possible defection of another Russian flight crew, this time with their country's most advanced experimental aircraft? If so, this was either the most outrageous scam ever dangled in front of the CIA . . . or a golden opportunity to pull off one of the most incredible espionage breakthroughs in modern history.

He read her confusion. "Obviously, we don't expect you to commit your government or its money on the basis of a single photograph," he assured her. "But if you would like to explore our offer further, I'll need a highly secure means of contacting you directly—one that avoids the usual delays involved in covert communications."

"I can arrange that," Reynolds said slowly, privately relieved that she wasn't being asked to make a spur-of-the-moment decision. She reached into her purse, selected a business card from among several in her wallet, and gave it to him. It was blank, except for a single email address, a collection of assorted characters using the domain name "spyder.biz." Messages sent to that address would be funneled to one of several covert servers CIA officials used for "private communications"—emails they wanted to hide from congressional scrutiny, nosy administration snoopers, and Freedom of Information Act requests from journalists and good-government groups. She made a mental note to make sure her tech people cut that particular server out of the loop, as a precaution to protect the rest of the dark network. After all, this might still be some kind of complicated con, or worse, a disinformation ploy run by Russia's own intelligence outfits.

With a nod of thanks, the young man slid the card into his jacket pocket. "One word of friendly warning, Ms. Reynolds: you understand that this is an extremely valuable property, so I cannot guarantee that our offer will be exclusive to your country. Quite naturally, others may prove equally intrigued." Then, without waiting for a response, he turned away from her and walked off through the gallery.

Miranda Reynolds stared after him with a frown. Con game or not, she didn't like the idea of a possible bidding war against Beijing. The People's Republic of China had its own stealth bomber program. Its agents would leap at the chance to acquire Russia's advanced prototype. The situation she now faced was complicated enough without turning into a possible high-stakes auction involving another of the world's great powers.

One of her aides materialized by her side. "Do you want him followed?" he asked quietly. His smartphone was already in his hand.

Impatiently, she shook her head. "Too risky. Whoever that guy really works for, he moves like a professional. We wouldn't learn anything that he doesn't already want us to know."

"So what's our next move?"

"We take the first available flight back to D.C., Charlie," she said. "And then we wait to see whether this trip was just a wild goose chase . . . or a real chance at the mother lode."

Minutes later, Pavel Voronin climbed into a taxi. He sat back with a pleased expression as it pulled away from Prague Castle. His meeting with the CIA had gone about as well as could be hoped. He reached into his jacket, pulled out his own phone, and texted a short report to Dmitri Grishin in Moscow. "*Kryuchok nazhivlen*. The hook is baited."

ELEVEN

THE NEXT DAY

Late in the afternoon, with the sun already low on the southwest horizon, a regularly scheduled Beechcraft 1900D twin-engine turboprop came in from the east on its final approach to the island's airport. Streamers of freshly fallen snow sprayed out from under its landing gear when it touched down. The pilot, used to winter flying in northern Alaska, slipped the props into beta, carefully used reverse thrust until his forward vision was being affected by blowing snow, then applied his brakes gently to avoid sliding off onto the tundra. Carefully, he tested their action on the slick surface as his aircraft rolled down the runway, gradually increasing his pressure on the pedals to decelerate slowly and steadily. After the turboprop came to a complete stop, it turned through a complete circle and taxied over to a small metal shed and gravel-topped parking apron that were the tiny airport's only permanent facilities.

Just four passengers deplaned from the Beechcraft, while its crew unloaded a few bags, boxes, and bundles of mail and other general cargo destined for Kaktovik and the Barter Island radar station. They were all lean, fit-looking men shielded against the harsh weather by colorful ski parkas and dark snow pants. Each man carried a large duffel bag and a small overnight backpack.

The town's yellow airport bus was already parked just off the apron with its engine running to provide heat for the driver, a middle-aged man with graying hair and a broad, weathered face. His vaguely Asiatic features marked him as one of the local Inuits. Smiling genially, he climbed down off the bus to help his passengers load their heavy luggage. "Don't usually get many tourists up here at this time of year," he commented politely. "The polar bears are all back north on the pack ice, and all we got otherwise is a whole lot of nothing much to see. Unless you got a thing for whale bones. Got a lot of them lying around in one big heap."

They all smiled ruefully. "As a matter of fact, that bone mound is why we're here," one of them explained. "We work for Fish and Wildlife and someone at headquarters back in D.C. wants an updated survey to pick up any significant changes from last season."

The bus driver nodded at that. Among its many other responsibilities, the U.S. Fish and Wildlife Service managed the Arctic National Wildlife Refuge, which included Barter Island. "Makes sense to map it out now, I guess," he allowed. "While the bears aren't around. They get seriously territorial when they're scavenging on those bones and scraps of spoiled blubber and skin."

Apparently satisfied with their stated reason for visiting the island, he climbed back aboard the bus and waited while his handful of passengers settled themselves. Then he put the vehicle in gear and drove off toward town. Kaktovik had two small hotels and a bed-and-breakfast inn. At this time of the year, any of them would be grateful to have paying guests, even at a reduced government rate.

S everal hours later, wearing a white camouflage smock over his cold weather gear, Captain Nick Flynn crouched behind a row of rusting, ice-covered oil drums on the outskirts of Kaktovik. This stretch of waste ground behind the town was covered with tarpaulin-sheathed whale boats, old cars up on blocks, abandoned shipping containers, and other junk. Clouds covered the night sky, and, except for a few lights shining among the town's ramshackle houses and buildings, it was pitch-dark. The temperature was well below zero. Despite his heavy clothing, his bones ached with cold, and he had to lock his jaws shut to keep his teeth from chattering. Every minute spent motionless here in the dark robbed him of precious body heat, but even the slightest movement could be fatal to his plans.

"*Comanche Six, this is Comanche One,*" Senior Airman Mark Mitchell's voice said quietly through his radio earpiece. There was an undercurrent of excitement in the young radioman's voice. *"I think the balloon is going up, sir. We just got a flash message from the RAOC. They report that our radar here is being jammed."*

"Copy that," Flynn replied, suddenly feeling warmer. The Regional Air Operations Center was located hundreds of miles south at Joint Base Elmendorf-Richardson. It was an underground command and communications center crammed full of sophisticated computers and displays. Every piece of data gathered by the North Warning System air defense radars lining Alaska's thousands of miles of frontier was fed straight back to the RAOC, where trained specialists sorted the wheat from the chaff—deciding which unidentified air contacts were genuine and which were nothing more than flocks of migratory birds or wind-driven ice crystals. So the center's report that signals from Barter Island's long-range radar were being turned into electronic hash was a sure sign of imminent trouble. "All Comanches, this is Six," he said into his mike. "Stand by. Don your owl eyes and scan your sectors."

Disciplined acknowledgments from the five two-man teams he'd deployed earlier that evening flooded smoothly over the radio. He felt a moment's pride. The soldiers and airmen of his small security team still had some rough edges that needed sanding, but the intensive physical and tactical training he and Andy Takirak had put them through was paying off now. And right when it mattered most.

Flynn opened an insulated pack, pulled out a pair

of night vision goggles, and put them on. In the Arctic, extreme cold depleted batteries with frightening speed, which was why it was essential to keep any electronic equipment as warm as possible until it was really needed. He switched the goggles on. Instantly, the world around him brightened into a monochrome vista that was almost as clear as natural daylight. Then he settled back to keep watch over his own chosen sector.

It shouldn't be long now, he thought calmly. That radar jamming had to be a trigger for some other enemy action.

Sure enough, only moments later, he spotted four figures as they slid cautiously around the corner of a small hotel about a hundred yards from his position. All four wore bulky equipment packs and carried weapons in their hands. "Hostiles in view," he whispered into his mike. "They're moving into Sector Bravo. Stand by."

Again, quiet responses ghosted through his radio earpiece.

Flynn crouched lower, watching closely while the four armed men drew nearer to his hiding place. They were moving along a bearing that would take them directly to the radar station, only a few hundred yards away across the tundra.

Sixty yards. Forty. Twenty.

Close enough, he decided, taking a deep breath. Letting it out in a whoosh, he reared up from behind the oil drums and leveled his weapon, sighting on the lead figure. "Now, Comanches! Hit 'em!" he shouted.

Flynn squeezed the trigger. As his weapon bucked backward with a muffled cough, he heard the same sound repeated from other scattered points around the iced-over junkyard, mixed in with excited whoops and yells.

Caught by surprise and completely out in the open, the four hostiles rocked under sudden, splattering impacts and went down in the snow. All around them, more rounds kicked up snow in brief spurts.

"Cease fire! Cease fire!" Flynn ordered. Smiling now, he flipped up his night vision goggles. "Y'all okay out there?" he called to the prone figures.

"Oh, for fuck's sake," a disgusted voice replied. "*Pink* paint? You hit us with fucking *pink* paint?"

Flynn hefted his paintball gun. "Sorry, guys," he said with an even bigger grin. "MILES gear freezes up in this climate." Like all battery-powered devices, the laser weapons and target sensors that were used in the U.S. military's Multiple Integrated Laser Engagement System drained fast in subzero temperatures. "So we had to improvise a little."

Later, back in the warmth of the radar station's rec room, Flynn apologized again to their disgruntled would-be attackers. They were U.S. Army Green Berets, part of the First Special Forces Group based at Fort Lewis in Washington State. Their parkas, ski masks, and snow pants were now stained bright pink by multiple paintball hits.

"I really wanted blue or even red ammunition," he told them. "But all the store down at Fairbanks had in stock was pink."

"*Neon* pink," the senior Green Beret noncom pointed out, still sounding aggrieved.

Flynn nodded, firmly controlling his own urge to laugh. "Yeah, but you've got to admit, it sure stands out in the dark."

The Special Forces sergeant looked down at himself for a moment. A wry smile twitched at the side of his hard-bitten face. "I can't deny that, sir." He shrugged. "What I don't quite get is how you tumbled to us so fast."

Flynn could understand the other man's dismay. Tonight's readiness exercise had been cooked up by overly eager staff officers down at Joint Base Elmendorf-Richardson. He'd been given a heads-up to get ready for a training drill, but nothing more. He certainly hadn't been warned about the possibility of a surprise attack on Barter Island by "Spetsnaz" commandos infiltrating the area disguised as American civilians. That "jamming" attack reported against the radar was a piece of misdirection intended to draw his security team out of position by suggesting the Russians planned an airborne drop from the north, from across the frozen Arctic Ocean. Instead, the highly trained Green Beret raiding party had run head-on into the buzz saw of Flynn's carefully planned ambush . . . winding up "dead" in the snow in seconds.

"Well, to be honest, I cheated," he explained. "I figured someone might try to secretly slip an assault force into Kaktovik ahead of time, so I took a few precautions of my own."

"Like what?" the Green Beret wondered.

In answer, Flynn raised his voice slightly. "Sergeant Takirak? Would you come in here for a second, please?"

Obeying, the National Guard sergeant entered the rec room. Although he was now back in uniform, the four Special Forces soldiers recognized him immediately. They shook their heads in disbelief.

"Ah, shit," one muttered. "The goddamned bus driver."

"Yep." Flynn nodded, smiling openly now. "I posted Andy at the airport to keep us in the loop on any new arrivals." He looked his paintball-stained guests over with a considering eye. "Particularly any fit, military-aged men. Fake Fish and Wildlife badges or not."

"Crap. No wonder you blew us away," the senior Green Beret noncom said, sounding even more disgusted. Flynn nodded again.

Ruefully, the Special Forces sergeant shook his head. "Well, sir, I've got to admit that you and your boys sure kicked our asses." Then he looked around the rec room, taking in its worn furnishings, old movie posters peeling off the insulated walls, and the faint smell of too many men crammed together in living quarters that weren't quite big enough. Outside, the wind rose to a howling pitch, shrieking through the guy wires supporting the radar platform and rattling loose pieces of metal siding. "On the other hand, I got a feeling tonight's show might just be the high point of excitement around here for the next couple of months."

Thinking about the fast-approaching and seemingly endless Arctic winter nights, Flynn had to concede that was probably true.

TWELVE

SEVERAL DAYS LATER

Russia's primary military command center occupied a massive white concrete compound of Stalinist-era buildings on the north bank of the Moskva River, roughly three kilometers from the Kremlin. Two six-story-high arches joined two wings to a central structure topped by the hammer-and-sickle coat of arms of the old Soviet Union and bas-reliefs of soldiers and flags. The imposing arches were closed off with triumphalist stained-glass windows. One bore the image of a sword-armed knight. The other depicted a modern female soldier carrying both a Kalashnikov assault rifle and a young child.

A new addition to the complex had been built in one of the older courtyards. It contained three large auditoriums equipped with wall-sized, wraparound screens and tiers of computer control stations with hardwired connections to an ultrafast supercomputer. Those were mostly for use as propaganda showcases and backdrops for political figures who wanted to impress their own people and those of other nations with images conveying high-tech Russian military prowess.

Smaller command centers and other facilities buried underground handled the real work of coordinating military action across Russia and around the globe. Now, inside a highly secure subterranean conference room, Colonel Alexei Petrov strode confidently to the podium set directly in front of a semicircular table. He looked out across his audience, comprised of the nation's most senior military leaders and government officials, including its president, Piotr Zhdanov. They were all men. Like the old Soviet Union, the Russian Federation paid a great deal of lip service to equality of the sexes, but its higher-echelon positions were always reserved for men with the right connections.

Zhdanov himself, usually depicted by a compliant government-controlled media as physically powerful and a paragon of perfect health, had aged rapidly over the past several months. His round face was pale and pudgy, and he looked thicker around the waist. There were visible shadows under his hard, brown eyes, and even his hair had thinned and turned gray. Well, Petrov thought dispassionately, death and illness come to us all sooner or later. If Russia's autocratic president had expected his run of good fortune to continue forever, recent events must have shown him how wrong he had been.

Now Zhdanov eagerly leaned forward in his chair. "I understand you have a special proposal to present to us this afternoon, Colonel?"

"*Da*, Mr. President," Petrov said. Outwardly calm,

inside he battled a storm of swirling emotions. In a very real sense, his fate now rested entirely on his ability to persuade these men, especially Zhdanov, to approve the plan he was about to present. He tapped a virtual control on the podium's computer display. Right away, the wall screen behind him lit up to show a detailed topographic map of the Russian Federation—all the way from its disputed land border with the Ukraine to the Pacific coast around Vladivostok.

He nodded to the junior officers waiting at the back of the room. They fanned out to present Zhdanov and the others with pairs of sleek, futuristic-looking eyewear. "Gentlemen, please put on the AR smart glasses you've been given."

They obeyed, and Petrov heard a series of stifled gasps as they saw the world around them instantly transform. The augmented-reality technology embedded in each pair of smart glasses had just studded the huge map with three-dimensional representations of the military hardware deployed across Russia—everything from fighter aircraft to main battle tanks, warships, submarines, surface-to-air missiles, strategic bombers, and nuclear-tipped ballistic missiles.

He smiled a bit, observing their awed reaction. Pavel Voronin was the one who had pressed him to make full use of this new technology in his briefing. "Salesmanship is showmanship," Grishin's urbane henchman had pointed out. "Dazzle those old farts and they'll be eating out of your hand by the time you're finished." It appeared that Voronin's cynical assessment might be correct.

Petrov tapped another control on the podium. In response, the map zoomed in to show the region of southern Russia around Akhtubinsk and the Chkalov State Flight Test Center. New three-dimensional pictures appeared. These showed the PAK-DA stealth bomber prototype effortlessly performing a series of complicated aerial maneuvers. They finished with image-enhanced video shot from one of the Su-34 chase planes when the bomber launched its Kh-102 practice cruise missile. That drew more excited murmurs, especially when the augmented-reality program depicted a realistic-looking nuclear fireball rising from the intended target.

"As you can see, Mr. President," Petrov said smoothly, "our flight tests of the new stealth bomber prototype are progressing rapidly and with complete success so far."

Zhdanov nodded gravely. "That is a testament to your own skills and courage, Colonel."

Petrov bowed his head slightly in acknowledgment of the president's fulsome praise. "But despite those successes, we still face a long road ahead to certify the design ready for operational deployment and full-scale production," he warned.

"How long a road?" Zhdanov asked.

"At least twelve more months," Petrov told him truthfully. "And perhaps as long as two full years, if we adhere slavishly to conventional flight-test procedures."

The president frowned. "Two years?" he muttered. "That's too long. Far too long." Based on current trends, he could easily be out of power, dead, in prison, or in exile by then. He needed a visible military success, and soon—an obvious triumph that would persuade Russia's fickle masses that his much-touted plans to rebuild their nation's greatness and its status as a world superpower were paying real dividends . . . despite these temporary economic hardships.

"I agree completely, Mr. President," Petrov told him. "But this is what we have left ahead of us if we follow ordinary, peacetime evaluation protocols." He activated another control. The sleek, manta-shaped PAK-DA bomber vanished from his audience's sight, replaced by a long, drearylooking, official Air Force timetable that listed, in mind-numbing detail, the remaining technical milestones required to qualify Tupolev's prototype aircraft for production. He watched the president's frown deepen to an exasperated scowl and exulted inside. "That's why I would like your permission to try something very different: a rigorous, complex, and realistic exercise designed to assess the full range of our new strategic bomber's strike capabilities. A single difficult flight test that would cut through much of the typical bureaucratic bullshit if it succeeds—and shave months off the timetable even if it fails."

With the ostentatious wave of a single hand, he erased the image of the official schedule from their smart glasses. In its place, a glowing phrase appeared, big enough to cover the digital map of Russia from west to east: *Operatsiya Prizrachnyy Udar.*

"Operation Ghost Strike?" Zhdanov said slowly.

Petrov nodded. He touched another control. It triggered a series of exciting, computer-generated visuals that matched his verbal presentation perfectly—thanks to advanced voice-recognition software that sent specific graphics to their high-tech eyewear whenever he used the appropriate keywords. "Under Ghost Strike, the PAK-DA prototype will be tasked with conducting a simulated cruise missile strike against the Pacific Fleet's anchorage and its Naval Aviation air bases around Vladivostok, in the Far East. To enhance the realism of this exercise, the aircraft will carry its full wartime payload of Kh-102 cruise missiles, K-74M2 heat-seeking missiles for self-defense, and fuel. Thus loaded, it will depart from base at seventeen-hundred hours and proceed toward its assigned targets in darkness, on a moonless night—"

As he laid out the plan, an image of the bomber prototype took off from Russia's primary strategic bomber base, Engels-2, seven hundred kilometers southeast of Moscow. It turned east, flying low across the Central Asian steppes and onward toward the towering Ural Mountains. "Naturally, the fleet itself and all of our other Eastern Military District air defense forces will be on full alert, ready for just such an attack."

More images appeared before the audience's eyes, depicting a web of intricate, layered defenses around Petrov's intended targets. These included sophisticated radars, surface-to-air missile regiments, and roving fighter patrols. "No easy task," the Russian Navy's senior admiral commented dryly. "One bomber against dozens of SAM launchers and some of our best interceptors? No matter how impressive the technology built into this new prototype of yours truly is, Colonel, you'll still be massively outnumbered. And after all, quantity has a quality all its own," he finished, quoting Stalin.

Petrov nodded. "That's precisely the point, Admiral." He turned to Zhdanov. "Win or lose, this exercise will yield a huge amount of invaluable real-world data on the PAK-DA—including its long-range endurance, air-to-air refueling capability, low-level penetrating stealth characteristics, and electronic warfare systems. We would be compressing months of more conventional testing and validation into a single demonstration flight."

"Allowing us to field a force of combat-ready stealth bombers that much more quickly?" the president asked.

"Yes, sir," Petrov said firmly.

Zhdanov was visibly impressed. Besides speeding up the progress of the PAK-DA program, the colonel's proposal offered the possibility of scoring a propaganda coup of the first magnitude—one that should rouse patriotic spirits here at home and unnerve potential enemies abroad. Best of all, it wouldn't matter whether or not the bomber prototype actually succeeded in scoring simulated hits on its targets this time. If Petrov and his copilot actually managed to penetrate the powerful defenses arrayed against them, it would show the world that Russia now had its own highly capable strategic stealth bomber. And even a failure could be spun to "prove" that America's own vaunted B-2 Spirit and B-21 Raider stealth aircraft were no match for Russia's combination of powerful radars, deadly surface-to-air missiles, and fast, agile interceptors.

The president glanced at those around him. "Comments, gentlemen?"

"The colonel's proposed Ghost Strike is certainly audacious, Mr. President. Who knows? It might even work out the way he hopes," a stocky, bullnecked man seated three chairs down from the president said bluntly. Major General Vasily Mavrichev was the chief of Russia's Long-Range Aviation Force. He had a vested interest in the PAK-DA program. Once the first stealth bombers reached operational status, they would fall under his direct command. But he was also known as an advocate for tried-and-true tactics and procedures, with an abiding distrust of anything new, let alone anything that might be considered revolutionary. "However, I don't like the idea of the PAK-DA carrying armed cruise missiles on what's really just a glorified training exercise. In my judgment, that's an unnecessary risk factor." He shrugged his broad shoulders. "I recommend that we load practice missiles with dummy warheads instead."

Petrov hid his irritation. Mavrichev's opposition to that part of his Ghost Strike plan was no surprise. But he could not afford to concede the point. Without real Kh-102s aboard the bomber when it took off, this whole operation was pointless. "Since we've already proved that the PAK-DA prototype is perfectly airworthy, the risk is minimal," he argued, aiming his words at Zhdanov rather than the general. "Besides, we don't have enough practice missiles in our arsenal to make up a complete weapons load. We'd be taking off light, which would not come close to replicating a real-life combat sortie."

"So we build more of the dummy weapons," Mavrichev countered stubbornly.

"Adding more delay and more expense," Petrov retorted. "And for no good reason. Sooner or later, we'll have to certify the PAK-DA's readiness to carry a full payload of live missiles. It's one of our key program milestones. Why not achieve it now if we can, considerably ahead of schedule?"

Zhdanov saw his point. "The colonel makes sense, Vasily Ivanovich," he said to Mavrichev. "As the Americans say, 'He's got the ball, let him run with it.'" Smiling broadly, he turned back to Petrov. "You won't let us down, will you, Colonel?"

"Absolutely not, Mr. President," Petrov promised. He matched Zhdanov's smile. "In fact, I can guarantee that you will be absolutely amazed by the results of Ghost Strike."

And that, he thought with carefully concealed pleasure, might have been the most truthful thing he'd said during this entire briefing.

SEVERAL HOURS LATER

Petrov stared moodily at the bronze bust of his father, Major General Vladimir Alexeyevich Petrov. Set atop a red granite tombstone, the sculpture's suitably heroic visage stared out at an open vista of empty grass squares, paths, and access roads. The national cemetery, a replacement for the Kremlin Wall Necropolis, was intended to serve as a burial place for Russian dignitaries and military heroes for the next two hundred years. So far, only a small fraction of its forty thousand plots had been filled.

He snorted. If the stubborn old bastard weren't dead, he'd probably be complaining about the lack of company. As befitted a true Hero of the Soviet Union, the general had always "modestly" believed he should be the center of everyone's attention.

Irreverently, Petrov lifted his father's old stainless-steel hip flask in a mock toast. "Here's to you, old man. I'm sure I'll see you in hell." He tossed back a quick swig and then retightened the cap.

"Was that a belated funeral libation?" a dryly

amused voice said from behind him. "Or simple thirst?"

Petrov turned around. Pavel Voronin stood a few paces away, dapper as always in a dark double-breasted wool coat.

"A bit of both." He offered the flask. "Care for one yourself?"

Voronin shook his head politely. "Thanks, but not right now. Perhaps another time. Somewhere more . . . cheerful." He glanced around the empty cemetery. There was no one else in sight. "Should I assume your presentation to the president went well?"

"Very well," Petrov confirmed. Quickly, he ran through the details of the Ghost Strike exercise Zhdanov had approved.

Voronin whistled under his breath when he heard that the PAK-DA would now be carrying nuclear-armed cruise missiles. "Wasn't that pressing your luck a little far?"

"Aren't you the one who's always emphasized the commercial aspects of this joint venture?" Petrov asked slyly.

"Your point?"

Petrov forced a laugh. "Having those weapons under our control only strengthens our bargaining position," he explained. "The fancier the goods in the shop window, the more a merchant can charge, right?"

The other man nodded slowly, acknowledging Petrov's point. Nevertheless, it was clear that he didn't particularly like the idea of a last-minute change in their plans. "Will loading those missiles affect the timetable?"

"Not in the slightest," Petrov assured him. "You can give your boss the green light." He checked his watch. "Tell him the show kicks off just a little over forty-eight hours from now."

THIRTEEN

Determined not to feel intimidated by the fact that she was meeting one-on-one with the man in charge of all U.S. intelligence activities, Miranda Reynolds, head of the CIA's Directorate of Operations, followed an aide into Jonas Murphy's office. Murphy, she reminded herself, was not an intelligence professional. Before being recently appointed as the DNI, the director of national intelligence, he had been a U.S. senator, and before that, a federal prosecutor. He undoubtedly had administrative, legal, and congressional know-how, but he lacked the experience that came naturally to those who'd spent their lives in the shadowy world of spies and counterspies.

His office itself was surprisingly small, with a single executive desk and a comfortable-looking swivel chair set between a pair of windows with the blinds drawn. A round conference table and several other government-issue chairs took up most of the rest of the room. A few prints, mostly of historical battles, lined the plain white walls, along with the usual photos of Murphy with the president of the United States and other high-ranking politicians.

Murphy himself, tall and lean, with faded red hair, stood up to greet her. He smiled politely. "Ms. Reynolds, it's a pleasure to see you today." He waved her into one of the chairs around the conference table and came over to join her. His aide departed as quietly and unobtrusively as he had appeared.

"Thank you, Director," she replied crisply.

Murphy held up a hand, smiling. "Please, call me Jonas. Let's leave that kind of stiff formality for places like Capitol Hill, where they thrive on titles instead of on what people actually *do*."

Briefly taken aback, she stuttered, "Uh, yes, sir . . . I mean, Jonas." If she hadn't studied Murphy's file first, she would have thought he was hitting on her. But the former senator was happily married, and, unlike many of his senatorial colleagues—both male and female—he actually seemed to be faithful to his vows. In a way, she thought that was too bad. She'd been divorced herself for nearly ten years. And it got harder and harder to date anyone the higher you rose in the CIA. Relationships carried too much chance of scandal or compromise, especially if you were a woman pushing ahead in what had once been largely a male-dominated preserve. Besides, she admitted to herself, having an in with the man who ran the entire intelligence community could have come in very handy during Langley's next round of cutthroat internal warfare.

"So, Miranda," the DNI continued, smiling faintly as though he'd discerned her thoughts, "as the saying goes, to what do I owe the honor of this visit?"

Reynolds forced herself back to the present. "Well, the truth is, I'm here to make what may seem like a very strange request."

"Sounds like a regular day at the office, then," Murphy joked. "I get those all the time. From your people at Langley. From the Pentagon. Heck, you can't even imagine the kind of oddball proposals that come in from the NSA or the National Geospatial-Intelligence Agency. I don't think those codebreakers and satellite geeks really live in the same universe with the rest of us." He saw her face and sobered up. "But you're serious."

She nodded her head. "Yes, I am. Dead serious."

"Okay," he said, leaning forward in his chair. "Shoot."

"I need a top secret alert sent out to all U.S.-controlled radar stations, AWACS planes, and other air units operating in Afghanistan, Iraq, and Turkey," Reynolds said bluntly. "Basically, if they detect an unidentified aircraft—*any* unidentified aircraft—in their zone of operations sometime in the next twenty-four hours, I need them to intercept and shadow it . . . but *not* to engage the bogey unless it takes hostile action. I also want them to immediately report any such contact directly to me. And if this unidentified aircraft tries to land at a friendly air base or even a civilian airport, they should allow it to do so—and then take immediate action to secure that aircraft against air or ground attack."

Murphy stared at her for a few seconds. Then he

shook his head in amazement. "Yeah, I guess you *weren't* kidding." He sat back a little. "And is there anything more you need?" he asked, with a hint of irony. "Short of operational control over . . . oh, let's say, a couple of Army divisions, or maybe a Navy aircraft carrier task force?"

Reynolds flushed slightly at his tone. Maybe she should have laid out more of the groundwork first, but what was done, was done. "Yes, I do need more," she said quietly.

"Such as?"

"Authorization to form a special 'go' team of CIA and U.S. Air Force security personnel and technical experts, including specialists from the Foreign Material Exploitation Squadron at Wright-Patterson Air Force Base," she told him. "A team that would be prepared to fly anywhere in the world at a moment's notice."

The Foreign Material Exploitation Squadron was exactly what it sounded like—a group of scientists, engineers, and other experts whose job was analyzing foreign-built aircraft and aerospace equipment captured on the battlefield or acquired by darker, less savory means. In earlier incarnations, it had pried open the secrets of captured Luftwaffe fighters and Soviet-era MiGs.

"That's a pretty long list," Murphy commented dryly. "So let's cut straight to the bottom line: what exactly is the deal here?"

Reynolds had known this question was coming. But she still found it surprisingly difficult to lay her cards on the table. Secrets were the currency of the intelligence community, and once you revealed them, their value diminished precipitously. For now, she decided to disclose most of what she knew, just not everything. "A new HUMINT source inside Russia has suggested that a pilot may be about to defect with one of their advanced military aircraft," she said cautiously. "Probably from a base somewhere in southern or central Russia. So I want to avoid the possibility that this attempt could end in tragedy, with one of our own fighters or missile units shooting the defecting aircraft down by mistake."

"Sensible," the DNI agreed. His eyes narrowed slightly. "What kind of aircraft are we talking here? One of their new Sukhoi fighters?"

She shook her head. "Bigger than that. In fact, the experimental version of their brand-new stealth bomber."

"Jesus," Murphy said in surprise. "You're kidding me."

"That's the word I've been given."

Murphy considered that for a few seconds. "Okay, so what's the motivation of this HUMINT source of yours?" he asked. "Is it something ideological? Personal? Or just plain mercenary?"

"Purely mercenary, I think," Reynolds admitted, feeling a measure of surprise that he knew enough to ask that particular question. Understanding the impulses that drove those willing to betray their country's secrets to the United States was a vital part of assessing their overall credibility and possible value as agents and sources. Those motivated by a desire for revenge for past crimes or slights or by gauzy ideals like freedom and world peace were more mercurial, and often harder to handle. Prospective agents who were primarily interested in money were usually more reliable—at least until greed got the better of them . . . or their own side made it more valuable to stay loyal.

The DNI sat back again. "Okay, Miranda, in your best judgment, what are we really looking at here?"

"You mean, is my source's claim about a possible defection true? Or is it just a piece of pie-in-the-sky bullshit peddled to score some quick cash from Uncle Sam?" Reynolds asked with a wry smile.

"That's about the size of it," Murphy agreed.

She shrugged. "Frankly, I'd put the odds that this is a genuine defection at only around one in four. But I figure it's better to be prepared . . . just in case this Russian is telling the honest-to-God truth."

Murphy considered that for a long moment. Then he nodded again. "Okay, that makes sense. I can sell both the alert and pulling a team of specialists together as a reasonable precaution." His gaze sharpened. "You say your source is all about money. If so, what's our exposure so far?"

"Minimal." Reynolds spread her hands. "But if it pans out, we'll need to dip pretty heavily into our black funds to secure exclusive access to the aircraft."

"'Heavily' is a pretty vague word," he said coolly. "What kind of real numbers are we talking about here?"

"My source is pushing for something on the order of a couple of billion dollars," she admitted.

"Holy crap!" Murphy blurted out in astonishment. He shook his head firmly. "That's considerably above my authority. There's no way in hell I can authorize anywhere close to that figure. Not without direct approval from the president himself."

Reynolds nodded. "Yes, sir, I know." Legally, the DNI could unilaterally transfer up to $150 million between different intelligence agency budgets. Securing anything above that amount would be far more complicated. "And that's why I want a security and evaluation team ready to pounce on that plane as quickly as possible."

"Ah," he said, taking her point. "Meaning that what this source of yours demands is not necessarily what they will get."

She smiled wolfishly. "Bingo. Because as soon as that aircraft is safely on the ground inside friendly territory, the negotiating power shifts pretty dramatically in our favor."

THAT SAME TIME

Captain Nick Flynn looked around the brightly lit vehicle maintenance bay. The center of the large, oil-stained concrete floor was now covered by a thick exercise mat, courtesy of the logistics personnel down at Joint Base Elmendorf-Richardson who'd finally filled one of his supply requisitions. He nodded in satisfaction. With the weather worsening day by day, he and Sergeant Andy Takirak had agreed they needed to move as much of their routine training indoors as possible. The maintenance bay might not be heated, but at least its prefab metal walls kept the wind and snow and ice outside. And he knew from their daily workouts that it was more than big enough for what he had in mind.

He unzipped one of the large duffel bags that had come up on the same flight with the exercise mat and started pulling out gear—mouth guards, boxing-style protective headgear, padded gloves, knee pads, and hard rubber training knives. This was the equipment he needed to run the team through a refresher course on what the U.S. Army and Air Force both referred to as "combatives"—the art of hand-to-hand combat. Far from being obsolete in an era of rapid-fire small arms, precision-guided munitions, and ever-more-destructive ranged weapons, hard-earned experience in Afghanistan and Iraq and other conflicts around the world had proved that the ability to survive and win in close-contact physical combat was a vital soldier skill. Hand-to-hand fighting could break out while troops were clearing buildings and villages, while they were manning security checkpoints, or even when trying to control prisoners taken on the battlefield.

Flynn heard the outer door behind him open and felt a swirl of freezing cold air. Suppressing a shiver, he got back to his feet and turned around.

First Sergeant Andy Takirak had come into the maintenance bay. The grizzled Alaskan brushed snow off his parka and stomped his boots to dislodge ice chunks wedged into their treads. "It's coming down pretty hard out there, sir," he reported. "Looks like that forecast was right."

Flynn nodded. Weather stations along the Arctic coast and satellites had been picking up indications of a large series of storms building up over the polar ice cap and starting to move south. Air Force and civilian meteorologists were all predicting an extended period of high winds, blowing snow and ice, and near-zero visibility. Which meant, in turn, that the training gear he'd requested had arrived just in time. There weren't likely to be any more supply flights arriving at the airport until the blizzards headed their way died out.

He indicated the equipment he'd unpacked. "What do you think, Andy?"

"I've always figured if you were close enough to

an enemy to reach out and touch him, you were already in a world of hurt," Takirak said calmly. He showed his teeth. "Give me my rifle and a couple hundred yards of distance any day."

Flynn nodded. "I can't argue with that." Then he smiled. "But I checked your records. You took the combatives instructor course and aced it a few years ago."

Takirak shrugged. "Well, that's because I learned a long time ago that wishes are one thing, and reality's another."

"Want a chance to brush up on your techniques before we run classes for the rest of the team?"

Takirak matched his smile. "Just the two of us, Captain?"

"Yep." Flynn picked up a pair of gloves and some headgear. "If I'm going to get dumped on my ass getting back up to speed on this stuff, I'd just as soon not have it happen in front of witnesses."

"Same here," Takirak allowed, starting to unzip his parka.

A few minutes later, decked out in protective sparring gear, they circled each other on the mat. They were each in a fighting stance, with chins tucked in and hands up, ready to strike or parry. Flynn eyed the other man cautiously. He had the longer reach, but the noncom was solid muscle and his reflexes seemed lightning-fast. "All set?" he murmured.

"Any time you are," Takirak assured him.

"Then . . . fight's on," Flynn called out, using the Air Force term to signal the beginning of a training engagement. He moved in fast, closing the range. The other man did the same.

The next moments flew by as they both delivered a flurry of blows and kicks with incredible speed and precision. Twice, Takirak got in past his attacks and defenses and slammed him down onto the mat. Once, Flynn broke free and reversed the advantage—setting up a choke hold that the older man had to acknowledge. The second time, the noncom swept his legs out from under him and then batted away all his attempts to get loose. This time, it was Flynn who had to slap the mat in surrender.

Shaking off pain and fatigue, they scrambled back to their feet and started circling again, each looking for an edge and not finding it. Another series of rapid-fire arm and elbow strikes and kicks left them both gasping.

BEEP-BEEP-BEEP.

The timer Flynn had set on his phone went off. He held out his hand and spat out his mouth guard. "Call it a draw, Sergeant?"

Panting slightly, Takirak nodded. "Sounds fair to me, sir." He shook his head with a quick smile. "Looks like I wasn't the only one who did well in the instructor course."

"I survived it," Flynn agreed. He eyed the other man. "I did get the feeling a couple of times that you were holding back a little, Andy. What was that, respect for my rank?"

Takirak shook his head. "No, sir. If I did, it was only natural caution. I always heard it was good tactics to keep a reserve—just in case the enemy's got something up his sleeve."

Flynn nodded. The other man was right. Which was why he'd done the same thing himself. He grinned, mentally calculating how the next couple of days of combatives training were likely to go. The rest of his team—younger, stronger, and bigger though some of them were—were about to learn the hard way that they were no match for the combination of greater experience and guile.

FOURTEEN

A SHORT TIME LATER

An olive-drab UAZ Hunter light utility vehicle sped past a row of gleaming white Tu-160M2 swing-wing supersonic bombers parked on the base's long apron. It turned right onto a taxiway that crossed both main runways and drove on toward a group of three large camouflaged hangars. In a squeal of brakes, it pulled up in front of the first hangar, whose armored rolling doors stood partly open. Through the gap, Tupolev's revolutionary PAK-DA stealth bomber was visible inside. Mechanics and weapons handlers in khaki fatigues bustled around the aircraft, completing their final checks.

Squads of stern-faced guards armed with 5.45mm AK-12 assault rifles were posted at the doors. Now that live nuclear weapons were loaded aboard the bomber, the base commander had instituted even stricter-than-usual security measures.

Colonel Alexei Petrov and Major Oleg Bunin hopped down out of the jeep-sized Hunter. Each wore a flight suit and carried his visored helmet under one arm. Casually, they acknowledged the driver's salute and then showed their IDs to the sentries. After being cleared through security, they strolled toward their waiting aircraft.

Suddenly, both of them faltered and came to a stop. They had unexpected company, another Air Force officer who was already there ahead of them. He wore a flight suit and helmet of his own and stood completely at ease, looking up at the PAK-DA with what could only be described as proprietorial pride. The stocky, barrel-chested figure of Major General Vasily Mavrichev was unmistakable.

"*Vot der'mo*. Oh, shit," Petrov muttered in a furious aside to his younger copilot. "Just shoot me now." Bunin nodded in dismay.

The commander of Russia's strategic bomber forces swung around toward them. His broad face wore an insincere smile that utterly failed to reach his eyes. They remained as sharp and wary as those of any peasant watching a tax collector counting sacks of grain in his barn. "Ah, Colonel Petrov and Major Bunin, there you are. And right on time!" he said cheerfully. "I appreciate junior officers with a sense of punctuality." He tapped his flight helmet. "As you can see, I've decided to ride along with you on this next mission. On your much-touted Ghost Strike combat exercise, eh? After all, I can't just sit back and let you young fellows have all the fun, now can I?"

"Technically, we're still in the test portion of this evaluation program, General," Petrov pointed out carefully. "Which means that it's well outside our safety protocols to carry anyone except trained flight crew who are completely familiar with all of the aircraft's systems."

If anything, Mavrichev's smile became even more disingenuous. "Technically, that is true," he allowed. Then he shrugged his burly shoulders. "But on the other hand, you personally assured the president that this prototype was completely airworthy, correct?"

Almost unwillingly, Petrov nodded. Damn the old bastard, he thought icily, suddenly he was arguing more like a lawyer than a high-ranking Air Force commander.

"So, by your own assessment, there is no great danger involved," Mavrichev concluded. "Besides, I'm coming along as a simple observer, not a crew member. And since the PAK-DA's cockpit is designed for four men, my presence won't exactly crowd you."

Like hell it wouldn't. Petrov's mind was running very fast now, first raising and then just as rapidly discarding options to handle this new problem. Having the general along on this flight added one more serious wrinkle to an already complicated plan. What was Mavrichev up to? he wondered. Did he somehow suspect what Petrov really intended?

Unlikely, the colonel decided. If that were the case, Mavrichev would have had him arrested the moment he set foot in the hangar. Most probably, the general, aware of President Zhdanov's enthusiasm for Ghost Strike, now wanted to horn in on the action—in the hope of reaping some of the resulting political benefits and glory for himself. It was an old maxim in Russia's armed forces: "Junior officers plan so that senior officers may profit."

"Have you cleared this with Lieutenant General Rogozin?" Petrov asked, still desperately casting around for some other reason to deny Mavrichev a seat on this flight. Yvgeny Rogozin, who commanded the whole Air Force, was Mavrichev's direct superior. And there were rumors the two men were bitter rivals. If so, it was just possible that he wouldn't be happy to see the head of Long-Range Aviation currying favor with the Kremlin this way. Maybe a quick call to Moscow would pay dividends—

"Of course I've cleared it with Rogozin," Mavrichev confirmed, crushing Petrov's faint hopes. "In fact, President Zhdanov himself has also approved my presence aboard the bomber for the duration of this exercise," he added with a thin smile.

Petrov kept his face immobile. "May I ask why?"

"Come now, Colonel," Mavrichev chided him. "Surely you can guess?"

And then Petrov understood. "It's our weapons payload," he said flatly.

"Precisely," the general said. "Just because the president approved your harebrained plan to carry nuclear warheads on this training exercise doesn't mean he's taken leave of all his senses. He understands the importance of tight control over such devices."

Glumly, Petrov nodded. Unlike all American nuclear weapons and some of Russia's own advanced ICBM warheads, Russian cruise missiles and tactical nuclear bombs were not equipped with permissive action links—electronic safeguards that required codes from two different sources before a weapon could be armed or detonated. Instead, as in the old Soviet Union, security over these nuclear warheads was maintained by "a man watching another man watching another man." Which meant Mavrichev had successfully persuaded Rogozin and Zhdanov that he needed to be aboard the bomber to provide a third layer of human command and control—a final safeguard over the twelve 250-kiloton missile warheads currently nestled inside the PAK-DA's weapons bays.

"Any other objections, Colonel?" the general asked pointedly.

Conceding defeat for the moment, Petrov shook his head. "No, sir." He forced a smile. "In that case, Major Bunin and I will be glad to have you on board. I think you'll find the experience . . . enlightening."

"I'm sure of that," Mavrichev agreed.

Studying the other man's bland expression, Petrov sourly wondered how many other unwelcome surprises the general had up his sleeve. With an almost imperceptible shrug of his shoulders aimed at Bunin, he led the way under the stealth bomber's broad, blended wing to its open belly hatch.

One after another, the three Russian officers climbed up the short ladder and made their way into the cockpit. While Petrov and Bunin strapped into their regular places, Mavrichev took the right-hand rear seat. If there had been a full operational crew of four aboard, that spot would have been filled by the bomber's weapons officer.

The older man shook his head in bemusement. Instead of the crowded banks of conventional switches, toggles, and dials he was familiar with from his days as a Tu-95 and Tu-160 bomber pilot, the console in front of him had only two large multifunction displays, which were currently blank, with a few gray buttons aligned below each screen. "*Mater' Bozh'ya!*" he muttered to himself. "Mother of God! This thing looks more like a flying video game machine than a serious combat aircraft."

Petrov noticed Bunin shoot him an amused, sidelong glance and shook his head slightly in warning. Mavrichev's apparent unfamiliarity with modern flight instrumentation wasn't all that surprising. He had been flying a desk for years now. And even Russia's upgraded Tu-160M2 bombers were mostly built around technology that was sometimes more than three decades old, a far cry from the high-tech systems built into their PAK-DA prototype.

Ignoring their unwanted guest for the moment, they quickly powered up their own displays and initiated a series of automated preflight and mission readiness checklists. The next few minutes passed in a blur of activity as they double-checked the aircraft's computers at every step.

"Our fuel tank readouts show seventy-five thousand kilograms loaded," Bunin reported, scanning his MFDs. "And we've got solid data links to all weapons in the bays. Everything's in the green."

Petrov nodded. "Very good." They were fully fueled, and all of their cruise missiles and air-to-air weapons were properly stowed and ready to receive targeting information from their attack computers. He checked his own display. "Our Ku-band targeting radar is on standby. All electronic countermeasures and other defensive systems are ready. Our secure satellite communications system is operational. I show available connections to Rodnik and Meridian-M satellites."

"Both engines look solid," Bunin told him. "There are no compressor, fan, or turbine problems."

"Copy that," Petrov acknowledged. He looked left outside the cockpit window and saw their crew chief give him the high sign. "All ground personnel are at a safe distance." He glanced back at Bunin. "We are go for engine start."

"I confirm, go for engine start," his copilot echoed.

Petrov pulled up a new menu on his display and tapped an icon. Two indicators flashed red and then turned green. "Ignition on both engines." He adjusted his throttles forward a notch, bringing the two big turbofans to idle. Slowly at first and then faster, the two jet engines spooled up, their noise deepening from a shrill whine to a low, rumbling roar. Through the canopy, they could see the armored hangar doors rolling all the way open. Directly off to the west, the sun hung low on the horizon.

"Good power readings," Bunin said, closely monitoring the readouts from both engines. "We're set."

"Let's get this bird airborne," Petrov agreed. He took a deep breath and keyed his mike. "Engels Tower, this is *Ten' Odin*, Shadow One. We're ready to roll."

"*Shadow One, Engels Tower, understood. You are cleared to taxi into position on runway two-two left*," the controller replied.

Petrov released the brakes and throttled up a little more. Slowly, the big blended-wing bomber moved out of the hangar and swung right onto the taxiway. Nearly four hundred meters farther on, it turned back to the left—perfectly positioned along the center line of the leftmost of the base's two long runways. "Engels Tower, this is Shadow One," he radioed. "In position, runway two-two left, ready for takeoff."

"*Shadow One, Tower*," he heard through his headset. "*Winds light at two-one-six, cleared for takeoff on runway two-two left. Good hunting!*"

"Shadow One cleared for takeoff," Petrov acknowledged. He set the brakes again and throttled up, running the bomber's twin engines all the way up to full military power. The rumbling roar outside the cockpit built in intensity.

"Compressors look good. Temperatures are good," Bunin reported from beside him.

Petrov nodded. "Copy that." He released the brakes. "Rolling."

Unshackled from artificial constraints, the PAK-DA almost leaped ahead, accelerating fast down the runway. Off to their right side, the long line of stationary Tu-160s blurred together into a continuous stream of bright white aircraft sliding past their speeding plane.

Less than halfway down the runway, Petrov saw the *Vr* symbol blink onto his heads-up display. They were now moving fast enough to take off safely. Gently, he pulled back on the stick. "Rotating."

Instantly, the bomber's nose came up. It soared off the tarmac and climbed rapidly into the air. Hydraulics whined below their feet as the landing gear whirred up and locked into position.

Petrov risked a quick glance over his shoulder at Mavrichev. The general sat transfixed in amazement, with his mouth slightly agape. And no wonder, the colonel thought with an inward laugh. Thanks to its advanced control surfaces and design, the PAK-DA prototype required considerably less runway than Russia's older Tu-160 bombers. Its takeoff performance was closer to that of a high-powered fighter than to a heavily loaded bomber.

Still climbing, the stealth bomber crossed the Volga and then banked hard right to turn back to the east as it flew over the city of Saratov. For a few moments, its oddly shaped wing was lit from behind by the last rays of the setting sun and then it vanished—swallowed up by the swiftly gathering dusk.

FIFTEEN

THREE HOURS LATER

Five thousand meters above a pitch-black landscape of primeval forests and a wide river that wound north toward the distant Arctic Ocean, four aircraft flew onward beneath the vast dome of a star-speckled sky. Green, red, and white navigation lights marked the relative positions of the PAK-DA bomber prototype, a four-engine Ilyushin IL-78M-90A refueling tanker, and the two Su-57 stealth fighters assigned to escort the tanker to this midair rendezvous.

Unhurriedly, with painstaking effort, Colonel Alexei Petrov maneuvered into position behind the humpbacked tanker aircraft. Small bright lights outlined the drogue basket streaming behind the IL-78. He'd locked the basket into the bomber's sophisticated IR targeting system. Steering, speed, and range indicators glowed across his HUD. They changed constantly as he closed in, making infinitesimally small adjustments to his stick and throttles.

Minutes earlier, he had extended their refueling

probe from its normal, stowed position inside a compartment along the right side of the PAK-DA's nose.
Now, it was just a question of mating the probe with
the drogue basket as it wobbled and danced in the
big Ilyushin's wake. Using a steerable boom system
like that pioneered by the U.S. Air Force would be
faster and more efficient, Petrov knew. Unfortunately, for some reason known only to its aircraft
designers, Russia had never bothered to adopt the
more advanced technique.

The lighted drogue basket grew steadily larger
through the canopy as he drew nearer. And now,
Petrov had become one with his aircraft. The PAK-
DA's stick and throttles were simply extensions of
his own body. Like a skilled dancer reacting instinctively to the improvised moves of his partner, he followed the movements of the drogue as it juddered
and bounced through turbulent air.

Easy, easy, he thought, almost there. Capture!
For a fraction of a second, the probe scraped along
the inside of the basket and then, with a soft *ca-
clunk*, it slid into the drogue's center receptacle and
locked in place.

"Contact," Bunin confirmed from his seat. Numbers started to change on one of his displays. "Taking on fuel."

More time passed while Petrov concentrated on
keeping station on the IL-78 tanker ahead. That
required continuous tiny adjustments to his flight
controls. Any sudden, unexpected movement could
rip their refueling probe out of the drogue and
damage both. Despite the cool air flowing from the

PAK-DA's climate control system, droplets of sweat were beading up under his flight helmet and oxygen mask.

"We're topped off," Bunin reported. "All fuel tanks are full."

"*Mat' Kuritsa*, Mother Hen, this is Shadow One," Petrov radioed. "We're gassed up and ready to break away."

"*Copy that, Shadow*," the tanker pilot replied. "*Clearing away on your signal.*"

"Mother Hen, execute breakaway . . . now!" Petrov ordered. At the same time, he pulled his engine throttles back a notch and pushed his stick forward slightly. The bomber's nose dipped a few degrees. The noise of their NK-65 turbofans diminished as they descended a couple hundred meters. In the same moment, the big Ilyushin up ahead of them increased its own speed and climbed away. The tanker was already banking into an easy left turn that would take it back west toward its home base southeast of Moscow. The big IL-78's two Su-57 fighter escorts rolled in behind it.

Instantly, the drogue and refueling probe separated in a quick plume of aerosolized fuel. Bunin tapped an icon on his display. The probe retracted back into the PAK-DA's nose. Numbers flickered across Petrov's HUD as their computer recalculated the aircraft's estimated RCS, its radar cross-section. Without the awkward, angular shape of the fuel probe sticking out in front, they should now appear to be only about the size of a large bird to any radar hunting them.

He glanced across the cockpit toward Bunin. "Now we get serious, Oleg."

His copilot nodded. Although they were still roughly four thousand kilometers from their planned targets—the Russian Pacific Fleet's warships at anchor in Vladivostok's harbor and the network of air bases around the same city—this air refueling point was the last certain safe haven along their flight route. From now on, every kilometer they flew took them closer to the vast region of Russia's Far East in which all "enemy" aircraft, radars, and SAM regiments assigned to defend against Ghost Strike were free to maneuver and deploy. Theoretically, their Kh-102 stealth cruise missiles could hit targets up to twenty-eight hundred kilometers away, but Petrov's mission plan anticipated a simulated launch at close range, no more than a few hundred kilometers from Vladivostok. A shorter flight time reduced the defenders' chances of detecting and destroying the incoming missiles. Besides, this exercise was supposed to simulate an over-the-pole attack on strategic targets deep inside the continental United States—where the PAK-DA would have to fly at least eight thousand kilometers just to reach a maximum range launch point. Pushing the bomber prototype to the very limits of its endurance was a key part of the proposal Petrov had sold to the president and his advisers.

"Okay, let's configure the aircraft for prolonged low-altitude flight," Petrov said matter-of-factly. "We're going to come in right on the deck, moving like a bat out of hell."

Bunin nodded. His fingers danced across displays as he brought up the bomber's digital terrain-following system and started entering waypoints.

From the seat behind the copilot, Major General Mavrichev leaned forward, unable to hide his surprise. "You plan to make your penetration run at low altitude? Why? The American B-2s fly and attack at high altitudes, don't they?"

"That's correct, General," Petrov said patiently. "But that's because the Americans have carried out most of their B-2 raids against terrorists—or against weaker nations without modern radars and high-altitude-capable SAMs. That's not who we're up against tonight. We're facing the first team. And every radar station, air defense regiment, and fighter interceptor between here and Vladivostok already knows we're coming. We *might* be stealthy enough to slip past them up high, but why press our luck when we don't have to? True, a low-level penetration flight will burn more fuel, but we've got plenty of gas right now, thanks to Mother Hen. And I'll trade fuel for surprise any day."

As if to confirm his words, a string of new alerts blinked into existence on one of his full-color displays. The same alerts also appeared on Bunin's screens.

"Multiple X-band and L-band airborne radars detected at high altitude ahead of us," his copilot reported. "The computer evaluates them as a mix of Su-27s, Su-30s, and Su-35s, all backed by at least one Beriev A-100 AWACS plane."

"Signal strength?" Petrov demanded sharply.

"Very weak," Bunin assured him. "They seem to be flying patrol patterns several hundred kilometers due east of us."

Petrov smiled narrowly. The air defense commanders assigned to find and "kill" them in tonight's exercise weren't taking any chances, either. They'd deployed a strong intercept force right on the edge of the allowed perimeter. Inside, he felt a moment's regret that Ghost Strike was nothing but a sham. Actually making an attempt to penetrate those tight defenses would have been a remarkable challenge, one requiring every ounce of his tactical and flying skills.

Then he stiffened as two high-pitched tones warbled in his headset. The PAK-DA's IR sensors had picked up two new contacts, this time moving in from behind them. He toggled a switch on his stick, switching to the view from one of the bomber's rear-facing thermal cameras. Two ghostly green-tinted images appeared on his helmet visor. They were closing fast.

"What the hell are those clowns doing?" Petrov growled. The two Su-57 stealth fighters that had been escorting the IL-78 air tanker had abandoned their charge and were now chasing after the PAK-DA.

Mavrichev leaned forward again, this time with a satisfied smile on his face. "I made a small alteration to your original operations plan, Colonel. Those fighters will accompany us as our escorts, at least until their fuel runs low. If any of those patrolling interceptors you've already detected ahead spot us in turn, the Su-57s will engage and destroy them—opening a clear path to your targets." He sat back in his seat, looking even more pleased with himself. "And as an added bonus, having friendly fighters along will let you test this aircraft's secure communications systems under realistic conditions."

Petrov's jaw tightened. Beside him, he noticed Bunin surreptitiously roll his eyes in disgust. The whole point of a stealth bomber was that it didn't need a fighter escort. If anything, adding more aircraft to the mission package only increased the odds they would be detected. But Mavrichev was a dinosaur who'd cut his teeth as a younger officer flying lumbering Tu-95 turboprops and supersonic Tu-160 swing-wing bombers—both aircraft types with enormous radar cross-sections. The general's understanding of strike tactics must have ossified years ago, Petrov concluded with justified contempt.

Outside, the two sleek-looking Su-57s separated and slid into positions four kilometers off the larger bomber's wingtips. *More uninvited guests at my private party*, he thought coldly. This situation was getting worse and worse. His brain went into overdrive as he frantically evaluated a new series of alternatives. He had the means to handle Bunin and Mavrichev. But those Su-57 pilots were beyond easy reach. At last, he shrugged and accepted reality. Things were going to get a lot messier than he would have preferred, but the stakes were far too high for him to back out now.

Petrov pulled down his oxygen mask and ostentatiously took out his father's old stainless-steel hip flask. With a quick jerk of his head, he mimed tossing back a shot, but he kept his teeth and tongue clenched tight to avoid swallowing any of the liquid inside. He lowered the flask with a strange sense of regret. He missed the sensation of high-proof vodka flowing down his throat like cold fire. Then, with his thumb held firmly over the top, he gave the flask a fast, hard shake to thoroughly mix all of its contents together.

Forcing a more genuine smile, he swung around in his seat and handed it back to Mavrichev. "One for the road, General?" he asked. "Before we get too busy to have any fun?"

The older man laughed and took a huge gulp before passing the flask up to Bunin, who did the same. "You surprise me, Petrov," he joked. "I had you pegged as a bloodless technocrat. But now I see that you're just as big a hell-raiser as your old man!"

Still smiling, Petrov retrieved his flask from Bunin and stowed it away again. Mavrichev had come very close to the truth there. Hell was precisely what he planned to raise. He toggled their secure tactical communications system. Like its strategic counterpart, it encrypted and compressed signals into millisecond-long blips before transmitting them. "*Prizrachnyy Polet*, Specter Flight, this is Shadow One," he radioed. "We are descending to five hundred meters. Suggest you take station ten kilometers out in front of me for now. Stay a little higher, though, say one thousand meters."

"*Affirmative, Shadow One*," the lead Su-57 pilot

replied. Even with the inherent distortion imposed by signals compression, he sounded confident, almost cocky. *"We'll swat any hostiles out of your way as needed."*

Petrov pushed his stick forward, beginning his descent. Through the canopy, he watched the two fighters pull out ahead. Seen from behind and below through the bomber's sensitive IR sensors, the Su-57s were marginally brighter against the cold, starlit sky. Despite design features that significantly reduced their engine heat signatures, they were still more detectable from the aft quarter.

He shot a quick glance at Bunin. His copilot's head slumped forward. The fast-acting drug he'd used to spike the vodka had taken effect. It was a fentanyl derivative, originally concocted by chemists for Russia's Spetsnaz hostage rescue units. Another swift look over his shoulder showed that Mavrichev was also unconscious. Or perhaps dead. Mixing any fentanyl variant with alcohol was incredibly dangerous, often leading to total respiratory failure. As Bunin's superior, he'd had access to the younger man's medical records. When he concocted this plan months ago, he'd run those records past shady medical experts provided by Grishin's go-between, Pavel Voronin. They'd assured him that his copilot's risk of a fatal overdose was reasonably low. Mavrichev had no such guarantee.

Petrov shrugged. One more death would make no great difference to his conscience.

He leaned forward and checked the readouts from his navigation and sensor systems again. They matched. Except for the distant interceptors and AWACS planes patrolling far off to the east, there were no other air contacts for hundreds of kilometers in any direction. To clear the skies for this top secret Ghost Strike exercise, Russia's air traffic controllers had temporarily diverted all routine civilian flights away from this isolated, almost uninhabited wilderness region. Effectively, his stealth bomber and its unwanted fighter escorts were all alone in the middle of nowhere.

Petrov grimaced. He was out of options. And almost out of time. Mavrichev's surprise move to assign those fighters to this mission had boxed him in. At last, with a frustrated sigh, he entered a new series of commands on one of his displays. Four warbling tones echoed through his headset. Data from the PAK-DA's thermal sensors had been successfully downloaded to four of the self-defense K-74M2 heat-seeking missiles carried in the bomber's internal weapons bays. They were locked on target.

Gently, he squeezed the trigger on his stick.

With a high-pitched whine, two bays under the wings cycled open. And one by one, four missiles were dropped into the air and ignited. Trailing smoke and fire, they slashed across the night sky—streaking toward their assigned targets at more than two and a half times the speed of sound.

All four missiles covered the distance in less than six seconds.

Taken completely by surprise by this treacherous attack, neither Su-57 pilot had time to realize what was happening—let alone take evasive or defensive action. Four blinding flashes lit the darkness. Ripped apart by proximity-fused warheads, both Su-57s tumbled out of the sky, strewing burning debris across the snow-covered forest below.

Horrified by what he had just done and yet strangely exultant, Petrov banked his stealth bomber to the left, rolling to the northeast toward the frozen Arctic coast now eighteen hundred kilometers ahead. He deleted Bunin's half-completed flight plan from the computer and substituted his own—one he had prepared over the course of the past several weeks. Whatever else happened, he was fully committed now. There was no going back.

SIXTEEN

SEVERAL HOURS LATER

President Piotr Zhdanov lit another cigarette, drew on it for a moment, and then, irritably, stubbed it out in an already-overflowing ashtray. The soft, background hum of the secure conference room's ventilation system rose slightly in pitch as overhead fans strained smoke out of the air. Sophisticated electronics and tobacco contaminants were not a good mix.

Zhdanov looked up at the wall-sized map display again. Glowing concentric rings showed the estimated detection ranges for active radar stations across Russia's Far East region. Other rings depicted the engagement zones for S-300 and S-400 surface-to-air missile units. Fighter icons showed the current reported locations for patrols scouring the skies for any sign of the PAK-DA stealth bomber prototype. He scowled. Nothing seemed to have changed.

At first, the apparent inability of Russia's alerted air defense networks to catch even a fleeting glimpse of Petrov's stealth aircraft had seemed like good news to Zhdanov and his military commanders. It was seen as a sign that Tupolev's vaunted bomber prototype was living up to its promise. But as the hours ticked past in silence, this early optimism had given way to a growing sense of unease.

Impatiently, Zhdanov swung around on Lieutenant General Yvgeny Rogozin. "Well? Where are they? What the devil is going on?"

"I'm not sure," Rogozin admitted hesitantly. The chief of Russia's Air Force used a control to sketch a glowing line across the digital wall map—one that crossed the coast considerably north of Vladivostok and then curved back over the Pacific Ocean toward Ghost Strike's assigned targets. "It's possible that Petrov has chosen a longer, more elaborate flight path to evade our defenses. Fully fueled, the aircraft has more than enough endurance to fly a route something along these lines. But there is a problem with this theory—"

"Which is the simple fact that those Su-57 fighters Mavrichev added to the strike package don't have anywhere near that kind of range," Zhdanov interrupted acidly.

Rogozin nodded. The corners of his mouth turned down. "Correct, Mr. President."

"And yet, we've heard nothing from them."

"No, sir." Rogozin tapped another control to highlight every military and civilian airfield between Moscow and Vladivostok. In response, pinpoints of light scattered across the wall map. "Nor are there reports that the Su-57s made emergency landings at any of our bases or airports."

"What about air-to-air refueling?" Zhdanov demanded.

Rogozin shook his head. "I contacted the commander of the Fourth Aviation Group at Ryazan personally. The IL-78 tanker that refueled Petrov's plane returned safely to base twenty minutes ago. And there are no other tankers currently in the air."

"Then we have a serious problem, Yvgeny," Zhdanov said darkly. "Contact Colonel Petrov immediately. I want to know *exactly* where he is right now . . . and just what in the hell has happened to those stealth fighters."

The sleek manta ray–shaped PAK-DA bomber raced over a vista of near-absolute desolation. Jagged, hummocky ridges of thick, compacted sea ice flashed below its wings and either vanished astern in the darkness or were swallowed by blinding curtains of gale-driven ice crystals that shrieked across the frozen wilderness.

Inside the cockpit, Petrov grimly held his course as the aircraft bounced and shuddered through increasingly turbulent air. The weather was growing steadily worse, just as the meteorological reports he'd studied had promised. Massive storms were brewing across the polar ice cap, with the promise of thickening clouds and high winds ahead.

Those developing storms were his allies, he knew. They would help hide his passage across this empty ocean of ice from prying eyes and satellites. And few of those who would soon be hunting him would believe he was crazy enough to risk flying through swirling maelstroms of wind and snow powerful enough to snatch his aircraft out of the sky and dash it into the sea in the blink of an eye.

Another gust slammed into the speeding bomber. Swearing under his breath, Petrov trimmed it back to level flight. In the seat on his right, Bunin's drooping head flopped toward him and then rolled back the other way. His copilot and Mavrichev were both still unconscious, but he'd taken the precaution of binding their hands and feet in case they recovered sooner than he expected. He'd also stowed their personal sidearms well out of reach. He had no intention of giving either of his prisoners the chance to do anything stupidly heroic and futile.

Red-flagged alert messages suddenly rippled across the large display he'd configured to manage the PAK-DA's sensors and defense systems. The bomber's radar warning receivers had just picked up new signals. These were from distant S-band phased array radars. Judging by their strength and bearing, they belonged to Sopka-2 air surveillance radars positioned on several of the rugged Arctic islands lining Russia's long north coast.

Petrov grunted. Somebody out there was waking up at last. It was far too late, of course. It was just possible that one of those radar stations might have detected his stealth aircraft, he supposed—but only if he'd been foolish enough to fly right past it at point-blank range. As it was, the PAK-DA was already well outside Russia's defense perimeter.

A sharp ping sounded in his headset. His secure satellite communications system had just received an urgent message. Moscow was demanding a situation update. A twisted smile tugged sharply at one side of Petrov's lean face. For a brief moment, he was actually tempted to reply, if only to see how much further he could exploit Zhdanov's misplaced trust in him. But then he shrugged. Why bother?

The president and his advisers would learn the horrifying truth soon enough.

Or at least part of it, he thought with eerily detached amusement. Like the malignant tumor inexorably gnawing away at his brain, the full truth of what he planned was something he intended to reserve for himself. For the time being, anyway.

Ignoring Moscow's increasingly frantic and repeated signals, Petrov flew on—racing north across the polar ice cap toward a darkening mass of storm clouds.

A pair of multirole, two-seater Su-30 fighters sped across the forest canopy at high speed. Their NO11M Bars pulse Doppler phased array radars were radiating in both air-to-air and air-to-ground modes. They had been urgently vectored to this area—the site of the missing PAK-DA's midair refueling rendezvous. It was the last place anyone could confirm seeing the stealth bomber prototype and its Su-57 fighter escorts.

Aboard the lead fighter, Major Valentin Yakunin scanned the night sky ahead of them and periodically checked his radar displays. He was searching for any sign of an air contact, no matter how faint or fleeting. So far, he had seen absolutely nothing. Which made sense, he thought disgustedly, because there was nothing to see. Considering how many hours had passed since the PAK-DA refueled over this uninhabited wilderness, this was the very definition of a wild goose chase. By now, the prototype stealth bomber could be thousands of kilometers away in any one of a dozen different directions. Moscow was clutching at straws.

"Are you getting anything significant back there, Ivan?" he asked his weapons officer.

In the Su-30's rear seat, Captain Ivan Saltikov had his head down to monitor his own instruments and displays. He was focused on returns from their ground-to-air radar and on the green-tinged thermal images captured by their forward-looking infrared sensor pod. "Not yet," he admitted. "So far, I've detected trees and more trees. Plus, a lot of trees. Oh, and some more trees."

"Well, make sure you don't miss the forest," Yakunin said dryly. "I understand there's supposed to be a very large one somewhere around here." A quick check of their navigation system showed that they were now more than fifty kilometers east of the stealth bomber's last reported position.

Suddenly, Saltikov snapped, "Hold on! I've got something, Major! I'm picking up a signal over the emergency channel." Quickly, he pushed a toggle on one of his panels to feed the incoming transmission to their shared intercom channel.

Through his headset, Yakunin heard a shrill, staccato series of beeps. The sequence faded briefly and then started up again, repeating the same tone pattern. "Christ, that's an emergency locator beacon!" he realized. Like their Western counterparts and most civilian airplanes, all Russian military aircraft carried a transmitter designed to activate automatically in the event of a crash.

"And I see where it's broadcasting from," Saltikov said, sounding sick to his stomach. Both the fighter's ground-to-air radar and its forward-looking infrared pod were showing the same thing—a wide scar torn through the forest. In and among the splintered and broken trees was a mass of wreckage, the mangled remains of an Su-57 fighter.

"*Hunter One, this is Two,*" Yakunin heard his wingman in the second Su-30 reply after he frantically relayed the news of what they'd seen on the ground. "*We just spotted more debris ourselves, several kilometers to the south of that first plane.*"

"Is it the stealth bomber?" he asked. My God, he wondered, could there have been some sort of disastrous midair collision between the PAK-DA and its escorts? One that destroyed all three aircraft before any of them could radio for help?

"*Negative, Hunter One. This second downed aircraft is definitely the other Su-57. There's no sign at all of the PAK-DA prototype.*"

Yakunin's eyes widened. Whatever had destroyed those two stealth fighters, it couldn't be an accident. He switched radio frequencies again to contact their home air base, near the border with Mongolia. "Domna Control, this is Hunter One. Patch me through to the NDMC in Moscow. And make it quick!"

MOMENTS LATER

When he understood what the Su-30 crews had discovered, Zhdanov slumped back in his chair. He felt the blood drain from his face. His pulse hammered wildly in his ears, louder even than the other equally shocked voices ringing out across the crowded conference room. Fighting for a small measure of self-control, he swung toward Lieutenant General Rogozin. "Yvgeny, are those pilots really claiming that our Su-57s were shot down?"

Looking pale himself, the Air Force commander nodded. "It appears so, Mr. President." He swallowed hard. "To confirm their assessment fully, we'll need to dispatch investigative teams by helicopter from Kansk Air Base. But the indications seem clear and unmistakable. Both fighters appear to have crashed almost simultaneously—as though they were struck by air-to-air missiles at virtually the same instant."

"Missiles fired from our own stealth bomber?" Zhdanov asked, unable to suppress the absurd hope that there was some other explanation for this catastrophe.

"Yes, Mr. President." Rogozin grimaced. "I'm afraid that is the only logical possibility."

Zhdanov stared at him. "Which means that the PAK-DA's crew has gone rogue."

Very reluctantly, Rogozin nodded again. "And they've taken our most advanced aircraft and a full load of nuclear-armed, long-range cruise missiles with them," he added quietly.

"And General Mavrichev? What about him?"

Rogozin frowned. "I suspect he's either a prisoner . . . or dead. Neither Petrov nor Bunin knew he would be aboard until the very last minute before they took off, so it's unlikely he was a member of their conspiracy."

"But why?" Zhdanov demanded. "What can these traitors possibly hope to gain?"

Rogozin sat silent.

"I asked you a question, General," Zhdanov snapped. Deep inside, he felt the faint stirring of white-hot rage. He welcomed it in place of the unreasoning fear that had gripped him only moments before. Fury was a leader's prerogative. Fear was only a mark of weakness.

The other man shook himself. He sighed. "Three horrifying possibilities suggest themselves, Mr. President," he said slowly.

"Go on," Zhdanov growled.

"First, Petrov and Bunin have decided to carry out a surprise attack against a foreign adversary, either the Americans or the Chinese . . . for some insane, unfathomable reason of their own."

Zhdanov stared at Rogozin in consternation. In total, the twelve cruise missiles aboard the experimental stealth bomber represented three megatons of explosive force—enough to destroy whole command centers, strategic bomber bases, and naval squadrons in port. Or kill hundreds of thousands, or even millions, of men, women, and children if they were launched against cities. And the deliberate detonation of even a single one of their 250-kiloton warheads could easily trigger an all-out nuclear confrontation. But of themselves, those twelve stolen missiles did not even come close to representing enough military power to actually win a war against either the United States or the People's Republic of China. Petrov and his copilot must know that, which would make any decision to fire the weapons an act of utter nihilism.

"The second possibility is that the bomber's crew has rebelled against Moscow and intends to decapitate the current government, again for some motive we do not yet understand," Rogozin continued grimly.

Zhdanov flinched. His eyes darted to the map. "If that's so, we could be under attack—"

"*Now*," Rogozin confirmed. "Given their low-altitude cruise speed, any missiles fired in our direction from maximum range may strike this complex and the Kremlin at any moment."

Zhdanov gritted his teeth. "You seem very calm about this situation, Yvgeny," he snarled.

Rogozin shook his head gravely. "No, just realistic, Mr. President. The Kh-102s have a circular error probability of less than ten meters. If Petrov has already fired missiles in our direction and they detonate on target, we'll be dead before we even know what's happening."

"How . . . comforting," Zhdanov ground out. "And your third nightmare scenario?"

"That the crew is defecting, with their aircraft, to either the United States or the People's Republic of China," Rogozin said flatly. "Of their three possible options, I consider this the most probable, since it does not require them to contemplate the murder of millions, including their own countrymen and families. One man's developing madness might have slipped past our psychological screening, but not two."

Unable to control his temper any further, Zhdanov slammed his fist down on the table, sending his ashtray skittering away in a cloud of cigarette butts and ash. "Fuck your bullshit probabilities, General! Whether Petrov and his copilot are lunatics or mere traitors and criminals doesn't matter! I want that prototype found and destroyed! Before this disaster completely blows up in our faces!" He stabbed his finger at the wall map. "Put every SAM regiment, radar station, and fighter unit across the whole country on the highest possible state of alert! That goes double for all our air defenses around Moscow itself!"

"There are a large number of foreign civilian airliners and cargo planes crossing through our airspace right now," Rogozin reminded him.

"Shut the transpolar air routes down. *All of them!*" Zhdanov ordered. "And closely monitor any aircraft still in our skies. If any of them deviates from its filed flight plan to the slightest degree, I want that plane intercepted immediately and forced to land for closer inspection. Understand?"

"Yes, sir," Rogozin agreed. He hesitated again. "But if the crew *is* defecting or if they're crazy enough to launch a sneak attack on the Americans or the Chinese, the PAK-DA stealth bomber could already be well beyond our borders."

"If they're defecting, our forces will hunt Petrov and Bunin down later and kill them—no matter where they've fled," Zhdanov said coldly. "I will not show mercy to traitors." He stood up. "But in case they *have* lost their minds and are trying to start a war or launch some sort of half-assed coup, we'll evacuate our key people. Starting now."

His movement sparked a general push toward the doors. Elevators ran deep underground from the National Defense Management Center. They connected with a secret labyrinth of subway tunnels built during the long Cold War. In the event of any attack on Moscow, trams were always on standby to hurry Russia's top civilian and military leaders to safety in one of two heavily protected command bunkers kilometers outside the city.

"It might be wise to contact Washington and Beijing by hotline to brief them on this situation," Rogozin pointed out carefully. "To avoid any unfortunate misunderstandings."

"Absolutely not!" Zhdanov snapped. "I will not humiliate myself in front of the Americans or the Chinese. Not until I have no other choice."

SEVENTEEN

A SHORT TIME LATER

The Emergency Conference Room lay buried several levels beneath the Pentagon. Roughly the size of a small theater or a school auditorium, it was dominated by a long, rectangular table. Every position at this central conference table had its own secure communications links to different military and intelligence commands around the globe. Large digital screens mounted on the far wall could be configured to show everything from orbital satellite views to live video streams from combat units, ships, and aircraft anywhere in the world. During any major crisis, the ECR served the secretary of defense, the Joint Chiefs of Staff, and other defense and intelligence officials as a war room, allowing them to make high-level command and control decisions on the basis of the best available information.

Late in the evening, Eastern Standard Time, Director of National Intelligence Jonas Murphy entered the ECR at a rapid walk. The room was filling up fast as Pentagon officials and senior officers representing all six uniformed military branches arrived for this hastily convened meeting. Murphy waved the two aides who'd accompanied him over to a row of chairs reserved for staff and took his own seat among the decisionmakers at the central table.

He nodded politely to Bill Taylor, the secretary of defense, who would chair this meeting. The other man's thick, black-framed glasses and unkempt white hair made him look a bit like an absentminded professor, but anyone who judged him on his appearance was in for a shock. A highly successful tech entrepreneur before coming to D.C., Taylor possessed a razor-sharp mind, one capable of juggling enormous amounts of detail without losing sight of the bigger picture. Murphy privately saw him as a huge improvement over the last incumbent at the Defense Department, a slick corporate type who'd seemed far more interested in self-promotion and favorable media reviews than in military readiness and the national interest.

Taylor pushed his glasses back up his nose and nodded in return. "You know anything about all this Russian shit that's just hit the fan, Jonas?" he asked conversationally.

"I may have a few ideas," Murphy allowed. How many of his cards he played during this meeting would depend entirely on the situation. The ECR was one of the most secure places in the Pentagon, perhaps in the whole world. But one of the most basic rules of intelligence was that secrets distributed too widely were very soon no longer secrets at all. There were an awful lot of people in this room right now, and leaking classified information to favorite journalists was an old, old game in Washington, D.C.

"Well, I just hope you brought enough intel to share with everybody," Taylor retorted with a lop-sided grin, obviously aware of the DNI's inner misgivings. Briskly, he activated the microphone in front of him and tapped at it. "Okay, folks, let's get started. The clock is running, and the president wants our recommendations on his desk, ASAP." As the room quieted down, he nodded to the briefer, a Navy two-star, up at the podium. "Go ahead and fill us in on what's been happening over the past several hours, Admiral."

Short, trim, and fearlessly direct, Rear Admiral Kristin Chao was the current head of the Pentagon's operations directorate. She pushed a control on her podium, dimming the lights. Simultaneously, screens lit up on the wall behind her. One showed a large-scale digital map of the entire Russian Federation. The rest showed smaller-scale maps of Moscow and its environs, the main bases of Russia's Aerospace Forces, and the primary ports of Russia's Northern, Baltic, Black Sea, and Pacific Fleets. A slew of icons representing surface-to-air missile units, fighter regiments, and air surveillance radars appeared across Russia's vast Far East region. "Beginning approximately eight hours ago, our reconnaissance satellites and other assets detected a much-higher operational tempo across this area," the admiral said tersely. "Combined with the temporary closure of Polar Route One across central Russia by Moscow, we assessed this activity as signaling the start of a large-scale air defense exercise of some kind."

"An exercise that we were *not* informed about in advance, despite the Kremlin's clear treaty obligations," Taylor commented dryly.

"No, sir," Chao agreed. Her expression was unreadable. "But as you know, Moscow honors its diplomatic obligations sparingly, if at all."

"And even then often only by accident," Taylor said with a cynical snort.

Chao smiled thinly. "So it seems, Mr. Secretary."

"So what's changed?"

"A great deal," the admiral said simply. She touched another control. Dozens of new icons flashed into existence across the map of Russia and the smaller screens which showed close-up views of its most important political, military, and industrial centers. "Approximately sixty-five minutes ago, SIGINT—signals intelligence—intercepts and new satellite imagery confirmed that Moscow has ordered *all* of its air defense regiments, radars, and combat air units to their highest alert status. At the same time, the Russians have also closed all transpolar air routes across their territory. No new international flights are being allowed into their airspace."

"What's the Kremlin's explanation for this sudden flurry of activity, Kristin?" the Air Force chief of staff, General Frank Neary, asked.

She shrugged. "There isn't one, sir." Her gaze was unwavering. "We've reached out on the hotline. But we're not getting responses from any senior Russian officials, either military or civilian."

"They're not taking our calls?" Neary asked in disbelief.

"Either that, or President Zhdanov and his top people are all still in transit to safe locations," Chao said bluntly. "Like the nuclear command and control bunkers outside Moscow. Or their new Mount Kosvinsky Kamen special facility deep in the northern Urals."

Neary stared at her, as did almost everyone else in the Emergency Conference Room. "Are you seriously suggesting that the Russians are preparing for war?"

"We can't ignore the possibility." She brought up a series of satellite images. They showed dozens of advanced fighter aircraft and Tu-160M2, Tu-22M, and Tu-95 heavy bombers being fueled and armed at bases across the Russian Federation. "There is a serious concern that all of this unprecedented activity could be the prelude to a surprise military move against the United States or some of our allies." That created a tremendous stir across the crowded room.

Taylor leaned forward. Behind his thick lenses, the secretary of defense's eyes were watchful. "Do we have any intelligence that might argue against that rather unnerving possibility, Admiral?"

"Yes, sir," Chao admitted. She tapped another button. New images appeared, these showing the docks and submarine pens around Murmansk and Vladivostok. "So far, we see no indications that Russia's ballistic missile submarines or surface combatants are changing their peacetime operational patterns." More detailed satellite pictures appeared, this time of major Russian army bases. Row after row of parked main battle tanks, infantry fighting vehicles, self-propelled artillery pieces, mobile anti-aircraft weapons, and other vehicles were visible. Plainly labeled "before" and "after" images showed no significant changes over the past several days. "Nor do we detect any evidence that its ground combat forces are moving to a higher state of readiness."

"What about their ICBM force?" Neary asked.

The admiral spread her hands. "It's difficult to say, General. We haven't yet picked up any firm evidence that their mobile and silo-based strategic nuclear missiles are moving to a higher state of readiness . . . but I'm not sure we would in any case."

Neary nodded grimly. Keeping track of Russia's road-mobile long-range missiles was a difficult task at any time, and Moscow had secure landline connections to its hardened ICBM silos. If the Kremlin actually issued strike orders to its land-based strategic nuclear forces, the U.S. probably wouldn't know anything until its satellites spotted the heat plumes from hundreds of separate missile launches. And at that point, Washington would have less than thirty minutes' warning before a devastating hail of nuclear warheads detonated across the United States. It was the nightmare scenario that had haunted

American presidents and military leaders for decades.

"But as far as we know *now*, this unprecedented level of military activity seems limited *solely* to Russia's Air Force, surface-to-air missile regiments, and surveillance radars?" Taylor asked pointedly.

Admiral Chao nodded firmly. "That's correct, Mr. Secretary."

Taylor looked along the table toward Jonas Murphy, favoring him with a shrewd, amused smile. "Which brings us around to you, Jonas."

"Me?" Murphy said, trying his best to sound surprised.

"Yes, you," the older man said wryly. "Earlier today, your office transmitted a top secret alert to all of our U.S. Air Force formations deployed in Turkey, Afghanistan, and Iraq, right? An alert that raised the possibility of a Russian aircraft making an unauthorized transit through their areas of operation?"

Crap, Murphy thought, feeling suddenly cornered. "That's true."

"So why did you send out this highly unusual alert?" Taylor asked bluntly, not bothering to beat around the bush.

Left with no other choice, Murphy fell back on partial truth. "The CIA received intelligence from what appears to be a high-level Russian source. Intelligence which suggested the possible defection of a pilot flying one of their most advanced military aircraft sometime in the next twenty-four hours."

"What type of aircraft?" Taylor pushed.

"Tupolev's PAK-DA experimental stealth bomber prototype," Murphy admitted.

That drew the reaction he'd expected. General Neary and the other Joint Chiefs of Staff seated at the table with him looked stunned at first and then somewhat predatory. The prospect of getting a close, hard look at the technology that Moscow had openly boasted would rival and even exceed that of America's own stealth bombers was irresistible.

"How reliable is the CIA's intelligence on this?" Taylor asked directly.

Murphy shrugged. "That's unknown, I'm afraid. We don't have any history with their source . . . yet."

"A defection attempt of that magnitude could certainly explain the frantic Russian air and radar activity we're seeing now," General Neary mused out loud, looking up at the wall screens. Then he turned back to Murphy. "But do you have any honest-to-God confirmation that such a defection is actually underway?"

The DNI glanced at the secure smartphone he'd laid faceup on the conference table in front of him. There were no new messages from Miranda Reynolds, the head of the CIA's clandestine operations service. He shook his head. "Unfortunately, I don't."

"Which means what you've been sold could be typical Russian disinformation," Neary pointed out. "Part of a deliberate plan to sow confusion and slow our response to the increase in military readiness we're seeing right now."

Murphy nodded uncomfortably. "That's certainly possible."

"Which leaves us with the question of how we're going to respond to what we *do* know right now," Taylor broke in. "Which is that the Russians are rapidly bringing their combat air units and ground-based air defenses to wartime levels of readiness." He looked along the table. "Suggestions?"

After a glance at his colleagues, Neary leaned forward. As the chief of staff for the Air Force, this was largely his bailiwick. "My recommendation to the president is that he immediately raise our own alert status to DEFCON Three, both here at home and abroad." The other senior officers around the table nodded, signaling their agreement. DEFCON Three would put the entire U.S. military on full alert, with the Air Force ready to move at fifteen minutes' notice. "And I also strongly recommend that he contact our allies and urge them to take similar precautionary measures."

Murphy interjected. "I concur, but with the caveat that we still urge caution by our air units operating near Russia's southern frontier. If a Russian pilot really *is* trying to defect, I'd rather that we weren't the ones who shot him down."

"Doing so carries risks of its own," Neary warned. "Even a single aircraft conducting a surprise strike can inflict a hell of a lot of damage using modern weapons."

Taylor considered that carefully. "That's true, General," he said after a few moments. "But Director Murphy has a good point, which I'll pass on to the president." The defense secretary spread his hands. "Anyway, if the Russians are preparing a serious attack against us, they aren't going to use just one plane—no matter how well it's armed—" He broke off abruptly as new digital maps opened on the far wall. These depicted regions of northern and western China. More symbols appeared, thickly clustered near the People's Republic of China's border with Russia.

"We've received new satellite and SIGINT data, sir," Admiral Chao confirmed. "All major fighter and SAM units assigned to the PRC's Western and Northern Theater Commands have just gone on high alert."

"Seems like Beijing's getting spooked by the Russians, too," Taylor said somberly. He reached for one of the secure links at his place. "It's time I called the president."

THAT SAME TIME

Staff Sergeant Peggy Baker sat up a little straighter in her swivel chair. She'd just caught a flash of movement on one of the multiple screens at her workstation. A small colored dot briefly appeared on the feed from the FPS-117 phased array radar at Barter Island. It faded out for a few seconds and then reappeared for another very short interval before disappearing completely.

For a moment, she was tempted to write off the blip as just a radar or weather anomaly. After all, seriously bad weather was closing in over the radar site and all of northern Alaska, complete with high winds and driving snow and ice storms. Then again, L-band radars weren't affected by storms to the same degree as high-frequency equipment. So whatever that unidentified object was, it could be something real. And from the size of the reflection, it was also very small, no larger than a good-sized bird—but no bird in nature moved at that kind of speed, almost 450 knots. She picked up the phone to her supervisor. "Ma'am," she told Lieutenant Colonel Carmen Reyes, "I may have picked up a bogey here. It could be nothing, but I think you should take a look at the track."

"On my way," Reyes said crisply. She hung up and trotted down the short flight of steps from the observation deck to the main floor of the operations center. It took her less than thirty seconds to reach Baker's station. "Okay, Peggy, show me what you've got," she ordered.

Rapidly, the sergeant entered a series of commands on her keyboard to pull up a recording of the data from Barter Island's radar. Reyes leaned over her shoulder, watching as the faint blip appeared, moved slightly across the screen, vanished, and popped up again for a few short seconds. Based on the short observed track, if that was a genuine bogey, it had been heading almost due south across the coast about twenty nautical miles east of Kaktovik. She pursed her lips in thought. "Contact Anchorage Center. See if they know anything about a private jet or commercial airliner that's gone astray up that way."

"Yes, ma'am." Baker picked up her direct line to the FAA's Air Route Traffic Control Center and relayed the colonel's question to one of the controllers on duty. On its face, the suggestion wasn't unreasonable. About an hour ago, the Russians had abruptly closed all the transpolar routes through their airspace. As a result, ARTCCs across the Northern Hemisphere were scrambling to divert dozens of civilian passenger jets and cargo planes to alternate routes. It was just possible that they'd lost track of one in all the confusion.

After a brief conversation, Baker hung up. She swiveled to Reyes. "Negative on that, ma'am. Anchorage says all the flights they were monitoring are accounted for. No civilian aircraft have been cleared through that sector."

Reyes tapped her foot on the tiled floor while she ran through her options. Although there weren't any aircraft currently on patrol, Third Wing did have two F-22 Raptor fighters on alert status. But even if this was a genuine bogey and not just some kind of equipment- or weather-related glitch, its last confirmed position was more than five hundred nautical miles from Joint Base Elmendorf-Richardson. That was very near the outside edge of a Raptor's subsonic combat range. Plus, by the time any F-22s arrived on scene, whatever the Barter Island radar had detected would be long gone. There was also one more significant factor to consider. "What's our latest read on the weather?" she asked.

"Horrible," Baker told her. "The Barter Island station reports strong winds from the north at forty knots, gusting to sixty, with a solid cloud layer down to less than five hundred feet. Conditions are worsening fast, with blowing snow and sleet. Visibility on the ground is only around fifty or sixty feet right now. And the storm front that's whacking them is headed straight our way."

Reyes shivered, suddenly very glad her command post was deep underground and centrally heated. She came to a decision and shook her head. "Right,

I'll buck this one up to Wing for their final call, but my recommendation will be that we let this bogey go. Given the weather conditions and the extreme range, there's almost no chance of making a successful or safe intercept."

EIGHTEEN

Buffeted by the storm howling down from the Arctic Ocean, the PAK-DA stealth bomber streaked
onward through a swirling torrent of wind-driven
snow and ice. Colonel Alexei Petrov fought to keep
his heavy aircraft under control, reacting almost instinctively to powerful gusts and unexpected pockets of severe turbulence that tugged and tore at the
edges of its wing. Through his canopy, he caught
only fleeting glimpses of the rugged, mountainous
maze he was navigating. Sheer limestone cliffs and
steep, boulder-strewn slopes towered above him on
all sides, rising higher and higher until they vanished in a thick, gray layer of low-hanging cloud.

The steering cue on his HUD slid sharply to
the right. Immediately, he yanked his stick in that
direction. The bomber banked sharply, narrowly
avoiding a cliff face that appeared suddenly out of
the darkness and then just as abruptly disappeared
astern, cloaked by falling snow.

Petrov felt his left eye twitch. Beneath his oxygen

mask, his facial muscles were locked in a manic grin. He'd plotted this low-altitude flight path weeks ago, using a combination of satellite photos and detailed topographic maps. But what had looked practical in the quiet, well-lit confines of his quarters was proving infinitely more difficult at night, in the middle of a raging storm. The course he'd chosen followed a series of narrow river valleys that writhed and twisted and wound their way deeper into this vast labyrinth of barren, snow-covered mountains and ridges. If he misjudged a single turn or lost control for even a fraction of a second, his stealth bomber would slam head-on into a mountainside or clip the edge of a precipice—disappearing forever in an enormous fireball that would briefly light up a few desolate peaks and gorges . . . and leave nothing but fragments of scorched wreckage as a monument. A quick death to be sure, he thought bleakly, but a singularly meaningless one.

Faintly, over the wailing sound of the wind and the roar of the PAK-DA's jet engines, he heard a groan from the seat next to him. It was echoed from farther back in the cockpit. Bunin and Mavrichev were starting to stir, slowly and painfully clawing their way back toward consciousness. After several hours, the fentanyl derivative he'd used to drug them was finally wearing off.

Petrov rolled the bomber back to the left, following the trace of an ice-covered river below as it curved back toward the southeast. Distances counted down on his HUD. He was very close to the Brooks Range divide, a geological boundary separating the rivers and streams that ran north out of the mountains toward the Arctic Ocean from those that meandered south, deeper into Alaska and Canada's Yukon Territory.

Now! His navigation cue spiked upward and he yanked back on the stick—pulling into a near-vertical climb. His left hand shoved the throttles forward, going to full military power. The PAK-DA skimmed just above the slope of an east–west razor-backed ridge that cut straight across his flight path. He cleared the top with only meters to spare and plunged into a wall of cloud. Ice pellets rattled off the cockpit canopy like machine-gun fire. Seconds later, his brightly lit steering indicator dipped toward the bottom of the HUD. He pushed forward, diving back out of the cloud and down into another gorge.

A new window opened on the multifunction display he'd set to manage the bomber's navigation system. TARGET RANGE: 90.5 KILOMETERS.

Petrov throttled back to significantly reduce his airspeed. He banked right and then left and back right again, following the narrow gorge as it snaked south through higher peaks and ridges. Little patches of stunted trees lined the banks of a frozen watercourse at its bottom. The howling winds and turbulence clawing at his aircraft diminished a little. He'd flown out ahead of the oncoming storm.

Gradually, the chasm widened. The mountains and rounded hills fell away on either side, revealing a broader valley ahead. Stretches of snow-covered tundra and clumps of woods appeared eerily green in the PAK-DA's infrared sensors.

Petrov glanced down at his MFD. TARGET RANGE: 15 KILOMETERS. He blinked, still scarcely able to believe that this nightmare run through the mountains was nearly over. He was just two minutes out. It was time to find out if Voronin's mercenaries were awake and attentive to their duties. His lips thinned. He disliked being forced to trust the competence of men he'd never met.

He reached forward and tapped a preset icon on the display. Obeying his command, the bomber's tactical communications system transmitted a short, encrypted radio signal at very low power. Without waiting for a response, he toggled on his landing lights. Powerful spotlights speared through the darkness. Control surfaces along the trailing edge of the PAK-DA's wing whined open, providing additional lift as his airspeed decreased. More hydraulics whirred as the landing gear came down and locked in position.

In the distance, glowing dots blinked into existence. Days before, Voronin's team had set up pairs of shielded infrared markers to outline the improvised runway they had built out of compacted snow. A parachute flare, blinding bright through falling snow, arced high into the air from the forward edge of the runway—giving him a visual indication of the wind direction and strength.

Gently, with tiny movements of the stick and his other controls, Petrov brought the big stealth bomber in to land. Ahead through his canopy, the twin rows of infrared markers grew steadily larger, taking on shape and definition as he skimmed low over the valley floor on final approach.

The first pair of markers slid past under his wing. He was just above the compacted snow field. It was time to set the bird down. Petrov throttled all the way back in one smooth motion. Robbed of the last lift keeping it in the air, the bomber dropped onto the runway. Curtains of snow sprayed outward as it thundered down the valley, shedding speed as he reversed thrust and carefully applied his brakes. Gradually, as the aircraft slowed, the trees and rock-littered hillsides blurring past his canopy sharpened into focus.

Petrov grinned more genuinely under his oxygen mask. He'd been confident this would work. His countrymen had successfully operated heavy four-engine IL-76 transport aircraft on similarly improvised snow and ice fields in the past. Their loaded weight was comparable to that of the PAK-DA prototype . . . and to the American B-2, for that matter. But the Americans were far too conventional to imagine anyone would risk pulling the same stunt with an armed stealth bomber—let alone using a makeshift runway secretly carved out inside their own national territory.

As he taxied toward the end of the field, a large white structure slowly emerged from the darkness and blowing snow. Shrouded in netting to break up its visual signature, it was a temporary aircraft shelter created with ultralight thermal and radar-reflective camouflage fabric. Two men were stationed near the entrance to guide him inside.

Slowly, directed by their glowing orange batons, Petrov carefully maneuvered the PAK-DA into position, set the brakes, and switched off both engines. The huge turbofans keened down to a stop, descending steadily in pitch until they fell silent. After so many hours spent in the air surrounded by their roar, this sudden quiet seemed unnatural.

He sat back with a relieved sigh, stripped off his headset, and unbuckled his straps. When he stood up, he noticed that both Bunin and Mavrichev were wide awake now. They glared at him. "Welcome to America," he said cheerfully.

"You fucking traitor," Mavrichev spat out in response.

Petrov shook his head. "I sincerely hope not, General." He shrugged his shoulders. "This is a purely private-enterprise operation. And if Moscow is wise, it will meet our price. Then you and Oleg there can fly the prototype home. You may not return as heroes, but at least you'll be the men returning a precious aircraft to its rightful owners."

Without waiting for a reply, he brushed past them and unlatched the hatch. When it swung open in a blast of bitterly cold air, he slid down the ladder and dropped lightly onto the aircraft shelter's hard-packed snow floor.

Shielded lanterns illuminated its cavernous interior. In their glow, Petrov saw a group of three hard-faced men waiting for him. They were bundled up against the subzero weather in parkas and fur-lined hoods. One stepped forward with a thin smile. "Congratulations on your success, Colonel. My name is Bondarovich. I'm in charge here."

Petrov nodded briefly. As a matter of operational security, he hadn't been briefed on any of their names. But he recognized their type—ex-soldiers who'd found a way to use the lethal skills they'd been taught by the state for their own personal profit. It amused him to realize they undoubtedly believed he was just the same.

Movement outside the tent caught his eye. A snowmobile was headed toward them from the far end of the runway.

"Another of my men," Bondarovich explained. "He fired that flare for you, and made sure none of our IR markers were blocked by drifting snow." He glanced up at the PAK-DA bomber looming over them. "I understand you have a prisoner you need us to handle?"

"Two of them, actually," Petrov said. He filled the other man in on Mavrichev's sudden decision to invite himself along on what was supposed to be a triumphant test of the prototype's capabilities.

Bondarovich whistled in amazement. "The commander of Long-Range Aviation himself? That's a devil of a big fish you landed, Colonel."

"More like a big pain in the ass," Petrov said with a sour grin. "I'll be glad to see the back of him once this is over."

The other man nodded in amusement and ordered his men into the plane to bring Bunin and Mavrichev out. While the two prisoners were hustled down the ladder, he asked quietly, "Have you contacted Moscow yet? To make our little proposition?"

Petrov shook his head. "Not yet. We'll let Zhdanov sweat awhile longer," he said. Suddenly aware of the piercing cold, he started to shiver. He zipped up his flight suit. "First, I need more suitable clothes, hot food, and some sleep. In that order."

"That we can arrange," Bondarovich assured him.

With the ex-Spetsnaz officer in the lead and Petrov right behind, the whole group headed outside toward a little cluster of tents hidden among some nearby trees. Bunin and Mavrichev, untied now, stumbled along at the rear, sandwiched between two watchful guards. Their flashlight beams danced across the ground, piercing the darkness and blowing snow.

Petrov noted that the wind was picking up fast. The storm he'd outrun in the mountains was almost on top of them. In thirty minutes or less, the landing he'd just made would have been completely impossible. He allowed himself to feel a moment of complete triumph. Despite all the unexpected obstacles thrown in his path, he'd succeeded in pulling off a masterpiece of operational planning and piloting skill. And as a result, Russia's most advanced combat aircraft was now effectively in his sole possession, along with twelve nuclear-armed cruise missiles. For one exultant instant, he understood what it must be like to be a demigod—a being far beyond the reach of other mortals.

And then everything went wrong.

As the snowmobile curved around to join the little group trudging toward camp, the shrill, high-pitched whine of its motor stabbed into Petrov's brain. Together with the stress accumulated during his long and dangerous flight and the tumor growing unchecked inside his skull, that was more than enough to trigger a cascade of unbearable pain. Gripped by a sudden, blinding headache, he doubled over and vomited into the snow. Unable to stop himself, he moaned aloud in agony.

Taken aback by his abrupt collapse, everyone else turned to stare at him in surprise.

Everyone except Mavrichev. Seizing his opportunity, the stocky, bullnecked general stiff-armed the nearest guard, knocking the man sprawling backward into the snow. Free suddenly, he sprinted toward the idling snowmobile. And with a guttural shout, he hurled its surprised rider out of the saddle. Then, before anyone could move to stop him, he threw his leg over the machine, opened its throttle wide, and skidded away across the tundra, bent low over the handlebars as he accelerated.

"God damn it!" Petrov snarled. Furious at the guards for their carelessness and at his own weakness for distracting them, he pushed Bondarovich away, lurched upright, and fumbled for his sidearm, a 9mm pistol. Fighting past the waves of pain still spiking through his brain, he leveled the weapon, aimed, and fired several times at the speeding snowmobile.

Most of his shots went wide. But at least one 9mm round slammed into Mavrichev's back, high up in the middle of his right shoulder blade. Bright red blood spurted into the air. A moment later, the fleeing general disappeared into a swirling curtain of windblown snow.

Still shaking, Petrov wiped distractedly at the vomit smearing his chin and then whirled toward Bondarovich. "Go on! Get after him!" he snapped.

"There's no need," the other man said callously. "That stupid son of a bitch won't get far. You pegged him. And in this storm, he'll either bleed to death or freeze soon enough." He looked up at the sky and then shook his head. "No, Colonel. Don't worry about it. We'll retrieve the body once the weather clears."

NINETEEN

A SHORT TIME LATER

Rank had its privileges at the Barter Island station—at least to the extent that Captain Nick Flynn got his own sleeping quarters. True, the same small space also doubled as his office, and it was really just an eight-by-eight cubicle slapped together out of thin plywood partitions. But at least it offered a modicum of privacy when he needed it. Except for Sergeant Takirak, everyone else on his Joint Force security team had to share a room with two or three others.

At the knock on his open door, Flynn closed the science fiction thriller he'd been reading on his tablet. "Come in," he said, fighting down an exasperated sigh. Between PT at what felt like oh dark thirty; a predawn foot patrol around the whole island in subzero temperatures; firing exercises out at their improvised range; a public relations–required Q-and-A session with kids at the local school; another of Takirak's regular lectures on wilderness and winter survival tricks and tips; and the routine mound of paperwork so beloved of higher-command echelons, he felt like he'd already had a pretty full day. His fatigue was compounded by the fact that they were now down to just a little over five hours of sunlight out of every twenty-four. Spending two-thirds of the usual waking day in darkness really screwed up circadian rhythms for most people—himself included.

"Uh, sir?" Senior Airman Mark Mitchell said cautiously, poking his head around the doorframe. The redheaded communications specialist had a knack for reading other people's emotions . . . or at least figuring out when they were pissed at him for pulling some boneheaded practical joke, usually after it was too late. Like the time a week ago when he'd excitedly brought Private First Class Hynes fake transfer orders to Hawaii's Schofield Barracks. Luckily, the team's brawny Carl Gustav recoilless rifle gunner, an Army specialist from New Mexico named Rafael Sanchez, had stepped between the two men before Hynes could go totally berserk.

"What is it, M-Squared?" Flynn asked patiently.

"We just got an alert message from JBER," Mitchell said.

Flynn looked pointedly at his watch. It was well after 1900, and the sun had been below the horizon for more than four hours. "The real thing, Airman?" he asked dryly.

For Mitchell's sake, he hoped this wasn't another lame attempt at humor. After all, there must be worse military duty posts than this isolated radar station. Though, admittedly, none sprang readily to mind. The enlisted man was a decent radioman, but there were definitely limits to the amount of juvenile crap Flynn was willing to put up with. If pushed too far, he'd boot M-Squared out of the unit first and worry about finding a new com specialist later.

"Honest to God, sir," Mitchell assured him earnestly. "This is the genuine article. And it's not just us. It's everyone. All over the whole world. The president or the Pentagon or whoever is ordering everybody—Air Force, Army, Navy, Marines, Space Force, the whole bunch—to DEFCON Three."

Flynn dropped his tablet and rolled off his cot in one smooth motion. The U.S. armed forces hadn't gone to DEFCON Three since 9/11, in the immediate aftermath of the terrorist attacks on New York and the Pentagon. That was more than twenty years ago. What the hell had just happened to trigger this kind of drastic move now? "Show me!" he snapped.

He followed Mitchell down the hall to the station's dining area in a hurry. Next to the kitchen, it was the largest open space in the station's ramshackle living quarters, big enough for up to twenty people to eat at the same time. The airman had taken over a corner table for his computers and other electronic gear. A sleeping bag nearby showed that he was sleeping there, too, probably to get away from his nominal roommate. Flynn had heard grousing that Army Private Wade Vucovich's snoring should be classed as a prohibited nonlethal weapon under international law.

The airman dropped into his chair and pulled up the encrypted message file they'd been sent from Alaskan Command down at Joint Base Elmendorf-Richardson. "See, sir?"

Quickly, Flynn scanned through the alert. Key phrases jumped out at him. "Unprecedented levels of military air activity observed across the entire Russian Federation." "No immediate confirmation of hostile intent." "Increase in readiness levels directly authorized by the National Command Authority," which meant the president and the secretary of defense acting jointly. But there was nothing about what might be behind these sudden Russian moves that had alarmed Washington.

His mouth tightened. He didn't know what was worse: the possibility that nobody in D.C. had a fricking clue as to why Moscow had just put its entire Air Force and air defense network on a wartime footing. Or the very real possibility that the Pentagon brass and the intel community had simply decided not to share their information with the grunts, squids, and zoomies posted out at the sharp end . . . figuring that they didn't need to know the whys and wherefores. Just like at the C-130 crash site in the Libyan desert, he thought bitterly.

Ditch that anger for now, Flynn told himself. His most immediate problem was figuring out how to translate this unexpected DEFCON Three directive into concrete action by the troops under his command. Older, more established Army formations and Air Force bases had thick manuals stashed away in their secure safes—manuals that laid out each and every action required to comply with the new, higher alert status, all the way down to precise rules of engagement for any extra guards posted at gates and perimeters. As a brand-new, completely untested unit, the men of his Joint Force security team didn't have any comparable manuals to tell them what to do in a sudden crisis. They were entirely dependent on his intellect, training, and instincts.

He looked up and saw the rest of the team filing into the dining room. Word that something was up had obviously gotten out fast. He supposed that wasn't much of a surprise. All twelve of them were basically living in one another's back pockets. Once the sun went down and temperatures plunged well below zero, their universe was essentially restricted to a small number of corridors and rooms. Certainly nobody sane had any incentive to go wandering off anywhere outside, even when they weren't on duty. It was the closest thing to a long-duration submarine patrol that anyone not in the U.S. Navy could ever experience.

"What's the word, sir?" one of them asked.

"As of this moment, we're moving to DEFCON Three," Flynn replied, "along with all other U.S. bases, ships, and air squadrons around the world. For some reason, our Russian friends have moved all of their own fighters, strike aircraft, strategic bombers, and SAM forces to full alert."

"Holy shit," Hynes said in amazement. "Are we at war?"

"Not as far as I know," Flynn told him. He glanced down at the time stamp on the alert message they'd been sent. He grinned crookedly. "Well, at least we weren't as of fifteen minutes ago."

"That isn't exactly comforting, Captain," Hynes said.

Flynn shrugged. "I didn't mean it to be, PFC." He looked around the crowded dining area. "Anyway, as of now, y'all are just as much in the loop as I am."

Effortlessly, Takirak shouldered his way through the group of suddenly nervous-looking soldiers and airmen. "What are your orders, sir?" he asked quietly. Alone of everyone, he seemed completely unfazed by the sudden turn of events.

Flynn nodded. "Glad you asked, Sergeant," he said, forcing himself to sound confident and in command. "As a first step, I want you to take a six-man patrol out pronto and set up a chain of two-man observation posts somewhere between here and the west end of the island. Make sure you've got decent fields of fire to cover the open ground around this station."

Takirak considered that. "It's pretty cold out there right now, Captain. Around ten below zero. Four hours outside is the maximum time I'd recommend—unless we're setting up camp."

"We'll rotate your team back inside after four hours," Flynn assured him. "I'll take over your OPs with the other half of the team for the next shift, while your guys get some hot food and rest. Then we'll trade off again."

"How long do you figure to keep this four-on, four-off rotation going?" the National Guard sergeant asked.

"However long it takes the geniuses in D.C. to pin down what the Russians are doing," Flynn said. "If Moscow's only running a big-assed readiness exercise, we ought to get the word to stand down pretty soon."

"And if this isn't just a drill?"

Flynn smiled thinly. "Then the weather will be the least of our problems, Sergeant."

Takirak shot him an equally tight grin in response. "Point taken, sir." He swung around and started jabbing fingers at some of the watching soldiers and airmen. "Hynes, Vucovich, Sanchez, Kim, and Boyd, you're with me. You've got ten minutes to report back here in full cold weather gear, with your weapons and ammunition. So move!"

They scattered instantly, heading for their racks to grab their equipment and then struggle into multiple layers of clothing designed to protect them from extreme cold—everything from long underwear, Gore-Tex pants, and fleece jackets to thick parkas, balaclavas, goggles, boots, and gloves. Even a few days under the veteran NCO's tutelage had taught them that "Takirak time" was precise. Ten minutes meant ten minutes and not a single second more, not unless you wanted to get seriously lit up in front of every other guy in the unit.

Flynn looked at the five men who were still left. "As for you guys, I suggest you grab some extra shut-eye while you can." Slowly, Mitchell and the others drifted away, talking the situation over in low, worried-sounding voices.

When they were gone, Takirak lowered his voice

and leaned closer to Flynn. "Just so I understand your thinking, sir, what's the real purpose behind deploying these observation posts?"

"Meaning, have I gone loco and actually started believing that the Russians might attack this radar site with helicopters or paratroops, instead of lobbing a couple of cruise missiles our way?" Flynn said wryly.

Takirak nodded. "Something along those lines."

"Then, no, I haven't gone nuts. I see this as a casualty reduction measure," Flynn told him very quietly. "If the shit really does hit the fan, this place is going to get blown to hell—and there won't be a damned thing we can do to stop that from happening. But at least any of our guys posted outside will have a decent shot at coming through alive and unhurt."

"Makes sense," the older man said. He shrugged. "Well, anyway, this'll be a good training opportunity for us."

Flynn looked at him curiously. "You don't think this alert could turn hot?"

"I suppose it could," Takirak said slowly. Then he shook his head. "But I don't see what the Russians would have to gain. Those men in Moscow aren't fools. Why would they start a war now? Over what? And doing it by massing a bunch of their bombers and fighters in plain view like this? So we have plenty of warning? That's nuts."

Flynn raised an eyebrow. "What would your plan be, Andy?"

"Hell, Captain, I'd just smuggle a nuke into D.C.

and set it off. Take out our top political and military leaders like *that*, without warning, and any war's already halfway to being won."

Flynn laughed. "I guess I should be glad you're not on the Russian General Staff."

"Who, me?" Takirak shook his head. "No, thanks. I have my hands full just keeping goofballs like Mitchell and Hynes squared away."

"Amen to that, Sergeant," Flynn agreed devoutly.

TWENTY

THE NEXT MORNING

Buried deep beneath the ground, the massive Sharapovo command bunker was roughly thirty-three kilometers southwest of the Kremlin, at the terminus of one of Russia's secret subway tunnels. It was also sited within a few kilometers of Vnukovo International, the oldest of the four airports around Moscow. Depending on events, that proximity allowed the possibility of evacuating some of the five thousand high-ranking officials, military officers, assistants, and dependents inside the bunker to even more distant, and presumably, safer regions.

At the moment, however, further flight was the last thing on the mind of Russia's president, Piotr Zhdanov. He was meeting with his closest military and political advisers inside a secure command center at the bunker's lowest level. Thick armored doors and squads of armed guards sealed this chamber off from the rest of the complex. Even in ordinary times, only those with the very highest security clearance were ever admitted inside. That was true now more than ever.

As hours passed without any sign of the missing PAK-DA stealth bomber, guesses about its possible fate had grown increasingly wild. By now, analysts concluded, its fuel reserves must be exhausted. And yet, no cruise missiles had been launched at any cities or military installations in the United States, China, or Russia itself. Nor had there been any triumphant news flashes from Washington or Beijing announcing the defection of pilots flying Russia's most advanced experimental aircraft. Now there was speculation by some that the bomber must have crashed somewhere, either accidentally or as an act of suicidal remorse by its traitorous crew. Others suggested that perhaps Major General Mavrichev, taken prisoner originally, had been able to break loose and bring the plane down in a final act of patriotic self-sacrifice.

But now all of those comforting theories had just come crashing back to earth. Moscow's most secure communications channels had received an encrypted signal—a signal that could only have been transmitted from the PAK-DA stealth bomber prototype. Hurriedly summoned from their quarters, barely an hour after their last futile conference broke up, Zhdanov and his most trusted advisers had convened again to hear this message.

"We're ready, Mr. President," the officer in charge of the command center's audiovisual systems said quietly. "My technical people have finished decrypting and decompressing the signal. Naturally, there may be some minimal degradation of video and audio quality."

"Screw the technobabble," Zhdanov rasped. With hands that shook slightly, he lit another cigarette. Nicotine and strong tea were taking the place of sleep during this crisis. He nodded angrily. "Go on, Colonel. Just play the damned video."

Silently, the colonel pushed a control on the console in front of him. A large screen mounted on one wall came to life. Seconds later, the faintly flickering, recorded image of Colonel Alexei Petrov appeared before them. The video had been shot inside the cockpit of the PAK-DA prototype.

"Good morning, Mr. President," Petrov began without preamble. His expression was serious. "By now, you must realize that I have taken control over this aircraft and its weapons. At this very moment, the bomber is safely on the ground, far outside your reach. You can no more hope to recover it through your own efforts than you can hope to put a man on the moon before the sun sets tonight."

Zhdanov bit down on a curse. This traitor was mocking him. His inability to promise a manned Russian lunar landing any time sooner than the next twenty years—at a time when both the American and Chinese space programs were racing ahead—was a source of long-standing irritation and shame.

"Which brings me to the crux of this matter," Petrov continued somberly. "If you want the PAK-DA stealth bomber, its deadly payload, and all of its many secrets back safely, you will have to pay for them all . . . and pay dearly. To the tune of two hundred billion rubles."

That created a stir of disbelief and dismay among the watching officers and government officials. Two hundred billion rubles was more than 2.6 billion U.S. dollars. Such a figure represented a huge sum for Russia's increasingly cash-strapped government and military.

"I have attached an additional file to this signal. It contains the detailed instructions required to make this payment," Petrov went on.

Zhdanov glanced at the colonel. The younger man nodded. "We found such a file, sir. It's been relayed to Federal Security Service experts for analysis."

Petrov leaned closer to the camera. "But let me be blunt. There will be no bargaining, no haggling. In fact, for every seventy-two hours that elapses from the transmission of this signal without full payment, the price you must pay will increase. The longer you delay, the more it will cost you to regain the stealth bomber and the twelve nuclear-armed Kh-102 cruise missiles currently in my sole possession." He shrugged. "Should you be tempted to play foolish games and ignore this warning, consider this: While I remain a Russian patriot, despite the weakened, corrupted state of your government and our society, my patience, and that of those who have backed me, is not limitless. If necessary, we will sell the PAK-DA prototype and its weapons to a foreign power—one that will welcome the opportunity to pry open our nation's most tightly held technological and military secrets." On the screen, the camera zoomed in on the renegade colonel's utterly determined face. "Consider the consequences carefully, Mr. President. Don't fuck this up. Petrov out." The screen blanked.

For a few moments more, Zhdanov said nothing. Then he glared around the table. "Well?" he demanded. "What do we do now?"

There was a long, uncomfortable silence. Somewhat understandably, none of the assembled generals and senior government officials wanted to be the first to stick his neck out on what could all too easily become the president's chopping block. Finally, Rogozin reluctantly cleared his throat. "I think it would be best if we took some additional time to analyze the available data, Mr. President." The Air Force chief looked pale. "The situation we now confront is . . . unprecedented." Other heads inclined marginally in agreement.

"True," Zhdanov said harshly. "If by *unprecedented*, you mean a complete catastrophe." He glanced at his watch. "Very well, you have one hour." The expression in his cold eyes hardened. "But not a single minute more. Clear?"

Then, without waiting for further responses, he got up and walked out—leaving his silent advisers still seated, warily staring at each other.

True to his word, Piotr Zhdanov returned to the command center precisely sixty minutes later. Briefly, he'd toyed with the idea of delaying longer, knowing the wait would further unnerve the generals and officials who'd failed him so singularly thus far. But faced with Petrov's own hard deadline, he'd finally decided the pleasure of making them sweat wasn't worth the loss of more time.

He dropped into his chair. "All right, gentlemen. Let's get started." He stabbed a finger at the now-blank wall screen. "First, can we trace that son of a bitch Petrov's message back to its point of transmission?"

Rogozin shook his head. "I'm afraid not. The PAK-DA prototype's strategic communications system is completely secure. We designed it specifically to handle signals between strike aircraft and higher headquarters under wartime conditions. It's essentially undetectable by any enemy, and, unfortunately, equally untraceable by us now."

"Explain that," Zhdanov said.

"The system automatically encrypts any message and compresses it to a microsecond burst," Rogozin said. "Those blips are then relayed to our orbiting Meridian-class military communications satellites and beamed back down to receiving stations here."

Zhdanov frowned. "Don't our satellites record where the signal originated?"

"No, sir," Rogozin said uncomfortably. "As a precaution against the possibility of American hacking which could allow them to track our bombers in flight, our programmers deleted that function."

"Wonderful," the Russian president said dryly. "A piece of brilliant software design that's just bitten us in the ass." He turned toward a paunchy, gray-haired man farther down the table. Konstantin Yumashev was the director of the Federal Security Service, the FSB. Largely responsible for counter-intelligence, counterterrorism, border security, and political surveillance, the FSB's ranks also included specialists in cybersecurity and financial crimes. "Can your people exploit that file containing Petrov's payment instructions, Yumashev?"

The FSB director looked apologetic. "It's highly unlikely, Mr. President. My experts tell me the funds transfer instruction the colonel attached appears uncrackable. If we agree to meet his demands, any money we deposit will undoubtedly vanish deeper into an intricate web of secret accounts within minutes, perhaps only seconds. With a tremendous expenditure of time and effort, my people might be able to pry their way into the top layer of financial institutions used as transfer nodes, but, ultimately, the odds are very much against our ever finding the ultimate destination."

Zhdanov nodded his understanding. Like many of those in this room, he maintained his own network of private, offshore bank accounts. So he was already intimately familiar with the methods required to shield certain . . . dubious . . . financial transactions from inconvenient public or regulatory scrutiny. His brow furrowed in thought. The fact that a relatively junior Air Force officer like Petrov apparently knew how to game the international banking system so effectively strongly suggested the colonel's boast about having powerful backers was accurate.

He frowned, wondering who they might be. Between enemies he'd made here at home and enemies he'd made abroad, the list of possible suspects would be very long. Then he shrugged. First things first, he reminded himself. Right now, recovering the PAK-DA bomber prototype had to be his top priority. For the moment, vengeance would have to take second place.

Once more, Zhdanov ran his cold gaze around the crowded table. "Recommendations?" he snapped.

Of them all, bald-headed Gennadiy Kokorin was the first one with the guts to speak up. The elderly minister of defense was very close to retirement. Perhaps between that and his long years of loyal service, he felt he had relatively little to lose. "Meeting Colonel Petrov's demands might be safest, Piotr," he said quietly. "Admittedly, his price is very steep, but seeing the Americans or the Chinese get their hands on our new bomber prototype would be much worse."

Zhdanov shook his head. "I will not pay this traitor so much as a single kopek, let alone two hundred *billion* rubles." His jaw tightened. No matter how hard they tried to keep such a decision secret, word that he'd yielded so tamely to blackmail would be sure to leak out. It would make him appear fatally weak at a time of growing political unrest. Essentially, if he caved in to Petrov's terms, he'd be signing his own political death warrant. Besides, such cowardice would also open the door to other greedy fools throughout Russia's armed forces and other government ministries—fools who might decide to imitate the colonel's criminal example for their own gains.

"But the Americans—" Kokorin began to protest.

"Screw the Americans," Zhdanov said coarsely, cutting the older man off. "And screw the Chinese, too. For the record, Gennadiy, we're not going to let Beijing or Washington buy the PAK-DA out from under our noses."

"Then what do you want us to do?" the defense minister asked.

"If possible, I want the stealth bomber recaptured," Zhdanov replied. "But if necessary, I want the aircraft completely destroyed. If we can't have it, no one else will." He saw his advisers nod enthusiastically in agreement. *Of course they agree*, he thought sourly. *Now that I've made the hard decision on my own, they'll back me up. And then deny having had any responsibility if things go wrong.* He turned back to Rogozin. "Which means our first step must be to find out where Petrov has landed."

"Yes, Mr. President," the Air Force commander agreed. He sighed. "One thing is clear: this is an organized conspiracy. While it might be possible for the colonel and his copilot to have stolen the PAK-DA on their own, it would be absolutely impossible for them to find a suitable landing field and then conceal the bomber without substantial help on the ground."

Kokorin nodded somberly. "Very true, General." He shook his head. "Since Petrov hasn't yet turned the aircraft over to a foreign government, he's almost certainly in league with a powerful criminal cabal." He rubbed a weary hand across his bald

scalp. "Probably the Mafiya or some other organized crime group."

Zhdanov noticed that some of his advisers looked
even more worried by that possibility. That was no
surprise, he supposed. Many of Moscow's political and military elites had at least an arm's-length
relationship with the capital's wealthier crime
bosses. Like was attracted to like, he thought cynically. Now, no doubt, some of them were nervously
considering the prospect that those ties might suddenly land them in very hot water, at least if any of
their Mafiya "friends" turned out to be involved in
Petrov's scheme. He made a note to himself to con-
sult with Yumashev after this meeting. Many of the
FSB's agents were probably on the take, too, but an
investigation might still bear fruit—especially if it
became a choice between a firing squad on the one
hand or losing a little extra under-the-table income
on the other.

"We'll worry about who's helping the traitor
later," he said impatiently. "Right now, I want your
best guesses as to where the PAK-DA could be."

In answer, Rogozin tapped a control on the computer keyboard at his place. The wall screen lit up
again, this time showing a digital map of the entire world. "Determining its hiding place will be
very difficult," he warned. "Fully fueled, the stealth
bomber prototype had a maximum range of eleven
thousand kilometers." On the screen, a bright red
circle centered on the bomber's last-known position, the refueling rendezvous point over the

Yenisei River in central Russia, rapidly expanded outward until it reached a radius of eleven thousand kilometers. "And, as you can see, that means almost all of the world's landmasses and major islands were within its reach."

Zhdanov nodded grimly, astonished despite himself at what he saw. Petrov could theoretically have flown anywhere in all of Russia, North America, Europe, Africa, the Middle East, Asia, and most of Australia. It was an enormous area, containing dozens of separate countries and close to two hundred million square kilometers, much of it sparsely populated forests, jungles, steppes, deserts, and mountains.

"Fortunately," Rogozin continued, "we can rule out certain major areas immediately." He touched another key. Europe blanked off the large digital map. "Given Europe's population density, high level of law enforcement, and the sheer numbers of other civilian and military aircraft operating inside its tightly monitored airspace last night, there is virtually no chance that Petrov could have flown anywhere there without being detected. Nor could he have hoped to land unobserved."

Another swipe by Rogozin's fingers eliminated a second large swath of the globe, this time the Middle East and Africa.

"How can you eliminate those regions as possible hiding places? Especially so quickly?" Zhdanov objected. "Huge portions of Africa and the Middle East are only thinly peopled. And in many of those

same areas, there are almost no functioning gov-
ernments, only warring tribes and rival religious
and political factions."

"That's true, Mr. President," Rogozin acknowledged. He entered a new command on his computer.
Icons depicting military aircraft, alerted air defense
radars, and missile sites suddenly appeared on the
wall map. They were deployed along a wide band
from Turkey and Georgia through Turkmenistan
and all the way to Afghanistan. "But we observed
intense American and American allied air activity
all across this zone last night. True, the PAK-DA's
stealth features might have allowed it to evade their
observation, but Petrov would know that he could
not count on that, at a time when even a fleeting
detection could lead to disaster."

The defense minister nodded his concurrence.
"Yvgeny is right, Piotr," Kokorin said. "Besides,
where could Petrov hope to find safety on the ground
in Africa or the Middle East, in places where the
real power is in the hands of terrorists, murderous
chieftains, and religious fanatics? It would be madness for him to assume he could hide a large aircraft
from such people for any real length of time."

Zhdanov shrugged. Perhaps they were right. He
waved a hand at the digital map. "What about some
isolated spot in Southeast Asia, then? Or maybe a
desert landing strip out in the empty Australian
Outback?"

Rogozin shook his head. "It's highly unlikely.
Reaching either place would have required the
PAK-DA to penetrate some of the most heavily de-

fended airspace in the world—by flying across the People's Republic of China, the Korean Peninsula, or Japan."

"So you believe Petrov flew our stolen bomber north," Zhdanov realized.

"Yes, Mr. President." The general touched more keys, highlighting all of northern Russia, the unclaimed Arctic, Alaska, and much of northern Canada. "Most of these regions are almost completely unsettled. And while the idea that anyone could have constructed a hidden airfield somewhere in these tens of millions of square kilometers of wilderness might seem far-fetched at first—"

"Some bastards have done it, nonetheless," Zhdanov said tersely.

Rogozin nodded. "So it appears."

Zhdanov stared at the highlighted zones of the map, almost mesmerized by its enormous extent. This was not a comparatively simple case of finding a needle in a farmer's haystack, he realized grimly. This was more like hunting for a single grain of sand in the wastes of the Gobi Desert. For a moment, he felt sure the task was impossible. But then he dismissed this feeling as unnecessarily pessimistic, the product of too little sleep and too much stress. He reminded himself that what one man could hide, other men, especially those equipped with sophisticated satellites, air-to-ground radars, and high-resolution cameras, could find.

He spun back to Rogozin and Kokorin. "All right! I want a full mobilization of every reconnaissance asset in our arsenal. All our satellites, all our aircraft, all our drones! Everything! Scour this entire area, starting with our own territory."

The Air Force general frowned, deep in thought. "We only have four of our frontline Tu-214R recon planes in service," he admitted. "But I can convert some of our Tu-95 strategic bombers for reconnaissance, perhaps as many as ten in the next twenty-four hours."

"That's not enough!" Zhdanov said curtly. "Only fourteen aircraft? You'd still be looking for Petrov when the Last Judgment arrives!" He swiveled toward a short, compact officer seated directly across the table. Admiral Nikolai Golitsyn commanded the Russian Navy. Throughout the entire discussion, he'd been very quiet—undoubtedly grateful that this was an Air Force mess and not one that involved his own officers and men. "How many Tu-142 and IL-38 maritime patrol planes can you provide, Golitsyn?"

Both the larger Tu-142 and smaller IL-38 multi-engine turboprops were equipped with powerful surface search radars and infrared sensors. While they were ordinarily tasked with hunting enemy warships and submarines at sea, it wouldn't be difficult for their crews to learn to use the same equipment to look for the PAK-DA bomber hidden somewhere in forests, mountains, or trackless tundra and ice fields.

The admiral looked blank for a moment. Then a junior aide seated behind him leaned forward and hurriedly whispered the answer in his ear. "Approximately twenty of each type, Mr. President," he said confidently.

"Good!" Zhdanov said. "Transfer them all to Rogozin immediately. I don't want any confusion caused by mixed chains of command."

For an instant, Golitsyn opened his mouth to protest, but then he closed it just as quickly. This was not a sensible time to insist on the Russian Navy's prerogatives, not with the president so obviously eager to find scapegoats to blame for this unfolding disaster.

Zhdanov's fingers drummed incessantly on the table while he considered other measures that would be necessary. The most obvious was to make sure they were ready to seize or destroy the stolen stealth bomber almost as soon as it was found. "I want every group of reconnaissance aircraft backed up by fighters, strike aircraft, and Spetsnaz commando teams," he ordered. Heads around the table nodded.

"What are your instructions if we fail to find the PAK-DA inside our own territory?" Rogozin asked carefully.

"You will press the search into American and Canadian airspace," Zhdanov replied.

"How far?"

Zhdanov barked, "As far as necessary, Yvgeny! We can't afford to pussyfoot around anymore."

"The Americans and the Canadians will protest any intrusion into their territory," Rogozin pointed out.

Zhdanov shrugged his shoulders. "Let them bitch. I don't give a rat's ass."

"They will also intercept our reconnaissance flights with fighter aircraft," Rogozin warned. "And our scout planes would be helpless in such a situation. A rear turret with a pair of 23mm cannons is no match for Sidewinder heat-seeking and AMRAAM radar-guided missiles."

The president bit at his lip in frustration. Much as he wanted to, he couldn't argue with Rogozin's chief point. Russian pilots were courageous enough, but he could not expect them to commit suicide, particularly for no possible gain. Moodily, Zhdanov stared up at the map, hunting for some possible solution. And then the answer came to him in a quick flash of inspiration. He slapped his hand down hard on the table. "All right! If your reconnaissance pilots are afraid to tangle with the enemy's interceptors, we'll escort them with fighters of our own!"

Rogozin stared at him. "That would be . . . difficult." He zoomed the display out so that it showed a view of northern Russia and North America, centered on the North Pole. A series of green lines appeared, originating at points just off Russia's northern coast and stretching deep into Canada, Alaska, and Greenland. "Even if we stage out of our Arctic island bases, escorting Tu-142 and IL-38 reconnaissance aircraft deep enough into North American airspace would require round-trip flights of more than six thousand kilometers. Our Su-27s, Su-35s, MiG-31s, and MiG-35s don't have anywhere near that kind of range."

"The Americans could do it easily," Zhdanov countered angrily.

"The American Air Force has almost five hundred air refueling tankers in its inventory," Rogozin replied. "Ours has fewer than twenty operational IL-78 aircraft."

Zhdanov's eyes glittered dangerously. "Then I suggest you make full use of every last one of those *operational* tankers, General. And if you can't or won't do so, I'll find some other officer who will." He leaned forward. "Do you understand me?"

Slowly, Rogozin nodded.

"Good then," Zhdanov said, pleased by the other man's acquiescence. "That's settled."

"The fighter pilots assigned to escort our patrol flights will need firm rules of engagement," Rogozin said carefully. "We don't want any unfortunate accidents."

"Certainly not," Zhdanov agreed. He shrugged. "Let's keep it simple: Your pilots are ordered to keep any NORAD combat aircraft a safe distance from our reconnaissance planes, so that the Tu-142s and IL-38s can complete their missions as directed. To do that, they're authorized to use every peaceful means necessary, including aggressive maneuvering of their own. Maybe these American and Canadian hotshots won't like a taste of their own medicine, eh? But your fighters are *not* to fire first under any circumstances, is that clear?" A thin, humorless smile crossed his face and then vanished. "After all, these shows of force are meant to let us to hunt down that bastard Petrov and our missing stealth bomber—not to set off some goddamned stupid air war over the polar ice cap!"

"Yes, sir," Rogozin agreed wholeheartedly. "But that still leaves the problem of what to do if Petrov *is* hiding somewhere in American or Canadian territory."

Zhdanov frowned. "How so?"

"Carrying out a Spetsnaz raid to recapture the bomber would be impossible," Rogozin warned. "Our helicopters don't have the necessary range."

"So refuel them in the air," Zhdanov snapped. "Just like your fighters."

"Their range is even shorter," Rogozin told him. "Which would force us to refuel them much closer to the North American coast. That would be extremely hazardous—and easily detectable by the North Warning System radars. The Americans and Canadians would have plenty of time to intercept our commando forces before they could reach their target."

Zhdanov clenched his teeth in frustration. Try as he might, he couldn't deny that the other man was probably right. If the traitorous colonel had really flown the PAK-DA prototype into the northern wastes of the United States or Canada, his only option would be to order its complete destruction by bombing or a missile strike. At best, that would be a hollow victory.

He noticed Golitsyn's aide whispering to the admiral again. "You have something to contribute, Nikolai?"

Golitsyn bobbed his head. "Yes, Mr. President." His aide leaned forward to enter a few commands on the keyboard in front of his superior.

A new image appeared, inset on the digital map showing northern Russia, the Arctic Ocean, Alaska, and northern Canada. It showed a large hump-backed nuclear submarine berthed beside a pier.

"This is *Podmoskovye*, one of our *Delfin*-class SSBNs, which the Americans called Delta IVs," Golitsyn explained. "Several years ago, we stripped out her ballistic missile tubes and converted her instead to carry commandos and unmanned mini-submarines."

"If you're suggesting using this submarine to carry a Spetsnaz team to the North American coast, that still leaves our men faced with a rather long walk," Zhdanov said wryly, holding his temper in check with difficulty. He'd long known the admiral wasn't that bright. But he'd hoped Golitsyn's younger, more educated subordinates would make up for their commander's shortcomings.

"No, sir, that's not my plan," the admiral assured him earnestly. His aide typed frantically, and now the photograph disappeared, replaced by a schematic showing all of *Podmoskovye*'s compartments. Besides her twin 180-megawatt nuclear reactors, the most noticeable was a very large compartment immediately aft of her sail. A label on the diagram indicated that was a hangar where the submarine's autonomous, unmanned minisubs were usually housed, enabling them to be launched secretly while below the surface. "What we *can* do is leave *Podmoskovye*'s smaller submersible vehicles behind and use this space instead to store collapsible bladders of helicopter aviation fuel. Then a high-speed run under the polar ice cap would bring the submarine to a point not far off the enemy coast, somewhere in the

Beaufort Sea. Once there, she could break through the ice sheet and establish an improvised refueling point. In case it proves necessary to send in a Spetsnaz raiding party."

Zhdanov considered the plan and asked, "How long would it take your submarine to reach its destination?"

Once again, Golitsyn held a short, hushed consultation with his aide. "A minimum of four days."

Four days? That might as well be an eternity in the present circumstances, Zhdanov thought wearily. Then again, what other options did he have? He nodded. "Very well, Admiral. Issue the necessary orders to the Northern Fleet and *Podmoskovye*'s captain."

At last, he turned his attention to two men seated just beyond Golitsyn. One, Sergei Veselovsky, headed the Foreign Intelligence Service, the SVR. The other, Aleksandr Ivashin, led the nation's military intelligence agency, the GRU. Each man looked more like a boring, middle-aged civil servant than a spymaster responsible for orchestrating the espionage and covert operations aimed at Russia's rivals around the globe. That was good cover, Zhdanov supposed. As it was, he made it a habit to keep a very close eye on the pair of them. Overly ambitious intelligence chiefs and secret policemen were always a potential threat to any Russian ruler. "Veselovsky! Ivashin!" he barked. "Listen up!" Caught off guard, they stiffened.

Tired as he was, Zhdanov hid a pleased smile. It was a useful practice to crack the whip every now and again, if only to remind these men of who was in charge. "You're going to immediately activate all of your intelligence assets inside the United States and the People's Republic of China—including every single one of the deep-cover agents we've planted over the past three decades. If either Washington or Beijing pick up any clues to the PAK-DA bomber's whereabouts, I'd better damned well find out exactly what they've learned just as soon as they've learned it!"

TWENTY-ONE

EMERGENCY CONFERENCE ROOM,
NATIONAL MILITARY COMMAND CENTER,
UNDER THE PENTAGON, WASHINGTON, D.C.

A SHORT TIME LATER

Under the ECR's bright overhead lighting, it was impossible to tell that it was still pitch-dark outside, with more than an hour remaining before the sun rose. But in a concession to the early morning hour, coffee carafes and china cups were set out along the large central conference table.

Jonas Murphy took a cautious sip from a steaming cup and then set it back down. Miranda Reynolds, seated next to him, raised an eyebrow. "Any good?" she asked.

"It seems to contain caffeine," the director of national intelligence said thoughtfully, after a moment's consideration. "Apart from that, I refuse to testify on the grounds that it might insult our hosts."

From his position at the head of the table, Bill Taylor chuckled. "Flattery won't get you anywhere, Jonas." Then the secretary of defense nodded to

Reynolds. "Glad you could join us this morning, Ms. Reynolds. I understand we have you to thank for the extraordinary video we've all seen?"

"Yes, Mr. Secretary," the CIA's chief of clandestine operations said. The short recording he referred to was from a Russian Air Force pilot, Colonel Alexei Petrov. In it, he claimed to have successfully stolen Moscow's much-touted stealth bomber prototype. The video had been emailed to her through the same covert server used by the shadowy Russian contact she'd met in Prague. She'd immediately relayed it to Murphy, who, in turn, had passed it straight on to the defense secretary and the Joint Chiefs. Before she'd even had time to finish dressing, she'd received a secure call summoning her to this early morning conference.

"So what's your assessment of this message?" Taylor asked, not beating around the bush. "Is it genuine?"

Reynolds pursed her lips. "The man speaking does appear to be the real Alexei Petrov," she said. "His facial features are a perfect match with other verified photos in our databases." The CIA, like other intelligence agencies, amassed huge amounts of information on foreign government officials, military officers, business leaders, and the like— most of it from publicly available sources, including newspaper and magazine articles, television news broadcasts, and even internet sites. "And we can confirm that he's regarded as one of Russia's top test pilots, especially for multi-engine aircraft. Given that, it would be logical to expect him to head up their stealth bomber flight test program."

"But is there anything in the guy's record to suggest that he'd pull a stunt like this?" General Frank Neary asked suspiciously. The Air Force chief looked plainly skeptical. "I mean, Jesus, actually flying away with the most expensive and advanced experimental aircraft in the whole Russian inventory? That's not exactly like walking into an embassy somewhere and asking for political asylum!"

"No, sir," Reynolds admitted. "From what we know, Colonel Petrov was a highly decorated, highly regarded officer, one of apparently unquestioned loyalty." She smiled slightly. "Then again, if there were any obvious reasons for Moscow to believe he might defect, Petrov would be in a Russian military prison or dead, and not sending us demand notes from a stolen high-tech aircraft."

Murphy leaned forward. "Plus, he's looking at a potential cut of several billion dollars," he pointed out. "That's a darned strong possible motivation, right there."

The other men and women around the table nodded in agreement. In his recorded message, the Russian pilot had made it clear that this was an auction, with the PAK-DA bomber going to the highest bidder.

"Then you think this is the real deal?" Taylor pressed. "That one of Russia's top test pilots is actually trying to sell us his country's most valuable aircraft? A stealth bomber that he's already got safely parked in some secret hiding place?"

Miranda Reynolds shot a quick sideways glance in Murphy's direction. The DNI shrugged slightly, as if to say that it was her call. Her mouth tightened. If she walked all the way out on a limb here, what were the odds that he wouldn't just saw it off behind her the moment anything went wrong? Along with selective leaking, blame shifting was almost a professional sport for senior government officials and politicians alike . . . and Jonas Murphy, she reminded herself, was a man who wore both hats. It was effectively a coin toss, she decided. Then again, her fingerprints were already all over this bizarre situation. She wasn't going to be able to duck the responsibility, no matter how things went down. So she raised her chin and looked straight at the secretary of defense. "Yes, sir, I do. Crazy as they sound, Petrov's claims fit the facts we see."

Taylor's eyes gleamed approvingly behind his thick, black-framed glasses. "Okay then. We'll proceed, for now, on the assumption that this Russian colonel has possession of an experimental stealth bomber that we'd sure like to have . . . and that Moscow desperately wants back." He turned to Neary. "If we want to find Petrov first, General, where should we be looking?"

"I had the Air Staff work the problem, using our best guesses as to the PAK-DA bomber's fuel load and flight characteristics," Neary told him. "Their analysis strongly indicates Petrov must have landed somewhere in the Northern Hemisphere—anywhere from Russia itself to Alaska, northern Canada, or possibly Greenland. Maybe even somewhere out on the polar ice cap itself."

"That's a hell of a big patch to search," Taylor commented wryly.

"Yes, sir," the Air Force chief of staff agreed. "Several million square miles of ice, tundra, mountains, and forests for a start."

Reynolds frowned. "Hold on, wouldn't Petrov need a runway to land on—one long enough to handle a very large aircraft? Doesn't that significantly limit the places we need to look? Even if he picked an abandoned airstrip or some remote, out-of-the-way airport—"

Neary shook his head. "It's not that simple, I'm afraid. The Russians put a lot of emphasis on designing their combat aircraft to fly out of rough, improvised airfields. Given some luck and skill, all this guy would need to set down safely was a long enough stretch of compacted snow or ice." He shrugged. "We fly C-130s onto a similar snowfield down at McMurdo Station in the Antarctic. Now, I sure wouldn't try that myself with a heavy bomber, but I'm not a test pilot . . . or a Russian."

"Can we task our satellites to do the job?" Taylor asked. "We've got a number of radar and photo-imaging platforms in orbit right now."

Murphy answered this one. As DNI, both the National Reconnaissance Office and the National Geospatial-Intelligence Agency fell under his authority. "We'd have to get very lucky," he warned.

"Satellite surveillance works best against fixed installations or other targets whose coordinates are at least generally known. Expecting our analysts to zero in on a single, heavily camouflaged aircraft out in the middle of all that territory would be like expecting them to win the lottery by buying one ticket."

"So, a fifty-fifty shot, then," Taylor said with a quirky grin.

Murphy matched him with a sardonic smile of his own. "I wouldn't know, Bill. You're the Pentagon's resident Silicon Valley math nerd. By training, I'm just a simple country lawyer."

"Coordinated searches by a large number of reconnaissance aircraft and drones equipped with air-to-ground radar would be a better bet," Neary said. "At least inside our own airspace."

Reynolds felt a frown cross her face. "Can we keep that kind of effort quiet?" she asked.

"From the media?" The Air Force chief of staff shook his head. "Probably not, ma'am. Any reasonably sized effort covering that much territory would involve dozens of aircraft and hundreds of aircrew. Word would be bound to leak out, no matter how big a classified label we slapped on the operation."

Reynolds shook her head in dismay. "Which means we could end up with nothing for all our pains. Nothing, that is, except a massive ecological and political disaster and a lot of egg on all our faces."

Taylor, Murphy, and the others nodded slowly, seeing her point. In his video, the Russian pilot had warned that any American attempt to seize the

PAK-DA prototype without payment would result in its immediate destruction, along with devastating radiological consequences, thanks to the multiple 250-kiloton thermonuclear warheads stored in its weapons bays.

"That's another thing," the defense secretary said. "Is Petrov's story about having a payload of nuclear-armed cruise missiles aboard that bomber even remotely plausible?"

"If this was an American experimental aircraft, I'd say there was no way in hell," Neary told him forcefully. "But the Russians play by very different rules, especially when it comes to nukes. Hell, back during the Cuban Missile Crisis, it turns out they deployed tactical nuclear weapons that some Cuban or Soviet general could have used against our troops if we ever invaded the island—even without an explicit okay from the Kremlin. So this guy's claim that they were trying to compress their flight test program by loading armed missiles as part of a war game isn't that far-fetched."

Taylor sighed. "Which makes Ms. Reynolds right. In the circumstances, a large-scale air search effort would be too risky. We wouldn't gain anything by provoking Colonel Petrov to destroy his aircraft, especially if it does carry nuclear weapons."

From the far end of the table, Rear Admiral Kristin Chao spoke up. "We do have one possible indication of the Russian stealth bomber's whereabouts," the head of the Pentagon's operations directorate reminded them. "Our North Warning System radar station at Barter Island picked up an unidentified contact last night. At least for a few seconds, anyway. This bogey might have been the PAK-DA bomber entering our airspace."

"Or just as likely an equipment glitch or some kind of weird weather phenomenon," Neary argued. "The whole Arctic region's getting hammered by snow and ice storms right now."

"Yes, sir," the admiral agreed calmly. "But it's at least a data point."

"One that doesn't get us much further," the Air Force chief of staff retorted. "The North Warning System radar network creates a relatively thin air surveillance zone along the northern frontier of both Alaska and Canada. Once the perimeter is penetrated, we have almost no ability to track an unidentified aircraft flying deeper into the North American interior, especially if it's coming in low or has stealth features."

Chao looked unmoved. "At the very least, it suggests Colonel Petrov has chosen to conceal the bomber in territory we control, rather than inside his own country's borders. That could provide us with a useful clue to his ultimate goals."

"For God's sake, Kristin," Neary snapped, "I don't see how you can possibly draw that conclusion—"

"Hold on there, you two," Taylor interrupted, jumping in to tamp down what was threatening to become an open argument between the two high-ranking military officers. "You can't fight in here. This is the War Room."

For a moment, both the general and the admiral stared at him in astonishment. But then, almost unwillingly, they grinned sheepishly. "Sorry about that, Mr. Secretary," Neary told him. Chao nodded her own mute apology.

"Don't sweat it," Taylor said mildly. "I don't imagine anyone here got much sleep last night, so it's no surprise if tempers are a little frayed." He looked carefully around the table. "Which is why, right now, I'd like to focus our limited energies on the biggest question we face."

"Which is: do we pay Petrov to get our hands on the PAK-DA prototype?" Miranda Reynolds said quietly.

"Score one for the CIA," Taylor said with a slight smile.

Absentmindedly, Murphy rubbed at his chin, frowning a little when he felt the patches of stubble his quick shave on the way to the Pentagon had missed. "There are a lot of pluses," he said carefully. "Sure Petrov's asking for a lot of money, but conventional intelligence efforts to acquire accurate data on Russia's stealth bomber program could easily end up costing us nearly as much over time. Not to mention taking years to produce results . . . and, in all probability, yielding far less useful information. The same goes for those advanced cruise missiles he says are aboard. Not only that, but just knowing that we've got their prototype, its electronics, and its weapons payload would compel Moscow to dramatically reengineer their stealth bomber and missile programs—at a huge expenditure in time and money." He turned to General Neary. "How much did the B-2 Spirit program cost us?"

"Somewhere north of forty billion in current dollars, not counting procurement," the Air Force chief of staff told him.

Murphy nodded. "Exactly. So by spending what's basically pocket change in the context of the federal budget, we could force the Russians to pony up billions more for a whole new bomber design. It's a win-win for us."

Neary frowned deeply.

"You have a problem with the director's analysis, General?" Taylor asked.

"Yes, sir, I do," Neary said. "What if we're wrong about this? What if Petrov didn't steal the PAK-DA bomber prototype at all? What if this is just an elaborate ruse orchestrated by Russian intelligence . . . and the aircraft that we're supposedly buying is still sitting safely inside a hangar on some Russian air base?"

"Jesus," Taylor muttered. "That would be . . . bad. Very bad."

Neary nodded. "We'd get caught paying billions of taxpayer dollars to Moscow for nothing. Not only would that inflict a lethal political blow to the president and his administration, it would humiliate the entire U.S. national security establishment as well. We'd be the laughingstock of the whole world." He shrugged. "Sure, the video sent to Ms. Reynolds shows this guy Petrov in some kind of fancy cockpit. But none of us knows what the inside of the real PAK-DA bomber looks like. Nor are there any shots of the outside. For all we really know, the whole thing could easily have been shot on a GRU- or SVR-built film set."

"There is another problem, even if Petrov's offer is genuine," Rear Admiral Chao commented. "It's pretty clear that he's getting a lot of help from someone we don't know anything about. If it turns out he's in league with Russian organized crime, or drug lords, or maybe even terrorists, the blowback from our funneling so much U.S. government money to them could be horrific."

Taylor winced, obviously imagining how that would play out in Congress and the press. The defense secretary wasn't a Washington insider by experience or inclination, but even a few short months on the job had taught him the savagery with which political war was waged in the nation's capital. He sighed. "Okay, it looks like whether or not we meet Colonel Petrov's demands is a decision that's way above all our pay grades. I'll brief the president as soon as I can, but my bet is that nobody in the White House is going to want to jump in with both feet on this. Not without a hell of a lot more information than we can give them right now."

"I do have one request, Mr. Secretary," Miranda Reynolds said. "I'd like your permission to deploy the specialist go team I've organized to Joint Base Elmendorf-Richardson in Alaska."

"The one with experts from the Air Force's Foreign Material squadron?" Taylor asked.

She nodded. "Plus CIA and Air Force security personnel." She looked down the table toward Chao. "If the rear admiral is correct, and Petrov has landed somewhere in northern Alaska or northern Canada, staging out of Elmendorf would put our team in position to move fast if we spot the PAK-DA bomber on the ground. Or in case we do strike a deal."

"Good thinking," Taylor said simply. "You've got my blessing. Get your team on its way to Anchorage as soon as possible."

TWENTY-TWO

THE NEXT DAY

Totem One, a four-engine HC-130J Super Hercules combat search-and-rescue aircraft assigned to the Alaska Air National Guard's 211th Rescue Squadron, rocked and jolted and bounced through the sky. It was flying through the upper fringes of a fierce winter storm blanketing the whole state. Patches of night sky sprinkled with stars appeared and disappeared whenever the plane crossed into towering cloud banks that cut visibility to nil and then came back out into clear air.

"Cripes," Major Jack "Ripper" Ingalls muttered, gripping the steering yoke tight. "I think General Arcaro hates me."

His copilot, Captain Laura "Skater" Van Horn, shook her head. "No, he doesn't hate you, Rip."

"He doesn't?"

She smiled. "Nope. His feelings toward you go way beyond simple hatred. In fact, I'd say he despises you with all the passion of a thousand hot, flaming suns." She nodded out the cockpit windows at the boiling sea of clouds. "I mean, why else assign us a 'routine' night training flight—right in the middle of the first really big storm of this season?"

Ingalls laughed. "Well, the general said he thought it'd be a good way to keep our flying skills honed."

Van Horn snorted. "Uh-huh. And King David told Bathsheba's husband, Uriah the Hittite, he wanted him to lead in battle because it was an honor."

"You know, your analysis of this situation isn't exactly making me feel better about myself, Skater," Ingalls said. He kept his eyes moving over the cockpit's multifunction displays and gauges. "Remind me to have you read that Air Force pamphlet on the importance of maintaining high crew morale once we get back to base."

She pretended to sigh loudly. "What, *again*?"

"Yes, *again*," the HC-130 pilot said firmly, with a quick, sidelong smile.

"You know, touchy-feely stuff like that is probably why Arcaro hates you so much," Van Horn said with a grin of her own.

Ingalls shrugged. "A man's gotta do what a—" A sudden alarm and a red caution and warning light cut him off short.

"Number Two engine shutdown," Van Horn said sharply. She toggled a switch. "Fire handle pulled." And then another. "Engine Start switch to stop. Fuel pump secured." Swiftly, she scanned their ACAWS— Advisory, Caution, and Warning System—message text. "Gearbox Two, no oil pressure."

Ingalls ran his eyes over his own display. "I confirm Gearbox Two, no oil pressure." He glanced out the cockpit window at their left wing. The six-bladed propeller on the inmost engine was stationary. "Number Two is feathered. No signs of a fire."

"For small favors, let us be very, very grateful," Van Horn said devoutly. She glanced at the pilot. "Okay, Rip, what now?"

"Now you take the aircraft," he said, sounding perfectly calm and in control. "Thus allowing me, as the august aircraft commander, to focus all my attention on managing this deplorable situation."

She nodded, settling her hands firmly on the yoke in front of her and giving it a quick shake to verify that she did indeed have her hands on the yoke. "Yes, sir. I have the aircraft."

"You have the aircraft, Captain," Ingalls confirmed formally, slightly relaxing his own grip. He keyed his radio mike. "Elmendorf Control, this is Totem One. I am declaring an in-flight emergency. We've lost our Number Two engine. No fire, repeat, no fire."

"*Copy that, Totem,*" an air traffic controller replied. "*Advise your intention.*"

Ingalls considered that. Technically, their HC-130J was rated to continue missions with the loss of a single engine. That was especially true for this training flight, without any heavy cargo or passengers aboard the aircraft. But the idea of trying to make it back to Joint Base Elmendorf-Richardson, nearly five hundred nautical miles away, in the middle of a storm, wasn't that appealing—especially down one engine for unknown causes. If one engine could crap out like this, there was no guarantee that a second and a third wouldn't do the same thing at the worst possible moment. Eielson Air Force Base at Fairbanks was considerably closer, but it would still take them forty-five minutes to get there. And the most direct flight path to Eielson meant crossing the Brooks Range, some of the highest and most rugged country in all of Alaska. Yeah, no thanks on that, he decided.

"What's the status of Deadhorse?" he radioed. The airport serving the Prudhoe Bay oil fields was just sixty nautical miles northeast of their current position. It didn't have a control tower, but at least the runway was paved.

"*Deadhorse is shut down,*" the controller reported. "*Visibility is currently nil, with blowing snow and very high winds.*"

"Crap," Ingalls muttered. "Okay, how about Barter Island?"

"*Wait one.*"

Van Horn shook her head. "Barter Island? Man, that's the back end of nowhere. I've flown in there a couple of times. It's just a gravel strip." The aircraft hit another pocket of turbulence and shook from end to end. "Which on a night like this is going to be ass-deep in snow and ice."

Ingalls shrugged. "Right now, I'll take just about any runway in a storm, Skater. And if we lose another engine, I'm gonna be happy if we can even find some relatively flat piece of tundra to set down on."

"*Totem, this is Elmendorf,*" the air controller's voice said through his headset. "*There's a small secu-*

*rity detachment posted at the radar station there. I just
checked with them. They report the storm's died down a
little there, with north winds diminishing to about half
of what they were an hour ago. The ceiling's only around
fifteen hundred feet and visibility's not great, maybe a
mile, maybe less. There may also be debris on the runway. Our guys are moving out now to check that and
clear the strip if necessary—but they say it'll take some
time.*"

"Copy that, Elmendorf," Ingalls said, pulling up
Barter Island on his navigation display. "Tell that
security detachment we're heading their way. We
should be overhead in about thirty minutes. Whatever they can do to clear the runway by then will
be much appreciated, but we're going to try to set
this crate down fast . . . before the storm closes in
again."

"*Understood, Totem,*" the controller replied. "*And
good luck.*"

Ingalls glanced across the cockpit. "Okay, Skater,
let's come to zero-four-five. But take it real easy
on your turn, okay? Keep your angle of bank well
under twenty-five degrees and watch your airspeed
and power settings."

"Copy that," Van Horn said tightly. They needed
to bank left, which meant turning into their dead
Number Two engine. With the aircraft's three other
engines still operational, that was doable. Still, extreme caution was necessary to avoid any risk of losing control due to asymmetric thrust. Slowly, she
turned her steering yoke. Her eyes darted across

her displays and gauges to make sure there were no other developing problems.

Gingerly, the Super Hercules rolled gently left—gradually coming around to the northeast as it headed directly toward Barter Island through a storm-cloud-covered night sky.

A SHORT TIME LATER

Through his night vision goggles, Captain Nick Flynn could just about make out the far end of the snow-covered runway. Beyond that, a glittering haze of blowing snow and ice crystals obscured everything. Since he was roughly two-thirds of the way down the strip, he estimated that put current visibility at a little more than half a mile. The wind must be starting to strengthen again, he thought grimly. Not exactly great timing, since that crippled HC-130J couldn't be more than a few minutes out.

Pairs of glowing yellow lights stretched away in both directions. They marked the edges of the hundred-foot-wide runway. Silhouetted against those lights, the soldiers and airmen of his Joint Force team were frantically clearing away pieces of windblown debris that littered the snow. The fierce blizzard that had been pounding Kaktovik and the radar station for more than two days had torn shingles, pieces of metal siding, canvas tarps, and even satellite dishes loose, along with bags of trash, broken-down cardboard boxes, empty barrels, and other abandoned objects—sending them all skittering across the open tundra. This mix of FOD, foreign object debris, was now a serious threat to the big turboprop headed here for an emergency landing. Metal shards or other solid trash sucked into the Super Hercules's propellers or engine intakes during landing could easily cause catastrophic damage.

Painfully aware that they were running very low on time to get this job done, Flynn got back to work. He leaned over, grabbed a bent section of siding half buried in the surface, and yanked hard. Nothing. The damn thing didn't move an inch. Grunting, he tightened his grip and yanked even harder. This time it broke free from the ice and came loose in his gloved hands. Like a discus thrower, he spun around in a single motion and hurled the piece of crumpled siding away from the runway as hard as he could. A powerful gust caught the warped metal panel and sent it spinning end over end through the air.

Senior Airman Mark Mitchell grabbed his arm. "Sir!" the radioman screamed into his ear to be heard over the north wind shrieking low across the island. He held up the handset connected to their AN/PRC-162 radio. "I've got contact with that Herky Bird. They're on final right now! They want our guys off the runway, ASAP!"

Flynn snapped his head around and looked west. He spotted a faint glow low in the sky there. The HC-130J had its high-intensity landing lights on, spearing through the darkness and the curtain of blowing snow and ice. That glow was growing brighter fast. The big aircraft must be coming straight in at more than 150 knots. "Pass the word, M-Squared," he yelled at the radioman. "Tell everyone to clear the strip! You go, too! Now!"

"Yes, sir!" Mitchell nodded frantically. Shouting into the handset to relay the order, he turned and jogged away.

Flynn swung around through a full circle and saw the rest of his men scattering off the runway. All except one. About a hundred yards away, the short, square-shouldered figure of Private First Class Cole Hynes hadn't budged. The soldier had his head down while he stubbornly wrestled with another big piece of debris. He didn't seem to have heard the order to get clear. And he was apparently too fixated on his task to notice that everybody else around him was bailing out.

Damn it, Flynn thought. Maybe the other man's radio was broken. Or maybe its batteries were dead, drained by the subzero temperatures. He cupped his hands and yelled as loudly as he could. "Hynes!"

It was useless. The howling wind caught his voice and tore it to shreds.

Down at the far end of the runway, the big HC-130J appeared suddenly out of the darkness and snow. It was no more than fifty feet above the ground and descending rapidly.

Shit, Flynn realized. He was out of time. Frantically, he sprinted toward Hynes, who had his back to the oncoming Super Hercules. He didn't waste any more breath yelling.

The aircraft touched down hard, bounced once, and then settled firmly onto the ground— thundering straight down the runway right at the two men. Plumes of pulverized snow and ice sprayed out behind its massive landing gear and whirling propellers.

At the last moment, Hynes looked up, brushing at the snow dusting his goggles with an irritated gesture. His mouth opened in surprise. "Hey, Cap—"

And Flynn, still running all out, threw himself forward—and slammed straight into the shorter enlisted man. The hard, diving tackle knocked Hynes backward off his feet, with Flynn ending up on top. Desperately, he buried his face into the icy surface of the runway . . . just as the left wing of the speeding Super Hercules slashed past right overhead.

For a split second, the whole universe became a hurricane-force maelstrom of shattering, deafening noise and pounding winds, snow, and razor-sharp fragments of ice. And then, blessedly, the noise and pummeling died away.

Dazed, Flynn slowly raised his head and looked behind him. The HC-130J was slowing fast as it neared the end of the runway. Painfully, he levered himself back up to his knees.

"Ow," Hynes said, sounding aggrieved. "Geez, that fucking *hurt*." His eyes focused on the man who'd just knocked him on his ass. "Uh, I mean, that fucking hurt, *sir*."

"Yeah, I bet it did," Flynn agreed with a wide grin. He climbed back to his feet and then helped the enlisted man up. He nodded toward where the big four-engine turboprop had finally come to a stop with its propellers still turning, just before it ran out of runway and risked skidding off across the icy tundra. "But maybe not as much as getting sliced into a bazillion pieces by one of those propeller blades, right?"

"No, sir," Hynes agreed fervently. "And thanks for not letting me get killed, sir."

"Too much paperwork involved, PFC," Flynn said, still smiling. "Fortunately for you, I'm lazy that way."

About an hour later, once they'd finished helping the HC-130J's aircrew tie their big plane down and cover its engine cowlings and sensor pods against possible flying ice and hail damage, Flynn had time to welcome the two Air National Guard pilots and their staff sergeant loadmaster a little more formally. Which, since they were all exhausted and freezing, pretty much consisted of a quick handshake and nod across the aisle of the bus as it drove away from the airport.

"Skater and I sure appreciate your guys' hard work out there, Nick," Ingalls told him tiredly. "If we'd had to try setting down with all that FOD still littering the runway, we'd have been in a world of hurt."

"Heck, I've been wanting to add my own aviation component to this half-assed command," Flynn said. "Now it looks like I'm finally getting my wish."

The copilot, a pretty brunette named Van Horn, choked back a laugh. "Just until the weather clears enough for JBER to fly in mechanics and spare parts to fix that dud engine of ours," she warned.

Flynn peered out through the windshield. Even with the headlights, it was now basically impossible to see more than a couple of dozen yards, if that. The brief lull in the storm was over and they were trapped again in the heart of a blizzard howling across the treeless, little island at full force. "That could be a while," he commented mildly.

The others nodded. "Welcome to winter in Alaska," Ingalls agreed with resignation. "Starts in the fall and doesn't end until sometime around summer. I figure we're probably stuck here for at least a couple of days, maybe more."

"Well, it's not all that bad around here," Flynn told them.

Van Horn looked surprised. "It's not?"

Flynn leaned back out of the way of the punch he thought might be coming his way in a second. "Nope," he said wryly. "It's much worse."

"I would kill you for that," Laura Van Horn said with an answering smile. "But I'm too darned tired. So maybe I'll take my revenge later, Captain Flynn."

TWENTY-THREE

THE NEXT DAY

Piotr Zhdanov watched in frustration as search area after search area shown on a large digital map of Russia turned green—indicating that concentrated sweeps by Tu-214R, Tu-142, and IL-38 reconnaissance planes had come up empty. "You're quite sure about these results?" he demanded. "After all, Petrov and his coconspirators have almost certainly camouflaged the PAK-DA prototype by now, and swept away any traces left by his landing on a snow or ice field. Couldn't your pilots and aircrews simply have missed them?"

"That is highly unlikely, Mr. President," Lieutenant General Rogozin said patiently. "We've subjected the most probable landing fields to repeated overflights. We've even done the same with many of those places that our planners consider far less suitable. In addition, we've deployed Spetsnaz units and other Army formations to multiple possible sites to confirm those negative results. So far, we haven't found a single trace of the stealth bomber inside our own national territory."

Zhdanov sighed. "So, then, where is he? And where is our missing stealth bomber?"

"Hidden somewhere on the North American continent," Rogozin said bluntly. "It's the safest place for Petrov, because it's the most difficult for us to search . . . or to attack."

"And how much progress have you made in carrying out reconnaissance flights over this region?" Zhdanov asked coldly.

"Not much," Rogozin admitted.

"Show me."

Wordlessly, the general brought up a new map on the command center's wall screen. It depicted the northern third of the North American continent—from Alaska in the west to the vast ice shelf of Greenland in the east. Comparatively tiny half circles colored green showed the areas probed by Russia's long-range reconnaissance aircraft so far. Fewer than half a dozen of them dotted North America's long coastline fronting the Arctic Ocean. In no case had a Tu-142 or an IL-38 succeeded in penetrating more than a few miles inside American or Canadian airspace before being intercepted and turned back by F-22 Raptors and CF-18 Hornets.

"*Mater' Bozh'ya!*" Zhdanov scoffed. "Mother of God! All you've done is nibble around the edges!" He glared at Rogozin. "Were your pilots and crews waiting for engraved invitations from Washington and Ottawa before doing their fucking jobs?"

"No, sir," Rogozin said quietly, not rising to the bait. "But it's taking time to move the air tankers and other assets needed by our fighter escorts into position—especially with the bad weather affecting the region. So up to now, all of our flights have been unescorted and vulnerable."

Zhdanov frowned. "How much longer will it take to assemble the necessary fighters and other planes?"

"One more day."

"Which will put us well beyond Petrov's first seventy-two-hour deadline," Zhdanov pointed out bitterly.

"Yes, sir," Rogozin said. "And his price to return the PAK-DA and its weapons payload to us will go up."

"Screw his price," Zhdanov growled. "The only thing that traitor's going to get from me is a missile down his throat or a bullet in the back of his skull. What worries me more is the possibility that he'll decide to sell out to the Americans first." His frown deepened. "We're not going to get too many more bites at the apple before that happens. So it's imperative that you concentrate these first fighter-escorted air searches on the most likely hiding places."

Rogozin stared back at him. "I'm not sure we can hope to do that," he said carefully. "Colonel Petrov had enough fuel on board to reach any possible landing site in several million square kilometers of North American wilderness. We simply don't have any evidence yet that would help us narrow that down significantly."

"That may not be quite true," another voice interrupted.

Startled, both Zhdanov and Rogozin swung around toward another of the several men seated around the table. On the principle that the less said the better when their leader was getting bad news, Kokorin, Yumashev, and the rest of the Russian president's senior military and civilian advisers had kept their mouths shut over the past several minutes. But now, Aleksandr Ivashin, the head of the GRU, had evidently decided it was worth the risk to join the discussion.

Zhdanov's eyes narrowed. That meant Ivashin had something up his sleeve, something he was confident would make him look good. Cautious by nature and training, the spymaster was not a fool. "You've picked up Petrov's trail?" he guessed.

"Part of it, perhaps," Ivashin said calmly. "Maybe enough to help General Rogozin's pilots refine their search parameters."

"Go on."

Ivashin indicated the computer console at his place. Through it he had secure communications links to the GRU's Moscow headquarters. "One of our deep-cover illegals in northern Alaska has reported in," he said. "According to this agent, one of the American air surveillance radars briefly picked up a faint, unidentified contact very close to the Alaska coast on the night Petrov disappeared. It was still flying south when it disappeared a short time later."

"Where would that take him?" Zhdanov demanded.

Responding to Ivashin's commands, the map display zoomed in to show the area between Prudhoe Bay and the western edge of Canada's Yukon Territory in the north and a little American town called Beaver and Ni'iinlii Njik, a Canadian national park, in the south. The enclosed region was still enormous, encompassing more than two hundred thousand square kilometers—mostly comprised of rugged mountains and uninhabited wilderness, including the Arctic National Wildlife Refuge. The head of the GRU pointed at the map. "Somewhere in there, possibly. Obviously, we can't be sure of that, but, assuming what the Americans picked up on their radar was, in fact, our stolen stealth bomber, this area seems the logical place to start looking."

Zhdanov sucked in his cheeks. "Is your agent reliable?"

"Completely reliable," Ivashin assured him. "We successfully infiltrated this particular illegal into Alaska years ago. And over that time, our agent has built up a very substantial network of useful information sources, including some inside the American military, local civilian government, and important regional private industries. The intelligence we've obtained has always proved to be accurate and extremely valuable."

Zhdanov nodded. He turned back to Rogozin. "Your opinion, Yvgeny?"

The Air Force commander studied the display very closely for a few moments more. He looked at Ivashin. "What is the Americans' own evaluation of this short radar trace? Do you know?"

"At the time, they seem to have assessed it as more likely to be a minor equipment malfunction or a natural phenomenon than a genuine air contact," Ivashin told him. "But my agent believes their views may have changed recently."

"Why?"

"Because the Americans have just flown a special team into their joint Army and Air Force base near Anchorage—a team that apparently includes intelligence specialists . . . and scientists and engineers trained in exploiting and analyzing foreign aircraft and aviation technology."

Rogozin took a short, sharp breath. "Well, that tears it," he said quietly. He turned to Zhdanov with a worried look. "I'll organize an armed reconnaissance mission over that area as rapidly as possible, Mr. President. We could be in a race now, a race where we're already starting out behind."

TWENTY-FOUR

The cavernous Emergency Conference Room seemed oddly vacant now to Jonas Murphy. Only the most senior members of the U.S. national security establishment—basically just the defense secretary, the members of the Joint Chiefs of Staff, and the director of national intelligence—had been allowed inside for this secure videoconference with NORAD's top commanders. The rows of chairs ordinarily set aside for aides and other officials sat empty. Instead, relayed by satellite from their command post inside Cheyenne Mountain, the televised images of General Keith Makowski and his Canadian deputy, Lieutenant General Peter Gowan, looked out from the ECR's large central screen.

"Your most recent reports don't exactly make reassuring reading, gentlemen," Defense Secretary Bill Taylor observed, holding up a sheaf of documents marked TOP SECRET.

On-screen, Makowski nodded. "That's true, Mr. Secretary." He looked dead serious. "Then again,

Pete and I didn't write them to be reassuring. Just accurate."

Beside him, Gowan leaned forward, bringing his lean features a little closer to the camera. "Unfortunately, happy talk from us won't change the situation we face," he said. "The harsh reality is that these repeated Russian probes of our airspace are imposing very serious strains on NORAD's forces and readiness levels. Remember, intercepting incoming Russian reconnaissance aircraft, especially those trying to penetrate the Arctic coastlines of our two countries, requires very long flights and multiple air refueling operations—all in potentially hazardous weather conditions. Put in the simplest terms, the current need to fly these missions virtually around the clock is rapidly exhausting the endurance of both our pilots and our ground crews."

"They're also wearing the shit out of our aircraft," Makowski added. "Look, it's hard enough to keep the Alaska-based F-22 Raptors flight-ready during normal winter conditions. They're beautiful machines, but they're doggone temperamental—especially with their stealth features, like those special radar-absorbent skin coatings."

Murphy knew that was true. As DNI, he had access to every piece of classified information produced by the U.S. military. Even at the best of times, some F-22 squadrons had only around half of their fighters ready to fly, with the rest down for needed maintenance.

"As of right now, this increased ops tempo is sidelining more and more of our Raptors, both with regular mechanical issues and weather-related skin damage," Makowski continued. "If Moscow keeps pushing this hard, in a week, or maybe less, I'll be damned lucky to be able to put a third of my aircraft out on the flight line."

"The same goes double for the RCAF," Gowan agreed. "Our CF-18 Hornets are more than forty years old now. Just to keep enough aircraft flight-ready at our four remote operating locations, we're constantly having to rotate fighters and pilots forward from our main bases at Cold Lake in Alberta and Bagotville in Quebec." His eyes darkened. "The situation simply isn't sustainable, at least not if the Russians continue probing our perimeter this way for much longer."

Taylor nodded somberly. "I get that, General Gowan." He looked up at the two faces on-screen. "What I need now from both of you is an assessment of Moscow's possible reasons for this sudden surge of air reconnaissance activity along our borders."

"Look, I don't have a crystal ball to read that asshole Zhdanov's mind," Makowski replied. "But I can tell you what Pete and I are most worried about."

Taylor nodded. "Go on, General."

"We're worried that Russians could be wearing our defenses down deliberately," Makowski said. "That they're using provocative measures just short of open hostilities to test our air defense system—and find its breaking point." He looked grim. "When you put that possibility together with the fact that the whole fricking Russian strategic bomber and fighter force has gone on high alert, well, it paints a real ugly picture."

Murphy lowered his own gaze to hide his expression. The CIA-provided intelligence which suggested that the Russian patrol aircraft were only searching for their own stolen stealth bomber prototype was tightly restricted, as was the video of Petrov supposedly offering to sell the PAK-DA to the United States. And as it was, neither Makowski nor Gowan were in that loop. He wondered how a fuller understanding of the possible situation might change their views. Then again, he thought with an inner shrug, maybe it wouldn't matter to them. Several of those who were already cleared to know about Petrov's claimed defection, including General Neary, the Air Force chief of staff, were inclined to think the whole story was nothing more than classic Russian disinformation, part of a typical *maskirovka* operation to mislead Moscow's adversaries about its true plans and intentions.

"We're drawing up plans now to reinforce you with fighter squadrons and more tankers from other bases in the continental United States," Taylor assured the two NORAD commanders.

Makowski nodded. "We appreciate that, Mr. Secretary. And we can sure use every new plane you send our way." He spread his hands. "But no matter how much you expedite those reinforcements, it's still going to take several days to move the aircraft, the equipment, spare parts, and munitions required to support them, and their personnel to where we need them. And even then, we'll have to run the arriving pilots and ground crews through some intensive refresher training before they can be assigned to intercept missions. Flying safely in the kind of severe weather conditions our guys are facing right now isn't easy."

"I imagine not," Taylor said quietly. He sighed. "All right, gentlemen, all we can ask is that your pilots continue to hold the line for now—at least until the additional squadrons we're deploying are ready to relieve them."

"We'll do our best," Makowski promised. "Our people are dead tired, for sure. But morale is still high. We're not going to let any Russian son of a bitch slip through unchallenged. Not while we have the watch."

A SHORT TIME LATER

Seated inside the PAK-DA's cockpit, Colonel Alexei Petrov plugged his portable computer into the stealth bomber's secure communications system and powered it up. Then he entered a code sequence provided by Pavel Voronin weeks ago. The screen flickered oddly for several seconds and then stabilized to show Voronin's face. Although the background was blurred out, Dmitri Grishin's top troubleshooter appeared relaxed and confident, as always.

"It's good to see you, Alexei," Voronin said with a faint smile. "Even if you do look like shit."

Petrov laughed bitterly. "If I do, at least I have a good excuse. You try getting any sleep in the middle of the worst fucking blizzard anyone's ever seen! Between the wind, the goddamned dark, and the balls-freezing cold, this place isn't exactly a rest camp, you know. I spend half my waking hours out there with Bondarovich and the rest of your security team, fixing wind and ice damage to our tents and the aircraft shelter. And the other half checking over this bomber's electronics and other systems to make sure everything's still working right."

"You have my sympathies," Voronin said insincerely. He shrugged. "On the other hand, all this terrible weather is perfect for our purposes, true?"

"True," Petrov allowed. Then he frowned. "But the same conditions that make us hard to find also make it impossible for me to take off again. These strong northerly crosswinds from out of the mountains basically pin my aircraft in place."

Voronin waved that away. "This storm will pass soon enough. Maybe even sometime in the next twenty-four hours. Or so the meteorologists promise." He shrugged his shoulders again. "Besides, where would you go right now?"

Petrov dodged answering what the other man only meant as a rhetorical question. What he ultimately planned and what he wanted Voronin and his oligarch employer to know were two very different things. He scowled. "That's another thing, Pavel. Why haven't we heard anything from Zhdanov or the Americans yet? What the devil are they waiting for? By now, they have to understand that we're not bullshitting here. And don't make the mistake of thinking that it's just my nerves that are starting to fray. Your ex-Spetsnaz commandos are getting pretty edgy, too."

"Patience, Alexei," the other man said coolly. "You can't expect politicians to part with such large sums of money so easily. Both sides just need a little more time to come to terms with the unpleasant reality they face. Once they understand that paying us is the only way to get control of the stealth bomber you've stolen, they'll cough up fast enough."

Petrov eyed him narrowly. "Do you have any proof of that?"

Voronin nodded. "My sources indicate that pressure is mounting on both Moscow and Washington. Soon enough, one side or the other will realize the silly-ass military games they're playing are counterproductive and very, very dangerous . . . and that meeting your stated price is the much-safer and much-easier option."

"I hope you're right," Petrov said tightly.

Voronin laughed. "Don't worry, Alexei. All you and the others need to do right now is keep your heads down for a little while longer. Except for those couple of minor glitches in the beginning, everything's gone according to plan." His expression turned slightly more serious. "Along those lines, though, has your unwanted passenger General Mavrichev's body turned up yet?"

Petrov shook his head. "Not yet. We took advantage of a short break in the storm yesterday to mount a quick search. Unfortunately, Bondarovich's men couldn't find any sign of him or the snowmobile before the weather closed in again."

"But you're sure he's dead?"

"Completely sure," Petrov said flatly. "Between the bullet I put in his back and the subzero temperatures, Mavrichev was effectively a corpse the moment he disappeared into the night. Even if it took him a while to die, there's nowhere he could have gone to find help. Not with the nearest village more than a hundred kilometers away."

Voronin nodded. "Good," he said with a pleased smile. "Then that's one less complication for us to worry about." He looked more closely at Petrov. "In the meantime, do your best to relax, Colonel—despite the hellish conditions. Think about the rather large fortune you're about to make, instead."

"Yes, because that will keep me warm when I'm outside freezing my ass off in the wind and trying to tie down another fucking camouflage panel that's ripped loose for the hundredth time," Petrov snapped sourly.

"It can't hurt, though, can it?" the other man said, not hiding his amusement. "Anyway, I'll contact you as soon as I have any news. For now, Voronin out." The screen went blank.

Impatiently, Petrov disconnected his computer from the PAK-DA's instrument panel and closed it down. Grishin and his suave assistant must think he was a complete fool, he thought in irritation, or else made blind by the prospect of riches and the power that wealth conveyed. Well, maybe that wasn't so surprising. Both the oligarch and Voronin were driven themselves by the desire for ever-greater wealth and power . . . and like many civilians they mistakenly believed the two things were one and the same.

But real power came in many different forms, Petrov knew. Soon enough, he would prove that—not just to Grishin and Voronin, but to the whole world.

Somewhere inside the back of his skull, he felt another wave of pressure building up. With a grimace, he shook out another couple of pain pills and forced himself to choke them down.

Then, oppressed by the sudden feeling that his time might be even shorter than he'd supposed, Petrov leaned forward and activated the PAK-DA's navigation system. One of the bomber's large multifunction displays lit up. Several more quick taps on the glowing touch screen retrieved an intricate mission plan that he'd been devising ever since he'd learned about the tumor growing inside his brain. Fittingly, he'd named this plan *Vikhr*, Whirlwind— after a malignant wind spirit in Russian folklore. And the day was fast approaching, he knew, when he would sow the wind, and leave millions of others to suffer the whirlwind that must follow in his wake. Almost obsessively, he started working through the plan again, checking and rechecking his calculations for flight times and fuel consumption.

TWENTY-FIVE

KAKTOVIK, ALASKA

A FEW HOURS LATER

Captain Nick Flynn glanced around the little hotel's dining room. It wasn't exactly fancy, but it was reasonably comfortable, warm, and well lit—though maybe a little too well lit for his present purposes. Meals were ordinarily served buffet style, but since he and Captain Laura Van Horn were the only ones eating here tonight, the cook had made a show of bringing plates of something resembling chicken marsala, rice pilaf, and steamed broccoli directly to their booth, even going so far as to adopt an outrageously fake French waiter's accent in the process.

That had sparked a strangled laugh from the stranded HC-130J's attractive brunette copilot. "Gosh, I didn't expect dinner theater," she remarked to Flynn once the inn's grinning cook had sauntered back to his kitchen.

"Kaktovik is a lot more sophisticated than you might first think," he responded with a smile.

Van Horn nodded. "So I gathered from the perfectly nice, store-bought curtains in my room here. Despite all the dire warnings you gave me on the bus last night, this quaint little inn does *not* actually use strips of cardboard cut from packing boxes for window coverings."

"They don't?" Flynn said, pretending to be surprised. "Well, there you go. Sophistication at its peak. After all, this *is* the biggest town for more than a hundred miles in any direction."

She wagged an accusing finger at him. "Uh, Nick, I hate to break it to you this way, but Kaktovik is also the *only* town for a hundred miles in any direction."

"Let's not quibble over the choice of a mere adjective," he said loftily. "I say *biggest*, you say *only*. What matters most is that we're both totally correct."

Van Horn laughed. "Fair enough." Then her expression turned more serious. She looked across her plate at him. "Which makes me wonder just how a regular U.S. Air Force officer, especially one who doesn't come across like he has his head stuck up his ass, ended up getting posted out here in the back of nowhere." She cocked her head to one side. "I'm kind of guessing it wasn't because you made a career-winning move in your last assignment."

To his surprise, Flynn wasn't as irritated by her probing question as he would have expected. Maybe it was the way she asked it, which seemed honestly sympathetic rather than judgmental. And maybe it was because she was the best-looking woman in uniform he'd seen for weeks. Well, admittedly, borrowing her own joke, she was also the *only* woman in uniform he'd seen for weeks. But there was something that made him want to trust her. "You'd guess right," he told her with a tight shrug.

"Care to fill me in?" Van Horn asked, genuinely curious now.

"I wish I could," he told her truthfully. "But I really can't. Let's just say I ended up in the wrong place, at the wrong time, with exactly the wrong people."

Her bright blue eyes widened a fraction. "Oh, wow. Don't tell me you got caught dallying with your commanding officer's wife/girlfriend/daughter?"

"Did you seriously just use 'dallying' in a sentence?" Flynn laughed.

Van Horn reddened slightly. "I read a lot of old British mysteries. Sorry."

"Don't worry, I won't tell anybody. Your secret is safe with me." Then he sobered up. "But, no, as it happens, I wasn't messing around with my senior officer's wife or daughter. Or his girlfriend." He raised an eyebrow. "So you think of me as a Don Juan type, huh?"

"'Don Juan'? Now look who's the nerd!"

Flynn gave her an abashed smile of his own. "Yeah, I majored in English Language and Literature and took tons of humanities courses in college. Definitely non-STEM." He tapped his chest. "Hence the lack of pilot's wings."

"I can see that I'm not the only one around here with a somewhat dubious background," she commented archly. "But no, Nick, to answer your sort of desperate question, you don't come across as a Don Juan." Then she chuckled. "Or maybe I just haven't gotten to know you well enough yet."

Well, that seemed promising, Flynn thought a bit smugly.

"So if you weren't caught with the wrong woman, what did you do to piss off the powers-that-be enough to get stuck out here? I mean, making sure the polar bears don't decide to walk off with Barter Island's nice, rusting radar station doesn't seem like a good match for your skills." Van Horn looked at him with a puzzled expression.

"It's classified."

"*Classified?* Classified as in 'It's embarrassing and I'd rather not tell you'? Or classified as in 'Seriously spooky stuff'?"

Flynn tried to adopt a casual attitude of indifference and knew he'd failed miserably. Finally, he said, "The spooky sort."

"And whatever happened still really pisses you off," she realized, reading the look on his face.

He made himself shrug. "Well, it has forced me to seriously reevaluate my military career. For example, my whole 'get promoted to general and live a life of idleness and luxury' plan might need to be scrapped."

"You know, civilian life isn't *so* bad," Van Horn said in an obvious bid to help change the subject. "Sometimes I don't even cry when I head out from Elmendorf-Richardson to go home."

Flynn couldn't help laughing. "Yeah, you've got a point there. So, uh, Laura . . . what do you do when you're not wearing a uniform?" Casually, he took a sip of his coffee.

Van Horn coughed out a laugh. "Is that your way

to wrangle an invitation to see me out of my uniform?"

Startled, Flynn said, "No, no, that's not what I meant! I mean, well . . . I just meant, um, what do you do in your civilian life?" He focused intently on his coffee.

Pleased at the reaction she'd provoked, Van Horn grinned broadly. "Sorry, but that was an easy setup. Actually, I fly for a company that hauls air freight between here and the Lower Forty-Eight. We handle a little bit of everything—airmail packages, crates of wine, medications . . . all kinds of stuff. Once we even hauled a red Corvette."

"A Corvette?" Flynn asked, surprised.

She nodded. "There was this oil company exec who wound up being transferred from Houston to Prudhoe Bay. Seems he couldn't bear to leave his baby behind. Or even wait for it to be shipped by sea." She shook her head in regret. "Man, I hate to think about what that beautiful car looked like after its first winter up here."

"Weren't you tempted to 'lose it' in transit?" he asked mischievously. "Just to save such a nice sports car from getting all banged-up and rusty, I mean."

"Oh hell yes!" Van Horn smiled to show she wasn't serious. "The only trouble was I couldn't quite figure out how to pull the Corvette off our plane without anyone noticing."

Flynn nodded slowly. "I see. So essentially you're telling me that you're a wannabe air pirate."

Van Horn leaned back in the booth and stared at

Flynn appraisingly. "I'm a woman with many talents."

For just a moment, he envisioned the curvy Laura Van Horn in skintight leather leaning against a red Corvette. His pants suddenly felt too tight and he realized he really had been stuck out here in the icy boonies for *way* too long. "Uh, yeah," he said hoarsely. "Sure." He was grateful that there was a table between them as he tried to change the image in his mind.

Van Horn took pity on him and changed the subject again. "So what's the deal with the guys in this security unit of yours? I know the military's gone all gung-ho on 'jointness' these days, but that's a pretty wild grab-bag assortment you've got there— Army, Air Force, and Army National Guard, right?"

Glad to be able to focus on work, he nodded. "I keep hoping to snag a Marine, a Coastie, and someone from the Space Force so I can make a full set." He shrugged. "No joy there, yet."

"And are they as good at causing trouble as you are?" she asked curiously, smiling slightly to take the sting away.

Flynn laughed. "Like you wouldn't believe!" And then, before he knew it, he found himself telling her funny stories about the assortment of military-grade-A oddballs, misfits, and overall "square peg in a round hole" types he'd found himself saddled with the day they all flew into Barter Island. Everything from M-Squared's elaborate pranks that almost always backfired on him to Private Vucovich's failed effort to set up an illicit moonshine still in one of the radar station's unused storage sheds. "Fortunately, no one was hurt when it exploded," he finished. "But Vucovich did find himself spending a couple of very cold and very lonely hours picking half-fermented potato slices out of the snow."

"Oh, holy *crap*," Van Horn choked. She dabbed at the tears of laughter in her eyes. "I sure wish I'd been there to see his face when that contraption blew sky-high!"

"It was truly a sight to behold," Flynn admitted. "It was all there, everything from the agony of defeat to the thrill of seeing a ten-foot-high ball of flame billow above the tundra, and knowing it was all his doing."

She shook her head helplessly, fighting down another wave of uncontrolled laughter. Then she looked straight across the table at him. "And despite all of this stuff, you're really proud of your team, aren't you, Nick? Or, at least proud of what you've made of them."

Caught off guard, Flynn thought about it for a long moment. Then he nodded. "Yeah," he said slowly. "Yeah, I guess I am. They've come a long way."

Over the past weeks, under the pressure of hard work and rigorous training, they'd gone from a bunch of discontented, doggedly separate individuals to a cohesive, effective military unit. It would be going too far to say that any of them were really happy about being stationed at Barter Island. In fact, if he ever heard someone singing the praises of the radar station, he'd probably be tempted to arrange an immediate psych eval. But his men had definitely come together as a group. And despite all the hardships, they appeared determined to do the job they'd been sent here to do and to do it well—no matter how crazy the Pentagon's idea of guarding the radar station against a physical attack still seemed.

"But that's mostly Andy Takirak's doing, I think," Flynn heard himself saying. "I really lucked out there. He's probably one of the best NCOs I've ever run into."

Van Horn smiled at him. "From your description of him earlier, he does sound like a true paragon of all the military virtues, combined with the wilderness survival skills of an Alaskan Inuit," she teased.

"He's not perfect," Flynn protested. "In fact, I just found out that he's got some personality quirks of his own." He looked sideways as if to make sure they were still alone and lowered his voice. "Horrible ones."

"Do tell," she said, with a wicked gleam in her eyes.

"Well, it turns out that one of M-Squared's most recent projects has been figuring out how to hack into everyone else's internet accounts," Flynn said.

"Which is a federal crime," Van Horn noted.

He nodded. "As I pointed out to Senior Airman Mitchell when I caught him red-handed. At great length. Along with a reminder that the military prison at Leavenworth might actually be one of the few places less appealing than Barter Island."

"And then you got him to spill what he'd learned?"

"I had to," Flynn said virtuously. "Just to make sure our unit's operational secrets were safe."

"Okay, so what's your NCO's terrible secret vice?" Van Horn wondered. "Porn?"

"Worse," Flynn said darkly. "Much, much worse." He lowered his voice even further and leaned across the table to whisper in her ear, noticing at the same time that it was a particularly beautiful, eminently kissable ear. "He's part of an online writing group."

Van Horn laughed, then her eyes widened again, this time in simulated dread. "Not . . . not . . . *Star Trek* fan fiction?"

"Oh, this goes way beyond a simple court-martial offense like that, I'm afraid," Flynn told her grimly. "No, they write poetry. Modern, nonrhyming poetry. All about the wonders of the Alaskan wilderness. And sunsets. And the ocean."

"You're kidding me," she said in disbelief.

He shook his head with a grin. "Nope. I swear it's the God's honest truth. And I kind of wish I hadn't looked at what M-Squared showed me. Some things should stay private."

"Definitely!"

For another long moment, they looked at each other in silence. Then Flynn cleared his throat awkwardly. "So, I've been meaning to ask—"

"Is this where you make your move, Nick?" she interrupted with a lazy smile.

"Huh? Er, no, that is . . . uh, well, if I did, would you slap me down?"

Her eyes crinkled with amusement. "Maybe.

Maybe not. How lucky do you feel right now, Captain Flynn?"

He glanced at his watch and sighed. "Not lucky at all, it turns out. Because I'm due on duty at our outpost line in about twenty minutes."

"Too bad."

Mentally, Flynn cursed the series of four-hours-on, four-hours-off patrol shifts he'd decreed in response to the Pentagon's order to go to DEF-CON Three. He never could have imagined he'd end up screwing up a date with a beautiful woman.

"But if we're still stuck here tomorrow, I just might be able to clear my calendar enough to have dinner with you again. Or maybe lunch, depending on when you're free," Van Horn said consolingly. "No promises, mind you."

"Noted," Flynn assured her. "But I do have one more quick question."

She raised an eyebrow. "Shoot."

"Why is your call sign 'Skater'?" he asked curiously.

Van Horn sighed. "Because pilots think they're really clever. My last name is Dutch, see . . . and speed skating is a big deal in the Netherlands, so—"

"You got tagged with 'Skater.' Well, I guess it could have been worse."

"Oh, back in the first weeks of flight school, it *was* worse," she told him with a twisted grin.

"Worse, how?"

"My last name is Van Horn," she pointed out. "Think about it."

Flynn winced. "Ouch." He looked at her. "So what happened?"

"A certain fellow pilot 'tripped' in the ladies' room and managed to bust her lip and get a black eye," Laura Van Horn said with a certain, deep-seated satisfaction.

"On a wet floor?"

If anything, her smile grew bigger. "Nope. That floor was bone-dry."

TWENTY-SIX

THE NEXT MORNING

One after another, two twin-tailed Su-35S fighters belonging to Russia's Twenty-Third Aviation Regiment sped down a snow-covered runway and lifted off into the hazy morning sky. Each aircraft was configured for long-range flight, equipped only with two external fuel tanks, a single pair of K-74M short-range heat-seeking missiles, and two KAB-500L laser-guided bombs. Streaking low over a stark white coastal plain, they flew northeast past a white radar dome sited on the lower slopes of Gora Sovetskaya, Wrangel Island's tallest mountain. The sleek jet fighters were camouflaged in jagged bands of white, light gray, and dark gray that blended with the bleak, ice-covered ocean ahead.

Aboard the lead Su-35S, Major Vadim Kuryokhin keyed his mike. "Moscow Operations Control, this is *Polet Telokhranitelya*, Bodyguard Flight. We're airborne and proceeding immediately to Rendezvous Point Alpha."

There was a short delay while his signal was relayed to Lieutenant General Rogozin, still deep underground in the Sharapovo command bunker. Then the general's voice came back through Kuryokhin's headset. He sounded strained. "*Bodyguard, this is Moscow Ops Control. Prospector and Mother Hen are in position at the rendezvous point. Good luck. Remember your mission. And remember your rules of engagement. Under no circumstances, repeat, under no circumstances are you to fire first at any American aircraft. Is that understood?*"

"Message clearly understood, Ops Control," the Russian fighter commander said distinctly. "Bodyguard out." He glanced out of his cockpit at the other Su-35, flying about a kilometer off his right wing. "Lead to Bodyguard Two," he radioed, making sure he was using a lower-powered tactical channel. "You heard the man, right?" he said wryly. "So keep your itchy finger off that trigger, Ilya. Or else Daddy Rogozin might give us both a spanking."

"*Two,*" his wingman, Captain Ilya Troitsky, acknowledged. "*What the hell does the general think we're going to do? Take on the whole damned American Air Force with a total of four missiles between the two of us?*"

"Apparently your aggressive reputation precedes you," Kuryokhin said with a grin.

Even over the static-laden tactical circuit, he could hear Troitsky's loud, exasperated sigh. "*For God's sake, Lead, it was one lousy bar fight. Just one. And no one even got killed.*"

Kuryokhin shrugged. "I think it was the fact that you were willing to take on four biker gang members by yourself that got some attention."

"*I* thought *there were only two of them,*" his wing-man said sulkily. "*Okay, Lead, I'll be on my best behavior. But are we still supposed to keep those F-22s off our guys? Or just wave politely at them as they zoom on by?*"

"We keep the *Americos* away," Kuryokhin confirmed. "We just can't shoot them in the process."

Over the circuit, Troitsky sighed again. "*Look, Major, you know these rules of engagement are stupid, right? Whoever came up with them must think you can screw a woman through your clothes and still get her pregnant.*"

"Stupid they may be, but they're still the orders we've been given," Kuryokhin said firmly. "Orders that we will both obey to the letter. Copy that?"

"*Two copies,*" his wingman replied.

The two Su-35s accelerated and raced on to the northeast across the frozen sea—staying at very low altitude to avoid any possibility of detection by American radar. Flying so low burned fuel fast, cutting their maximum range by more than half. Which was why the rendezvous they were headed toward was so critical to the success of this mission. Ahead of the two Russian fighters, a band of dark clouds stretched across the sky. They were at the western edge of what seemed to be a never-ending sequence of snow and ice storms surging down out of the polar region to pummel Alaska and northern Canada.

One thousand kilometers northeast of Wrangel Island and five hundred kilometers due north of the Alaska coast, two other Russian aircraft flew a fuel-conserving racetrack pattern. One was a very large, swept-wing aircraft with four eight-bladed propellers, a Russian Tu-142 maritime reconnaissance plane. The other, almost as big, was an IL-78M-90A refueling tanker. They were several thousand meters above the solid cloud layer, orbiting high enough to make out a pale orange glow off to the southeast. In these polar latitudes, so close to the beginning of true winter, the sun never actually appeared above the horizon.

Colonel Iosif Zinchuk looked out the left side of the Tu-142's cockpit as he banked gently into yet another turn. Far below, he saw the two Su-35s break out of the clouds and streak toward them, climbing almost vertically. He keyed his mike. "Bodyguard, this is Prospector," he said. "I have you in sight."

"*Copy that, Prospector*," the lead fighter pilot, Major Vadim Kuryokhin, acknowledged. "*Permission to tank from Mother Hen. We're not exactly flying on fumes, but we could be a lot more comfortable.*"

Zinchuk knew the other man wasn't exaggerating. Reaching this distant midair rendezvous without being spotted by American radar had required both Su-35s to fly well beyond their normal combat radius. Without additional fuel from the IL-78, they would be doomed to ditch somewhere in the icy wastes below, or, worse yet, make a humiliating emergency landing at the nearest American airport. "Permission granted," he radioed immediately. He throttled back all four of the Tu-142's big engines, slowing down to make room for them behind the humpbacked tanker aircraft.

For a time, the four Russian aircraft flew together in formation. Zinchuk watched closely as the two Su-35s carefully edged in behind the much-larger IL-78, each aiming for one of the drogue baskets streaming behind its left and right wing. Through his headset, he could hear a calm, running radio commentary between the three aircraft as they helped guide each other into position. Despite air currents that set the baskets bouncing and swaying in the tanker's wake, both fighter pilots succeeded in making contact after only a couple of failed attempts. And once they were solidly connected, the task of refueling itself took comparatively little time. The IL-78's pumps could transfer more than thirty liters of fuel per second, enough to fully replenish both fighters in less than eight minutes.

One after the other, the Su-35s broke contact and peeled away from the tanker. "*Prospector, Bodyguard,*" Zinchuk heard Kuryokhin say. "*We're ready to proceed when you are.*"

"Copy that, Bodyguard," he replied. "I'm starting our run now. Give me plenty of room until we break out of the clouds." Slowly, he turned the Tu-142's steering yoke back to the right and pushed forward. In response, the huge aircraft banked toward the south-southeast and descended. Moments later, they crossed into the cloud layer and the world outside the cockpit vanished—swallowed up in a sea of unrelieved gray. The buffeting increased, accompanied by a staccato fusillade of ice droplets spattering across the wings, canopy, and fuselage.

Zinchuk watched his altimeter very, very closely as it spun down, hoping like hell that the meteorology reports he'd been given were halfway accurate. If these clouds went all the way down to the ocean, he'd have to abort this mission—which would definitely not endear him to anyone in Moscow.

Then, at a little over five hundred meters, they came back out of the storm clouds into a faded, murky half-light. Through driving flurries of snow, the Tu-142's command pilot caught glimpses of a desolate, windswept vista stretching away in all directions. Ridges of rafted sea ice unrolled below the reconnaissance aircraft's enormous wings, growing larger as they lost still more altitude. Tight-lipped, he took his aircraft down even more before leveling off only two hundred meters above the barren ice cap.

This was a form of madness, Zinchuk knew. For all its many virtues—sheer endurance, payload, and powerful, long-range sensors among them— his mammoth turboprop was not at all designed to make low-level penetrating flights through enemy air defenses. Without any form of terrain-following radar or computer navigation, the slightest lapse in his concentration or control could lead to utter disaster.

But coming in practically right on the deck was the only way the Tu-142 could possibly hope to escape detection by the chain of American radars lining Alaska's northern coast. Behind him, the two Su-35s reappeared, emerging out of the cloud layer again. Smoothly, the twin-tailed fighters slid forward into their assigned slots, one to his right, the other to his left.

"I'm picking up weak signals from an airborne radar!" Captain Sukachov, the Tu-142's defense systems operator, abruptly reported over the intercom. With all of their active sensor systems still on standby to avoid prematurely revealing their presence, Sukachov's radar warning receivers were their primary means of figuring out what the Americans ahead of them might be doing. "It's a pulse Doppler system. Our computer evaluates it as an AN/APY-2 type."

"What's your assessment?" Zinchuk demanded.

"It's an American E-3 Sentry AWACS aircraft," Sukachov told him. "From the bearing and signal strength, I'd estimate that it's orbiting somewhere over western Alaska, probably near Nome."

Based on prior experience, Zinchuk judged that was likely to be true. Any U.S. Air Force early-warning plane operating in that area was perfectly positioned to pick up Russian reconnaissance probes coming east from the Chukchi Peninsula,

Asia's easternmost point—one only a little over a hundred kilometers from American territory. "Can that E-3 spot us?" he asked.

"No, sir," Sukachov said with complete assurance. "We're well outside its radar's effective range and much too low. As far as that enemy AWACS plane is concerned, we might as well be on the far side of the moon."

THAT SAME TIME

Eighty nautical miles west of Fairbanks, a large four-engine Boeing-designed aircraft orbited at high altitude. Antennas studded its exterior, allowing it to sift the airwaves for even the faintest electronic signal. Inside the RC-135V's electronic-equipment-crammed aft cabin, Captain Amanda Jaffe knelt down next to Technical Sergeant Philip Kijac, one of the fourteen cryptologic language analysts aboard Exult One-Five. As the information integration officer aboard this flight, it was her job to fit together all the disparate fragments of intelligence its specialists gathered and somehow use them to develop a coherent picture. All too often that was like trying to put together a jigsaw puzzle where all the pieces were gray and half of them were missing.

"What have you got for me, Kij?" she asked.

In answer, he brought up a recording of the weak radio transmissions several of their antennas had picked up a few minutes earlier. Jaffe plugged her headset into his console and listened along to the series of hissing crackles, squeaks, and pops. "Encrypted voice transmissions?" she guessed.

Kijac nodded. "Yes, ma'am, that's my read."

"Coming from where?"

He opened a map on his computer screen. "Those signals originated somewhere along a bearing of roughly zero-zero-five degrees from our current position. Triangulating backward and judging by the signal strength when we picked them up, I'd estimate those transmissions were coming from around . . . *here*." With a stylus, he tapped a point near the top of his digital map. It was far north of their RC-135V, well out over the ocean.

Jaffe frowned. "That's what? Nearly three hundred nautical miles off our coast?"

"Yes, ma'am," Kijac agreed. "Which also puts them outside the range of any of our North Warning System sites."

Reflexively, she tapped a finger against her lips, thinking things through. "Could that have been one of those big Russian recon aircraft reporting back to its home base?"

The specialist shook his head. "I don't think so. A signal like that would have been a lot more powerful and much easier for us to pick up. No, ma'am, this sounds more to me like multiple aircraft talking to each other, using a real low-powered tactical frequency."

Jaffe nodded, seeing his point. "Can you match those transmissions with anything else in our databases?" she asked.

Radio transmissions and other electronic signals recorded by RC-135V Rivet Joint ELINT flights all went into giant computer data archives for later analysis and comparison against other intelligence. Transmissions that could be definitively paired with types of aircraft performing distinct activities—things like landings and takeoffs, bombing runs, simulated dogfights and missile launches, and air reconnaissance reports, for example—were especially valuable, since they could be matched against new signals to speed up the process of figuring out what they meant. The system was similar to that used by the U.S. Navy to identify other submarines from passive sonar recordings of their unique acoustic signatures.

"I think so," Kijac said. "I've got the computer running a comparison screen now." As he spoke, a series of lights lit up along the side of his display. Rapidly, his fingers tapped the touch screen, opening a series of graphs that showed the signal characteristics of the transmissions they'd just detected matched against earlier recordings. He expanded one. "There we go. That's a match, all right, with a ninety-plus percent certainty."

Jaffe eyed the computer's assessment with interest. "So it thinks the signals we picked up were from Russian multirole combat aircraft, either Su-27s or Su-35s, carrying out some kind of air-to-air refueling exercise?" The specialist nodded.

She frowned. Why were the Russians sending frontline fighters so far out from their usual bases? She checked the meteorology plot and her frown grew even deeper. Those faint radio signals had come from right in the middle of a developing storm front. Air-to-air refueling was never a trivial maneuver, even in good weather. And in bad weather, even at high altitude, the aircraft involved would have been contending with high winds and significant turbulence. She shook her head. Whatever was going on out there, this was no routine training mission. Not even the Russians were crazy enough to try a risky refueling op so far from any friendly base, not when a failure would likely doom both the fighter itself and its pilot. Not without a really pressing reason.

Making a decision, Jaffe picked up one of the RC-135's secure communications handsets. "Air Operations Center, this is the IIO aboard Exult One-Five. We've just picked up indications of at least three and possibly more Russian aircraft operating three hundred and fifty–plus nautical miles due north of Umiat. Be advised that we believe these aircraft include at least one air refueling tanker and two multirole combat fighters, probably Su-27s or Su-35s."

THAT SAME TIME

The Third Wing's commander, U.S. Air Force
Colonel Leonard Huber, listened closely to the report relayed from the RC-135V ELINT plane. He
didn't like the idea of Russian fighters operating
so far north, out on his flank. His defenses were
mostly oriented to detect and intercept combat
aircraft sortieing from Moscow's air bases on the
Chukchi and Kamchatka peninsulas. But fully refueled Su-27s or Su-35s coming south out of the Beaufort Sea would be in a great position to slide past his
command's defenses without being detected.

He studied the board. Third Wing didn't have
many aircraft up right now, just an E-3 Sentry
AWACS plane with the call sign Anvil Four-Five
over the Seward Peninsula and the RC-135 west of
Fairbanks. The colonel swung to his operations officer. "Contact Anvil and tell them to shift eastward
toward Fairbanks. I want airborne radar coverage of
that corridor across the Brooks Range in case our
Russian comrades are trying something sneaky."

"Yes, sir."

Huber turned back to the board. His jaw tightened. "And I want all four of the F-22s we've got on
ready alert in the air," he said firmly. "Send one pair

to escort the E-3 and assign the other two Raptors to bird-dog Exult One-Five."

"You think the Russians might be planning to bushwhack them?" his ops officer asked.

Huber shrugged. "Maybe. Maybe not. But if they are, I'm not interested in making things easy for them." His eyes narrowed. "Because I do know that if we lose those AEW and ELINT aircraft, we'd be suddenly blind and deaf—which strikes me as a real good way to end up getting our asses kicked if Moscow's got bigger and nastier plans today."

TWENTY-SEVEN

A SHORT TIME LATER

Colonel Iosif Zinchuk peered ahead through the Tu-142's cockpit windows, straining to see clearly through a dim, gray half-light. Ahead of his big patrol plane, the clouds were thickening, as were the torrents of snow and sleet now driven almost straight across the icebound sea by shrieking, gale-force winds. The closer they came to the coast, the worse this storm got. He gripped his steering yoke tight, making constant, small adjustments to keep the Tu-142 from veering suddenly off course or slamming a wing or propeller blade into the jagged surface not far below them. Every muscle in his arms, shoulders, and face felt on fire with the strain involved in this prolonged, low-altitude flight.

"Colonel, that American AWACS plane is moving," Sukachov reported again over the intercom. "Both the strength and bearing of its radar emissions have changed."

"Moving where?" Zinchuk snapped.

"Due east from its previous position," the Tu-142's defense systems operator said.

Zinchuk frowned. "Heading back to its base?"

"No, sir," Sukachov told him. "The E-3's course would take it more southeast if that were the case. This looks like a change in deployment instead."

"Is that usual?"

Sukachov hesitated and then admitted, "I'm afraid not, Colonel. In fact, it's a definite departure from the standard operational patterns we've observed in the past."

"Which could indicate that the Americans are onto us," Zinchuk guessed.

"That is a possibility," the other man said. He cleared his throat uncomfortably. "If their AWACS plane continues eastward on its present heading, it will be in a position to detect us once we cross the coast and have to climb over the mountains."

Zinchuk fought down the urge to rattle off a string of violent, profane curses. Doing so might make him feel better, but hearing their commander lose control of his temper would only unnerve the rest of the Tu-142's eleven-man crew. As it was, several days of long, difficult patrols across the polar ice cap had already put them all on edge.

He winced. Had this hazardous, borderline insane flight just above the ice been for nothing? "How could the Americans know what we're doing?" he demanded angrily. "Were we spotted by that fixed radar site at Barter Island?" On their present course, they were drawing ever closer to the American FPS-117 long-range array just off the Alaska mainland.

"No, sir," Sukachov promised. "At this altitude, we're still well below its horizon."

Impatiently, Zinchuk forced himself to set aside the question of how the Americans apparently knew what they were doing. That was something for intelligence officers in Moscow to sort out later—once he and his crew returned and were debriefed. Maybe their plane had been spotted by an American spy satellite in orbit, as hard as that seemed to believe. Or maybe the CIA had its own spies inside the Ministry of Defense. What mattered now was that he do whatever was necessary to press onward with this risky reconnaissance mission . . . and to preserve whatever was left of their most important tactical surprise.

He glanced out the left side of the Tu-142's cockpit. There, about a kilometer off his wing, he could just barely make out the needle-nosed profile of one of the two Su-35s assigned to escort him deep into the American interior. Between the fighter's winter camouflage and blinding flurries of snow howling across the windswept ice, it was incredibly difficult to spot. Unfortunately, he knew, visual detection and radar detection were two very different things. Su-35s were incredibly agile combat aircraft, but they were not stealth fighters.

Nevertheless, Zinchuk thought, there were still a few tricks he could play to confuse the enemy's radar picture. He keyed his mike. "Bodyguard Lead, this is Prospector. Close in on my aircraft. Tuck yourselves in as tight as you can, right behind each wing."

"*Prospector, Bodyguard,*" he heard Major Kuryokhin reply. "*Copy that. Moving into your shadow now.*"

Zinchuk concentrated on holding the big reconnaissance plane straight and level while the two much-smaller jet fighters carefully maneuvered into position—closing on the Tu-142 until they were flying only a couple of dozen meters away on each side. With luck and skill, their smaller radar signatures would blend with that of the much-larger aircraft, presenting the Americans with what should appear on their screens as only a single bogey.

Several minutes later, Zinchuk heard Lieutenant Gorsheniov, the Tu-142's navigator, call out over the intercom, "Feet dry!" They had just crossed the Alaska coast and were now back over land.

With a touch of weary cynicism, the colonel considered how little practical difference there was between the sea's ice-covered expanses and the snow-and-ice-layered frozen tundra stretching ahead of them. Colliding with either surface—solid land or solid water—meant sudden death. Slowly, he pulled back on the yoke, bringing the Tu-142's nose up a few degrees to begin a steady climb to higher altitude. The northernmost slopes of the rugged mountains making up the Brooks Range were only sixty kilometers away.

THAT SAME TIME

Two dark gray F-22 Raptors from the Ninetieth Fighter Squadron flew north-northeast from Joint Base Elmendorf-Richardson. Both carried twin six-hundred-gallon external fuel tanks mounted on underwing pylons and a full internal weapons payload of six AIM-120 AMRAAM radar-guided missiles and two AIM-9X Sidewinder heat-seekers. They were headed toward a midair rendezvous with Exult One-Five, the RC-135V Rivet Joint electronic intelligence aircraft currently orbiting west of Fairbanks.

Aboard the lead Raptor, Captain Connor "Doc" McFadden suddenly heard the voice of an air controller from Elmendorf-Richardson come up over his radio. *"Casino Lead, this is Air Ops Center,"* the controller said. *"We're changing your mission. Both our E-3 Sentry and Barter Island have picked up the same new air contact—probably another Tu-142 patrol plane. It just crossed the coast east of Barter Island, heading south-southeast at around three hundred and eighty knots. Bearing zero-one-five, range three hundred and forty miles, altitude six thousand and climbing. We need you to intercept, positively identify, and warn off that Russian aircraft."*

McFadden clicked his mike. "Copy that, Ops," he said tersely. "Anything else we should know about?"

"*Affirmative, Casino,*" the controller told him. "*Signals intelligence from Exult One-Five strongly suggests the Russian recon plane could be accompanied by combat aircraft, probably Su-35s. And the E-3 says that bogey may be a little too big to be just one aircraft. So stay sharp.*"

McFadden whistled softly off-mike. So the Russians had figured out a way to provide fighter escorts for their patrol planes coming over the Arctic? Well, that was a new twist, and not a good one. "Lead to Casino Two," he radioed. "Let's punch it, Cat. The closer we intercept these guys to the coast, the more maneuvering room we'll have."

"*Copy that, Doc,*" his wingman, Lieutenant Allison "Cat" Parilla, acknowledged. "*But that blizzard coming across the mountains is really nasty.*"

McFadden nodded to himself. The quick meteorology brief they'd been given just before takeoff had shown yet another severe winter storm headed across the state, with fierce winds and bands of thick clouds. "Well, let's just hope these guys play it smart and come in above the weather," he said, advancing his throttles. Instantly, he was pressed back deeper into his seat as the F-22's powerful twin Pratt & Whitney turbofans spooled up.

Accelerating smoothly to nine hundred knots, both Raptors streaked toward the distant Brooks Range.

A SHORT TIME LATER

As the Tu-142 climbed steadily through a swirling sea of gray cloud, Zinchuk was sure that his lumbering aircraft had now been detected. Sukachov's reports of steadily increasing signal strengths from both the American E-3 AWACS plane and their ground radar station could yield no other possible conclusion. He spoke over the intercom. "Very well. The *Americos* know we're here, so there's no point in staying quiet. Activate all sensors!"

Acknowledgments from the electronics officers stationed in the forward and aft cabins rattled through his headset. Satisfied, he radioed his two fighter escorts. "Bodyguard, Prospector. Recommend you break away now. Use the mountains for cover and take station ahead of us."

Aboard the rightmost Su-35, Major Vadim Kuryokhin heard Zinchuk's suggestion with relief. Maintaining a safe distance from the colonel's reconnaissance aircraft was incredibly difficult in this solid cloud layer, even with his fighter's IRST, its infrared search and track system, picking up the other aircraft's enormous heat signature. He'd been dreading the possibility of a fatal midair collision ever since they'd started climbing into this low-hanging mass of snow- and ice-swollen storm clouds.

He raised Troitsky in the other Su-35. "Okay, Ilya. Switch your radar on at low power and set synthetic aperture mode. We're going down to play hide-and-seek ahead of Prospector. Stand by."

"*Two, standing by,*" his wingman replied.

Kuryokhin pushed a button on the side of his left-hand multifunction display. Half the display lit up, showing a highly detailed, three-dimensional image of the surrounding mountains and twisting river valleys. Using its synthetic aperture mode, the Su-35's IRBIS-E passive electronically scanned array radar mapped the ground ahead—making very low-altitude flight possible even in poor visibility. Swiftly, he sketched out a suggested flight path and sent it via data link to Troitsky.

He took a deep breath. This was going to be . . . a little hairy. "Very well, Two! Break away . . . now!" He pulled his stick sharply right, rolling the fighter into a diving turn away from the huge Tu-142. Down and down he plunged through the clouds with his eyes practically glued to the images on his glowing MFD. A jagged mass of rock, the spire of a thousand-meter-high peak, loomed ahead, growing with alarming speed, and he quickly rolled back to the left to dodge around it.

Then Kuryokhin banked hard right again and pulled back on the stick a little, leveling off as he broke out of the clouds only a few hundred meters above the ground. There, in a widening gap

between steep, ice-sheathed slopes and even higher
rocky cliffs, he picked out the trace of a frozen river
through the snow—like a gray-silver snake winding
through white sand. His Su-35 turned to follow it,
and he pushed his throttles forward to accelerate
out ahead of Zinchuk's now-invisible Tu-142 as it
climbed higher above the clouds. In his rearview
mirror, he saw Troitsky's plane swing in behind
him. Curving back and forth along the meandering
valley, the two twin-tailed Russian jets flew onward.

Still more than two hundred nautical miles south
of the oncoming Tu-142, the American F-22 pilots, Doc McFadden and Cat Parilla, both heard the
same high-pitched, chirping tone in their headsets.
Their radar warning receivers had just detected the
Russian reconnaissance plane's powerful active sensors lighting up.

"Guess that guy's not trying to hide anymore,"
McFadden commented laconically.

"*Nope,*" his wingman agreed. Parilla checked her
RWR display. "*He still can't see us, though, even with
these honking big gas tanks hanging off our wings.*"

McFadden nodded, scanning his own display.
External fuel tanks made their Raptors a lot less
stealthy, but they were still outside the range at
which that Russian radar should be able to spot
them. On the other hand, they were closing that gap
fast. With the propeller-driven Tu-142 and their
F-22s now headed straight for each other at a combined speed of more than twelve hundred knots,

they were shaving off nearly twenty-two nautical miles every minute.

"Anvil Four-Five, this is Casino Lead," he radioed the E-3 Sentry, now orbiting well behind them over Fairbanks. "Any confirmation yet on those possible Russian fighters?"

"*Casino, this is Anvil,*" the radar controller aboard the AWACS plane replied. "*Negative on that. We thought we saw a couple of smaller contacts break away from the Tu-142 a few seconds ago. But we've got nothing else on our screens right now.*"

McFadden frowned. He didn't like not knowing where those Su-35s were—or even if they were real, and not just a figment of the RC-135 Rivet Joint crew's collective imagination. He opened a terrain map on one of his displays. His mouth turned down even more as he scanned the rugged topography of the Brooks Range. Air search radars couldn't see through solid rock. Which meant that jumble of mountains and valleys and gorges offered a number of possible hidden avenues of approach for pilots willing to take chances.

He made a decision. Their Raptors weren't supposed to sneak up on that big, lumbering Russian patrol plane. Far from it. The whole point of this intercept mission was to swoop in hard and fast and make it very clear to that SOB that he wasn't going to parade around unchallenged through U.S. airspace. Besides, if there were Russian fighters out there somewhere up ahead, the more eyes looking for them, the better. Situational awareness mattered more right now than stealth. "Okay, Cat," he said.

"Let's not be coy. It's time to let these guys know we're coming their way. Light 'em up!"

And then, suiting his actions to his own words, Mc-Fadden activated the F-22's powerful AN/APG-77 radar. As an active electronically scanned array, it randomly changed frequencies with every radar pulse, making it a lot harder for any enemy to pick out its emissions from ordinary background noise in the electromagnetic spectrum. But harder wasn't the same thing as impossible.

THAT SAME TIME

Alexei Petrov followed Bondarovich into the aircraft shelter at a run. Inside, the hanging lanterns used to provide illumination swayed crazily in swirling currents of freezing air. Distorted shadows danced across the fabric walls and hard-packed snow floor. Wind-whipped ice crystals spattered against the parked PAK-DA bomber's wing and fuselage.

Petrov stared up at the shelter's roof and swore. More of the camouflage cloth panels had ripped loose. Still attached at one end, they flailed wildly in the blizzard. Straps that had tied the panels to overhead aluminum trusses whipped back and forth from the loose side of each panel. He grabbed Bondarovich's shoulder and pointed upward, screaming into the other man's ear to be heard over the shrieking wind. "Get your men! All of them! Bunin, too! If we don't tie those damned panels back in place, this fucking storm will tear the whole shelter to pieces!" He shoved the ex-Spetsnaz soldier back toward the outside. "Move, damn it!"

The other man nodded anxiously. He turned and plunged back into the maelstrom outside.

Petrov scrambled up a ladder and out onto the PAK-DA bomber's wing. His boots might damage a few sections of the plane's advanced, radar-absorbent skin, but that was nothing compared to what would happen if the shelter came apart around it. Even an hour or two of exposure to subzero temperatures, hundred-kilometer winds, and blowing snow and ice could render the aircraft completely unflyable. Frantically, he grabbed for one end of a strap as it snapped through the air, and missed.

Again and again, he tried to get a hold on one of the flailing straps and failed. His face darkened in fury. To come so close to changing the world forever and then to be defeated by a wind-whipped piece of cloth? How his father must be laughing at him, he thought grimly. Laughing at him out of the icy depths of hell.

TWENTY-EIGHT

OVER THE BROOKS RANGE, NORTHERN ALASKA

A SHORT TIME LATER

Connor "Doc" McFadden eyed the green diamond in the center of his HUD. It marked the radar-designated position of the Tu-142 reconnaissance aircraft they were heading toward at high speed. Glowing numbers next to the diamond showed the range counting down fast. They were now only about forty nautical miles apart, less than two minutes out at their present closure rate. Time to slow that down a little, he thought, especially since the sky over this part of the mountains was a wall-to-wall winter storm front marked by masses of dark cumulonimbus clouds soaring tens of thousands of feet above the ground. Getting any kind of visual lock on that big Russian turboprop was going to be tough in the present circumstances—and it would be impossible if they blitzed right past each other at twelve hundred–plus knots.

"Casino Two, Lead," he radioed to Cat Parilla. The lieutenant's F-22 was positioned a few hundred yards off his right wing and about a thousand feet higher. Sometimes he could see her aircraft visually. Sometimes he couldn't. Visibility dropped to near zero whenever they punched through one of the towering cloud masses. "Let's rein it in some, to avoid an overshoot."

"*Copy that,*" his wingman replied. "*Getting to be kind of a rough ride up here, anyway.*" Strong turbulence and winds were pummeling the two fighters, subjecting them to sudden jolts and buffets, especially inside the clouds.

"Yeah, I hear you, Cat," McFadden agreed. "Easing off, now." He pulled back on his throttles, simultaneously banking left and right in a flat scissors to shake off even more airspeed. Alerted by the data link connecting their two Raptors, Parilla followed his maneuvers. Gradually, both F-22s slowed their headlong rush, dropping from more than 900 knots to around 450.

McFadden checked the diamond icon in his HUD again. It hadn't budged an inch to either side. That Tu-142 was still flying straight on, showing absolutely no sign of turning back out of U.S. airspace. And by now, those Russians must know they were about to be intercepted by a pair of American jets. Their APG-77s had been locked on to the slower turboprop for several minutes, giving its crew plenty of time to realize they were being painted by radar. One more thing was certain. Wherever those hypothetical Su-35 escorts were, they certainly weren't hiding in that recon plane's radar shadow. At this range, any Russian fighters there would have stood out like deer caught in a pair of high-beam headlights.

It was high time he and Cat announced themselves, McFadden decided. He changed frequencies
to the guard channel. "Russian Tu-142 military
aircraft, this is one of the American F-22 fighters
headed your way. You are deep inside our airspace
and violating international law. Turn back now. Repeat, withdraw now. Radio your intention to comply with this order immediately, over." He clicked
off his mike and listened. For a few seconds, there
was only the hiss of static.

"Russian Tu-142, you are violating—" McFadden
started again, now allowing a distinctly hostile edge
to creep into his voice.

"*American F-22, this is the Russian Tu-142,*" the
other plane suddenly replied. "*We regret that we are
unable to comply with your request. We are only conducting a peaceful search for a missing aircraft—one of our
polar research UAVs which may have strayed accidentally into this area. We have no hostile intent. Repeat,
this is a peaceful search mission.*"

McFadden scowled under his oxygen mask. Son
of a bitch! These clowns were trying to play games.
He stabbed his mike button again. "Listen up, pal,
I'm not 'requesting' a damned thing. You will turn
around immediately and get the hell out of U.S. airspace as quickly as you entered it. Understood?"

Five thousand meters below and twenty kilometers ahead of the four-engine Tu-142, Major
Vadim Kuryokhin shrugged his shoulders. There
had never been any real chance that the Americans

would let Zinchuk and his crew probe so deeply into their national territory without interference. Or that they would buy the ridiculous cover story about some missing drone. This was going to come down to a duel of pilot skill . . . and guts.

His eyes swept the upper edge of his HUD. Two icons were visible, one for each of the oncoming F-22 Raptors. They were accompanied by rapidly changing numbers showing the estimated range and altitude of the American jets computed by his IRST system. Between their powered-up radars, radio transmissions, and external fuel tanks, neither Raptor was especially stealthy at the moment. But they were getting very, very close, and pretty soon their radars would spot the two Russian Su-35s twisting and turning down among these sharp-edged mountains and icy gorges.

A predatory grin flashed across Kuryokhin's face. Better to act now, he thought, before the Americans figured things out and had time to react. "Lead to Bodyguard Two," he radioed. "You take the high man. I'll take the low."

"*Two*," Ilya Troitsky said immediately.

"Make them piss their flight suits, but no shooting!" Kuryokhin warned again. "Remember, we're here to keep them off Prospector's back, not to start World War Three."

His wingman snorted over the radio. "*Yes, Papa Bear. I'll be good.*"

"Then follow me!" Kuryokhin ordered. He yanked back on his stick and went to afterburner. His Su-35 streaked upward, climbing vertically at more than a thousand kilometers per hour. He broke out of the lower layer seconds later and spotted his chosen target, the lead F-22, almost directly above him, flying through a valley of clearer air between two towering masses of cumulonimbus storm clouds. The American stealth fighter grew larger in his canopy with astonishing speed. He thumbed his radar to air combat mode.

*B*EEP-BEEP-BEEP.

"*Holy crap!*" McFadden blurted, startled by the rapid-fire sequence of high-pitched tones pulsing through his headset. His Raptor was being painted by an enemy radar at close range. Madly, he scanned the sky in all directions. Where the hell—

Suddenly, a blur of white and gray flashed past his canopy just ahead of him and kept on climbing. Jesus, that was an Su-35, he realized, noting the other aircraft's twin tails and sleek, swept-back wings in a split second. And then the Russian fighter's wake slammed into him, rattling the F-22 from end to end.

Shaking off the stunning impact, McFadden pulled into a hard, climbing turn toward the Su-35 that had just bounced him. G-forces slammed him back into his seat and his vision grayed out a little. Straining against the g's, he spotted Cat Parilla's Raptor rolling away as she dodged a second Su-35 spearing up at them out of the clouds. Her rapid evasive maneuver carried her straight into a column of cloud and she disappeared from sight.

Above him, the first Russian fighter came out of its own turn and then abruptly banked tightly in the opposite direction—maneuvering with incredible speed and agility. It vanished into another cloud.

"Anvil, this is Casino Lead," McFadden grunted, reporting in to the E-3 AWACS while he reversed back after the Su-35. Everything outside his cockpit turned dark as he entered the clouds himself. He locked his radar onto the Russian. A new diamond blinked onto his HUD, sliding fast down and back to the right again. He slammed his stick hard in that direction, rolling inverted to dive after the still-invisible enemy fighter. "Two bandits just jumped us," he forced out against the strain of continual tight turns. "No missiles in the air. Maybe these guys want to play, not fight."

"*Copy that, Casino,*" the radar controller aboard the distant E-3 Sentry acknowledged. "*Sure looks like a tight furball from here.*"

For "furball," read "fucking mess," McFadden thought fuzzily, as he tightened his next turn even more, now pulling eight g's and using his F-22's thrust-vectoring engine nozzles to pull the aircraft's nose around even faster. He couldn't see shit in all of these clouds. And he'd lost track of Parilla. Sure, their data link threw a steering cue to her fighter onto his HUD, but it was jinking all over the place as they each maneuvered wildly, trying to pick up an advantage over the two Su-35s that had just bushwhacked them . . . or to break away from trouble if the bad guys gained a favorable position on them.

He leaned forward, trying hard to see something, anything, through the swirling gray haze ahead of his Raptor. His radar said an Su-35 was out there ahead of him, no more than a few hundred yards away. But he couldn't make out anything, not even a quick, fleeting glimpse of a camouflaged wingtip or tail fins or a clear canopy. His teeth clenched hard. Chasing these Russian fighters around this storm front was like playing blindman's bluff with *everybody* blindfolded, not just whoever was "it" . . . and stuck at the same time inside one of those whirligig carnival rides that spun unpredictably in every direction.

Inside the Tu-142 reconnaissance aircraft's forward cabin, Captain Yuri Bashalachev peered intently at his hooded scope. As the plane's bombardier-navigator, he had primary control over its powerful Korshun-KN-N search radar. Ever since Colonel Zinchuk ordered their sensors to activate, he'd been using the system to scan the terrain below them. From this altitude, the Korshun had a search radius of more than 250 kilometers, even through the intervening haze of obscuring cloud and wind-driven snow and ice. Around and around, the radar's rotating beam swept hypnotically—turning up nothing but a seemingly endless jumble of mountain peaks and low-lying valleys.

And then something flashed briefly on the screen. Something that didn't look at all natural.

Suddenly excited, Bashalachev pressed his face even harder against the radar display's hood. His fingers raced across his controls, tweaking them to focus in on what appeared to be a wider valley on the southern fringe of this vast range of higher peaks and lower ridges and hills. And then he saw it again, near one end of the valley. He froze the image, staring hard at what he saw.

Those straight and angled shapes, partial and oddly blurred though they were, were definitely *not* natural, the bombardier-navigator decided instantly. He checked the coordinates against the map pinned up next to his station. Just as he'd thought, this entire region was supposed to be nothing but uninhabited wilderness. Excitedly, he toggled his intercom mike. "Colonel, radar here! Contact, contact, contact! Probable man-made structure. I think it might be what we've been looking for!"

"Where?" the Tu-142 commander pilot demanded.

Bashalachev peered down again at his scope. "At our nine o'clock now," he reported. "About twenty kilometers to the east."

"Nice work, Yuri! We're coming around to make another pass over the target," Zinchuk told him.

Immediately, the huge plane banked sharply to the left, turning steeply to circle back toward what its radar had picked up. Over the intercom, Bashalachev heard the colonel on the radio to Moscow. "Operations Control, this is Prospector. Silver Lode. Repeat, Silver Lode."

"Silver Lode" was the short code phrase indicating the possible—but not certain—discovery of the stolen PAK-DA stealth bomber on the ground.

A t that same moment, Captain Connor "Doc" McFadden saw one of the Su-35s emerge out of the murk—headed straight at him. Desperately, he yanked his stick hard right, hurling the F-22 into another brutal, high-g, diving turn to avoid a possible collision. The Russian fighter roared past no more than a few yards above him and then disappeared as suddenly as it had come.

McFadden craned his neck around hard against the enormous forces pinning him against his seat, desperately searching for any sign of the enemy aircraft that might already be swinging around to slot in right behind him. But there was nothing. Just a churning cauldron of dark gray cloud.

Halfway through its tight, diving turn, his Raptor burst back out into the open air. Alarms blared through the cockpit. Alerted too late, McFadden whipped his head back around to the front . . . just in time to see the huge, propeller-driven Tu-142 directly ahead. "Oh, shit—"

Moving at more than five hundred knots, the F-22 slammed into the Russian reconnaissance plane's right wing and sheared it off. McFadden was dimly aware of a tremendous, shattering impact that seemed to go on forever, but that could really only have lasted for milliseconds at most. Thrown forward against his straps with rib-smashing force, he saw a mass of blurred red caution and warning lights ripple across the cockpit.

Horrified, he looked up through his canopy and saw the Tu-142 tumbling out of control. Slowly, the huge aircraft rolled over on its left side, trailing debris and burning fuel from the jagged stub of its missing wing. *Time to go*, he thought groggily. Moving in what felt like slow motion, he reached down between his legs, gripped the ejection seat handle, and yanked hard.

Above McFadden, the F-22's canopy blew off and spun away to one side. And then the ejection seat's rocket motor fired. It hurled him up and out of the stricken Raptor—directly into the path of the razor-edged shards of metal spiraling down from the stricken Russian turboprop. Several fragments ripped through the ejection seat's parachute before it could fully deploy. Others tore into the seat itself and killed him instantly.

A thousand meters higher, Major Vadim Kuryokhin's Su-35 raced out of one of the towering columns of cloud—still hunting for the highly maneuverable American stealth fighter he'd been tangling with over the past few minutes. To his horror, he saw the Tu-142 spinning toward the ground, wreathed in flames from nose to tail as it fell. "My God, Ilya," he shouted over the radio. "Those bastards just shot down our recon plane!"

"*Two copies. Arming missiles,*" his wingman replied

coldly. Moments later, Troitsky called out, *"Target locked. Missiles fired!"*

Shit-shit-shit-shit," Lieutenant Allison "Cat" Parilla snarled, seeing the two heat-seeking missiles fall away from under the wings of the Su-35 that had just swung in a couple of miles behind her. Their motors ignited in bursts of flame. Trailing smoke, they streaked across the intervening sky, moving at more than two and a half times the speed of sound.

Immediately, she broke hard left, spiraling upward in a tight, climbing turn. Her thumb stroked the countermeasures button. Dozens of white-hot flares streamed out behind the F-22, each a miniature sun against the glowering mass of dark storm clouds on all sides. Seduced by the flares, both Russian missiles veered away and detonated harmlessly.

Parilla reversed her evasive turn and rolled into the clouds again. She'd seen the steering cue for McFadden's Raptor vanish suddenly off her HUD. Now she knew why. The Russians had decided, for reasons of their own, to turn this cold air war hot. The green diamond identifying the Su-35 that had just tried to kill her slid into view, pulling out ahead of her aircraft as the other pilot desperately turned in an effort to bring her back into his sights.

"Too late, asshole," she snapped, squeezing the trigger on her stick. One AIM-120 AMRAAM and then a second dropped out of her main weapons bay. They flashed away into the gray haze at Mach

Four, already guided by their own internal active radar seekers, since the range was so short, essentially point-blank for missiles designed to reach out and kill at more than eighty nautical miles.

A dazzling orange flash lit the clouds. In that same moment, the target diamond blinked off her HUD, signaling the destruction of the enemy aircraft. But before she could fully savor the kill, shrill, chirping tones through her headset warned that the second Su-35 had locked on.

Reacting fast, Cat Parilla dove for the deck. More flares rippled out behind her violently maneuvering Raptor. One of the two missiles closing in on her chose a decoy instead and went off harmlessly in her curving wake. She never saw the second, which arrowed on through the spreading cloud of tiny suns and detonated just above her cockpit.

Major Vadim Kuryokhin saw the American F-22 stagger when his missile exploded. Slowly at first, and then faster, the Raptor rolled over and fell away, spewing smoke and fire. Eager to confirm his kill, he followed the stricken aircraft down into the clouds, tracking it by the red-tinged glow. Abruptly, it flashed brightly, spraying glittering sparks outward through the concealing gray mists.

Had that dying F-22 just blown up? he wondered. Deciding he'd seen enough, the Russian Su-35 pilot started to turn away—and slammed head-on into a jagged mountain peak shrouded in cloud. His fighter disintegrated in a ball of fire.

Some kilometers away, Alexei Petrov came outside into the blizzard's unnatural darkness and freezing winds. Bondarovich's men finally had the necessary repairs to their aircraft shelter in hand, freeing him to head back to camp for a short rest. He straightened up to his full height to stretch aching muscles . . . and then he stopped dead, staring off to the west.

A bright white glow lit the sky there, slowly falling through the darkness and thick clouds. Then, suddenly, it vanished with a blinding flash, followed by a dull red gleam in the distance that slowly faded away.

"What was that?" one of the exhausted mercenaries who'd followed him out of the shelter asked in astonishment. "Some sort of weird lightning from the storm?"

Petrov shook his head in dismay. "No," he ground out slowly. "I think that was trouble for us. Very serious trouble."

TWENTY-NINE

For several seconds, a shocked silence pervaded the crowded operations center. One moment, they'd been observing five aircraft—two American and three Russian—on the radar feed relayed from the E-3 Sentry AWACS plane over Fairbanks. And the next, all five aircraft were gone, wiped off the display as quickly as if some unseen giant's hand had swatted them out of the sky with one mighty stroke.

Colonel Leonard Huber, Third Wing's commander, shook his head in disbelief and then turned to his assembled officers. "Can anyone tell me what the hell just happened up there?"

Helplessly, they all shrugged. "Whatever it was, it went down awfully fast," one of them said at last. "The RC-135 ELINT plane picked up a few fragmentary transmissions from the two Russian Su-35s, but they're encrypted and unreadable. We didn't get anything from our own aircraft."

Huber nodded gloomily. That was not a good sign. At least one of the F-22 pilots, McFadden or

Parilla, should have been able to call out a warning, even if their mock dogfight with the Su-35s had suddenly turned hot for some weird reason. He sighed. "Well, one thing's clear, anyway. A bunch of different aircraft, ours and theirs, just crashed in the middle of a god-awful wilderness."

"And during a blizzard," his operations officer pointed out quietly. "One of the worst in years."

"Yeah, that, too," Huber agreed tersely. A screen depicting the most recent meteorology reports for the Brooks Range showed the entire area socked in, with strong winds, near-zero visibility thanks to blowing snow, and subzero temperatures. "Mounting a combat search-and-rescue operation up there is going to be a bitch," he said thoughtfully.

"Yes, sir."

Huber's eyes sought out his liaison with the Alaska Air National Guard. The ANG's 176th Wing ran the ARCC, the Alaska Rescue Coordination Center, which managed all the various military and civil aviation resources needed for search-and-rescue operations. "Major King, what kind of CSAR assets can your people rustle up fast?"

The major looked up from the computer link she'd been intently studying. "Colonel, the ARCC says we can have a pararescue team and a pair of HH-60G Pave Hawks from the 210th Rescue Squadron ready for takeoff in ninety minutes."

"But your helicopters can't make it out that far unrefueled, can they?"

"No, sir," King agreed. "The area where those planes went down is more than a hundred miles beyond our birds' maximum range. Ordinarily, they'd tank on the way, but the blizzard is moving south fast across the whole state. Midair refueling would be far too hazardous in these conditions. So our helicopters will have to stage through Fairbanks and then Fort Yukon, stopping to refuel on the ground at both places."

Huber nodded again. Those refueling stops would make slow going, further adding to the time it would take the pararescue team to reach any crash sites. On the other hand, recent forecasts predicted some minor improvement in the weather over the mountains later on today. So, assuming ANG's Pave Hawk helicopters could somehow fight their way through the storm in the first place, those hoped-for lower winds and better visibility should significantly aid any recovery operations. "All right, Major," he said to King. "Activate your search-and-rescue units and get them in the air as quickly as possible."

One of the airmen manning their secure communications board turned toward him. "Sir? The Pentagon is on the line asking for you."

Huber hid a grimace. Both NORAD headquarters and the Pentagon were receiving live feeds from the operations center here—which was normal, especially considering the extraordinarily high level of Russian air activity around Alaska's perimeter. It had been a coin toss to guess which group of senior brass would be faster off the mark to horn in on this crisis situation. He took the phone. "Third Wing, Colonel Huber speaking."

"Colonel?" a woman's voice said in reply. "We've never met, but my name is Miranda Reynolds. I'm in charge of the CIA's operations directorate."

Huber felt his eyebrows go up. Of all the people he'd expected to be speaking to today, the chief of the CIA's clandestine service definitely had *not* been on his list. "What can I do for you, Ms. Reynolds?" he asked cautiously, strongly suspecting that whatever it was, he wasn't going to like it much. And the more he listened, the more he knew just how right he'd been.

THAT SAME TIME

Miranda Reynolds hung up the secure phone and looked around the table at the others present—who included Jonas Murphy, Bill Taylor, and the entire Joint Chiefs of Staff. "Well, the colonel bought it," she said with a shrug. "He certainly wasn't thrilled by the idea, but he's okayed including members of our specialist go team in the search-and-rescue mission force. He thinks we want them along so they can comb through the wreckage of those Russian fighters and their reconnaissance plane."

"Those downed aircraft might be all your people find," General Frank Neary told her.

"That's certainly possible," Reynolds agreed coolly. "On the other hand, that Russian reconnaissance probe was pushed a lot harder than any of the others we've seen so far, wasn't it?"

Neary and the others nodded somberly. Not only had the presence of Su-35s so far from the Russian mainland come as a very unwelcome surprise, but so had the willingness of those fighter pilots to mix it up so aggressively with the American aircraft sent to intercept them—aggression that had clearly led to disaster for both sides.

"My strong suspicion is that level of determination is itself evidence that Moscow knows something we don't about the area their Tu-142 was searching," Reynolds continued. "The Russians must have solid intelligence indicating their missing stealth bomber is hidden somewhere in the Arctic National Wildlife Refuge."

From her position at the far end of the table, the Pentagon's operations staff chief, Rear Admiral Kristin Chao, nodded. "I see your point. ANWR checks off all the boxes as a good place for this Colonel Petrov to conceal the PAK-DA prototype he stole."

"Which is why I want our go team on the scene, ready to move in fast if it turns out I'm right," Reynolds said firmly. "As bad as it was to suddenly lose all those aircraft, it may just have given us the chance we needed to beat Moscow to the prize."

Neary stared coldly at her. "Maybe so, Ms. Reynolds. Assuming, of course, that we don't find ourselves in a shooting war with the Russians over what just happened out there. In which case, there won't be much of a *prize* left for your experts to pick over."

THIRTY MINUTES LATER

Piotr Zhdanov listened to Lieutenant General Rogozin's grim report in stony silence. Although controllers at air bases along the Arctic coast and eastern Siberia were still trying to raise Colonel Zinchuk's Tu-142 and its two Su-35 fighter escorts by radio, there seemed little doubt that all three aircraft had crashed—and within just a few minutes of the colonel transmitting a coded phrase suggesting his crew might have found the PAK-DA stealth bomber's hiding place.

"This tells all we need to know," the Russian president said when Rogozin finished. "That sighting report was genuine. And now the Americans have the same information."

Rogozin looked puzzled. "Sir?"

Zhdanov stubbed his cigarette out in irritation. "Come now, Yvgeny. It's obvious, isn't it? Why else would the Americans order their fighters to shoot down our planes?"

"Except that we are not yet certain of exactly what happened to our aircraft," the general reminded him carefully.

Zhdanov raised an eyebrow. "The pilots you assigned to this mission had strict orders not to fire first, correct?"

"Of course, Mr. President," Rogozin said.

"And were they reliable, disciplined officers?" the president asked pointedly.

Too late, Rogozin saw the trap into which he'd just walked. "Yes, sir," he agreed reluctantly, obviously knowing there was only one acceptable answer. "Aggressive, of course, as the best fighter pilots must be. But Major Kuryokhin and Captain Troitsky were both loyal, trustworthy men."

Zhdanov nodded in vindication. "There you are, then. The Americans had to have started this mess by firing on our planes. It's the only logical conclusion. Washington wants to make sure it seizes Petrov and the PAK-DA bomber first."

On his side of the conference table, Aleksandr Ivashin nodded vigorously. Ordinarily dour and undemonstrative, the head of the GRU suddenly appeared unusually animated. "I may be able to confirm your hypothesis, Mr. President."

"How?"

"We've just received an emergency signal from one of our two-man, deep-cover Spetsnaz teams," the spymaster said. Given enough time during any major crisis, it was Russian practice to deploy small covert commando units into rival nations—tiny groups of highly trained operatives who were expected to provide intelligence in the runup to open hostilities, and to conduct sabotage missions and targeted assassinations once war broke out. "These agents are stationed outside the large American military base near Anchorage, the one they call Joint Base Elmendorf-Richardson. They've reported signs that the Americans are readying helicopters for immediate deployment to northern Alaska. And they believe this force includes elements of the CIA black ops team recently flown to the base."

Zhdanov stared at him. "They're sure of this?"

Ivashin nodded. "Their report indicates a high level of confidence in this assessment."

"Can you contact this Spetsnaz team directly?" the president demanded. "Without wasting time going through cutouts or your other usual security procedures?"

A trace of worry appeared on the GRU director's face. "Yes, but doing so would significantly increase the risk of American intelligence detecting their presence."

"I don't give a shit about the risks," Zhdanov said coldly. "We've gone far beyond the point where individual lives matter." He lit another cigarette and then stabbed it at Ivashin. "Your team is to take immediate, preemptive action against those American helicopters. I don't care how they do it, but they are to stop this CIA operation before it gets off the ground. Is that clear?"

Ivashin's mouth opened in surprise.

"I will not listen to any objections," Zhdanov warned him. He glared around the table at his senior advisers and military commanders. "We have one overriding objective right now: the Americans must *not* be allowed to get their hands on our stealth bomber and its weapons payload. While I still want to avoid open war if at all possible, no one here can deny that this situation has already escalated dangerously, thanks to the Americans' own warlike actions against our reconnaissance aircraft!"

Slowly, they nodded.

Now Zhdanov's mouth compressed into a tight, thin line—as though he were being forced to swallow something extraordinarily unpleasant. "One thing more. We're going to have to agree to meet the traitor Petrov's demands, while still assembling air units and commando forces to retake or destroy the stolen bomber if the opportunity arises." He saw their astonishment and scowled. "Don't act so surprised! What other choice do we have? Now that we know the aircraft is already on American soil, it's essential that we get it safely back to Russia . . . even if it means temporarily yielding to blackmail."

THAT SAME TIME

In a deserted subterranean corridor outside the ECR, Jonas Murphy signaled Miranda Reynolds over. "I just heard from the president directly," he said quietly, without any preamble.

She raised an eyebrow. "Yes?"

"The aggressive actions of those Russian aircraft searching for their stealth bomber have convinced him, and his whole White House team, that this Colonel Petrov's offer is not a scam or one of Moscow's disinformation operations," Murphy told her.

Reynolds nodded. It seemed a little late to draw that fairly obvious conclusion, she thought wryly, though she supposed almost every politician had an ingrained instinct to play it safe—especially with so many influential voices in the Pentagon urging caution.

Murphy sighed. "And all of the State Department's efforts to persuade the Russians to step back from the brink of open hostilities have been rebuffed so far. So have the president's own personal attempts to reach out to Zhdanov."

"Is this heading where I think it is?" Reynolds asked, keeping her voice even lower.

The DNI nodded again. "The president's decided to meet the financial demands made by this would-be defector and his backers." He shrugged. "In the circumstances, he's willing to take the chance that we might be dealing with some very unsavory characters."

"If it means avoiding war, funneling money to criminals might not seem so bad," Reynolds agreed.

"Exactly," Murphy said. "Anyway, as far as the president is concerned, the sooner that stealth bomber is firmly in our hands, the better. Once that happens, Zhdanov will have to come to terms and negotiate for its return." He smiled tightly. "Which we will gladly do . . . once our technical experts have finished studying its avionics and other systems."

She eyed him closely. "So you want me to . . ." she said slowly, drawing it out. Like his boss, Murphy was a politician first. In the past, CIA officers had gotten into a lot of trouble for acting on the basis of winks and nods from occupants of the Oval Office and their subordinates—only to have the ground cut out from under their feet when things went sour.

"Signal our agreement by encrypted email through that secret server of yours," he confirmed, with a crooked grin of his own that told her he knew exactly what she was doing. "Treasury officials are already transferring the necessary funds, three billion dollars, to your agency's 'black accounts.' Now we just need you to let Petrov's backers know that they've won."

THIRTY

A SHORT TIME LATER

Not far from Naples, a sleek, hundred-meter-long ship rode at anchor off the volcanic island of Ischia. Though it was as large as a naval frigate, the vessel's big, gleaming windows, luxurious fittings, swimming pool, and aft helicopter pad marked it as a rich man's plaything.

High up on the megayacht's top deck, Dmitri Grishin stood at a railing. Through half-closed eyes, the Russian oligarch surveyed the glittering, moonlit waters of the Tyrrhenian Sea. Streetlamps illuminated the faded stucco facades of the restaurants, shops, and hotels that lined Ischia's beaches and small harbor. He rolled his shoulders, in an effort to ease some of the tension eating away at him from the inside.

Abruptly, he turned as he heard quiet footsteps behind him.

It was Pavel Voronin. In a concession to the Mediterranean fall climate and his employer's desire for discretion, he'd traded in his usual tailored business suits for an open-necked shirt, blazer, and khaki slacks. He'd flown in from Moscow the day before, and as far as Grishin's family and the ship's crew were concerned, the younger man was just another of the junior corporate executives the oligarch sometimes rewarded with brief stays on his yacht.

"Well?" Grishin asked.

"They've met our price," Voronin told him with a slight smile. "I just confirmed it with our financial networks. All the required funds have been securely transferred."

Grishin breathed out in relief. "Who met our demands? Moscow or Washington?"

"Both of them," Voronin said, smiling more broadly now.

For a moment, the oligarch stared at him in astonishment, taken completely by surprise. But then a sly, triumphant grin spread slowly across his own face. This was beyond his wildest and most optimistic expectations. In the blink of an eye, the operation he'd dubbed Vanishing Act had just netted him close to six billion U.S. dollars. True, on paper, that was still less than his publicly declared net worth. But until now, most of his nominal fortune had consisted of hard assets—of factories, mines, oil and gas wells, ships, and fleets of trucks and railcars. Unfortunately, in Piotr Zhdanov's Russia, tangible possessions and investments were not real wealth. They were only hostages: hostages to a government that could seize them by decree, either on a whim or to appease an angry mob looking for scapegoats for their country's increasingly dire economic conditions. Under Moscow's despotic and unpredictable rule, today's billionaire could all too easily become tomorrow's imprisoned pauper.

But now, Grishin thought with growing delight, he'd broken free. Close to six billion dollars, sheltered in an impenetrable web of dozens of secret accounts, represented both security and continued power and influence for himself and for his family. Even if Zhdanov tried to throw him to the wolves, he would fail. Grishin could safely ride out the coming economic and political storm abroad— biding his time until the moment arrived to choose the next winner in Russia's ongoing cycle of internecine power struggles.

Jubilantly, he clapped Voronin on the shoulder. "Well done, Pavel!" He chuckled out loud. "Now you're a rich man, too!"

Voronin had been promised a 1 percent share for his work in coordinating and orchestrating Vanishing Act. Perhaps such a sum was not true wealth when compared to that possessed by his employer, but it was a fortune nonetheless and ample reward for his labors, Grishin believed. Somewhat smaller shares had been promised to Bondarovich and the other ex-Spetsnaz soldiers Voronin had hired for the real dirty work. More, naturally, had been promised to Colonel Alexei Petrov for his part in the conspiracy.

"Which nation's payment will we honor?" Voronin asked dryly. "After all, I need to let Petrov know in which direction the bomber should fly—once the winds ease up enough for it to take off again."

Grishin shrugged. "Tell him to return the PAK-DA prototype to our own country, of course." He turned back to the rail and looked out across the water again. "I'm willing to bleed Zhdanov and his cronies, but I'm no traitor. Not to the Motherland." He glanced at the younger man. "The Americans were dupes, leverage to use against Moscow—never anything more."

"Naturally," Voronin agreed.

Grishin eyed him. "Once the stealth bomber takes off, are your men ready to clear off themselves?"

The other man nodded. "Bondarovich and the others have their orders. They'll head for the Canadian border by snowmobile, where I have a bush plane waiting to pick them up. Nothing at the camp can be traced back to us."

"And Colonel Petrov?" the oligarch asked quietly. "What arrangements have you made for him?"

Casually, Voronin leaned against the railing. His eyes were hooded. "Regrettably, Alexei is a proud and volatile man," he said reflectively. "Somehow, I don't think he's really suited to a quiet, discreet life of luxury. It would be very hard for him to accept the need to disappear completely."

"Perhaps so," Grishin agreed.

"Which is why my men will take the necessary action on their way to the border," Voronin assured him. "You can be very sure that no one will ever see the colonel again."

THAT SAME TIME

On the slope of a hill climbing steeply two hundred feet above a frozen stream, two men crouched near the base of a Sitka spruce tree. They wore thick parkas, ski pants, and fur-lined hoods against the intensifying cold. Besides their civilian winter clothing, they also had powerful night vision–capable binoculars slung around their necks. As storm clouds rolled across the sky above them, driven by high winds whistling down out of the north, daylight was fading fast.

One of them, Spetsnaz Captain Arkady Timonov, zoomed in on the pair of American HH-60G Pave Hawk helicopters parked on the apron near one of the air base's two runways. Both had their rotors turning. "They're spooling up," he said to his companion. "Better get ready."

"This is madness," the other man, Lieutenant Leonid Brykin, muttered, more to himself than to Timonov. He knelt beside a large equipment bag and started unzipping it.

"Madness or not, we have our orders," Timonov growled. Privately, he agreed with his subordinate, but Moscow's urgent instructions left them with no real latitude. What made it even worse was that their superiors in the GRU had chosen to relay those instructions using encrypted text messages sent directly to their smartphones. Given the eavesdropping and code-breaking capabilities of the American National Security Agency, that was almost as bad as emailing their cover identities and pictures straight to the FBI. As it was, the Spetsnaz captain figured he and Brykin had no more than a day before federal law enforcement officers started looking for Mr. Pindar and Mr. Jones in earnest.

Still grumbling under his breath, Brykin finished unzipping the bag and hauled out a long, green fiberglass tube with a handgrip and trigger mechanism near the midpoint. It was a Pakistani-made Anza Mk III surface-to-air missile launcher. Based on a Chinese model derived from Russia's own 9K38 system, this particular weapon had been captured from Muslim extremists in Chechnya and then smuggled covertly into Alaska years ago. Quickly, he set the tube in place on his right shoulder and flipped a switch to power up the missile's seeker head and gyros. A soft hum confirmed the system was ready.

Next to him, Timonov peered intently through his binoculars. The first helicopter lifted off, climbed to about a hundred meters, and then dropped its nose slightly to gain airspeed as it crossed the runway. Accelerating, it swung north, heading straight toward them. The second Pave Hawk trailed close behind. Red, white, and green navigation lights blinked rapidly on both helicopters. He lowered the binoculars. "Here they come, Leonid. Make your shot count."

The lieutenant nodded tightly. He pressed his eye into the SAM launcher's sight and turned through a short arc, until he had the crosshairs settled squarely on the trailing helicopter. A speaker behind his right ear buzzed. Steadily, the buzz grew louder and shriller. "I have tone," he confirmed. The missile's infrared seeker head had locked on to the Pave Hawk's heat signature.

Through the sight, Brykin saw the second Pave Hawk grow progressively larger. He estimated that it was now approximately three kilometers away and closing fast. Slowly, he pulled the launch trigger halfway back. That "uncaged" the missile's IR sensor, allowing it to swivel freely inside the nose cone so that he didn't have to aim manually anymore. The buzzing noise intensified. Satisfied that he had a solid lock on his target, Brykin angled the launch tube up at forty-five degrees. Anything lower risked having the missile strike the ground when it launched.

"Any day now, Leonid," Timonov growled.

Ignoring him, Brykin squeezed the trigger all the way. Instantly, the Anza Mk III's booster motor ignited, hurling it out of the launch tube in a dense, choking cloud of acrid smoke. The missile itself burst out of the cloud and soared skyward as its main rocket motor kicked in. Visible as a bright white dot riding a plume of smoke, it climbed high above the hill, arced over, and then darted straight at the trailing American helicopter.

Three seconds after launch, the SAM slammed head-on into the Pave Hawk's main rotor assembly and exploded in a blinding red-and-orange flash. Trailing torn shards of rotor and fuselage, the stricken helicopter rolled over and plunged into the forest not far beyond the runway. Flames and darker black smoke eddied away from the crash site.

"Nice shot!" Timonov exulted. "Now, let's get the hell out of here!"

Obeying, Brykin tossed the spent launcher away and followed his leader upslope and deeper into the woods. With luck, they hoped to make it back to their parked car and speed away before the base's security personnel could react to this sudden ambush. Behind them, the surviving Pave Hawk took evasive action, spewing flares as it circled back toward the runway.

The American search-and-rescue mission had just been ruthlessly aborted.

Rear Admiral Kristin Chao tapped a control on her console, bringing up a live video feed from Joint Base Elmendorf-Richardson on the Emergency Conference Room's largest display screen. It showed a pillar of thick, oily smoke rising from the woods just beyond the air base. The smoke column curved sharply, swept southward by rising winds from the approaching blizzard.

"Approximately thirty minutes ago, one of the two helicopters assigned to our search-and-rescue mission was shot down—apparently by a handheld SAM fired from outside the base perimeter," she said crisply. She looked sympathetically at Miranda Reynolds. The CIA official looked sick to her stomach. "I'm afraid that was the Pave Hawk carrying your go team."

"Are there any survivors from the downed helicopter?" Bill Taylor asked gravely. The white-haired defense secretary, who was usually more energetic than far younger men and women, appeared to have aged visibly over the past several hours.

"A handful, Mr. Secretary," Chao replied. "All critically injured, many with severe burns."

General Neary, the Air Force chief of staff,

stirred in his seat. "And the sons of bitches who shot our bird down? Any luck finding them yet?"

Regretfully, the rear admiral shook her head. "No, sir. Personnel from the 673rd Security Forces Squadron are combing the area where that missile was launched. They found this"—she brought up a picture of the discarded SAM launcher—"but that's it, so far."

Jonas Murphy stared at the image. "Is that a Russian-made weapon?"

"It's a Pakistani copy of a Chinese-designed derivative of the Russian 9K38 *Igla*," Chao told him. "The type NATO labels an SA-18."

Miranda Reynolds glowered. "That missile's a goddamned blind. This wasn't some random terrorist attack by Muslim extremists. This was a Russian Spetsnaz operation, from beginning to end."

Chao nodded. "That's almost certain, Ms. Reynolds." She sighed. "What's much less certain is whether this Russian special forces operation is actually at an end."

"Meaning what?" Murphy asked.

"Meaning that we cannot be sure yet that they had only one missile team deployed outside Elmendorf-Richardson," she said bluntly. With the press of another key, she brought up a map hurriedly put together by her operations directorate staff experts. It showed all the areas around the air base where concealed enemy SAM teams might reasonably hope to take a shot at aircraft and helicopters while they were most vulnerable—at takeoff, on landing, and in the early stages of any flight.

A quick study of this map elicited dismayed-sounding murmurs from all of the military professionals present.

Chao nodded. "You see the point." She turned to Taylor, Murphy, and Reynolds, the only three civilians now allowed into this cavernous war room, and explained. "Even using units from the Army and Army National Guard, it will take us a minimum of several hours to search and secure these areas. And until we've done that, launching another search-and-rescue mission toward those crash sites would be like ordering our people to play Russian roulette."

"Literally, in this case," Taylor said grimly.

"I'm afraid so," the rear admiral agreed.

"But by the time our troops manage to secure the base perimeter against a missile ambush—" Murphy began.

"That storm front will be directly overhead," Chao confirmed. "Making further flight operations impossible until the weather clears."

Miranda Reynolds scowled. "Don't we have any other assets—troops, aircraft, something, for God's sake—anywhere else in Alaska we could send into the Brooks Range to look for those downed aircraft . . . and the stealth bomber?" Her fingers drummed nervously on the conference table. "Just because we've paid Petrov's price doesn't mean Moscow's going to give up on getting the PAK-DA back. And if the Russians beat us to the punch while we're sitting on our asses waiting for better weather conditions, we've just thrown away billions of dollars and a bunch of lives for nothing!"

In answer, Chao brought up another map, this one centered on northern Alaska. "My staff has found one possibility," she said quietly. Her fingers touched a control, highlighting Kaktovik and Barter Island. "There's a Joint Force security team deployed here, at one of our North Warning System's long-range radar stations. We've checked the records and all the personnel attached to this force have parachute training. In fact, they've recently completed a practice jump."

Neary shook his head. "All the airborne training in the world's no good without a plane to jump from. And with that blizzard socking in both Eielson and Elmendorf-Richardson, we're screwed on that front."

"Not quite, sir," Chao said coolly. "There's an Air National Guard HC-130J on the ground now at Barter Island."

The Air Force chief of staff stared at her. "On the ground there? Why?"

"Because it lost an engine in-flight and had to make an emergency landing," she answered. "But we've checked the specifications and that Super Hercules is rated to fly, even with a dud engine."

"You'd be asking the flight crew to take a hell of a risk," Neary commented. "Not to mention the troops you're asking to parachute into the middle of nowhere in the tail end of a blizzard."

Miranda Reynolds broke in impatiently. "Everything about this mess involves risk. I say we tell them to go." She looked at Chao. "Who's in charge of this security team?"

The rear admiral smiled oddly at her. "A U.S. Air Force officer it appears that your agency has had some dealings with in the not-so-distant past, Ms. Reynolds. The officer in question is a certain Captain Nicholas Flynn."

Reynolds's mouth fell open in consternation. "You're kidding me," she managed to get out at last.

Chao shook her head, still smiling wryly. "No, Ms. Reynolds," she said. "I most certainly am not."

THIRTY-ONE

Captain Nick Flynn unzipped his parka and stripped off his thick gloves as he sat down at the dining area table set aside for his unit's computers and other electronic gear. He'd just been called in from a duty shift outside the radar station, freezing his ass off on outpost duty. Apparently, an encrypted message had just arrived over their link to Alaskan Command—one that only he could read.

After blowing on his hands to restore some semblance of feeling, he entered the necessary codes. Lines of text and embedded maps and images appeared on the screen. It was a task order assigning them a new mission. But any faint hope that he could stand his unit down for some much-needed rest vanished the moment he read the message header. Good news did not carry the IMMEDIATE precedence designator. That was almost always reserved for situations involving serious military matters.

His mouth tightened as he read further. What

the brass wanted them to do now went way beyond ordinary crazy. In fact, it was off-the-charts lunacy. Stripping out all the happy talk about achieving vitally important national security objectives, the operations staff officers cozily forted up at Joint Base Elmendorf-Richardson expected Flynn and his men to parachute deep into the Arctic National Wildlife Refuge. Then, assuming they survived this hazardous nighttime drop, they were supposed to begin an immediate search-and-rescue operation— hunting for combat aircraft, two American F-22s, a big Russian Tu-142 recon plane, and two more Su-35 fighters, which had crashed somewhere among those jagged peaks and rocky valleys during an air intercept that had gone horribly wrong.

He shook his head angrily. There was no way in hell he would ask his soldiers and airmen to commit suicide chasing some staff weenie's whim, not without pushing back as hard as he dared first. Without waiting to start second-guessing himself, Flynn stabbed the screen icon that would open a direct, secure video connection to Anchorage.

There was a moment's delay while his signal was uplinked through a satellite and stabilized, and then a new window opened on-screen. A senior Army noncom looked back out of it at Flynn. "Yes, sir?" the NCO asked.

"This is Captain Flynn at Barter Island. I need to talk to—"

"Wait one, sir," the other man interrupted. "I'm switching you to General Rosenthal, now."

Flynn felt his eyebrows go up. Lieutenant General

David Rosenthal was the top dog, the overall commander for every airman, soldier, sailor, and member of the Space Force based in Alaska. And despite that, he'd apparently just been sitting around anticipating this video call from a junior officer posted to the back end of nowhere? This deal looked worse and worse.

Rosenthal's lean, squared-jawed visage flickered onto the screen. "Good afternoon, Captain. I assume you've got some questions about your orders?"

Flynn stiffened. "Not exactly questions, sir."

The general smiled dryly. "More like a protest, then. As in, what kind of stupid SOB dreamed up this nightmare and dumped it in your undeserving lap?"

Despite his anger, Flynn felt an answering ironic grin flit across his own face. "Not exactly in those words, sir. But I guess that's basically the gist of it." He leaned a little closer to the screen. "Look, General, between the crappy weather and the prevailing winter darkness, asking my guys to make a parachute drop into those mountains goes way beyond the call of duty. Risk is one thing. They all signed on the dotted line when they enlisted. But this is more like a kamikaze run. My troops aren't even trained for combat search-and-rescue operations."

Rosenthal nodded grimly. "I'm well aware of that, Captain," he said. "Unfortunately, the pararescue team we dispatched first was ambushed shortly after takeoff. A SAM brought down one of their two helicopters, with heavy casualties." His gaze hardened. "Which makes your team it, I'm afraid. You and your men are the only airborne-qualified force we've got that can reach those crash sites sometime in the next twenty-four hours."

"Someone shot down one of our helicopters?" Flynn said, staggered by the news. Carrying out a missile attack just outside the largest military base in Alaska represented an almost unthinkable escalation. "Who? The Russians?"

"Probably," the general said tersely. He shrugged. "Look, son, for what it's worth, your orders come straight from the top—from the SecDef and the Joint Chiefs. Their assessment is that your mission is of the utmost importance. If we're going to have any hope of avoiding an all-out war with Russia, we've got to learn more about what really happened out there, both to our planes and to theirs. So it's vital that you find any surviving aircrew and retrieve the flight recorders from every crash site you can reach."

Flynn frowned. "That's one hell of a tall order, sir."

"Yes, it is," Rosenthal said flatly. "And I don't like this much more than you do. But there it is." His chin came up as he looked Flynn straight in the eyes. "Your country is counting on you and your team right now. I know that may sound corny as hell, but it also happens to be true."

Shit, shit, shit, Flynn thought irritably. He really hated these kinds of appeals to his patriotism, especially since they were practically guaranteed to work on him. *Just stick a flea collar around my darned neck and call me Uncle Sam's Pavlovian dog,* he mused in disgust. That was how they got you, he knew, by invoking the danger to a land and a people you loved. And the trouble was, sometimes the danger was real. If the Russians were suddenly shooting down American planes and helicopters practically at will, it was harder and harder to see how the U.S. could avoid a major armed clash with Moscow.

"There's one more thing that wasn't included in the first draft of your orders," Rosenthal continued. "But it comes straight from the Joint Chiefs, too. Apparently, there's also a chance that you might run across another aircraft on the ground out there. An intact aircraft. And if you do, you're to report its presence and location immediately, but you are not, repeat not, to take any further action . . . not without direct orders from either the SecDef or the JCS."

"Exactly what *kind* of intact aircraft are we talking about?" Flynn asked carefully. Inside his mind, a whole new set of alarm bells were now going off. "One of ours? One of the Russians? Or one made by little green men from Mars?"

The general winced. "You now know as much about this as I do, Captain." His expression was not happy. "I'm pushing hard for more data, especially since it may have some bearing on what happened to our Raptors and the other missing planes. And on why the Russians are being so goddamned aggressive all of a sudden. So far, though, I'm not getting very far."

If those internal alarm bells got any louder, Flynn judged, he'd be metaphorically deaf real soon. He scowled. "Just for the record, sir, this sort of 'need to know' bullshit really pisses me off."

"You're not alone in that feeling, son," Rosenthal said. A hint of frustration crept into his voice, confirming what he said. "And I fully understand your own particular aversion to this level of strict secrecy."

That was true enough, Flynn realized. No matter how "prettied up" the orders justifying his exile to Barter Island may have been, the Pentagon's version of the old boys' network undoubtedly meant Rosenthal knew all about his earlier run-in with the CIA and its Libyan black ops arms smuggling.

"If it's any consolation, Captain Flynn," the general continued, "my strong suspicion is that there are a number of people back in Washington right now who are almost equally unhappy that you're in charge of this mission."

Flynn shook his head. "Frankly, sir, that's not much consolation at all." He sat back with a resigned sigh. "Okay, we'll do our best."

"I know you will, Captain," Rosenthal said. "Now, from what I understand, there's supposed to be a lull in this blizzard later tonight, but it may not last long. So organize your team and pull together any gear you'll need fast. We're putting Major Ingalls and Captain Van Horn and their HC-130J on standby out at the Barter Island airport right now. They'll be ready to take off as soon as your men are on board."

Sweating in the station's steam heat, Flynn strode down the corridor toward Sergeant Andy Takirak's tiny quarters. He'd thought briefly about stopping by his own room to wriggle out of his parka and the rest of his cold weather gear to get more comfortable, but he'd resisted the temptation. They were already on the clock, without any time to waste. And any layers he took off now were only ones he'd have to squeeze back into before they headed out to the airport.

Behind him, he heard a solid door bang open. Deep voices echoed through the station as the soldiers who'd been on outpost duty came hurrying back into the dining area to get out of the bitter, bone-chilling cold.

"Hey, what are you guys doing back inside?" he heard Cole Hynes ask, sounding annoyed. "You're not due for another couple of hours."

"The captain called us back in," Vucovich told him. "He said we should grab some hot food and stand by for new orders."

"What new orders?" Hynes demanded.

"Hell if we know," Sanchez's bass baritone rumbled. "I was freezing my balls off out there, so I'm sure not planning on bitching."

That would change soon enough, Flynn thought somberly. Nobody in their right mind was going to be thrilled about the prospect of a night jump—let alone a night jump into the wilderness in the tail end of a blizzard. In fact, he might be lucky if he got out of this without a full-fledged mutiny on his hands. Or was mutiny only something that ever happened to the Navy?

He reached Takirak's door, knocked once perfunctorily, and then pushed it open. "Sorry to bust in on you, Andy. But we've got a situation," he said quickly.

Obviously caught off guard, Takirak looked up sharply from his tablet. He'd been sitting upright on his cot, apparently concentrating intently on something displayed on the tiny device. Hurriedly, he put the tablet facedown beside him. "Excuse me, sir? What kind of a situation?"

"A bad one," Flynn said quietly. He kicked the door shut behind him and ran through a quick summary of their new orders.

When he was done, Takirak whistled softly and shook his head. "You weren't kidding."

"Oh, how I wish I was," Flynn said with a twisted grin. "So, anyway, we've got a crapload of work to do and no time to do it in." He nodded at the noncom's tablet. "I'm sorry to cut into your poetry writing time, but there it is."

Takirak stared at him with a puzzled expression. "Poetry, sir? Me?"

Flynn colored slightly. "Ah, shit, Andy. M-Squared hacked us all a while back, and he blew the whistle on that amateur writing group you're part of. Forget I mentioned it."

For a moment, the older man looked furious. It was not an expression Flynn had ever seen on him before and it made the powerfully built National Guard NCO seem strangely dangerous. But then, visibly, Takirak forced himself to calm down. He donned a half-abashed grin instead. "Already forgotten, Captain." He shook his head slowly. "Somehow, Senior Airman Mitchell keeps managing to surprise me. I must be losing my touch."

"He's trouble with a capital *T*," Flynn agreed. "Speaking of whom, where is M-Squared, anyway? I haven't seen him since I got back inside."

"In town," Takirak said. "Along with Pedersen. They were next on the leave roster."

Flynn nodded. Although they were still at DEFCON Three, his soldiers and airmen needed some occasional downtime to blow off steam if they were going to stay even half-sane in this remote, frozen outpost. Four-hour passes into Kaktovik were the best he could do for them. There wasn't exactly any hell-raising nightlife in the little village, not with all alcohol sales and possession strictly banned, but at least they could eat different food and see different faces for a change.

"Look, I'll go round those two up," the sergeant volunteered. "Alert status or not, their phones are probably off, or out of battery. And I know most of their likely haunts."

Flynn nodded. "Yeah." He grinned crookedly. "That'll give me a chance to spring the glad tidings on everybody else while you're gone. Though maybe I should put on my body armor first."

"Mission briefings are a prerogative of rank, Captain," Takirak said stolidly.

"Which you wouldn't dream of horning in on," Flynn guessed.

"Not in a million years," the sergeant said devoutly. "Yours is to reason why. Mine is but to do or die." He stood up and started pulling on layers of cold weather gear, pausing only to slide his tablet into an inner pocket of his parka.

That took Flynn aback for a split second. He wouldn't have guessed that the veteran noncom was a slave to tech gadgets, the way so many of the younger soldiers and airmen were. Then he shrugged inwardly. After all, he wouldn't have ever pegged Takirak as a would-be poet, either. But maybe the National Guardsman just figured they might not be coming back to the radar station anytime soon, depending on how this hazardous search-and-rescue mission went.

Nearly an hour later, in the middle of supervising his men as they finished stowing their weapons and other equipment aboard the airport bus, Flynn checked his watch for what seemed the hundredth time. He frowned. Where the hell were Takirak and Mitchell?

Private First Class Torvald Pedersen, the team's designated rifle marksman, had checked in a while back and was now busy helping the others. When asked, the dark-haired rancher's son from South Dakota confirmed that the sergeant had found him first, as he was just finishing dinner at one of Kaktovik's small hotels. Takirak had ordered him straight back to base, before heading farther into town to track down M-Squared. Since then, nobody had seen hide nor hair of either man. Nor were they answering repeated calls to their phones.

Flynn swung away from the bus and stared down the icy track leading into Kaktovik, hoping that he would see two figures trudging toward the radar station. But there was nothing moving. In the distance, the little village's street and house lights twinkled brightly against a night sky speckled with thousands upon thousands of stars.

At least some of the meteorologists' predictions of improving weather had panned out, he realized. Thick clouds still obscured most of the mountain peaks south of the small island, but the skies overhead were clearing and the north winds had calmed down some. If similar conditions held over their drop zone, the jump might not be quite as suicidal as he'd feared. But that still seemed like a big "if" when there were so many lives on the line.

Two of his men, Vucovich and Airman Peter Kim, steered their snow machines out of the station's large-vehicle maintenance bay. Each vehicle towed an empty sled behind it. With a flourish of loud, lawnmower-like motors, they pulled up beside Flynn.

Vucovich pushed his goggles up onto his forehead. "Want us to scout the town for the sarge and M-Squared, Captain?" he asked. "It ain't that big."

Flynn thought about that and then shook his head. As it was, it would take more time than they could easily afford to secure the two snow machines and their sleds aboard the HC-130J's single available equipment pallet. And the aircraft's loadmaster, Staff Sergeant Tim Wahl, was already waiting for them with growing impatience. "Takirak knows we're headed to the airport," he said, more confidently than he felt. "Once he's got Airman Mitchell in hand, he'll meet us there. In the meantime, you guys go report to Wahl and help him load your vehicles."

Vucovich nodded. He pulled his goggles back down and thumped Kim in the shoulder. "Let's hit it, Pete. Last man to the airport has to do all the grunt work." Grinning widely, they opened their throttles and sped away across the tundra, trailing plumes of ice and snow from under their ski runners.

Flynn watched them go with a bemused grin. He'd completely misread his team's likely reaction to their new orders. Far from plunging them into gloom, the prospect of action—even incredibly hazardous action, like making a parachute jump at night over mountains—had them all pumped up. He guessed that was a combination of the same craving for adventure that had caused most of them to enlist in the first place—plus the natural, wild-eyed optimism of youth, and a desperate willingness to do anything that would get them out of the dull, grinding routine of sentry duty on this isolated island.

He turned back to find Sanchez looming over him. The big New Mexican was the only one who looked even a little disgruntled. But that was because Flynn was making him leave his beloved Carl Gustaf 84mm recoilless rifle behind. On a search-and-rescue mission, they would need extra supplies and medical equipment more than a heavy weapon designed to blow open bunkers and kill armored vehicles.

"Everything's loaded on the bus, sir," Sanchez reported. "The sergeant and M-Squared's stuff, too."

Flynn nodded. He looked down the track toward Kaktovik one more time and then shrugged. They couldn't wait here any longer. "Then let's mount up, Specialist," he said. "But pass the word for everyone to keep their eyes peeled on the way through town. Our two missing guys can't have gone far."

SOME TIME LATER

Flynn felt a hand on his upper arm. He turned to find Laura Van Horn looking up at him with a concerned expression. She also looked half-frozen to death. Her flight jacket was fine inside a cockpit, but it wasn't made to stand up to subzero temperatures.

"Rip says if we're going to go at all, we should go soon," she shouted over the steadily rising roar from the HC-130's three working Rolls-Royce turboprops. Ingalls was busy running a slew of checks, closely monitoring his gauges and displays for the slightest sign of any more engine trouble. "We can't tell how long this break in the storm's really going to last." She waved a hand at the runway, where little swirls of snow crystals were dancing across the surface. "If the wind picks up even another ten knots, there's no way we could drop you safely. We'd have to abort the mission."

Flynn nodded grimly. "And that's not an option."

"I sure wish it was, Nick," Van Horn told him, sounding even more worried. "As it is, JBER's on the radio every five minutes, asking for a status update." With an obvious effort, she forced herself to appear more confident. "I've gotta say, though, this 'Hey, sorry, Skater, but I have to make a parachute jump into the wilderness' deal is kind of a sleazy way to duck out on that next gourmet meal you promised me."

He couldn't stop a short, sharp laugh. "Yeah, well, that did take some serious organizing. I had to pull strings all the way to Moscow and the Pentagon to set up this stunt."

Van Horn reached up and thwacked him gently in the forehead. "Idiot. Most guys would just have said they'd lost my phone number."

"Oh, crap," Flynn said in mock horror. "That would have been smarter. And much, much easier to arrange." Then he sobered up again. "Is everything else set?"

She nodded. "Everybody else is aboard and strapped in. Sergeant Wahl's got the anchor cables rigged for your parachutes. He says the pallet with your snow machines and sleds and extra gear is ready to drop, too. Or, in his words, as ready as he can make it with a bunch of amateurs for helpers."

Flynn glanced at his watch one last time. He sighed. "Okay, then. I guess that's it. But it sure sucks to have to go without my NCO or my radioman."

"Uh, Nick?" Van Horn said suddenly, turning him back around to face the road from Kaktovik. She pointed at a figure trotting toward them from out of the darkness. "Isn't that Sergeant Takirak?"

His eyes widened in relief. "Yeah, it is." Without thinking, he gave her a quick kiss on the cheek. "Tell Major Ingalls we're go for takeoff as soon as Andy's had time to get into his parachute harness and check over his weapons and equipment."

With a wry glint in her eye, Van Horn nodded and hurried away.

Flynn moved out to meet Takirak. The other man had a jagged cut across his forehead, and he was pale and drawn.

"Jesus Christ, Andy!" Flynn exclaimed. "What happened to you? And where's M-Squared?"

"Mitchell happened to me," the National Guard sergeant said angrily. "I found him okay, but when I briefed him on the mission, that son of a bitch said he wouldn't go. He said it was nuts and he hadn't signed up to kill himself."

Flynn frowned. It figured that Mitchell would be the one man to react so strongly. The red-headed airman probably had a more vivid imagination than anyone else on the team—certainly vivid enough to see all the ways this night drop and planned trek through the wilderness could go very badly wrong. "Then what?"

"I told him I didn't give a crap about what he thought," Takirak said tightly. "And that he was going whether he liked it or not. And that's when the bastard cold-cocked me with a loose board and took off." He reached up, gingerly felt the cut on his forehead, and winced. "By the time I got back to my feet, Mitchell was long gone." He looked embarrassed. "I'm really sorry I let him jump me like that, Captain. I never saw it coming."

"It wasn't your fault, Andy," Flynn assured him. He shrugged. "I wouldn't have expected M-Squared to pull something like that, either." For one thing, assault and desertion seemed wildly out of character for the usually happy-go-lucky young airman. Then again, he thought somberly, every man has his own breaking point.

"Let me go back into town and dig the son of a bitch out," Takirak pleaded. "There aren't many places he can hide."

Flynn shook his head. "Not happening. We don't have time for a manhunt, even if I wanted to drag Mitchell along under arrest." He pointed at the big Super Hercules with its six-bladed propellers already spinning. "See?"

"Yes, sir," Takirak agreed flatly. "I see." He grimaced. "About Mitchell's radio, Captain, the PRC-162?"

Flynn nodded. "That's a problem. With the battery, the darned thing adds another thirteen pounds to our load. I hate to dump it on one of the other men, especially since we're all going to be toting extra weight. But we sure as shit are going to need communications, so—"

"I'll carry it, sir," Takirak said gruffly. "I took the radio operator's course a while back, and, anyway, it's my fault that we're down a man. So if anyone's going to haul the extra weight, it should be me."

Flynn nodded, understanding the older man's need to prove himself. Letting himself get jumped by a junior enlisted man was the first crack in Takirak's hard-won aura of invincibility. And it couldn't have come at a worse time, right at the start of a highly risky mission. "Okay, Andy," he said briskly. "You've got the radio."

THAT SAME TIME

"Come up slowly to one hundred meters," Captain First Rank Mikhail Nakhimov ordered quietly.

"Coming up to one hundred meters, aye, sir," his diving officer intoned. He pushed controls. With a faint hiss, compressed air pushed water out of *Podmoskovye*'s ballast tanks. Gently, with constant adjustments to maintain an even trim, the eighteen-thousand-ton nuclear submarine edged upward toward the ice-covered surface.

"Holding at one hundred meters," the diving officer reported at last.

Nakhimov nodded. Now came the hard part. Or rather, the dangerous part. Side-scan sonar, temperature, and pressure detectors all strongly suggested they had found a comparatively thin section of the polar ice cap—one where the ice was somewhere between one and two meters thick. But even the thinnest-seeming stretch of ice could hold hidden hazards, jagged-edged ridges, or stalactites pushed down by pressure from above . . . massive spears of ice that could shear open a submarine's pressure hull on impact. "Activate our video cameras and turn on all the outer lights," he said.

More officers around the control room obeyed.

Screens brightened, showing a murky, half-lit view of the underside of the ice cap above. Nakhimov ran his gaze over each screen, closely studying the images they showed. He glanced at his executive officer. "Well, Maxim? What do you think?"

"It looks good," the other man replied. He tapped one of the screens. "There are some pressure ridges off our starboard bow, but they're well away from us." He glanced at the diving officer. "If Senior Lieutenant Yalinsky can take us up straight, instead of weaving like a drunken whore, we shouldn't have any trouble."

Anatoly Yalinsky smiled self-consciously. "I should be able to manage that, sir."

Nakhimov nodded. "Very well." He reached out and gripped the railing around the plot table. Other officers and sailors around the control room did the same with other holds. "Sail planes to vertical," he ordered. On camera, they saw the huge, winglike hydroplanes mounted on *Podmoskovye*'s sail swivel upward and lock in a vertical position. He signaled Yalinsky with a nod. "Surface, but like a genteel lady," he ordered. "Not like Maxim's drunken whore." That drew the laughs he'd hoped for.

More air hissed into their ballast tanks, giving the submarine positive buoyancy. Gradually, it rose, covering the remaining distance between the top of the sail and the underside of the ice cap in about twenty seconds. There was a sudden, sharp little jolt. *Podmoskovye* stopped dead, now pinned against the ice above her. "Increase buoyancy," Nakhimov said calmly.

Still more air flooded the tanks, expelling water. Steadily, the pressure against the ice layer built up, until, with a sudden *craacckk* that reverberated through the hull, it gave way. Instantly, *Podmoskovye* bobbed through the shattered ice like a cork, bouncing high into the open air. Yalinsky sprang into action, opening valves to allow more water back into her ballast tanks until she rode evenly, at rest in the center of a raised mound of broken blocks of meter-thick ice.

At Nakhimov's next orders, more sailors and officers went to work, climbing out through a hatch at the top of the sail and then slithering down onto the ice-sheathed hull. Quickly, they started clearing away the blocks of ice covering another, larger hatch farther back along the submarine's 166-meter-long hull. Once it was clear, sailors began hauling thick hoses up through the hatch and out onto the ice cap. These hoses were connected to the aviation fuel bladders and pumps occupying *Podmoskovye*'s minisub hangar.

"Send a signal to Saint Petersburg," Nakhimov ordered, turning away from the edge of the sail with a satisfied smile. "Inform Fleet Headquarters that we are on station one hundred and sixty kilometers from the American coast, and ready to assist in flight operations."

THIRTY-TWO

A SHORT TIME LATER

Major Jack "Ripper" Ingalls looked out through the HC-130J's cockpit windows. Through breaks in the clouds scudding southward, he caught glimpses of a vast sea of rugged, snow-capped peaks spreading out ahead of them as far as the eye could see. Pale light from the nearly full moon low in the east created an eerie patchwork of gleaming white snowfields and impenetrable shadow. The Super Hercules was at seven thousand feet, high enough to clear the tallest mountains on their flight path, but not by much.

Beside him, Laura Van Horn had her head down while she keenly studied their navigation display. After taking off from Barter Island, they'd made a slow, climbing turn over the coastal plain, babying the aircraft since their left inboard engine was still out of action. Now they were headed due south, taking the most direct possible route toward the drop zone for Nick Flynn's team. "We're ten minutes out, Rip," she said. "Time to start our descent."

"Copy that, descending," Ingalls said with a tight

nod. He pushed the steering yoke forward very gradually, not by much, no more than a degree or two. This approach to the drop zone was a tricky one. Past the midpoint of the Brooks Range, the highest peaks tended to diminish in elevation, but some of them still spiked nearly a mile into the sky. If the HC-130J came in too low, it risked slamming head-on into a mountainside. If it came in too high, there'd be no way to descend rapidly enough to drop Flynn and his men from a safe height.

Ingalls saw the airspeed indicator on his HUD rising and throttled back a bit. Ideally, he wanted to cross the drop zone at no more than 130 knots. Much faster and any parachute jump would be far too hazardous. Much slower and he risked stalling out, especially with the drag from their dead Number Two engine. He blinked away a bead of sweat. This was a high-wire act from beginning to end, with no safety net waiting to save anyone if he screwed up.

Aft of the HC-130J's cockpit, Flynn sat hunched over in one of the mesh seats that lined the sides of the cargo compartment. Between his parachute harness, weapons, and other gear, he was carrying well over a hundred pounds of extra weight strapped to his back, chest, and thighs. Add the tendency of the big aircraft to shimmy and shake in turbulence every few seconds, and there was no way he could hope to get comfortable. Thank God this was such a short flight, he decided.

He turned his head to look at the rest of his team. Soldiers and airmen gave him answering grins or flashed thumbs-up signs. Another positive of the quick trip, Flynn thought dryly. Nobody'd had much time yet to consider what a really dumbass idea this was.

And then Staff Sergeant Wahl was leaning over him, holding on to a seat frame. "Six-minute warning, sir," the HC-130 crewman yelled into Flynn's ear. For the purposes of this flight, Wahl was acting as both loadmaster and jumpmaster. Despite the half-inch-thick insulation covering almost every exposed metal inch of the aircraft's fuselage, the deafening roar from the Super Hercules's big engines made it sound like the other man was a hundred yards away.

Wahl saw his answering nod and moved out into the middle of the compartment. He waved his arms to get everyone's attention. "Get ready!" He used hand signals to make sure he could be understood over all the pounding racket.

Obeying the command, Flynn and the others unbuckled their seat belts.

"Port-side personnel, stand up!"

Made awkward by all their heavy equipment, Flynn and the five men with him on the HC-130's left side staggered upright and turned toward the rear of the plane. As the first man slated to jump, he was at the head of the line.

"Starboard-side personnel, stand up!" Wahl shouted next.

Now those seated on the right side clambered to

their feet. Sergeant Andy Takirak, who would be the last man out, was at the back. A gauze bandage covered the jagged cut on his forehead. He met Flynn's gaze and nodded confidently, as if to confirm that he was ready to go despite his minor injury.

Wahl spoke briefly into the intercom mike attached to his flight helmet, checking in with the cockpit crew. He nodded sharply at what they told him and then looked back at the waiting paratroopers. "Hook up!"

Flynn grabbed his static line and snapped its hook over the anchor cable stretched above his head. Behind him, the others in his stick did the same. Those to his right followed suit, hooking onto another anchor cable running down that side of the aircraft.

Wahl moved down the line of heavily burdened soldiers and airmen, watching closely as they checked their static lines and equipment and then did the same for the man in front of them. Satisfied by what he saw, he nodded to Flynn. Then he moved around to the side of the equipment pallet loaded with their two snow machines, sleds, and other heavy gear. The jumpmaster clipped his own safety line to a bracket. "We're opening the rear ramp now! Get set!"

Flynn and the others shuffled carefully into position several feet behind the pallet.

The tail section of the HC-130J split in two, with the top half elevating out of the way as the big rear ramp whirred down and locked in position. The whole process took just twenty seconds. Immediately, the noise level ratcheted up to an almost unimaginable level. Between the suddenly magnified roar of the huge Rolls-Royce turboprops and the howling ice-cold wind gusts whipping down the length of the compartment, it was now virtually impossible to hear anything.

Crouched beside the equipment pallet, Wahl signaled the waiting men to stand by. They were ten seconds out from the drop zone. Abruptly, he yanked a restraining cord away. Freed, the pallet rolled smoothly down the ramp, tipped over, and vanished into thin air.

Given the "go" signal by Wahl the moment the ramp was clear, Flynn didn't hesitate. He moved forward down the ramp and stepped off into space.

Instantly hurled away from the HC-130J by its freezing prop blast, Flynn tumbled through the night sky like a gale-borne leaf . . . until his parachute snapped open with a tooth-rattling jolt. Jesus, he thought dazedly, that *hurt*. Dangling under the chute's billowing canopy, he slid downwind at a dizzying pace. Looking down past his boots, he saw a darkened landscape lit silver in places by moonlight spilling through fissures in the cloud layer overhead. Steep-sided hills and ridges rose on all sides of the snow-covered valley below. And the boulder-strewn slopes lining its southern edge were growing ever larger with alarming speed.

Flynn held tight to his risers and twisted around, trying to find the rest of his team as they jumped behind him. He had time to catch only a brief glimpse of other moonlit parachutes scattering across the sky on the wind.

Everything after that happened very fast. The

silvery snowpack below him took on shape and definition with horrifying swiftness. Hurriedly, he released his rucksack and weapons case, bent his knees, tucked his chin, and—

Whummp.

Flynn thumped down with a bone-jarring thud and rolled sideways. Despite the hard landing, this time he was able to unclip his left-side riser attach and spill the wind from his fluttering canopy before it could drag him very far across the snow. Moving quickly, he stowed his used parachute, shrugged out of his jump harness, and then checked over his weapons and other gear—pausing only to spit blood from a cut lip into the snow.

Clambering to his feet, Flynn turned through a complete circle to get his bearings. As best he could judge, he'd come down about two-thirds of the way across the valley. He strapped on a pair of snowshoes and set off back to the north, plowing determinedly through foot-deep snow toward where he judged their equipment pallet should have come down. Since the pallet held their only motorized vehicles and additional supplies, he'd told his team that would be their rally point. Gusts of wind whipped up glittering waves of snow and ice crystals that stung every exposed bit of skin on his face. Hurriedly, he pulled up his face mask, ducked his head down, and kept moving.

He found the pallet about 250 yards away, lying canted over at a forty-five-degree angle under its collapsed parachutes. Drifting down out of the sky, it had smacked straight into a little clump of dwarf willow trees with disastrous results. Both snow machines had broken loose on impact. Slammed against tree trunks with tremendous force, they were little more than crumpled masses of metal and fractured fiberglass. One of the two towed sleds was probably salvageable. The other was a complete wreck, with both its runners torn off and twisted out of recognition. Bags and boxes of medical and other supplies were strewn across the snow, most of them ripped open.

"Well, shit," Flynn muttered with feeling, staring at the mess. The emergency search-and-rescue effort he'd been ordered to mount had just been knocked back to a nineteenth-century technological level. He was now entirely dependent on men on foot using snowshoes and cross-country skis to traverse difficult terrain.

Over the next several minutes, in ones and twos, more of his men straggled in, bowed down under the weight of their own weapons and gear. They all stopped dead when they saw the shattered pallet and its wrecked cargo. Growled profanity blistered the freezing air, most of it directed at the "goddamn Air Force" for "managing to score a bull's-eye on the one fucking clump of trees in a couple hundred fucking miles."

"Now what?" Hynes asked bluntly. "Sir."

Flynn forced himself to smile back at the square-shouldered, Army enlisted man. Boosting morale with stupid jokes and determined optimism was one of the most important tasks for any military officer, even when everyone knew it was total bullshit.

"Now we all hoof it, PFC. Just like in the good old days. You joined the infantry first, didn't you? Trekking through the wilderness on your own two feet ought to be right up your alley."

"Yeah, cheer up, Cole," one of the others said with a crooked smile of his own. "Sure, it's fricking cold out. And it's dark. *And* we're all gonna have to drag our sorry asses through the snow for miles and miles—"

"I'm waiting for the 'but' here, Boyd," Hynes said darkly.

"Well, I mean, how much worse could it get?" the other man finished.

"A lot worse," another soldier said suddenly, looking off to the south.

Flynn turned and saw a little party trudging slowly toward them out of the darkness. Wade Vucovich was staggering along under the weight not only of his own equipment, but also that of Sanchez and Torvald Pedersen. The big New Mexican had Pedersen slung over his shoulder in a fireman's carry. In a rush, everyone moved to join them.

With a grunt, Sanchez stopped and kneeled down. Then, gently, he rolled the dark-haired sniper off his shoulder and set him carefully on the snow.

"What happened?" Flynn asked, squatting next to Pedersen.

"Screwed up my landing, sir," the marksman said blearily. "I think I busted my leg."

Sanchez nodded. "Me and Wade here splinted it and gave him some painkillers, but Tor can't walk on that broken leg, so I had to carry him." He saw the astonished look on Flynn's face and said quickly, "It wasn't that far, Captain. Not more than a half a mile."

Flynn stared at him blankly. A half a mile. Through snow and ice in below-freezing temperatures. Damn, he thought with sudden pride, these men were *good*. And to think he'd first seen these guys as the Grimy Ten, a bunch of no-hopers foisted on him by other officers who were smart enough to get rid of them. He felt a moment's regret that Airman Mitchell had been the one man who'd folded up in the crunch. Despite M-Squared's occasional goofball tendencies, he'd seemed to be shaping up well.

"You're not going to leave me here, are you, sir?" Pedersen asked suddenly, sounding worried.

"Oh hell no," Flynn assured him, as a way to solve this problem abruptly unfolded inside his mind. It was just a question of applying their very limited but very real resources to the task in hand. "You can ride on the one sled that mostly survived the drop. We'll fix it up and rig a couple of rope harnesses so we can take turns pulling you, like sled dogs."

Behind him, he heard Hynes mutter, "Geez, M-Squared on the run, all our snow machines wrecked, and now a busted leg to top it off. Crap, the sarge is going to be really, really pissed off."

Flynn raised his head in sudden concern. He looked around the circle of faces. Everyone else except Takirak had already arrived at the rally point. So where *was* the veteran NCO? Lying out there somewhere in the dark, injured himself or maybe dead? He scrambled back to his feet, ready to order out a search party to go look.

At that moment, Takirak came gliding into view, moving across the snow on snowshoes with easy, practiced strides. Despite the fact that he had the PRC-162 manpack radio slung over one shoulder, and his own rucksack and M4 carbine on the other, he looked surprisingly fresh.

"Sorry I'm late, sir," he told Flynn apologetically. "The wind carried me a ways farther than I hoped."

"Glad you could finally join us, Sergeant," Flynn replied with a slight smile to take away some of the sting of his words. Quickly, he outlined their current situation.

Takirak nodded stoically. "Well, it could be worse, I suppose," he allowed.

Flynn saw Hynes roll his eyes dramatically and stifled a laugh. "I guess so, Andy." He nodded to the radio the sergeant carried. "But if that thing's still working, we need to report in."

While the rest of the unit moved off to gather up any surviving supplies and work on the damaged sled, he and Takirak squatted down on the snow around the radio. Working efficiently, the sergeant unfolded the unit's satellite communications antenna, angled it toward the horizon, and plugged in a battery pack.

As soon as he was done, Flynn flipped the power switches to on. They didn't have any time to waste. The PRC-162's batteries were rated to minus twenty-two degrees Fahrenheit, but prolonged exposure to extreme low temperatures would reduce their effectiveness. He picked up the handset. "Kodiak Six to Jaybird One. Kodiak Six to Jaybird One. Come in, Jaybird."

A squeal of static was the only answer.

With a frown, Takirak adjusted the antenna position. Above the Arctic Circle, it was often difficult to link with communications satellites in geosynchronous orbit over the equator. The extremely low angle required meant signals had to cross more atmosphere, with all the resulting distortion and loss of power. Plus, these high latitudes also adversely affected the refraction of radio signals. The Russians had far fewer communications problems in the Arctic, thanks to their own constellation of satellites in special polar orbits.

"Kodiak Six to Jaybird One," Flynn tried again.

This time, a static-laden voice replied. "*Jaybird One copies, Kodiak Six.*" They'd reached Alaskan Command, six hundred miles south at Joint Base Elmendorf-Richardson.

Swiftly and concisely, Flynn outlined their current status and location.

"*Understood, Kodiak. Suggest you proceed to Site Alpha*—" More high-pitched static squealed across their weak connection.

Flynn clicked his mike. "Affirmative on that, Jaybird." Before it failed, satellites had picked up an F-22 Raptor's emergency locator beacon about four miles southeast of their current position, somewhere near a range of steep hills that separated this particular valley from the next one over. It was labeled Site Alpha on their mission planning map.

"*Recommend extreme caution,*" Alaskan Command continued. "*The Russians have already engaged in open hostilities to prevent CSAR operations in your area. Our runways here are still closed. We can't provide any re-inforcements or air support if you run into trouble.*"

"Copy that, Jaybird One," Flynn acknowledged. "Kodiak Six, out."

He shut off the radio and waited while Takirak disconnected the battery and stuffed it back in his rucksack to stay warmer. "Nice to know they're worried about us. Now, at least," he commented.

The sergeant shrugged his shoulders. "Ass cover-ing is a fine art," he said irreverently. He looked at Flynn. "What are your orders, Captain?"

"We'll march southeast along the valley toward that downed F-22," Flynn decided. "But not until ev-eryone's gotten some food into them." Extreme cold and exertion burned calories far more rapidly than anyone not used to Arctic conditions could imagine. And fatigue could easily become a lethal weapon in this climate. "Then we'll move out, deployed in a skirmish line. I want to cover as much ground as we can. We know where one wrecked aircraft might be, but there are at least four others out there some-where."

Takirak nodded. "Sounds sensible, sir." He stood up and slung the radio over his shoulder again. "With your permission, I'll take point."

"Good idea, Andy," Flynn agreed. The older man had decades of experience surviving in this type of rugged terrain and severe winter weather. Relying on him to be their advance scout made perfect sense.

THIRTY-THREE

THAT SAME TIME

Alexei Petrov stood in the shelter of the trees near their camouflaged encampment. He had his head cocked, listening intently as the sound of a large turboprop faded slowly in the distance. The aircraft, invisible in the clouds and darkness, had made one slow pass over the neighboring valley to the west before turning away to the north. He glanced at Bondarovich, standing next to him looking up at the sky. "You can relax now, Sergei. Whoever that was knocking on our door, they're leaving now."

The ex-Spetsnaz soldier scowled. "That was too close, Colonel." He nodded toward the camouflaged aircraft shelter. "When can the PAK-DA take off? The sooner that bomber's in the air and flying back to Russia, the sooner the rest of us can get out of here."

"Not long now," Petrov assured him. "No more than a few hours, so long as the winds continue to moderate." He dug his boot into the snow layer, testing it. "Even after this storm, our improvised runway is still solid. So it's just a question of waiting for the crosswinds to die down a bit." He looked at Bondarovich. "I suggest you and your men grab some shut-eye while you can. Your prisoner, too. Poor Major Bunin has a long flight ahead, with the prospect of a cold welcome waiting for him at home. And the rest of us face what will certainly be a long, hard trek to Canada through these mountains, correct?"

The other man nodded in agreement. "True enough." He smiled thinly. "Though at least our welcome will be much warmer than the major's." He raised an eyebrow. "What about you, Colonel?"

Petrov shrugged. "I want to refine the bomber's return flight plan some more. Just to make sure Bunin won't get picked up by American radar or patrols on his way out. After all, it would be bad business to take President Zhdanov's money and then fail to return his property." He waggled his steel hip flask with a knowing grin. "And if I get tired, I've always got a little pick-me-up to keep the party going."

Eyeing the colonel's vodka flask with barely concealed contempt, Bondarovich shrugged. He'd made no secret that he found Petrov's drinking habits unprofessional. "It's your funeral, I guess." Wearily, he plodded off through the snow toward the large tent he and Grishin's other mercenaries used as sleeping quarters. They kept Bunin tied up on a cot there, too, except when they let him eat and attend to matters of nature.

Petrov stood watching him go. *My funeral?* he

thought. His grin twisted. That was truer than the other man knew, and in more ways than one. He shoved the hip flask back into his parka and headed out toward the aircraft shelter. His time here was running out fast and he had preparations to make—preparations that would clear any potential obstacles from his path.

THAT SAME TIME

Fourteen heavily equipped Spetsnaz commandos assembled outside what would appear from the air to be mounds of snow and ice. In reality, they were cunningly camouflaged shelters, the core of a small military camp established secretly out on the polar ice cap two days before—hundreds of kilometers off the Russian and American coasts and far outside the detection range of NORAD's air surveillance radars. A satellite dish angled toward the horizon provided direct communication to Moscow.

Just beyond the tents, aircrews had finished stripping away the netting used to conceal two helicopters. One was a twin-turbine Kamov Ka-60 *Kosatka* (Killer Whale) troop transport. Russia had transport helicopters with more range and payload capacity, but the Ka-60 was designed for stealth, with special coatings to reduce its radar and thermal signatures. The other machine was a massive Mil Mi-26T2 heavy-lift helicopter that had been converted into an air refueling tanker. The extra fuel it provided en route had allowed the smaller, shorter-ranged Ka-60 to reach this distant hidden base in the first place.

Spetsnaz Major Gennady Korenev squinted against the bitter wind keening across the ice. He was glad that Moscow had finally made up its mind to deploy his detachment. Forty-eight hours spent sheltering against brutal temperatures that routinely dropped to more than forty degrees below zero was more than enough to convince any rational man that this vast desolation was best left to the polar bears.

With Korenev in the lead, his group of elite troops marched briskly toward the waiting Ka-60. Its engines were already spooling up. Slowly at first, and then gradually faster, its rotor blades began turning.

Just before they climbed into the helicopter, Korenev's second-in-command, Captain Primakov, touched his arm and pointed back toward the camp. "We've got company coming," he yelled over the shrill, growing whine of the helicopter's twin turbines.

Korenev turned and saw one of the Air Force officers who'd flown in to man this temporary camp hurrying toward them across the ice. His mouth twisted in frustration. "Oh, for God's sake, has Moscow gotten cold feet?"

"Can't be as cold as mine right now," Primakov joked. "Maybe one of our guys left his toothbrush behind."

Unwilling to be amused, Korenev shook his head. "Get the men on board, Captain. It's too fucking cold to fart around out here. If the mission's been called off, at least we can warm up a little first." He moved out from the helicopter to meet the newcomer halfway.

It was the ice camp's communications specialist. He held out a message folder and map overlay. "This just came in from Moscow, Major," he panted, trying to catch his breath in the bitter, lung-freezing chill. "Highest priority."

Korenev read through the message with growing interest. The GRU had just received new intelligence from one of its most reliable agents, a source code-named *SIROTA*, Orphan. A small force of American troops—an irregular mix of active-duty Army and Air Force personnel and National Guard reservists—had reached the target zone ahead of them. The map overlay showed the U.S. unit's last reported position. As a consequence, his original orders to deploy for a covert reconnaissance into the region had been altered. Now he was to hunt down these Americans and eliminate them first. He shrugged, taking this ruthless directive in stride. Like his men, Korenev was a hardened veteran of the war against terrorists in Syria, where prisoners were rarely taken by any side. Pocketing the map overlay, the Spetsnaz major moved on toward his waiting helicopter. As soon as he buckled into his seat, the Ka-60 lifted off and darted southeast, skimming just above the polar ice to avoid detection by enemy radar.

Ninety minutes later, the helicopter slowed in its headlong rush and turned toward an eerie black monolith rising starkly above a gleaming mound of ice. A signal lamp blinked repeatedly from the top

of the monolith, which was actually the SSBN
Podmoskovye's large sail.

The Ka-60 orbited once around the surfaced nuclear submarine and then settled in to land nearby.
Before its rotors stopped turning, sailors bundled
up in thick coats and fur caps against the cold
dragged hoses across the ice to begin refilling its
nearly empty fuel tanks. Soon, fully refueled, the
helicopter lifted off again. Now it flew south, carrying Korenev and his Spetsnaz commandos toward
the coast of Alaska and the mountainous wilderness
beyond.

A SHORT TIME LATER

Scorched and torn pieces of metal and fragments of half-melted composites were strewn for dozens of yards around a fire-blackened crater a couple of meters deep. The dying F-22 must have augered in almost vertically and at very high speed, Flynn judged. One gruesome check of the crumpled mass of fuselage half buried in the bottom of the crater had confirmed that the Raptor's pilot hadn't managed to eject before her aircraft slammed nose-first into the frozen tundra. At least her death was quick, he thought sadly.

Now he and his team were probing the debris field for some sign of the fighter's mission data recorder—which should have captured everything from cockpit voice and video recordings to detailed data from its engines, flight computers, and other avionics. That was exactly the kind of information Air Force investigators needed. With it, they might be able to piece together a reasonably accurate picture of what had happened during the clash between the American F-22s and the three downed Russian aircraft. In the pale glow cast by the low, full moon poking above the eastern hills, flashlight beams darted here and there through the tangled wreckage.

Flynn crouched beside a blackened metal panel wedged into the dirt. Holding his flashlight in one gloved hand, he gently brushed away flakes of carbonized composites with the other. The panel might have a serial number or an identifier code that could help determine which section of the Raptor it came from.

"*Sir!*" a voice hissed softly through his headset. "*Hey, Captain! It's me, Hynes. I think I got something here. There's something weird upslope, maybe a few hundred yards out.*"

Flynn looked toward where he'd posted the Army PFC as a sentry at the eastern edge of the debris field. The enlisted man had dropped to one knee, sighting along the barrel of his M249 Para light machine gun up at the steep, rocky hillside looming over the crash site.

Quickly, Flynn moved toward Hynes, staying low himself. He went prone next to the shorter man. "What did you spot? Movement?" he asked sharply.

"No, sir," the other man said. "Just some kind of lumpy shape up there on that slope. And it hasn't moved an inch since I first noticed it. But whatever it is, it sure as shit isn't anything natural."

Takirak dropped prone on the other side of Hynes. "Trouble?" he asked quietly.

Flynn shrugged. "Could be." He grinned tightly. "Or maybe PFC Hynes here needs an eye exam."

"Hey, I was twenty-twenty the last time the docs checked me over," the enlisted man protested.

Flynn readied his own carbine and nodded to Takirak. "Let's go check it out, Andy." He glanced at Hynes. "You cover us, PFC."

"Yes, sir," the younger man promised, still sighting through his scope. "If whatever that thing is so much as twitches, I'll blow the shit out of it."

Cautiously, Flynn led the way uphill, veering wide to stay out of Hynes's line of fire. By the time they were about a hundred yards out, he could see what the enlisted man was talking about—a darker, oddly shaped mass nestled in among a field of ice- and snow-covered boulders that must have been deposited across the slope by some retreating glacier thousands of years ago. He and Takirak kept going, planting their feet carefully to avoid sliding back down the steep slope.

When they got within twenty yards, Flynn flicked on his flashlight. His eyes widened slightly as the beam illuminated an unsettling sight—a corpse sheathed in ice and slumped over the handlebars of a snow machine that seemed to have wedged itself between two larger rocks.

"Son of a bitch," he muttered in amazement, hearing an equally astonished murmur from Takirak a little behind him. He moved closer and carefully set his M4 down against a boulder.

Gingerly, they eased the dead man off the machine, laid him down, and then rolled him over. His pale blue flight suit was marked by a dark, reddish-brown stain of dried blood around an ugly exit wound high up on his chest. Flynn's light settled on the name tag fixed below this wound. генералмайор василий мавричев, дальняя авиация, it read. Slowly, he translated the Cyrillic letters out loud, "Major General Vasily Mavrichev, Long-Range Aviation." His jaw tightened. "Okay, this is bullshit," he growled. "Total, absolute, *complete* bullshit."

"Sir? What's the problem?" Takirak asked, sounding puzzled.

Still frowning hugely, Flynn looked across the corpse at the noncom. "Our ice man here just happens to be the commander of Russia's Long-Range Aviation Force, Sergeant," he explained. "The head of their whole goddamned strategic bomber force."

He squatted back on his haunches, thinking fast. How the hell would a senior Russian Air Force commander end up all the way out here in the middle of nowhere in the first place? Let alone dead with a bullet wound in the back? And riding a snow machine manufactured in America or Canada? He shook his head. Nothing about this weird situation jibed with the briefing he'd been given about a downed Tu-142 reconnaissance aircraft and the Su-35 and F-22 fighters. He said as much out loud.

"Maybe this Mavrichev bailed out of that Russian recon plane before it crashed?" Takirak suggested.

"And you think he just happened to land right next to a working snow machine?" Flynn said, not hiding his skepticism. "Dead-smack in the middle of a few million acres of totally uninhabited wilderness?"

"There are a couple of lone-wolf trappers working parts of the refuge. Or at least there used to be,"

Takirak said stubbornly. "And those guys can get mighty trigger-happy if they think someone's stealing from them. If one of 'em saw this Russian general zooming off on his snow machine, he'd shoot him dead in a heartbeat."

Flynn stared at him in surprise. He'd expected more from the sergeant's common sense and intelligence. The other man had to know how unlikely his theory sounded. "Pretty thin odds on that, Andy," he commented dryly. "Somewhere around a billion-to-one against, I'd guess."

"Well, he had to come from somewhere, didn't he?" Takirak pointed out, with a shrug. "I mean, it's not like he just fell out of an empty sky." He shook his head. "Look, Captain, I agree this is odd. But the guy's dead. He's not a threat, and he's sure not going anywhere. Right now, we've got bigger problems on our plate—between Pedersen's busted leg and finding those other downed aircraft before the weather closes in on us again."

Flynn frowned. Part of him agreed with the older man. But only part. The other half of his mind was remembering what General Rosenthal had said about maybe coming across an intact aircraft on the ground. He had a sudden conviction that the two things—this mystery plane and their frozen corpse—must be connected somehow. Which made the dead man potentially far more important than Takirak seemed to want to believe. He looked up. "We still need to call this in, Andy. Pronto."

"If you say so, Captain," the sergeant said dubiously. He eyed their surroundings. "Could be tough to get a connection around here, though," he warned. "Got a lot of high ground in the way that might block our link to the satellite." With obvious and surprising reluctance, he went through the process of setting up the radio and its small dish antenna.

When Takirak finished, Flynn lifted the handset to his ear. "Kodiak Six to Jaybird One." In answer, a crackling squealing of high-pitched static blasted his eardrum. He winced and held the handset a little farther away before trying again. "Kodiak Six to Jaybird One," he repeated. More meaningless noise screeched out of the receiver.

Tight-lipped, Takirak tried adjusting the angle of the antenna. He even switched frequencies. Nothing worked to establish a solid satellite link. After repeated failures, he looked apologetically at Flynn. "Sorry, sir. I can try moving to a different spot. Like I said, these hills could be blocking our signal."

Frustrated, Flynn nodded. "Do what you can, Sergeant." He got back to his feet. "Meanwhile, I'm going to go round up the rest of the men." More than ever, he wished Mitchell hadn't cut and run on them. The young airman had a real gift for electronics, one that the older National Guard noncom, for all his many other military and wilderness survival skills, obviously did not share.

"We're moving out?" Takirak asked, sounding surprised. "Before we finish looking for that F-22's flight recorder?"

"Yep," Flynn said. He prodded the dead Russian general with the toe of his boot. "My bet is that this guy's the key to a lot of the strange shit that's been going on. The blizzard probably wiped out most of the tracks from his snow machine. But maybe we can find traces of blood or ski trails across pockets of snow where they were sheltered from the wind." He retrieved his carbine. "So my plan now is to follow those traces and see just where they lead."

THIRTY-FOUR

OVER THE BROOKS RANGE

A FEW MINUTES LATER

The Ka-60 *Kosatka* helicopter clattered low above a frozen stream, following the gorge the watercourse had cut through solid stone and shale over untold millennia. Streamers of snow cascaded off cliff faces and whirled away through the air in its wake.

Spetsnaz Major Gennady Korenev glanced around the crowded troop compartment. His men were packed in like sardines, crammed shoulder to shoulder in the helicopter's folding seats. Above their protective thermal masks, expressionless eyes returned his gaze. They were all trained and experienced killers. No one had any illusions left. This operation was going to be messy.

"Major! We've got a priority signal for you!" one of the Ka-60's two pilots called over the intercom suddenly. "From GRU headquarters."

"Patch it through," Korenev ordered. The background noise through his headset changed to a thin, reedy whistling, indicating a live secure satellite connection. "Raven here," he said. "Go ahead."

"We've just received critical new intelligence from

SIROTA," the mission coordinator back in Moscow told him. *"The situation has changed—"*

Korenev listened attentively while the coordinator gave him the details. His eyes widened very slightly. Then, when Moscow signed off, he unbuckled and squirmed forward to crouch right behind the two pilots.

"What is it, Major?" one of them asked, peering back over his shoulder.

"Show me the planned LZ on your navigation display," Korenev demanded.

Obeying, the pilot opened a digital map on the helicopter's large central multifunction display. A blinking green dot indicated the place they'd picked out to land the major and his commandos, near the northwestern end of a valley.

Korenev shook his head. "We need to land a few kilometers more to the southeast." He reached out and tapped a spot on the map. It was in a gap between two hills. "Somewhere around here."

The pilot leaned forward and studied the terrain. "That shouldn't be a problem. The terrain looks pretty clear." He glanced back at the Spetsnaz officer. "So what's going on?"

"This mission just went from what was planned as a quiet, little manhunt to an all-out sprint for the prize," Korenev said tightly in reply. "Discretion's gone out the window. Now Moscow doesn't give a damn about how much noise we make."

The helicopter pilot shook his head in disgust. "Nice of them to let us know, I guess. Even if it's pretty late in the game." He jerked a thumb over his shoulder. "Those guns we left behind might have come in handy."

Korenev grunted in agreement. Combat models of the Ka-60 were often equipped with two pod-mounted 12.7mm machine guns. They'd been taken off to save weight for this long-range, low-level penetrating flight into hostile territory. And even though he didn't expect the ragtag American unit they were targeting to put up much of a fight, there was no question that the extra firepower would have been useful. He shrugged his shoulders. "No plan survives contact with the enemy. This one won't be any different."

THAT SAME TIME

Colonel Alexei Petrov gunned the motor of the snowmobile to force the vehicle up the last few meters of the hill overlooking their camp. He came out over the crest moving too fast and braked hard, skidding and weaving across the hard-packed snow as he slid to a stop. With a feeling of relief, he shut down the motor and brushed off his goggles.

One of Bondarovich's ex-soldiers came over to greet him, pushing up the night vision goggles he'd been using to scan the surrounding terrain. "A little trickier running one of those snowmobiles than flying a plane, eh?" he said with obvious amusement.

Petrov forced himself to smile. "Trickier, no. Different, yes." He climbed down off the machine.

The mercenary shrugged. "Well, you'll have time to pick up the technique during the trek out to Canada." His eyes flickered a little when he said that.

You're a poor liar, friend, Petrov thought with hidden amusement. He was surprised that Bondarovich had let Grishin and Voronin's plan for him slip like this. The former Spetsnaz officer should have kept that to himself until the very last second, right before they put a bullet into the back of Petrov's skull. The old proverb "Three men can keep a secret if two of them are dead" floated through the colonel's memory. It seemed particularly apt, just now. Neither the oligarch nor Voronin were foolish enough to leave him alive a moment longer than necessary. To them, Petrov was just a tool—someone to be used and then discarded when his particular skills were no longer needed.

Then again, perhaps that was fair. After all, his own views of Voronin and Grishin were just the same. All along, this had simply been a race to see whose goals were achieved first. And what the other two men could never have realized was that his own hidden plan was always bound to come to fruition before theirs.

"Where's everybody else?" the sentry asked.

Petrov nodded toward their camp. The camouflaged tents were completely invisible in among the trees. "Getting some rest."

"Lucky bastards," the other man said enviously. "Guess I pulled the short straw."

Petrov laughed. "Maybe." He turned away to look out across the valley. "Any more signs of trouble?"

"Nothing, Colonel," the sentry assured him. "It's been quiet ever since that other big plane made its pass and flew away." He slapped at his arms and legs. "Mother of God, though, it's cold enough to freeze my ex-wife solid." His mouth twisted in a sour grin. "And I can tell you that she was one hot-blooded woman."

"Well, cheer up, you'll be warm soon enough," Petrov assured him smoothly. "And rich, too."

The other man's smile broadened. "There is that."

Pleasantly, Petrov held out the steel hip flask in his left hand. "Since that's the case, how about a little nip to celebrate?"

The sentry's eyes lit up with anticipated pleasure. Everyone in camp knew the colonel only drank the best. "Absolutely." He pulled down his face mask and tilted his head back to drink.

Without hesitation, Petrov drew his 9mm pistol, shoved it hard against the other man's stomach, and squeezed the trigger. Muffled by close contact, the sound of the shot was no louder than a car backfire might be somewhere far off.

The sentry's eyes widened in horror. He dropped the flask and staggered backward. Brutally, Petrov kicked his legs out from under him. Then he raised his booted foot high and stomped down hard on the other man's exposed neck, crushing his trachea with one swift, savage motion. For a few seconds, the dying man's heels drummed spastically, kicking up snow . . . and then they stopped.

Petrov looked down at the blood spattered across his fur-lined parka with a hint of disgust. Then he shrugged. Before long, he would no longer need the coat to shield him from this miserable weather. He bent down to retrieve his flask, remounted the snowmobile, and sped off down the hill toward the sleeping camp.

THIRTY-FIVE

A SHORT TIME LATER

Nick Flynn moved cautiously out onto a patch of dark ice just below a massive boulder half-buried in the hillside. One misstep and he'd take a long, painful spill down the steep side of this rugged spur. Slowly, he edged out into the middle of the ice patch and crouched down. His flashlight beam flicked out, catching what looked like a trail of rust splotches across the surface.

More dried blood, he thought with satisfaction. Along with parallel depressions sliced into the top layer of ice. Which meant they were still headed the right way. He shook his head in amazement. To have made it across this part of the slope without tipping over and tumbling end over end downhill, Major General Mavrichev must have been driving that snow machine flat out at top speed. The Russian general had also been incredibly lucky, Flynn decided, though that was probably the wrong way to look at it—considering that he was almost certainly dying at the time.

Flynn rose back to his feet and looked around.

Counting him, eight men were spread in a skirmish line along the flank of this half-mile-long spur. It ran roughly south off a longer, higher ridge that separated this valley from the next. A couple of hundred feet below and a few hundred yards to the southwest, he could make out the small moonlit shapes of two more of his troops, Rafael Sanchez and Noah Boyd, as they moved slowly across more level ground, hauling a sled with Torvald Pedersen strapped aboard. He didn't like the need to disperse his small command so widely, but it wouldn't have been safe to try pulling that sled across this hillside. Not unless he wanted to risk adding a broken neck to Pedersen's already-fractured leg.

He took a moment to check the digital map stored in his tablet. Past this spur, the terrain opened up onto a somewhat wider plain, one cut through by curving, shallow, gravel-banked streams that eventually merged to become the Old Crow River. Considering Mavrichev had taken a pistol-caliber-sized round through his right lung, the Russian general had likely been shot somewhere in that next valley. Which meant whoever it was that had put a bullet into him was probably close, no more than a few miles up ahead. And that, in turn, meant it was time to start being a hell of a lot more cautious.

Flynn edged off the ice patch onto firmer ground and then keyed his tactical radio. "Kodiak Six to all Kodiaks on this hill. Close up on my position. Sanchez and Boyd, you guys hold where you are for now. Six out."

Acknowledgments flooded through his headset.

Both ends of his skirmish line began curling toward him, with the men higher on the spur sliding carefully downhill and those lower down painstakingly working their way back up. It took time to complete the maneuver, but finally, Flynn found himself at the center of a group of closely clustered, curious faces. All but one. Takirak stayed a couple of yards away, as if he wanted to both physically and mentally distance himself from the others.

Flynn frowned inside at that. Something had seemed off with the grizzled noncom ever since they'd found that dead Russian Air Force general. Maybe it was the head wound he'd taken, though that hadn't seemed more than a surface gash. Or maybe, he thought sadly, the older man was one of those recruiting-poster soldiers who excelled in peacetime training and then folded under the stress of real action. Whatever it was, it was a serious problem. He'd come to depend heavily on Takirak's advice and local knowledge. Realizing he could no longer fully trust his second-in-command felt an awful lot like losing his right arm.

"What's up, sir?" Hynes asked at last.

Aware that he'd been silent for too long, Flynn shook himself. Soldiers didn't like being stared at by their officers. It made them nervous, both because they started wondering how they might've screwed up, and worse, because it could mean they were being led by someone who had no fucking clue of what to do next. And enlisted men knew all too well that an indecisive officer was the one most likely to get them all killed.

"Here's the deal," he said calmly, facing his men. "Somebody out in front of us seems kind of trigger-happy. Now, they might technically be on our side—"

"Like maybe the CIA?" Airman Kim asked curiously.

Flynn nodded. "Possibly." Then he shrugged. "Or they may be outright hostile." He saw Hynes's mouth open and beat him to the punch. "Yes, as in the Russians, PFC Hynes. Either way, I want the chance to take a good, hard look at whoever they are *before* they see us coming. So we're switching to night vision gear starting now."

Heads nodded in understanding. From their current position, in the hills above these intertwined valleys, the ordinary flashlights they'd been using could be seen for miles.

"Using the NVGs in this cold will drain their batteries pretty fast," Takirak warned.

Flynn stared at him. "I'm aware of that, Sergeant," he said quietly. "Do you have an alternative that I've missed?"

The older man nodded. "We'd make better time down on the flat with the guys hauling the sled," he said, pointing downslope. "Movement would be easier, faster, and a heck of a lot safer. There's less chance of someone twisting an ankle on that tundra . . . and any lights we need won't be as obvious at a distance."

Flynn shook his head. "We'll stick to the high ground for now," he said firmly. "At least until we know more about what we could be facing up ahead.

If we are heading into trouble, I want every tactical advantage I can get."

"It's your call, sir," Takirak allowed stiffly. But the disapproving set of his shoulders and the undercurrent of skepticism in his voice both left no doubt that he believed his commander was making a mistake.

Flynn ignored that. Trying to argue the sergeant into agreement would only waste time. And making it even more obvious that their two leaders weren't seeing eye to eye would only unnerve the rest of his soldiers and airmen. Instead, he pulled his own night vision goggles out of an insulated pouch attached to his body armor and slid them on over his helmet. He powered them up. Instantly, the darkness brightened into a monochrome semblance of daylight. The men around him did the same, though Takirak donned his own vision gear with an obvious lack of enthusiasm.

"Okay," Flynn said. "We're going to tighten up our skirmish line from here on out. I want two-man fighting pairs, with a twenty-yard separation between pairs. We'll follow this spur around back to the northeast and continue on along the main ridge. Keep your eyes peeled and move as quietly as you can. Once we're back on the main ridge, pay attention to our right flank. That's the most likely threat axis. If anybody is camped up ahead, they're probably down there on the valley floor—somewhere close to one of those iced-over streams for water and shelter."

Hynes held up a hand. "What do we do if we spot someone, sir?"

"You take cover and report the contact, PFC," Flynn told him. "But nobody opens fire unless I give a direct order. Is that clear?" They nodded.

Flynn swung his M4 carbine off his shoulder. "Right. Let's move out—" And then he broke off suddenly, holding up a hand for quiet. He thought he'd heard something behind them, off in the north—a faint, rhythmic whirring sound. In the abrupt hush, he heard the noise more clearly as it grew louder. It was the fast, thudding noise made by a helicopter's rotors and turbines.

"Down!" he hissed. Everybody on the hillside dropped flat and froze in place. In their white camouflage smocks and heavy rucksacks, they looked more like snow-covered rocks than anything else. He glanced downslope. The two men pulling the sled had stopped and were staring up at the sky back the way they'd come. He tapped the push on his tactical radio. "Sanchez and Boyd. Grab Pedersen and find some cover. Now!"

That kicked them into gear. With the injured man's arms slung over their shoulders, the two soldiers hurried into a small depression lined with snow-covered bushes and went to ground.

"Friendlies?" Kim whispered.

"Not likely," Flynn replied. That helicopter sounded like it was coming from the north, and there weren't any U.S. military helicopters closer than Joint Base Elmendorf-Richardson—which was hundreds of miles to the south and currently socked in by that big blizzard.

Takirak wriggled around to face him. "You could be wrong about that, Captain," he said pointedly. "There are a lot of civilian helicopter operators working out of the Prudhoe Bay oil fields. I used to fly with them a lot when I worked as a guide up around Deadhorse. Maybe our guys at JBER hired one of those birds to bring in reinforcements for us."

"Reinforcements from where exactly, Andy?" Flynn asked, working to hide his irritation. For some reason, Takirak seemed to be trying very hard to sow doubts about every decision he made. What the hell was the noncom's problem? "In case you forgot, there aren't other U.S. troops stationed this far north." That hit home. He saw the older man's eyes flash angrily.

The *thwapping* sound of spinning rotors slowed suddenly and then faded away. It was replaced by a low, shrill whine of engines spooling down.

Flynn raised his head. The helicopter had landed behind them, somewhere out of sight around the curve of this rocky spur. Reacting quickly, he waved his men back up onto their feet. Pushing on ahead the way he'd originally planned would be foolhardy now. The last thing he wanted was to be surprised by a potentially hostile force closing in from the rear. He clicked his mike. "Sanchez and Boyd, stick tight where you are. And stay off the radio. Six out," he murmured. He looked at the others. "The same goes for everybody else. Voice commands and hand signals only from here on out. We don't know who else might be listening to our net."

His men nodded. Maybe the idea that someone could have broken into their tactical net was crazy, but it felt like a hell of a weird coincidence for that helicopter to have landed so close to them. It was almost as though it had been guided straight to this particular spot, which was otherwise just one of thousands of square miles of virtually identical wilderness. One thing was for sure, Flynn knew. All of his instincts were screaming danger warnings right now. And he didn't plan to ignore them.

Quickly, he issued new orders. They would backtrack along this spur toward where that helicopter had landed—deployed and ready to conduct a hasty ambush against anyone who might be following their trail. He half expected Andy Takirak to bitch some more, but instead the noncom merely nodded. "Good plan, Captain." Takirak unslung his own weapon and started to move out ahead of the rest of the unit. "I'll go scout," he said, with a quick, unreadable glance over his shoulder. "I can reach a decent observation point faster on my own."

"Hold on, Andy!" Flynn said sharply.

Almost unwillingly, the older man halted in his tracks. "Sir?"

"Leave the radio," Flynn ordered, nodding at the bulky PRC-162 still slung over Takirak's other shoulder. "You don't need the weight. And that antenna sticking up might give you away." For a moment, he had the strangest sense that the sergeant might disobey him.

But then, with a fleeting half smile, Takirak pulled the radio off his shoulder and set it down on the snowy slope. Without another word, he turned and loped away over a low rise, swiftly vanishing from sight.

Watching him go, Flynn felt the hairs go up on the back of his neck. Takirak's native name, *Amaruq*, Gray Wolf, had never before seemed so apt. He had the sudden, eerie impression that the older man had just revealed himself as a complete stranger— someone he'd never actually known. And as though that revelation was a sort of key to unlock his intuition, Flynn abruptly saw an answer for many of the odd events that had worried him over the past several hours.

Seconds passed while he stood frozen in place, feeling sick at heart and trying to make the pieces to this puzzle fit in some other way. Flynn couldn't fight down the sudden, terrible certainty that he'd never see M-Squared, his red-haired radioman, again . . . at least not alive. But then he breathed out. There was only one way to be sure, and in the meantime, he wasn't going to gamble with the lives of his men in the hope that he was wrong.

Flynn turned quickly to the half-dozen soldiers and airmen still with him. "Change of plan," he told them quietly. He pointed at the top of the spur, a couple of hundred feet above where they were now. A tumbled mass of rocks and larger boulders marked the crest and continued on down the far side. "We'll set up there instead," he ordered. "Now, drop your packs here and follow me!"

Obeying, they shrugged out of their rucksacks and then hurried after him as he plowed upward through the snow and ice.

THIRTY-SIX

THAT SAME TIME

As soon as the Ka-60 touched down, Spetsnaz troops slammed both side doors open and poured out in a rush. Bent low, the fourteen Russian commandos fanned out around the helicopter and then dropped flat in the snow with their weapons ready. Camouflage smocks and white helmet covers helped them blend with their surroundings.

Major Gennady Korenev carefully scanned the steep, treeless hill rising several hundred meters away. A narrow saddle of bare rock tied it to a larger ridge running off to the northeast. He couldn't make out any movement on that southern spur, but trampled patches in the snow roughly halfway up its slope showed that several men at least had moved across that flank and then around to the other side. He lowered his night vision binoculars and nodded. The Americans, as he'd expected, were somewhere ahead of them.

Getting back to his feet, he trotted back to the grounded Ka-60. With its engines off, the big main rotors had almost stopped turning. He leaned in through one of the side doors to speak to the two pilots. "Keep your eyes open. We're moving out after the enemy now, but we'll be back once that little job's done. Then we'll all push on to pinpoint the main objective, the PAK-DA bomber."

They nodded. "Good hunting, Major," the lead pilot said. "We'll be ready to take off again when you return."

With a soft whistle, Korenev signaled his men back up out of the snow. More rapid hand signals started them moving toward the higher ground. The Spetsnaz troops went forward in short rushes, sprinting ahead by twos and then going prone to cover the men coming up behind them. It was a tactic that guaranteed his detachment always had a solid base of fire waiting on overwatch—ready to immediately engage any enemies who showed themselves.

Korenev stayed a few meters behind the right flank of the advancing troops, while Captain Primakov, his second-in-command, did the same over on the left. This physical separation helped ensure that a sudden burst of enemy fire couldn't take them both out at once. It also allowed tighter control over the Spetsnaz unit as it maneuvered.

So the major was close by when one of his men suddenly stopped and dropped to a knee to peer at something in the moonlit snow just ahead. And when the soldier signaled him over, he was there in seconds. "What've you got, Vanya?"

The other man pointed to a pair of thin, rail-like tracks and two sets of deeper boot prints running roughly southeast toward a gap in the hills between this valley and the next. "More of the Americans," he said quietly. "Two of them towing something on a sled."

"Supplies," Korenev guessed. "Or perhaps heavier weapons." The intelligence reports provided by Moscow's prized source had claimed that the Americans had left their larger-caliber weapons, a recoilless rifle, and man-portable antiair missiles behind for this mission. But he was experienced enough to understand the limitations of even the most perfect-seeming intelligence. He shrugged. "If they've split their forces, so much the better for us. We'll finish off the larger group and then mop these two up for dessert."

The other man smiled wolfishly and then darted forward, obeying his commander's silent hand signal to resume the advance. Korenev drifted along in his wake, allowing the gap between them to widen.

Suddenly, higher up on the hill they were advancing toward, a small bright light began blinking at them in short, rhythmic flashes. Startled, the major threw himself prone again. Ahead and to his left, his soldiers did the same, bringing their mix of assault rifles and automatic weapons to bear. But then Korenev realized those flashes were in the same shorthand code used for silent communication between Russian special forces units. And that this message carried the prefix *SIROTA*, to verify that it came directly from the GRU's most prized agent. He mouthed the words as they were spelled out by that blinking light: ENEMY FORCE DEPLOYING

IN AMBUSH ON FLANK OF HILL SOUTHEAST OF MY PO-
SITION. CAUTION ADVISED.

Slowly, the major stood up, making sure he could be seen. Then he crossed his clenched fists over his head twice—confirming that he'd received the warning. The light blinked off immediately, leaving the dark mass of the hill once more cloaked in shadows and thin strips of moonlight.

Korenev waved Primakov over to join him. "What now?" the younger officer asked.

The major bared his teeth in a predatory grin. "Simple, while the Americans wait like imbeciles for us to walk blindly into their trap, we'll veer to the left." He indicated the main ridge to the northeast of the spur. "And climb up that way instead. Then we'll swing back to the right and come in to hit them from above and behind." He hefted his AK-12 assault rifle and patted the stock. "With the tables turned, it shouldn't take long to finish off our American friends."

THAT SAME TIME

Flynn moved warily downhill through the icy boulder field that covered this part of the slope, careful to watch where he placed his feet to avoid any unnecessary noise. Before heading here on his own, he'd ordered the rest of his men to take up concealed firing positions in the jumble of rocks and boulders farther up the slope. And he'd left his M4 carbine behind a while back, worried that the longer weapon might clatter against rock surfaces and give him away. Instead, he'd drawn his Glock 19 sidearm. That left him with one hand free for balance on this uneven, slippery surface.

He halted at the base of a weathered granite boulder twice the size of a man and stood listening. The soft, clicking noises he'd heard coming from ahead had just stopped, as suddenly as they had started. Cautiously, Flynn edged around the side of the boulder . . . and found Takirak crouched a couple of yards away, staring down into the valley. Soldiers camouflaged in snow smocks were on the move there, turning to parallel the high ground as they advanced to the northeast. Their helmets and other gear gave them a look almost identical to that of American special forces troops, but their weapons were clearly Russian.

And the National Guard sergeant still held the flashlight he'd been using as a signaling device.

Flynn sighed. There were moments when he really hated being right. This was probably the worst of them. He sighted along the barrel of his pistol, aiming at Takirak's back. "So, Andy," he said quietly, almost conversationally. "Just how long have you been betraying your country?"

For a long, seemingly endless moment, the other man froze solid, not moving a muscle. But then he turned his head slowly toward Flynn. "I have never betrayed *my* country, Captain," he replied with a thin, tight smile on his face. *"Ya russkiy, chlen sibirskogo plemeni yupikov.* I am a Russian, a member of the Siberian Yupik tribe." He shrugged. "And for what it matters, a colonel in the GRU."

Flynn whistled softly under his breath, suddenly seeing the bigger picture they'd all missed. Along with the Inuits and Aleuts, the Yupiks were one of the three main groups of native peoples spread over the sprawling northern regions from Russia's Far East to Alaska, Canada, and Greenland. They shared related languages and common cultures. Recruiting one of them to act as a deep-cover agent in Alaska, with a lack of family ties explained by his supposed status as an orphan fostered down in the Lower Forty-Eight, was a brilliant move by Russia's military intelligence service.

With his cover established, Takirak had been perfectly placed for years to spy on the vital oil fields and pipelines at Prudhoe Bay—and, through his service with the Alaska National Guard, on U.S.

military installations across the state. No doubt, in the event of war, he would have been ordered to carry out sabotage missions against them. Flynn shook his head slightly in dismay. *Man, we let the fox, or rather* Amaruq *the Gray Wolf, saunter right into the henhouse*, he thought coldly, imagining how pleased the men in Moscow must have been when Takirak wangled his way into this assignment to guard the radars making up Alaska's portion of the North Warning System.

Abruptly, Takirak whirled toward him—hurling his flashlight like a missile. It crashed into Flynn's shoulder, sending him staggering back a couple of steps, partially off-balance. Before he could bring his Glock back on target, the Russian sprang to his feet, crashed into him, and chopped down hard at his right hand. Flynn's pistol went flying, clattering away into the rocks somewhere out of his reach.

Shit. Not good. Shaking off the stinging pain from his hand, Flynn shoved the older man back a couple of paces and then went for him. Takirak lunged to meet him head-on. Grunting with effort, they exchanged a flurry of short, vicious strikes aimed at vulnerable points—turning and twisting to absorb some painful blows, while parrying others. Neither gained a decisive edge. At last, almost by mutual accord, they separated slightly and crouched staring at each other, panting, scraped up, and bloody.

Takirak spat blood out of his mouth, without taking his cold, hard eyes off Flynn. Both men drew the combat knives they carried on their body armor and closed in again. There was no holding back now—only one of them would walk away from this.

Jesus, the Russian was fast, Flynn realized desperately, rolling away from a lightning-quick thrust that flickered right past his face. Backpedaling now, he narrowly blocked a second strike, but only at the cost of a ragged gash across the outside of his left forearm. He clenched his teeth hard against a sudden flare of white-hot pain from the wound.

Frantically, he thrust back at Takirak. Almost contemptuously, the enemy agent parried his strike. Then he hammered his fist into the inside of Flynn's right wrist—briefly paralyzing the nerves there.

Horrified, Flynn saw his blade fall out of his numbed fingers. Inside, he knew the advantage was shifting irreversibly to his enemy. *So get off your ass and fight*, he growled silently to himself.

Or die.

Furious now, he lowered his head and charged. Ignoring a knife slash that glanced off his helmet, he body-slammed the Russian, driving him back against a boulder with enormous force. He heard Takirak cry out in sudden agony. They both went down again, but this time Flynn ended up on top.

Quickly, he pinned the other man's knife hand with his left knee. Grim-faced now, Takirak heaved up against him. Flynn bore down. His fingers closed on a piece of broken rock and he smashed it across the Russian's face. He heard bone crunch. Spatters of blood flew across the trampled snow.

Takirak's eyes glinted fiercely above the red mask

of his stone-shattered face. Again, ferociously, he heaved up with frightening strength. This time, Flynn couldn't keep his hold. He was hurled away from the other man, and fell sprawling on his back.

Furiously muttering obscenities through his ruined mouth, Takirak rolled back upright with terrifying speed. He dove toward Flynn, who desperately scrabbled through the snow beside him. His hand closed on his combat knife. Blindly, he stabbed upward with everything he had . . . and buried the blade in the Russian's throat, all the way to the hilt. A bright scarlet fountain of blood, steaming in the freezing air, sprayed across Flynn's face. Above him, Takirak arched backward, clawing at the knife handle protruding from his neck. His eyes opened wide in horror, and then all the light went out of them. He slumped forward, shuddered once, and died.

THAT SAME TIME

Alexei Petrov stalked silently toward the tent where Bondarovich, the other mercenaries, and his former copilot, Oleg Bunin, were sleeping. He carried a green steel jerry can containing twenty liters of gasoline. It was one of those they used to refuel their snowmobiles. Several of the fuel cans had been stockpiled at one end of the camp in preparation for their escape to Canada. One side of his mouth quirked upward in an ironic grin. Never let it be said that he had allowed any of the resources so thoughtfully provided by Pavel Voronin and his master, Dmitri Grishin, to go to waste.

Just outside the tent, he set down the jerry can, unlatched its cap, and pulled it open, wrinkling his nose at the sharp tang of raw gasoline. Then, squatting beside the tent door, he carefully unzipped it from the bottom—not far, just a few centimeters. He heard a faint noise from inside as some of the four drowsing men bundled up in their sleeping bags stirred suddenly, apparently disturbed by the icy wind now whipping through the tiny opening.

Unhurriedly, Petrov tipped the jerry can over and watched the gasoline pour out. It sloshed out in waves, flowed through the unzipped door, and rippled across the tent's polypropylene fabric floor in an amber tide. Satisfied, he stood up and moved back a few meters. Then he pulled out a loaded flare pistol, cocked the hammer, and fired downward through the door.

With a crackling hiss, the flare exploded. A blinding, red-tinged flash lit the inside of the tent, replaced by a flickering orange glow as burning gasoline sprayed everywhere. Coolly, Petrov dropped the spent flare gun and pulled out his pistol. He ignored the agonized screams echoing from Bondarovich and the others. They'd been abruptly jolted out of sleep . . . only to find themselves trapped in a hell of whirling, wind-driven fire. Already blazing like torches, burning men stumbled toward the door, frantically trying to squeeze out through the narrow opening. Methodically, Petrov shot them one by one.

When the screams finally stopped, he lowered his pistol, turned, and walked away toward the distant aircraft shelter. Behind him, dancing tongues of fire licked up into the sky.

THIRTY-SEVEN

ON THE SPUR

THAT SAME TIME

Flynn doubled up his thermal mask and used it to mop Takirak's blood from his eyes, the rest of his face, and the razor-sharp blade of his combat knife. Finished, he tossed the sodden mask away in disgust. Then he took out a field dressing from his first aid kit and wrapped it around his gashed left forearm. Finally, he retrieved his pistol from the ground, brushing off the ice and snow that coated its muzzle and slide before slipping it back into his chest rig.

Off to his right, a little higher up the spur, Flynn heard the faint clatter and rattle of equipment. Six soldiers and airmen, all he had left under his direct command, were moving into position. Below the other side of this hill, his remaining men, Sanchez, Boyd, and the injured Torvald Pedersen, had gone to ground in some bushes a few hundred yards away. He would have liked to order them back to the main unit, but radioing them would be the only means of doing that. It was too risky. For all Flynn knew, their tactical frequencies and encryption systems were one of the secrets Takirak had already passed on to his fellow Russians.

Staying low, Flynn risked a quick look out across the open slope. The white-camouflaged Russian Spetsnaz commandos were still advancing along the valley. Apparently, they hadn't heard his brutal, hand-to-hand fight with Takirak, probably thanks to the noise made by the northerly winds hissing across hard-packed snow.

Flynn watched the enemy soldiers for a few more moments. It was pretty clear that they planned to bypass this particular piece of high ground—probably intending to climb the main ridge instead, before turning to hit the unsuspecting Americans from behind. Their plan would have worked, if he hadn't already figured out that Takirak had betrayed the ambush positions he'd first chosen. As it was, leapfrogging forward along the valley floor only exposed the Russian flank to attack from this rocky spur.

He left Takirak's corpse crumpled in the snow and moved back around through the jumble of boulders to rejoin his troops—reclaiming his M4 carbine on the way. The first man he came to was Private First Class Cole Hynes. Hynes was crouched behind a cairn of smaller rocks that formed a natural breastwork about waist-high. His bipod-mounted M249 Para light machine gun was positioned on the pile of rock, aimed straight downhill. "You find the sarge, sir?" he asked quietly.

Flynn nodded. "Yep."

"Is he coming?"

Flynn shook his head. "Sergeant Takirak's just fine where he is, Hynes." Even if he'd felt up to it right now, there wasn't time for any complicated, morale-busting explanations about Takirak's real identity as a Russian spy.

"So, those guys?" Hynes nodded at the snow-camouflaged shapes still moving by bounds along the foot of the hill. "Are they who I think they are?"

"They're definitely Russians," Flynn confirmed.

"So I can shoot 'em?" Hynes asked hopefully.

Flynn nodded. "But only on my order, PFC." He clapped the younger man on the shoulder. "Hold tight for a few more seconds, okay?"

Hynes nodded enthusiastically. "Copy that, Captain."

Flynn moved on down the line, quickly making sure that the rest of his troops—Airman Peter Kim, and Army Privates Wade Vucovich, Mike Sims, Floyd Leffert, and Gene Santarelli—were in position and understood the situation. Sims, Leffert, and Santarelli were known in the unit by the collective nickname of the Three Amigos, because they seemed perfectly content to spend most of their waking hours—both on duty and off duty—in one another's company. Most of that, from what Flynn could tell, was due to a shared passion for video games and the same Swedish heavy metal band. He figured that was as good a basis for camaraderie as any other.

One by one, all five gave him a tight nod or a swift thumbs-up signal. Satisfied, he reversed back down the line and took up a position just to Hynes's right, prone between two gray boulders. Another quick look down the slope showed that the Spetsnaz commandos were right where he wanted them—directly in front of his men and out in the open. They were a little over two hundred yards away. Carefully, he sighted on one of the Russians, a soldier carrying an AKM equipped with a 40mm grenade launcher. "All Kodiaks," he said loudly, raising his voice to be heard down the line. "Hit 'em! Now!"

Flynn squeezed off three quick shots. Snow spurted up behind his chosen target as the first two rounds missed, but the third hit the Russian in the side. The enemy soldier went down hard. On his left, Hynes opened up with his M249 light machine gun, firing short bursts down the hill—walking them across the Spetsnaz formation. Two more of them crumpled right away. Blood pooled red on the white snow.

Across the hillside, the other Americans joined in, firing down at the enemy commandos caught in the valley. Flashes lit the night. Another Russian fell. The rest, reacting fast, dove for whatever cover they could find and started shooting back—aiming toward the muzzle flashes.

5.45mm and 7.62mm rounds whip-cracked just over Flynn's head, smacking into boulders and then ricocheting away with weird, keening wails. Shards and splinters of pulverized rock spun away after them. "Stay low, Kodiaks!" he called. "And pour it into them!"

Sighting through his scope, Flynn found another target, a Russian prone behind a low rise. Only the man's helmet and rifle were visible. He squeezed the trigger several times. More chunks of snow and ice sprayed up, torn by bullets striking home at nearly three times the speed of sound. The Russian soldier disappeared, either hit or scrambling for new cover.

One of the enemy commandos got a grenade launcher in action. It coughed, hurling a 40mm caseless grenade up the slope.

Craack. The grenade detonated several meters behind the American line with a dazzling flash. Fragments whistled across the hill. "Shit!" one of the Three Amigos said suddenly, sounding surprised. "I'm hit." From the deep Alabama twang, that was Leffert. His friend Sims reared up to take a look and then took a bullet in the shoulder, falling back with another shocked cry.

"For Christ's sake, stay down!" Flynn yelled. He glanced to his left, toward the clump of rocks occupied by the two wounded Amigos. "Sims? Leffert? You okay?"

"I'm not hit bad, sir," Leffert called back. "I can still fight. But Mike's pretty bad. He's losing a whole lotta blood and his damn shoulder looks like it's hanging by a thread."

Flynn gritted his teeth. Besides being their radio and coms expert, M-Squared had also been tapped to be their unit medic. One more crime to lay at Takirak's feet, he thought bitterly.

Down in the valley, the Spetsnaz grenadier popped back up, ready to fire again. This time, Hynes was waiting for him. The machine gunner put a three-round burst right into his chest. The

Russian fell backward in a red mist of blood and shattered bone.

Flynn fired again at another commando darting uphill to gain a better position. He missed, and the enemy soldier threw himself down into a small depression on the slope, disappearing from sight. His jaw tightened. From the number of bodies now strewn across the valley floor, they'd already inflicted heavy losses on the Spetsnaz force. That wasn't shocking, since surprise and cover both favored the Americans. But enough Russians had survived the opening fusillade and found cover of their own to turn this into a pitched battle—one whose outcome was still seriously in doubt. Now they were trying to establish a firm base of fire of their own, one that would allow them to keep Flynn and his men pinned down long enough for an assault force to close in and wipe them out in a close-quarters fight.

The M4 went dry. Rapidly, he hit the mag release, let the empty fall out, and slapped in another full magazine. Immediately, he opened fire again. At the same time, he felt as though his mind had split in half, with one part fully occupied by the need to find and kill the enemy . . . and the other busy weighing different tactical options. Breaking contact and falling back up the hill was a nonstarter. As soon as the Russians got into these rocks, they'd have all the advantages superior numbers and training could provide. And with Leffert and Sims wounded, he didn't have enough able-bodied troops left to maneuver to the right or left in the hope of taking those Spetsnaz bastards in the flank again.

"Which leaves what, Nick?" Flynn muttered, squeezing off more shots and feeling his M4 thud back repeatedly against his shoulder. "Pray . . . and hope for luck? Real good plan there, genius." But then again, he thought grimly, what other options did he really have?

In the narrow, brush-choked gully around the other side of the spur hill, Torvald Pedersen heard the sudden crackle of automatic-weapons fire when Flynn and the others sprang their ambush. The noise only grew in intensity as more and more rifles and machine guns joined the fray. Startled by the explosion of noise where there had been only silence and the hiss of the wind, he sat bolt upright, ignoring the stab of pain from his fractured leg. "Holy shit! You guys hear that? There's one big, mother-humping battle going on!" He grabbed Rafael Sanchez by the shoulder. "Rafe! We've gotta go help the rest of the team."

The big New Mexican nodded slowly, but then he frowned. "Yeah, but the captain told us to stay put."

"Maybe we should call in and ask for new orders?" Boyd suggested from the other side. He'd unslung his own M4 and was crouched at the lip of the shallow gully, watching the north. Dozens of split-second flashes brightened the night sky along the crest of the hill above them.

"Can't," Sanchez reminded them. "The captain ordered radio silence, remember?"

Pedersen nodded. "Exactly! Which is why we

need to use our initiative, just like they trained us to do. Right?" he demanded.

Boyd pulled at his jaw. "Yeah, you're right." But then he waved a hand out across the open expanse of snow. "Trouble is, crossing that valley right now looks a lot like suicide to me. If just one bad guy pops up and catches us out there without any cover, we're fucking toast."

"That's why we stick to this streambed," Pedersen argued. A frozen stream ran along the middle of the shallow, brush-lined depression. It snaked down into the valley and then swung north.

"The sled won't make it through that rough ground," Sanchez said. "And you've got a busted leg."

Pedersen grinned up at him. "That's why you're going to sling me over your shoulder again, big guy." He lifted his weapon. "And my rifle, too, this time." As the team's designated marksman, Pedersen carried an M14 Enhanced Battle Rifle—a vastly modified and improved version of the old 7.62mm weapon last used in the field by U.S. troops in South Vietnam. When equipped with a telescopic sight, it had an effective range of more than eight hundred yards.

Spetsnaz Major Gennady Korenev risked a quick look up at the hill towering above them and ducked back again. More enemy rounds snapped through the air just over his head. Little geysers of snow and frozen clumps of earth erupted behind him. He scowled. The Americans were better shots than he'd imagined. And, barricaded in their improvised fortress of stone up there on that damned spur, they had a tremendous advantage over his handful of survivors. All he and his troops could make out were the deadly flashes stabbing out of that boulder field—as their rifle and machine-gun fire swept the valley and this barren slope from end to end.

He glanced to his left and then shook his head. There was no way to gain any ground there. Primakov and most of the men on that flank had been killed or badly wounded in the first few seconds of this firefight. That left a shift to the right. He belly-crawled over that way, careful to keep his head below the little hummock of ground that was his only piece of cover. One of his commandos was there, periodically popping up to pepper the rocks above them with short bursts from his AKM assault rifle.

"Hot work, Vanya," he murmured.

The soldier spat to one side, sliding another curved thirty-round magazine into his rifle. "Worse than Syria," he agreed.

Korenev raised himself up slightly, high enough to scan the terrain to the west and southwest through his night vision binoculars. Farther out across the valley floor, he could see the dark line of a stream-bed snaking across the open ground. There was good cover there, he judged, but it was too far away, more than three hundred meters. If he tried to redeploy his men there, the Americans would cut them down before they'd run off even a quarter of the distance.

Instead, he angled his binoculars, sweeping the hillside as it curved around to the southwest. And then, for the first time since the Americans had ambushed them, he felt a faint stirring of optimism. There was a fold on the surface of the hill there, within easy reach from this position. It looked like a patch of dead ground to him, one that offered a comparatively sheltered approach up the side of the spur. Assault troops moving up that dead ground ought to be able to get into the rocks on the Americans' left flank without being fired on.

He thumped his fist into the snow in sudden excitement and turned toward the other Spetsnaz commando. "Vanya! We've got those bastards! I see—" And a 7.62mm rifle round moving at more than 850 meters a second hit Korenev in the right side of his head, punched through his helmet, and tore out the other side in a spray of blood, brain matter, and splintered skull. He flopped over into the snow, killed instantly.

The surviving Russian whirled around and opened fire on full automatic, hosing down the distant streambed around where he thought that shot must have come from. He could see snow and bits of torn brush pinwheeling away as his bullets tore at the ground. His eyes narrowed as he leaned into the burst. Accuracy was important, but there were times when you needed to throw lead downrange, hoping to get lucky . . . or to at least make the enemy eat dirt.

His AKM stopped firing when it ran through its thirtieth round. Quickly, the Spetsnaz soldier grabbed for another magazine. But before he could reload, he slumped forward, hit high in the chest by another American bullet that penetrated his body armor.

T hree hundred yards away, Torvald Pedersen lowered his M14 and spat out a mouthful of gravel and twigs. "Geez, that was close." He pulled his eye away from the scope and glanced toward Sanchez and Boyd with a grin. "But I got both of those bastards. Did you see them—"

His smile froze. Boyd was dead, lying facedown on the lip of the streambed. Sanchez, ashen-faced, had slid back down a few feet. He was fumbling to stuff a field dressing into the gaping hole blown in his upper arm.

"Ah, hell," Pedersen muttered. He sighted back through the rifle scope. From what he could see, there weren't many Russians still moving. But from here, he could draw a bead on every last one of the sons of bitches. He tracked left a little, settled his sights on a new target, breathed out, and very, very gently, squeezed the trigger.

Out on the valley floor, another Spetsnaz commando went down.

F lynn climbed slowly to his feet. The staccato rattle of gunfire and the sharp crack of exploding grenades had finally stopped. But now the sounds of war had been replaced by eerie moans rising from the horribly wounded men—both American and Russian alike—sprawled across the hillside or huddled among the rocks.

Still holding his light machine gun, Hynes came over. "What do we do now, Captain?" he asked. "We sure kicked the shit out of those guys, but they kicked the shit out of us, too."

Flynn nodded wearily. His best guess was that only three or four of the Russian Spetsnaz troops were alive, though badly wounded. They were certainly in no condition to keep fighting. The rest were dead.

His tactical radio crackled suddenly to life. "Sir, I know you said not to use this thing, but I've got a situation down here," he heard Pedersen say. "Boyd is dead. And Rafe's hurt pretty bad. And I can't make it far on my own with this doggone busted leg."

Flynn keyed his mike. "Roger that, Private. Hang tight. We'll come get you."

Hynes whistled softly in dismay. "Jesus, sir. Boyd and Sims makes two dead. And with Leffert and Sanchez wounded, that just leaves six of us on our feet."

Flynn sighed. "Five, PFC. Sergeant Takirak is dead, too."

The other man's eyes widened in shock. "The sarge? Killed? How?"

"Enemy action," Flynn said tiredly. That was true enough, for a certain definition of "enemy," he thought. This still wasn't the right time to break the news that Takirak had actually been a GRU deep-cover agent. The moment for that would come later, when they were all safe—and after he'd had a chance to brief Alaskan Command's counterintelligence people. Takirak must have been running a network of other spies. To keep them from bolting for safety before they could be pinpointed and arrested, it was vital to keep the information about his death and real identity tightly held.

"So what's the plan, sir?" Hynes asked somberly.

"We need to get that satellite connection working and contact JBER," Flynn told him. "We need medevac ASAP for our injured guys and for our prisoners. No one who's been wounded will last long in this cold."

Hynes took a deep breath. "That ain't happening, sir." He jerked a thumb toward the boulder field. "Sims had the radio with him. It took a bunch of splinters when that Russian grenade went off."

"Well . . ." Flynn thought about swearing and then just shrugged. There just weren't enough cuss words in the English language to cover this situation.

From farther up the slope, Vucovich suddenly shouted. "Hey, Captain! Look at that!"

Flynn lifted his head and stared toward where the other man was pointing. There, off to the east, a flickering orange glow lit the darkness. Something was on fire out there, some miles away. Something where nothing should be. The isolated clumps of dwarf willows and spruce trees in this part of the world did not burn down in the icy, arctic winters. Not naturally anyway.

His eyes narrowed. One more damned mystery,

he thought angrily. And probably one connected to that dead Russian general they'd been tracking before this battle erupted. He scuffed furiously at the snow with his boot cap. What the hell was he supposed to do now? They were dozens of miles from the nearest possible help, with no way to communicate with anyone. But if he didn't do something soon, every injured man now in his charge was going to die—from either shock, their wounds, or the brutal, bone-chilling cold.

Thinking hard, Flynn walked down the slope to where the first of the Russians had fallen. He squatted down beside the dead man, noticing again how similar their uniforms and gear looked to those worn by his own troops. From a distance and in the dark, there was almost no way to tell them apart. His eyes widened slightly as the ghost of an idea wafted into his mind. Maybe there was a way he could solve several of his problems . . . with one risky move.

Suddenly excited, he straightened up. "Vucovich," he snapped. "You and Santarelli and Kim start gathering up all the wounded. Heat up some MREs and get some food into them." He whirled toward Hynes. "Put that MG down and grab a couple of those Russian weapons. You're coming with me."

Hynes stared at him. "Where to, sir? Where are we going?"

Flynn grinned at him. "We're going to arrange a ride out of this hellhole, PFC."

THIRTY-EIGHT

THAT SAME TIME

Ferociously, Piotr Zhdanov ground out another cigarette. He fumbled the pack out of his jacket pocket. It was empty. Angrily, he balled it up and tossed it aside. From behind, one of his aides diffidently offered him a fresh pack. He waved it away. As it was, the inside of his mouth tasted like dust and ashes.

He glared across the table at Lieutenant General Rogozin and the head of the GRU, Aleksandr Ivashin. "Well?" he demanded. "Still nothing?"

Helplessly, both men shrugged. As yet, there were no new reports—either from the Spetsnaz raiding party they'd sent into Alaska, or from the stolen stealth bomber to confirm that it was headed back to Russia, now that they'd paid the ransom demanded for its release. Their last news from Major Korenev indicated that his troops had landed deep in enemy territory and were ready to pursue, intercept, and destroy the ragtag American security unit ahead of them. Nothing at all had been heard from Petrov or his mysterious backers.

A soft chime came from the computer at Rogozin's place. The general leaned forward, reading the alert he'd just been forwarded. "Our satellites have received a new secure message from the PAK-DA stealth bomber," he reported.

Zhdanov breathed out. "Finally." He thrust a finger at the Air Force commander. "Put it up on-screen, Yvgeny."

With a nod, Rogozin signaled the colonel in charge of the underground command center's audiovisuals. The large wall screen flickered to life.

"Damn it," Zhdanov growled, seeing the face of Alexei Petrov materialize. He was again sitting in the futuristic-looking cockpit of the PAK-DA prototype. There was no conceivable circumstance in which the traitor could imagine he would return to Russia and survive the experience. Which meant that plane was still sitting on the ground inside the United States when this message had been recorded. And from the time stamp shown in the lower left-hand corner of the screen, that was less than five minutes ago.

"By now, you must have realized that I have no intention of returning this aircraft," the image of Petrov said coldly, confirming the Russian president's worst fears. "Sadly, our beloved Motherland—under your slovenly governance—is unworthy of such a gift." His expression darkened. "For decades now, our nation has been in decline—with its demoralized population aging and increasingly infirm; its economic strength decaying; and its military power nothing more than a facade, a thin shield for the dying body behind it. What have you achieved since the Soviet Union, once the world's mightiest superpower, crumbled to ruin?

"Nothing!" Petrov sneered. "You constantly boast about the 'New Russia,' but what do you have to back up such crowing? A population now only a third the size of the United States? And less than a tenth that of the People's Republic of China? An economy in ruins, more dependent on oil than even the Arab kleptocracies?" He leaned closer to the camera so that almost all they could see was his contempt-filled face. "It is time, Zhdanov, that you and your boot-lickers faced facts. You and all of your policies and plans are nothing but miserable, criminal failures."

Zhdanov stared at the screen, scarcely able to believe what he was hearing. No one in the past two decades had dared to insult him so openly—at least, no one who expected to live outside the gray walls of a prison, if allowed to live at all. From the rigid, horrified silence around him, he knew others were thinking the same thing.

"But because I am a true Russian patriot," Petrov continued, "I am offering you—unworthy though you are—a chance offered to no other Russian government since the fall of the Soviet Union: the opportunity to strip our most dangerous enemy, the United States, of most of its nuclear arsenal. The opportunity, moreover, to do so with minimal damage to our Motherland's own military and industrial might."

Zhdanov grimaced. What the hell was this madman talking about?

As if in answer, Petrov sat back again, allowing them to see the detailed map filling one of the stealth bomber's large, sophisticated digital displays. It showed the interior of the United States. "This plan is code-named *Vikhr*, Whirlwind," the traitor colonel said conversationally.

Whirlwind? Zhdanov darted a questioning glance at Rogozin. The general shrugged helplessly, as if to confirm this was nothing he'd ever heard of before, either.

On-screen, the recorded image of Alexei Petrov kept talking. "Very shortly, I will take off from this hidden airfield," he told them. "Once safely airborne, I will fly a stealthy course deep into American airspace." He smiled grimly. "There, approximately five hours from now, I will launch the twelve long-range, nuclear-armed stealth cruise missiles that you, perhaps foolishly, have entrusted to my care."

That drew startled gasps from around the room. All along, the prospect of a rogue commander in control of live nuclear weapons had been their worst nightmare—a fear that had faded only when it seemed Petrov was more interested in money than in sparking a nuclear holocaust.

"These missiles will be targeted on American military command and control centers in and around the Washington, D.C., area, their B-2 bomber base in Missouri, their B-52 bomber bases in Louisiana and North Dakota, and the U.S. Navy's ballistic missile submarine bases at Kitsap, Washington, and Kings Bay, Georgia," Petrov said calmly, apparently wholly unconcerned that he was announcing the probable deaths of hundreds of thousands and perhaps millions of people, soldiers, airmen, sailors, and civilians alike. "They will be carefully timed to arrive and detonate simultaneously."

Zhdanov saw Rogozin's head nod slowly. What the colonel proposed was technically possible. It was simply a matter of setting the necessary navigation points so that missiles aimed at closer targets would fly somewhat longer, more circuitous paths to arrive at their chosen destinations. While that increased the chances that the Americans might detect some of the incoming attacks, the risk was minimal. Their ability to spot stealth weapons fired from so deep inside their national territory was negligible.

Petrov reached out and tapped the display. The digital map of the United States blanked and then disappeared. "My attacks will decapitate America's political and military leadership," he said bluntly. "They will also wipe out its strategic bomber force and sink much of its ballistic missile submarine fleet in port."

"My God," Zhdanov muttered, seeing in his mind's eye fire-laced mushroom clouds towering above American ports, airfields, and its national capital. It was the old dream so often pictured by Soviet strategists during the long Cold War. And, at the same time, the old nightmare of those who understood the risks involved.

Petrov's mouth thinned. "Even men of limited imagination, like yourselves, should be able to see the opportunity offered by the chaos and confusion this bolt-from-the-blue strike will create," he went on. "Perhaps even to realize that an immediate follow-on attack by Russia's strategic rocket forces could destroy the remaining American ICBMs in their silos . . . before any of the dazed survivors can order a retaliatory launch."

Again, Zhdanov saw Rogozin nod his head in agreement, though almost unwillingly now. With Washington, D.C., in radioactive ruins and the American president and his top military leaders dead, the Americans simply would not be able to react in the thirty short minutes between the time Russia's own ICBMs rippled out of their silos and off their mobile launchers and the lethal moment their hundreds of multiple nuclear warheads detonated over U.S. missile fields.

"At that point, the United States will be left with only a handful of missile-armed submarines at sea," Petrov said coldly. "If you threaten to destroy America's cities in case those submarines launch their own weapons, the surviving elements of its weak-kneed governing elites will stand down in fear . . . leaving Russia the nuclear master of the world." He shrugged. "The choice," he added icily, "is yours. Either cast the die with me and win. Or die as ineffectual cowards when American ICBMs rain down on you in retaliation for my actions."

The screen went dark as his message ended.

For a long, seemingly endless moment, there was only stunned silence in the crowded command center. Then, finally, Zhdanov slammed his fist down on the table, rattling cups and saucers and startling his advisers and military commanders, who appeared sunk in gloom and uncertainty. "Well, what do we do *now*?" he snapped.

"There is still a chance that our Spetsnaz troops will find Petrov and the stealth bomber," Rogozin tentatively suggested.

Like a striking snake, Zhdanov whipped around on Ivashin. "Is there?"

The head of the GRU swallowed hard. During Petrov's recorded tirade, he'd been frantically texting his headquarters for a mission update. His face was pale. "Unfortunately, we've lost contact with the raiding party . . . and with the crew of their helicopter, Mr. President."

Zhdanov glared at him. "Which means your Major Korenev—and your *brilliant* deep-cover agent Orphan—have both failed."

"Yes," Ivashin admitted miserably.

Zhdanov turned back to Rogozin. "Can the Americans intercept the stealth bomber and shoot it down? Before Petrov can launch those cruise missiles?"

The Air Force commander shook his head. "It's highly unlikely, Mr. President. NORAD's radars and air defenses are concentrated along the perimeter of American and Canadian airspace. Petrov and his aircraft have already penetrated those defenses."

"What if we warned the Americans ourselves?" one of the other generals asked.

Rogozin shook his head. "Petrov's missiles have a range of more than twenty-eight hundred kilometers. He can strike his chosen targets from anyplace in a huge volume of space, across tens of millions of square kilometers. In effect, his planned launch point could be literally anywhere over the continental United States . . . or even over southern Canada. It would take a miracle for any American interceptor to find his stealth bomber in time."

"And miracles have been in short supply lately," Zhdanov said acidly. He scowled. "More to the point, what do we gain by warning the Americans?" He glared around the room, seeing their sudden, alarmed comprehension. He nodded. "Exactly. We gain nothing. The Americans can't stop Petrov. But by warning them of what's coming, we would just give them time to evacuate their military and political leaders, disperse their bombers and submarines, and put their ICBMs on full alert." His fist crashed down again, making them all jump. "So, in the end, we would only find ourselves confronted by a fully armed and ready enemy—an enemy bound to seek vengeance for Petrov's sneak attack."

Rogozin and the others were visibly shaken. In many ways, that would be the worst of all possible outcomes. Even a failed cruise missile attack on the target cities and bases Petrov had listed would still kill hundreds of thousands of American civilians. War would be inevitable. "What, then, are our options, Mr. President?" the Air Force general asked finally.

Zhdanov's eyes were hooded. "Options?" He shook his head in disgust, staring down at the surface of the table. "There are none."

"Sir?"

Slowly, the Russian president looked up. "We have no choice but to ride this nuclear whirlwind Petrov plans to unleash. Every other path leads inevitably to disaster."

"If you're wrong, millions of our countrymen may die," Rogozin warned.

Zhdanov nodded heavily. "True enough." Then he shrugged. "But if we sit here and do nothing, those same millions may die—and all for nothing." He turned to the commander of Russia's Strategic Rocket Forces, Colonel General Anatoly Gruzdev. "Bring your missiles to their highest state of launch readiness, General. But discreetly. The Americans must not find out what we're up to."

Somberly, Gruzdev nodded his understanding.

"The moment our early-warning satellites confirm nuclear detonations on targets inside the United States, you will launch an all-out attack on America's ICBM fields," Zhdanov continued. "Destroy every single one of those enemy missiles in their silos, Anatoly. Make the rubble bounce. We'll only get one chance at this."

THIRTY-NINE

Inside the cockpit of the PAK-DA stealth bomber, Alexei Petrov leaned forward and finished keying in the last elements of his flight plan. Lights along the top of the central multifunction display flashed from amber to green as the aircraft's computers checked his orders and signaled their acceptance. He watched them closely, aware of more pressure building up in the back of his brain. The headaches triggered by his malignant brain tumor were coming more rapidly now, held at bay only by increasing doses of medication.

Fortunately, Petrov thought with cool irony, very soon now, he would no longer need to worry about his disease. Death, after all, was the final solution for all human illness. But in the meantime, the need to numb himself against crippling pain required him to rely on the bomber's autonomous systems to manage this final mission. Through the haze induced by medicines, his own reflexes were no longer up to the task.

He checked his flight instruments and panels one

last time, just to be sure. Without a copilot to help him run through his checklists, precision was even more essential. Satisfied, he tapped a code sequence on the screen's virtual keyboard to set his VIKHR program in motion.

Immediately, a new window opened on the MFD. An icon blinked. GO FOR ENGINE START, the bomber's computer reported. Two indicators flashed red and then green. IGNITION ON BOTH ENGINES. Petrov glanced at his throttles. Eerily, both moved on their own accord, going to idle without any command input from him. Through the aircraft's open belly hatch, he heard the two big turbofans powering up. Their noise deepened from a high-pitched whine to a growling rumble.

Oppressed suddenly by a sense of urgency, Petrov got up and moved back through the short interior tunnel to the open hatch. He climbed down the ladder there, dropped awkwardly onto the hard-packed snow floor, and then hurried over to the controls for the camouflaged aircraft shelter's large central door. It was a simple, small box dangling from a power cord connected to electric motors mounted near the roof. He flipped the single switch and heard the motors hum. For a few moments, he stood watching just to make sure nothing went wrong as they slowly winched the hangar's fabric covering upward.

In the moonlight, far across the gleaming white surface of his improvised runway, flames still danced amid the burning wreckage of the tent camp he'd set ablaze. A thick column of oily black smoke, lit from the inside by flickering sparks crackling off the gasoline-fed fire, curled away on the wind.

And then Petrov's eyes widened in shock. A camouflaged military helicopter had just clattered straight through the smoke. Sleek-nosed, with a four-bladed main rotor, it was already flaring out to land close to the hangar. Someone had found him! He whirled around and scrambled under the PAK-DA bomber's broad, blended wing to get back to the hatch.

Aboard the Ka-60 *Kosatka* helicopter, Flynn snapped an order to Hynes. He and the square-shouldered enlisted man were the only Americans aboard. He'd been forced to leave the other three able-bodied troops under his command, Vucovich, Kim, and Santarelli, behind at the spur to do their best to keep the wounded and injured alive until he could get back to them. "Keep the crew covered, Cole. Once we're down, this bird doesn't go anywhere without my say-so!"

The Army PFC nodded. "You got it, sir. One twitch I don't like and both of these guys will end up splattered across that windshield." He had the Russian-made AKM he'd picked up back on the battlefield angled to sweep the entire cockpit at the slightest sign of trouble from either of the helicopter's two pilots. Fortunately, the Russian aviators still seemed to be in a state of shock at how easily the tables had been turned on them. When Flynn and Hynes came hurrying out of the darkness, they'd seen what they'd expected to see—two

Spetsnaz commandos coming to report the destruction of the American force. Instead, they'd suddenly had assault rifles shoved in their faces and found out the hard way that they were now prisoners.

Once Flynn checked out this burning wilderness camp where no camp should be, he planned to use the captured helicopter to fly his men and the wounded Russian survivors south to Fairbanks, the nearest place with an emergency trauma center. With a little luck, he hoped, the blizzard would have eased up enough by then to make the flight possible. If not, some of the more severely injured would be dead before too long.

So time was short, he reminded himself sharply. But he still needed to find out what the hell was going on here. Too many men had died for him to walk away from here without answers. Not waiting any longer, he slammed the Ka-60's side door wide open and dropped out onto the ground—ducking his head against a howling torrent of rotor-blown snow and ice.

Cradling his own captured AKM rifle, Flynn moved out from under the spinning blades . . . and then stopped dead, taken completely by surprise at what he saw ahead of him. They'd landed about fifty yards from the only intact structure left, a very large fabric tent of some kind. It was a faded white that matched the snow-covered terrain, and draped in camouflage netting to break up its silhouette. But the whole front of the tent had just rolled upward, allowing him to see the huge blended-wing aircraft hidden inside.

"Jesus Christ," Flynn muttered to himself, staggered by the sheer size of this plane. It was as big as a B-2 Spirit stealth bomber and shaped pretty much the same way. But it was just as obviously *not* an American aircraft design. Which meant it belonged to the Russians. His eyes narrowed in speculation. What kind of war game was Moscow playing here? Why secretly station a brand-new strategic bomber of some kind—for this could be nothing else—so deep inside American territory?

He felt a shiver down his spine. Whatever the reason, he was pretty sure it was nothing good, at least not from an American perspective. For a split second, Flynn stood frozen in place, remembering the earlier, explicit orders relayed to him from the Pentagon: *Observe and report any unidentified aircraft on the ground, but under no circumstances take any other action without further instructions.* Then he shook his head decisively. Yeah, screw that, he thought with a mental shrug. There was no way he was just going to sit back and watch the Russians finish whatever they were up to here, because he could hear that stealth bomber's engines spooling up right now.

Besides, Flynn asked himself with a sudden grin, what more could the spooks and the Joint Chiefs do to him for disobeying orders? Exile him to the back end of Alaska again?

He started to trot across the snow toward the hangar. But then he spotted movement under the aircraft's fuselage. A man in one of those pale blue Russian flight suits—the same kind worn by Mavrichev, the dead general they'd found—was already climbing up a short crew ladder into the bomber.

Without hesitating, Flynn raised the AKM rifle to his shoulder and pulled the trigger. A clump of snow kicked up under the fuselage. Too low. He raised his aim slightly and squeezed off several more shots. This time he saw sparks cascading off the metal ladder. But the crewman he'd been shooting at had already disappeared through the open hatch.

Flynn lowered his weapon and sprinted toward the hangar, acting almost entirely on instinct. He couldn't tell if he'd scored any hits on that guy, but whether he had or not didn't seem to matter. Somebody was still inside that Russian stealth aircraft, and unless he wanted to just stand here and watch it fly away, he needed to get a lot closer.

Gritting his teeth in pain, Petrov dragged himself up the ladder and flopped over onto the deck. His right arm, torn open by a rifle round, now hung useless at his side. Straining, he struggled back to his feet. But when he tried to turn the manual hatch control, he almost blacked out.

Giving up with a muttered curse, he reeled into the cockpit and dropped into his pilot's seat. Sickeningly aware of the hot blood soaking the sleeve of his flight suit, Petrov reached out with his left hand and quickly brought up a menu on one of the MFDs. Blurry shapes appeared, and he tapped an icon that would retract the ladder and close and seal the belly hatch. With a sigh, he released the brakes and sat back in a daze—feeling the PAK-DA bomber start its programmed takeoff roll.

Flynn saw the big aircraft lurch into motion, lumbering forward out of the tentlike hangar, accompanied by a steadily increasing roar from its jet engines. The crew ladder extending from its hatch had started to slide upward and out of sight. "No fucking way," he snarled. He threw the rifle aside, lowered his head, and ran even faster, plunging across the snow with rapidly lengthening strides.

Moving all out now, he raced under the bomber's fuselage—heading for the open hatch he'd seen. It was already swinging shut. Frantically, he jumped high, caught hold of the coaming, and hauled himself up through a rapidly narrowing gap. He wriggled away onto a metal deck just as the hatch slammed shut and latched tight behind him. From the vibration and noise all around him, it was clear that the Russian aircraft was still moving . . . bouncing up and down as it trundled onto a rough runway created out of compacted snow and ice.

Oh, smooth move, Flynn thought wryly. He'd just managed to scramble aboard an enemy aircraft that was obviously getting ready to take off. That was all well and good, except that his personal piloting skills had topped somewhere around the model airplane stage. Maybe he should have stopped to think about this whole idea first. Now what was he supposed to do?

Well, when in doubt, improvise like hell, he decided. And, like Teddy Roosevelt said, carry a big stick. Or, in this case, a 9mm Glock 19. He got to his feet and drew his pistol before moving forward into the cockpit.

To Flynn's surprise, although there were seats for four crewmen, only one, the pilot's position, was occupied. A Russian Air Force officer, a colonel named Petrov according to the name tag on his flight suit, sat strapped in, bleeding profusely, ashen-faced, and clearly in terrible pain. Through the clear canopy, Flynn could see the snow-covered landscape sliding past at increasing speed as the stealth bomber rolled down the runway. He leveled his pistol at the pilot's head. "*Ostanovi etot samolet seychas zhe!*" he snapped. "Stop this aircraft, now!"

To his surprise, Petrov forced an agonized smile. "Or what?" he retorted in lightly accented English. "You will shoot me? And then we crash?"

"Yeah, if that's what it takes," Flynn growled.

Still smiling crookedly, the Russian held up his empty left hand. His shattered right arm was immobile. "Shooting me will not change anything, Captain . . . Flynn," he said tiredly, reading the name off Flynn's own uniform. "I am no longer in control. The computers are."

At that moment, the bomber lifted off, shuddering and shaking as it plowed through wind gusts and low-altitude turbulence. Flynn hurriedly grabbed hold of the back of the copilot's seat while still keeping his pistol aimed at Petrov's head. Hydraulic thumps and whines from behind the cockpit signaled that the landing gear had retracted and locked inside.

Slowly, the aircraft banked, turning toward the south as it sped low over snow-capped ridges and hills. With difficulty, Flynn tore his eyes away from the bleak and empty landscape. He set the Glock's muzzle directly against the Russian colonel's temple. "Then turn those computers off and land this big son of a bitch."

Petrov laughed harshly. "I will not." He shrugged. "I am already dying anyway." Sardonic amusement flickered in his icy blue eyes. "What you do not understand is that you are dying with me. Though you may live long enough to see the missiles fly."

"Missiles? What missiles?" Flynn demanded sharply. *Oh, shit*, he thought, feeling cold.

"This bomber prototype carries twelve nuclear-tipped cruise missiles," Petrov told him calmly. "Missiles that I have already armed. In a few short hours, once this undetectable stealth aircraft reaches its preprogrammed coordinates, those missiles will launch against strategic targets in your country—"

Flynn listened with mounting shock and horror while the Russian laid out his plan. And, from the smug expression on his gray, bloodless face, Petrov enjoyed seeing his reaction. "You must be fucking insane," Flynn ground out between clenched teeth when he'd finished.

The other man shrugged again. "Perhaps." His eyes were half-closed now. "Then again, it could simply be that knowledge of approaching death clarifies the mind, stripping away everything that is useless—concern for mere individuals and so-called morality, for example . . . in favor of more important matters like the fate of nations and the application of raw power in its most elemental, atomic form."

"Like I said, you're nuts," Flynn said bluntly.

Petrov's eyes opened fully again. "Insult me all you like," he said coolly. "It changes nothing." He waved his left hand at the white wilderness visible ahead of the speeding bomber. "Enjoy the ride, Captain."

Swiftly, Flynn looked around the cramped cockpit. There had to be something he could try, he thought desperately. Something he could use to stop this lunatic from triggering a war that would kill millions. Faster and faster, he scanned displays, dials, buttons, and switches. There was nothing. No control helpfully marked "Pull to stop nuclear holocaust" in Russian and English. No magic off switch.

He swallowed hard against a sharp, acid taste in his mouth. For one thing, he decided there was no way he was going to ride this bird all the way to the point where it fired its missiles. Especially not strapped in beside this smug Russian son of a bitch. He glanced down at his pistol. If worst came to worst, he always had at least one way out.

A way out. The thought echoed in Flynn's mind, bright and clear like a bugle call on a windless summer morning. Carefully, he looked around the cockpit again. And this time, he saw what he was looking for.

"Sorry, but your big plan's a bust, Colonel," he said quietly. "It's not going to happen." He slid into the copilot's seat next to Petrov and strapped himself in.

The Russian snorted, watching him through narrowed eyes. "What? You imagine you can somehow hack into this aircraft's computer systems?" He sneered. "Please, take all the time you wish."

Flynn grinned back at him, feeling suddenly fully alive and in control. "Computer hacking is for subtle, clever guys." Then he reached down and grabbed the yellow-and-black-tape-wrapped ejection seat handle between his legs. "But I'm not that subtle or clever. *Do svidaniya*, Colonel."

He yanked the ejection handle just as Petrov screamed in sudden, horrified comprehension.

Everything after that happened in milliseconds. First, tiny explosive charges shattered the canopy over Flynn's head. And then the rocket motor below his seat ignited, lobbing him out of the stealth bomber and away into the frigid slipstream with tremendous force. Petrov's distorted face shrank into a tiny dot, while the cockpit's computer control panels—smashed by the shock wave—shattered, shorted out, and went dark.

Slowly, with Petrov still strapped into his seat and screaming in helpless terror, the fatally damaged PAK-DA bomber rolled over on one wing and then, completely out of control, whirled end over end down out of the sky. Seconds later, it smashed into a jagged, saw-toothed ridge and blew up with a flash that lit the night sky for miles around.

Flynn, knocked out by the bone-jolting shock of a rough, low-altitude ejection, clawed his way up out of nothingness just in time to see the parachute above him snap open. He looked down and saw the ground rushing up at him at high speed. "Ah, hell—"

Then all he felt was an enormous, shattering impact. The whole world around him went black. Still tumbling downward, Nick Flynn fell endlessly into the darkness.

EPILOGUE

SOME DAYS LATER

Captain Nick Flynn resisted looking at the wall clock for what seemed the thousandth time in just the past couple of hours. Frantically, he wriggled his back against the pillows, trying again to scratch an itch somewhere inside the bulky upper body cast they'd put him in while his badly broken shoulder healed. No joy. He sighed.

He'd gone far beyond being ordinarily bored at being stuck alone in this hospital room. In fact, Flynn had now moved on to the next stage of boredom, a stage he privately referred to as the "So help me God, the first chance I get I'm going to grab someone's weapon and shoot my way out of this fricking place" phase. Although that was mostly a joke, he couldn't shake the uncomfortable feeling that no one planned to let him out of this isolated wing any time soon.

The only people Flynn saw regularly were doctors and nurses . . . and the armed guards posted outside his door. He'd had to do a lot of arguing even to get a rundown on what had happened after he'd ejected from the Russian aircraft. Fortunately for him, PFC Hynes, who should have his sergeant's stripes back now as a reward, had reacted instantly to the sight of his commander vanishing into an enemy bomber by ordering the Ka-60 helicopter crew to "follow that plane!" And while falling farther and farther behind the speeding PAK-DA, they'd still been close enough to see Flynn's ejection seat parachute open, and retrieve him before he froze to death. After that, the helicopter had returned to the battlefield at the spur hill, picked up the wounded and other survivors, and then made it safely through the tail end of the blizzard to Fairbanks. Thankfully, Floyd Leffert, Rafe Sanchez, and Tor Pedersen were expected to recover fully from their injuries. One of the four badly wounded Spetsnaz commandos hadn't been so lucky, but the other three were still alive—and apparently the subject of a lot of heated diplomatic negotiations between Moscow and Washington, D.C. The same thing went for the two captured Russian pilots and their Ka-60 helicopter.

In the meantime, here he was, Flynn thought gloomily, stuck in isolation—unable to communicate with anyone, not the surviving members of his team and not even his own family. At least the food was decent, for hospital food. Then again, that might only be an omen that they were fattening him up for the bureaucratic kill. What felt like endless hours of debriefings since he'd been flown here from the trauma center in Fairbanks had made a couple of things painfully clear: First, the U.S. intelligence community had desperately wanted to get its grubby hands on that Russian stealth bomber in an intact condition. And second, the spooks were really pissed that the superadvanced aircraft was now scattered in highly radioactive pieces across some desolate slope in the Alaskan Never-Never instead.

Flynn wasn't sure anyone believed what he'd told them about the Russian colonel's real plans to blow the hell out of strategic targets from Washington, D.C., to Barksdale Air Force Base in Louisiana. One of the CIA debriefers had even snidely wondered why Flynn hadn't had the foresight to record Petrov's demented ramblings on his smartphone as evidence. His quick, smart-ass rejoinder that he'd been kind of too busy "doing all that running and shooting and not dying shit" hadn't gone over very well. His mouth quirked upward in a wry grin. It might be time he reread that book on how to make friends and influence people. Its lessons obviously hadn't stuck.

There was a soft knock on his door. Flynn looked up warily. It wasn't anywhere near lunchtime yet, which left only a series of unpleasant alternatives ranging from the next round of painful physical therapy for the injuries he'd sustained while ejecting . . . to another mind-numbing debriefing session where intelligence officers asked him the same damned questions over and over and over again, obviously hoping they could trip him up somehow. For just a moment, he was tempted to call out "Go away!" just to see what would happen. But then he shrugged. Anything, painful or not, was probably better than just lying here. And not, not, *not* thinking about the itch between his shoulder blades that he could not scratch.

The door opened.

And Captain Laura Van Horn came in. The attractive, dark-haired National Guard pilot grinned cheerfully at the surprised expression on his face. "Wow, Nick. I heard you'd had a tough time, but I have to say that you really do look like hell."

With an effort, Flynn closed his mouth. "It's camouflage," he told her, smiling back. "I'm only lulling the sentries out there by looking helpless like this. That way I can catch them off guard when I make my move to break out of this joint."

Van Horn came over and gently tapped the solid plaster cast encasing his chest and arms. "Pretty good camouflage," she commented dryly.

"I may have gone a bit overboard," Flynn admitted. He raised an eyebrow. "Which leads me to wonder just how you got in here. From what I can tell, I'm sort of off-limits to just about everyone."

She nodded. "That you are." She shrugged. "But I told you I was a woman of many talents, remember?"

"Yeah," Flynn said tightly, trying very hard not to summon up the mental image he'd created the last time she said that. Stuck in a hospital bed with twenty pounds of plaster immobilizing his arms was definitely not the right moment to imagine Laura Van Horn in a sexy outfit.

"Plus, I have some friends in high places," she said as the door opened behind her. A thin, middle-aged man in a dark jacket and tie quietly entered. He had graying hair and pale eyes that peered out knowingly behind a pair of wire-rimmed glasses.

Flynn looked him over with a skeptical eye. "You don't strike me as being a doctor. And you're sure as hell not a nurse. Which makes you—"

"My boss," Van Horn finished for him. "Mr. Fox."

"Fox? Seriously?" Flynn said. "And now you're going to tell me that Mr. Fox here heads up a civilian air freight company in Alaska? Flying people's mail orders and gift boxes between there and Seattle?"

She had the grace to redden slightly. "That may not have been completely accurate." She folded her arms. "Our range of operations is actually a little more . . . global."

"I bet," Flynn said, starting to feel a little angry at having been played for a sucker when they first met. "I guess what you really do is more like delivering weapons and explosives to a bunch of rebels or terrorists or freedom fighters in faraway, godforsaken places—depending on what they're calling themselves on any particular day of the week."

"Not at all, Captain Flynn," the older man said with a dry laugh. "We leave idiocy along those lines to the amateurs, like the CIA."

"So who are you?" Flynn challenged him. "Defense Intelligence Agency? Homeland Security? FBI?"

"None of those," Fox said with some amusement. "I run a little outfit of my own."

Flynn looked at him. "Called what?"

The older man shrugged. "Many different names, depending on the task in hand." Casually, he seated himself in one of the chairs next to the bed. "What matters is that I'm always on the lookout for people who might be useful."

Flynn glanced up at Laura Van Horn. "So, our whole dinner date? What was that, just an artfully managed job interview? Complete with a carefully arranged dud aircraft engine?"

Reddening a bit more, she shook her head.

"*That*, Captain Flynn," Fox said calmly, "was serendipity." He shrugged his narrow shoulders. "Oh, given time, I would have asked Laura here to find a way to talk to you . . . to size you up, one could say. You've been on my radar as a possible recruit to our little band of brothers and sisters for quite a while."

Flynn stared at him. "Why me?"

"You have language skills, high intelligence, intuition, tenacity, and daring," Fox told him frankly. He smiled. "Those aren't common anywhere, and certainly not in our government's more . . . *established* . . . intelligence bureaucracies." Behind his lenses, his pale eyes gleamed. "Besides, you've demonstrated a remarkable talent for pissing off all the wrong people by doing exactly the right thing. A talent like that should be put to even wider use."

Flynn looked across at Van Horn. "You work for this guy," he said quietly. "What does it really involve?"

"No bullshit this time?" she asked, with the faint echo of a laugh.

"No bullshit," he confirmed.

Van Horn nodded, looking relieved at his change in tone. "Well, Nick, basically the job involves travel to a variety of unsavory, exotic places, frequent danger, and the occasional risk of getting killed. All for relatively low pay and uncertain benefits."

"So, pretty much the same as serving in the armed forces, then," Flynn pointed out with a quick, sidelong grin.

Fox nodded. "True enough," he allowed, with a fleeting smile of his own. "But with one rather significant exception . . . especially to someone like you."

"And what's that?" Flynn wondered.

"The opportunity for truly independent action, without being held back or second-guessed by superiors who are more interested in protecting their careers than in accomplishing the mission," Fox said bluntly.

For a time, Flynn considered that, looking back and forth between Laura Van Horn and Fox. How far could he trust them? Maybe not far, he thought. At least not yet. Then again, if even half of what they said was accurate, it could turn out to be one hell of a ride. He nodded. "Okay, count me in."

THAT SAME TIME

Dmitri Grishin's huge luxury yacht was anchored off a small, cliff-circled harbor on the French coast. One of the hundred-meter-long vessel's auxiliary craft, a beautiful teak motorboat, rumbled softly across the azure waters of the Mediterranean, swung through a graceful curve, and glided in alongside a centuries-old stone quay. Quickly, crewmen tied the motorboat up and then turned to help their only passenger, the oligarch himself, up a short ladder.

At the top, Grishin paused to thank them. "Your service during this vacation has been superb, and will be amply rewarded," he said cheerfully. "I only wish the press of business didn't require me to return so soon to Moscow."

They bobbed their heads in gratitude. Their employer, though demanding, paid well—and tipped even better when he was pleased. And everyone aboard the yacht had noticed the sea change in his mood over the last few days. With a final, genial wave, Grishin turned toward the limousine that would take him back to the airport in Nice.

And then his head exploded—blown apart by a subsonic 9mm round. Without a sound, his corpse toppled off the quay and splashed into the Mediterranean.

Three hundred meters away, high up on the rocky cliff overlooking the little village, the man who'd shot him began methodically disassembling his scoped VSS Vintorez sniper rifle. This silenced weapon had been specially developed for use by Spetsnaz-trained assassins.

Two other men stood nearby, watching impassively while the murderer quietly and efficiently stowed the tools of his trade in a carrying case. One of them was a senior officer in Russia's Foreign Intelligence Service, the SVR. He turned to the tall, elegantly dressed younger man at his side. "Moscow is grateful for your cooperation and patriotism, Mr. Voronin," he said. "Without your information, this traitor might have managed to escape detection. And only your inside knowledge enabled us to retrieve the two hundred billion rubles he had been paid as ransom."

Pavel Voronin smiled modestly. "What else could I have done, once I learned the true extent of Grishin's crimes?" he said. He sighed. "The old man betrayed us all in the end, every single one of those who trusted him."

Somberly, the SVR officer nodded. "A nasty business, indeed. President Zhdanov took the news of this treachery on Grishin's part very badly."

"Please assure the president that both he and Mother Russia can always count on my loyal service," Voronin assured him earnestly.

Later, watching the two other Russians depart, Pavel Voronin smiled more genuinely. With a single, simple act, he had freed himself from his unnecessary apprenticeship to Grishin. The oligarch had always been too cautious, too narrow in his thinking. Soon, Voronin thought coldly, he would be able to realize the full extent of his own personal ambitions—a task that would be made considerably easier by the billions of dollars the Americans had so generously and foolishly paid into secret accounts that were now his . . . and his alone. Whistling softly, Voronin turned and walked away from the cliff.

Behind him, in the gathering darkness, Dmitri Grishin's body floated slowly out to sea.

WEAPONS AND ACRONYMS

WEAPONS

- AIM-9X—American heat-seeking air-to-air missile

- AK-12—Russian assault rifle

- AMRAAM—Advanced Medium-Range Air-to-Air Missile, American radar-guided air-to-air missile

- AN/APG-77—American advanced aircraft radar system

- AN/PRC-162—American handheld tactical radio

- Anza Mk III—Pakistani shoulder-fired antiaircraft missile

- F-22 Raptor—American fifth-generation fighter aircraft

- FPS-117—American phased array air surveillance radar

- HC-130J—American combat search-and-rescue aircraft

- IL-38—Russian radar-equipped patrol plane

- IL-78M-90A—Russian aerial refueling aircraft

- IRBIS-E—Russian advanced passively scanned phased array fighter radar

- IRST—Infrared Search and Track, Russian passive air detection and tracking system

- Kamov Ka-60 *Kosatka*—Russian medium-range troop transport helicopter

- Korshun-KN-N—Russian long-range aerial search radar

- Mil Mi-26T2—Russian heavy-lift helicopter

- RC-135V—American reconnaissance aircraft

- Tu-95—Russian long-range bomber aircraft

- Tu-142—Russian long-range reconnaissance aircraft, converted from the Tu-95 bomber

- Tu-214R—Russian advanced long-range reconnaissance aircraft

ACRONYMS

- ACAWS—Advisory, Caution, and Warning System; aircraft systems alerting system

- ARCC—Alaska Rescue Coordination Center, directs rescue responses in Alaska

- ARTCC—Air Route Traffic Control Center, American wide-range air traffic control

- AWACS—Airborne Warning and Control System, American aerial radar system

- CSAR—Combat Search and Rescue

- DEFCON—Defense Condition, a series of coordinated actions in response to a military crisis

- DNI—Director of National Intelligence, American executive in charge of all intelligence agencies

- ECR—Emergency Conference Room, American Pentagon meeting area

- ELINT—Electronic Intelligence

- GRU—*Glavnoje Razvedyvatel'noje Upravlenije*, Russian military intelligence

- HUD—Heads-Up Display, a system that displays flight and weapons information so a pilot does not have to look down to read it

- HUMINT—Human Intelligence

- JBER—abbreviation for Joint Base Elmendorf-Richardson, American military installation near Anchorage, Alaska

- JCS—Joint Chiefs of Staff, the senior uniformed leaders of the six branches of the American military

- MILES—Multiple Integrated Laser Engagement System, a "laser tag" infantry training system

- NORAD—North American Aerospace Defense Command, the joint American-Canadian command that directs air defense of North America

- RAOC—Regional Air Operations Center, a U.S.

Air Force unit that directs airborne air defense activities

- RCAF—Royal Canadian Air Force

- RCS—radar cross-section, a value relating to an object being detected by radar

- RWR—radar warning receiver, a device that detects and classifies radar energy

- SecDef—abbreviation for the American secretary of defense

- SIGINT—Signals Intelligence, the process of obtaining, identifying, and disseminating radio signals

- SVR—*Sluzhba Vneshney Razvedki*, Russian Foreign Intelligence Service

If you enjoyed **ARCTIC STORM RISING**,
keep reading for a sneak peek at
the next thrilling Nick Flynn adventure

COUNTDOWN
TO MIDNIGHT

Available in hardcover Spring 2022
from William Morrow

ONE

JANUARY

Shadows cast by the setting sun stretched across a long, winding ski trail bordered by snow-dusted pines. Down in the narrow valley at the foot of the mountain, the Kitzbüheler Horn, lights were beginning to glow—outlining the streets and buildings of one of Austria's most popular and charming Alpine villages. The forested heights of another peak, the Hahnenkamm, the Rooster's Comb, climbed skyward on the other side of the town. Curving white trails crisscrossed the slopes of that mountain as well. Kitzbühel was the center of one of the largest ski areas in the Tyrolean Alps, attracting crowds of competitive skiers and the world's jet-setters during the winter months.

Nicholas Flynn came gliding around a curve in the trail and turned to a quick stop off to one side. His skis sent a little curl of loose powder pattering downhill. He raised his goggles briefly, squinting down the slope ahead. This late in the day, the light was going flat—making it difficult to spot any bumps or dips along the surface. Fortunately, this was a trail designed for intermediate skiers, and not one of the steep, rugged runs favored by experts or amateurs with lots of medical insurance and a death wish.

He looked across at the Hahnenkamm. One of the sheer twisting and turning trails he could see was known as the *Streif*, the Streak. Since 1937, it had been the site of the World Cup's most challenging race. Skiers plunging down the run's two-mile length routinely topped more than sixty miles an hour—with nothing between them and a catastrophic crash but their own skill, agility, and experience.

Flynn felt a wry grin tug at the side of his mouth. Fighting hand-to-hand against Russian Spetsnaz commandos and parachuting into winter storms was one thing, but there was no way in hell he'd ever be crazy enough to believe he could handle a race on something like the *Streif*. "After all, a man's gotta know his own limitations," he murmured. As a kid growing up in mostly snowless Central Texas, family winter vacations to Colorado and Utah had taught him enough to make it downhill without face-planting . . . and to realize that any thoughts of hurtling straight down the local equivalent of a double black diamond slope were purely delusions of grandeur.

Fortunately, he wasn't here to show off. Far from it, in fact.

About a hundred yards farther along, Flynn spotted another skier pulled off on the same side of the trail, apparently taking pictures of the spectacular Alpine views with his cell phone. The other man's white parka, dark green ski pants, and a red knit cap signaled that he was Flynn's contact for this clandestine rendezvous. Arif Khavari was a high-ranking official in Iran's state-owned shipping company. He'd come to Austria as part of an Iranian delegation to an OPEC meeting in Vienna. A short ski excursion had given Khavari a chance to escape the constant scrutiny of his compatriots and their official security detail.

Flynn glanced back the way he'd come. There were no other people in sight. The lifts would close at four o'clock, and with the light fading and temperatures falling fast, most skiers were already headed off the mountain to get ready for a busy evening of *après-ski* drinking, dining, and dancing in Kitzbühel and the even smaller neighboring villages. Satisfied for the moment that they were as alone as it was possible to be in a public place, he swung around and skied down to join the Iranian. He stopped again a few feet below Khavari—not far from the edge of the woods lining the trail.

The other man, shorter by a few inches and dark-eyed, looked nervous.

Flynn donned a friendly smile. "Excuse me?" he asked, in plainly American-accented English. "Can you tell me the time?" He nodded over his shoulder. "I've got a business call at five, but I'd still like to make one more run down the mountain if I can."

Khavari made a show of checking his phone screen. "The Hornbahn gondola stops running in minutes," he said hurriedly, rushing through the agreed-upon recognition phrase selected for this rendezvous. "I do not believe you could reach it soon enough to ride back up."

"Too bad, but I guess those are the breaks," Flynn answered with a shrug, finishing the protocol. He allowed his easy smile to tighten just a bit. "Okay, Mr. Khavari, now that we've confirmed our respective *bona fides*, maybe you can clue me in on just why you needed to see someone in person, instead of communicating through the usual secure channels. We can't take a lot of time here." In the shadowy world of espionage and counterespionage, any face-to-face contact was highly risky, no matter how many precautions those involved took. It was something that should be done only when absolutely necessary. And keeping any meeting as short and to the point as possible was one way to minimize those inevitable hazards.

The Iranian swallowed hard. "You represent your decision-makers in Washington?" he asked quietly.

Flynn nodded, opting for discretion over the absolute truth. If Khavari was under the mistaken impression that he was in touch with an official U.S. government intelligence agency, so much the better for operational security. What the Iranian didn't know couldn't be forced out of him if the Revolutionary Guard's goons ever figured out that he'd turned against the regime.

Besides, Flynn thought dryly, up to about a year ago, he *had* been working for the government—as a captain assigned to U.S. Air Force intelligence activities. Unfortunately, acting boldly to salvage things when the CIA's own people screwed up not just one, but two, of the agency's sketchy covert operations in a row turned out to be a really bad career move. The bureaucrats at Langley needed a scapegoat to blame for their own blunders. And Nick Flynn, a junior military officer without a drop of influence in D.C.'s political circles, must have seemed perfect for the part.

So he'd been laid up under guard in a military hospital, recuperating from his last brush with one of the CIA's "brilliant" plans, when the mysterious Mr. Fox arrived to recruit him to join what the older man had modestly described as a "little private intelligence outfit." Months later, after intensive courses to further hone his language, espionage tradecraft, weapons, and other skills, Flynn had come to understand that the Quartet Directorate—commonly referred to as Four by those in the loop—was actually something considerably larger and more important. This mountainside rendezvous with Arif Khavari was his first solo operational assignment for his new employer.

"I have a friend, a good friend," the Iranian said, lowering his voice even further. "Like me, he secretly despises the corrupt men who are ruining our country." He hesitated briefly before going on. "First, you should know that we both love our nation and our people. We are *not* traitors. The insane mullahs in Tehran and their evil servants are the real traitors."

Flynn nodded his understanding. No one except

the utterly mercenary or sociopathic could find it easy to break faith with his or her own native land, no matter how vile its current government might be. He fought down an urge to hurry the other man along again. Spooking Khavari or unintentionally insulting him now would do more harm than good.

"My friend is a naval architect," the Iranian went on. "He works at our state-owned shipyards west of Bandar Abbas. Recently, he approached me with strange news about one of their current projects. Strange and disturbing news."

Flynn hid his surprise. Iran's seemingly perpetual quest for nuclear weapons was the hot topic in Western intelligence circles, not its ship construction plans. "Go on," he prompted.

Quickly, Khavari explained. According to his friend, Navid Daneshvar, major modifications had been ordered to a large oil tanker named *Gulf Venture* now under repair at the Shahid Darvishi shipyards—modifications which made no sense for any vessel genuinely intended to carry petroleum products to ports around the world. No commercial oil tanker needed concealed compartments, hydraulic cranes, special ship stabilizers, and additional high-speed pumps.

Equally troubling were strict new security measures that seemed intended to shroud this project in absolute secrecy. Among other things, Tehran had ordained the construction of a huge temporary roof over the yard's largest dry dock in order to block any satellite imagery of the work in progress.

And all shipyard personnel assigned to the project were being kept under close watch in special housing, forbidden to communicate with their families or anyone on the outside, except under very limited circumstances. The only exceptions to this policy were a handful of senior staff believed to be absolutely loyal to the regime, like his friend Daneshvar. Finally, large numbers of special commandos from the Revolutionary Guard's Quds Force had been deployed as guards around the Darvishi complex—backed up by foreign "mercenaries," probably Russians.

"Russians?" Flynn said, unable to hide his surprise at the thought of Iran's notoriously xenophobic rulers allowing armed foreigners of any stripe to operate inside their jealously guarded territory.

Khavari nodded darkly. "So Daneshvar says. Either Russians or maybe Eastern Europeans. Slavs of some kind, for sure."

Flynn thought for a moment and then asked, "Can you get your hands on blueprints that show the specific alterations being made to this ship? That'd give our analysts a much better shot at figuring out what your government is planning."

Sorrowfully, Khavari shook his head. "It's proved impossible to smuggle out any documentation from the shipyard complex. Everyone is thoroughly searched on entry and departure. And it's strictly forbidden to take anything, whether on paper or a USB drive, beyond the gates. Or to bring any data storage devices inside. Even the main computer systems are 'air-gapped'—cut off from any physical or wireless connection to the internet. So far, Daneshvar has been forced to relay every scrap of information to me solely by word of mouth. And even that is incredibly dangerous."

"Yeah." Flynn frowned. If only half of the security measures the Iranian described were actually in place, Tehran was taking no chances. Besides a defense against espionage, blocking both physical and internet access to the shipyard's computers would also prevent cyberattacks like those periodically used by the Israelis and other hostile countries to sabotage Iran's nuclear and missile development facilities. Thinking hard, he dug one of his ski poles a little deeper into the snow. "Look, what's the time frame on this project? When are the modifications to this tanker supposed to be complete?"

"Not long," Khavari told him gravely. "Perhaps only a matter of weeks. Two months at the outside. The yard is working around-the-clock to finish its work on the *Gulf Venture*. No delays are tolerated."

Flynn's jaw tightened. "A couple of months? That's not much time to—" He stopped abruptly, aware that his subconscious had just sent up a warning flare. Something was off, somewhere. He stared over the Iranian's shoulder, peering at the slope higher up the trail. Was that movement in the trees over on the other side? Maybe around a couple of hundred yards off?

Suddenly, Khavari's chest exploded high up, right over his heart—spraying bright red blood and bits of pulverized bone across the white surface of the snow. He'd been shot in the back.

Shit, shit, shit, Flynn thought furiously. He threw himself prone, just as another bullet ripped past his own head and smacked into a tree further downslope. A third round slammed into the Iranian, who was already dead. His corpse toppled sideways and fell in a heap just uphill.

Flynn reacted without hesitation. Khavari's body wasn't good cover. Not for long, anyway. It wouldn't take whoever'd just bushwhacked them more than a few seconds to find a new vantage point, one with a clear angle on him. So, it was move and move fast. Or die right here.

He punched the tip of one of his poles into the binding release levers on his skis—popping them free. Then he curled around, grabbed both skis, and tossed them sideways into the woods lining this side of the run. Frantically, he rolled after them across the slope. Ice crystals spurted up near his face from another near miss.

Swearing under his breath, Flynn reached the wood line and scrambled behind the trunk of a pine tree, whose heavy, snow-covered lower branches almost brushed the ground. "Son of a bitch," he muttered through clenched teeth. Being shot at sure got old fast. Especially since he wasn't armed himself right now. Austrian gun laws were more relaxed than those of many other European countries, but he'd still figured the local authorities would pretty seriously frown on a foreign

"business consultant" carrying a concealed pisto
if he were caught. Well, mark that decision dow
as a triumph of excessive caution over commo
sense, he thought bitterly.

Then again, he realized, the assassin who'd jus
killed Khavari and tried to blow his own brains ou
had to be using a scoped rifle. And one with a hel
laciously effective suppressor at that. Even throug
the crystal-clear Alpine air, the sound of the shot
had been remarkably muffled, more like the me
chanical *snap* of a bolt cycling than the sharp-edge
crack usually made by a high-powered round explod
ing outward from a rifle barrel. So even if he had
sidearm right now, charging back up the mountain
through the snow to go *mano a mano* with a traine
sniper would be a terminally stupid plan. The en
emy would nail him the instant he broke cover and
came out into the open.

No, Flynn decided. There were situations wher
attacking into an ambush was the least bad option
But this was most definitely *not* one of those situa
tions. Instead, much as he hated it, the smart pla
now was to bail out and get clear.

Swiftly, he scooted downhill to where his ski
had slid, careful to keep the trees between him
and that unseen, distant gunman. It took onl
moments to brush away the caked snow from hi
boots and bindings and snap back into his skis. H
paused for another few seconds to get his bearings
He'd ducked into the woods on the northwester
edge of the trail. And according to the trail map
he'd studied before meeting Khavari, there wa

another run just on the other side of this thin strip of forest, one that would get him off the mountain.

Flynn's mouth twisted in a self-conscious grin. So much for his earlier plan of taking the easier way down the Kitzbühler Horn. His chosen alternate route was marked as a more advanced slope, a lot steeper and more rugged than he ordinarily found comfortable. Still, he was okay with taking the risk of sprawling flat on his ass in front of more experienced skiers if it meant staying out of the rifle sights of an assassin. Moving carefully through the softer, deeper snow under the trees, he glided away at an angle, heading for the neighboring run.

He stopped again just before coming back out into the open. Both native caution and his training dictated that he make a few rapid changes to his appearance. For one thing, the bright blue outer shell of his ski jacket was spattered with Khavari's blood. That was bound to draw unwanted attention, whether from the ski area's security personnel, the general public, or, just as conceivably, other members of the hit team who might already be looking for him near the lower lifts.

Quickly, Flynn unzipped the shell from its insulating layer and then reversed it to show the black inner lining instead. Next, he pulled off his goggles and stuffed them out of sight in a pocket. This late in the day, they were more hindrance than help anyway. Finally, he tugged a ski hat down over his bare head. Taken separately, none of these tiny alterations were exactly major measures of disguise. But together, he hoped they would alter his visual

profile just enough to confuse anyone hunting for
the man who'd been seen talking to Khavari right
before he was shot.

Satisfied that he'd done all he could for now, Nick
Flynn squared his shoulders and skied out from the
tree line.